A SPELL OF SWALLOWS

Sarah Harrison

WINDSOR
PARAGON

First published 2007
by
Hodder and Stoughton
This Large Print edition published 2007
by
BBC Audiobooks Ltd by arrangement with
Hodder and Stoughton

Hardcover ISBN: 978 1 405 61838 0
Softcover   ISBN: 978 1 405 61839 7

British Library Cataloguing in Publication Data available

Printed and bound in Great Britain by
Antony Rowe Ltd., Chippenham, Wiltshire

A SPELL OF SWALLOWS

Vivien Mariner loves her husband, and is adored by him in return. So why does she find herself so strongly drawn to John Ashe, the enigmatic stranger who appears in Eadenford, as if from nowhere, the summer after the Great War ends?

Helping around the house and garden, Ashe quickly makes himself indispensable at the vicarage, insinuating himself ever deeper into village life. As the vicar's wife, Vivien must be above suspicion, but will the dark, dangerous pull of passion prove too strong for her to resist?

Interweaving a devastating account of the bloody chaos of war with the ruthless seduction of a principled woman, *A Spell of Swallows* paints an absorbing picture of the vulnerability of love.

For Boz, Fan and Thea—
love always

CHAPTER ONE

The girl, carrying the cake wrapped in a cloth, walked along the river bank towards the ford. She walked briskly, partly because in April it was still fresh at this time in the morning, but mainly because this was one of only six days off in the year and she wanted to make the most of it. Eaden Place had changed in many ways, but some of the old traditions were kept up. The girl's mother had worked at the house twenty-five years ago, in the eighteen-nineties, and had always been given a simnel cake, made by cook, to take home at Eastertime: she said that judging by last year's cake standards in the big kitchen had slipped, but the cake had disappeared anyway.

The girl could have continued to follow the river round the side of the hill and had an easy, if slightly longer, walk home. But being young and strong, and in a hurry, she had decided to wade across and take the short cut over Fort Hill. On the other side she would turn south, and it was then only a mile and a half to her parents' small farm.

The water chuckled along next to her, going the same way. She whispered to herself: *Watch out for the swallows!* Her great-grandmother used to say that to her when she was off to play by the river as a child, because there was some old wives' tale about the swallows spending the winter under water, and flying out in the spring. She'd known even then that it was nonsense, that the swallows flew south, but as the river widened towards the ford, which was now in sight, she found herself imagining what that would look like: all the swallows bursting from the surface with the water shooting off their feathers—

She stopped. Beneath her straw hat, her hair stirred with apprehension. On the far side, in the deeper part of the river where the trout lurked in green shadows under the bank, the surface of the water was troubled. It began to churn, a small whirlpool formed, bubbles spun and burst—and then something sleek and dark broke the surface. Could it be? The girl started to move away, backwards at first, because she didn't want to take her eyes off whatever it was.

And then—oh my good God!—now she could see, and she let out a shriek, turned tail and ran hell for leather along the track. She dropped the cake, damn! but never mind that, and never mind the short cut, wild horses wouldn't have dragged her over the other side now; all she wanted was to put as much distance as possible between her and that *thing* from beneath the water.

*   *   *

As Ashe emerged, he saw there was a girl on the far bank, watching him, moving backwards with a bundle clutched to her chest, her eyes like organ stops. The next moment she screamed and fled, arms pumping and feet flying, even dropping her bundle in her haste to get away.

Not to add to her terror, he stood still until she was out of sight. Then he waded across, retrieved the bundle—something round and solid tied up in a kitchen cloth—and returned to where his clothes and haversack lay beneath the trees. Once he'd dried himself as thoroughly as possible on his neckerchief he dressed with care and put on his boots, and a tie. The damp neckerchief he folded and put in his pocket. Only then did he sit down and undo the bundle, and his eyes closed as he inhaled the sweet, spicy smell of fruit cake and almonds.

Ashe was very hungry. He'd taken the milk train as far as he could reasonably afford, and been walking for three hours since. He pulled the cake apart with both hands as if it had been a bread roll, and ate about a quarter of it right off before wrapping the rest up again, and even that was a struggle. Full, but somewhat disgusted with himself, he stood up, dusted off the crumbs and wiped his sticky mouth and hands on the damp neckerchief.

What with his cold river-bath, the sun climbing in the sky and the warm weight of cake inside him Ashe felt drowsy, and lay down with his head on his haversack, to catch some sleep. Which he did, like a baby.

*   *   *

An hour later he set off again. His bag wasn't full and he'd managed to cram in the cake—an unlooked-for bonus—with his few other possessions. It was a morning of shining, new-minted perfection, such as you only got in England, early in the year. Ashe's step was light; he felt full of walking, he could have walked to Land's End and probably on the water after that. This last idea amused him and he began at first to hum, then to sing out loud, an obscene army song that silenced the carolling birds and sent several small animals scurrying for cover.

It wasn't long before he emerged from the woods to find himself on a gentle green hillside; a dozen black and white cows lifted their heads and gazed at him, jaws rotating. Away to his left a road wound up the southern slope of the hill and disappeared into the trees. A couple of hundred yards below him was a hedgerow frothing with flowering blackthorn amongst which, about halfway along, he could see a stile. On the far side of the stile lay a shaggy, ungrazed hay meadow, its lush spring growth sparked with early wild flowers, yellow, blue and white; off to right and left, rich brown plough dusted with the brilliant green of new crops. In the gentle valley he noted exactly what he was looking for: the quiet gathering of cottages and larger houses that comprised the village of Eadenford, cradled in the curve of the river. From its centre rose a church tower shaped like a dunce's cap, topped with a cockerel weathervane.

Ashe paused to survey the scene: picturesque, peaceful, unsuspecting, a village populated by nice, quiet people who kept themselves to themselves and hung on tight to their secrets. People who would want to keep it that way. Rich pickings: easy money.

Yes, he said to himself. This'll do.

*   *   *

He began to make his way down the slope, fastidiously avoiding the cowpats. In the distance, someone was shooting rabbits and the crack of the

4

gun in the still blue air made him twitch. When he drew level with the staring cows he made a sudden leap towards them, teeth bared and snarling, brandishing his haversack overhead, and they trotted away, jostling each other in their anxiety to escape, their swollen early-morning udders swinging and bouncing.

Ashe reached the stile, dropped his bag on the other side, and climbed over after it. Hoisting it over his shoulder he went on his way towards the village, his long measured strides thrashing the meadow grass.

*   *   *

The Reverend Saxon Mariner, still lying inside his wife, could see the whimsical church tower of St Catherine's through the window. The weathervane might have been drawn with pen and ink on the pale blue sky. He savoured the contrast—Vivien's body beneath him, soft, sweet and white, and the sharp black image of the strutting cockerel—and felt himself stiffen a little in response. Vivien nuzzled her mouth against his chest; she called it 'kissing his heart'. He put his arms round her and rolled on to his side so that they were facing one another. Her eyes were still closed, but she put up a hand and stroked his cheek.

It was a rare day on which they did not spend some time in the bedroom. The cook-housekeeper, Hilda, if her employers were not in any of the downstairs rooms, knew better than to come looking for them. Nothing short of fire, flood or invasion by a foreign power would have been accounted sufficient reason. She was a stolid,

5

childless woman who had lost her husband in the South African war, and was not a gossip. Her lack of interest in matters marital was watertight, except insofar as they directly affected her duties— mealtimes, visitors and so on—and in those departments she had no cause for complaint; the Mariners were exemplary employers.

Slowly, Saxon withdrew from his wife; her eyes opened. He got out of bed, leaving her lying in exactly the same position, like the sloughed skin of a snake. Only her eyes, a shortsighted speedwell blue, followed him as he went into his dressing room and closed the door.

*　　　*　　　*

When he'd gone, Vivien closed her eyes once more. These moments of separation after lovemaking served as a kind of mental antechamber, a period in which each of them recalibrated and returned to their other, outward selves. She thought about her husband in that little room which was a foreign land to her, and one with closed borders. When he emerged, everything would be different. One of the questions which exercised Vivien was which married state was the true one: that which they had just experienced or the one they were now entering? They moved between the two so often, and on each occasion the transformation was complete. Though she could not be absolutely sure (she had no woman friend with whom she was intimate enough to discuss such things) she suspected that she and Saxon were unusual, and that most other couples, while they might or might not enjoy as much passion, had greater intimacy, an everyday sharing of thoughts and jokes and gossip and endearments.

She might have liked that. There was a fluidity in such relationships, a sense of partnership . . . Vivien turned on to her other side and gazed out of the window. On the other hand theirs was a partnership, albeit of a different kind. They may not in reality have been equals, but they aspired to equality. They respected one another. Her role in running the house and dealing with parishioners was accorded as much weight and value as Saxon's ministry to the people of Eadenford, and his poetry, which she could not always fully grasp but which she believed, in spite or because of this, to be good. He never invited her to read his work, but neither did he prevent her, and when she did look at it he always asked her opinion and listened with serious attention. She was neither patronised nor criticised. For a country vicar's wife, she had considerable freedom.

As she got out of bed and began to dress, it did not occur to Vivien that it was the half-expectation of patronage and criticism which made her appreciate their absence.

*   *   *

Saxon stood in front of the mirror on his chest of drawers, brushing his hair with ivory-backed brushes. He heard his wife moving about in the bedroom and as always allowed her time to put her clothes on before himself emerging. His dressing room had a door on to the landing as well as one into the bedroom, and contained an austere camp bed for those nights when he worked late, was out on parish business, or when either one of them was ill and wanted peace and quiet. The room was monastic, its walls painted a dark cream, the floor of bare boards, with a small rag rug by the bed. A washbasin stood in one corner. The only decorations were Saxon's Hogarth and Beardsley prints, and his green brocade dressing gown hanging on the back of the door.

He turned his head this way and that, touching the brushes lightly to the odd stray hair. He liked a neat head, inside and out. When he was satisfied, he took his dove-grey tweed jacket from its hanger and shrugged it on over his black clerical shirt. From habit, he spread his hands and examined the backs, then the palms. Immaculate hands were important for a priest. They were the bearers of blessings, baptismal water, bridal rings, the body and blood of Christ . . . the focus of so much faith and hope. Taking a last look in the mirror, he admitted a little vanity. There was nothing the matter with taking a pride in one's appearance. If he had a criticism of his wife it was that she, who had so many natural advantages, cared very little for presentation. She was not interested in clothes, and her exceptionally pretty brown hair, was generally untidy and without style. She stumped about the garden—and the village—in boots and a smock, to the occasional dismay of Saxon, who couldn't help picturing the splendour of a *soignée* Vivien. And yet no one could have called his wife frumpy. She looked lovely in whatever she wore, and he was sufficiently observant to realise that he was not the only one who thought so.

His own reflection showed a tall, slim man with the colouring of a fox, and the face of one, too—

narrow, the eyes a little close together on either side of a long nose, mouth thin-lipped but wide; a face that was sharp, alert, self-possessed and (something Saxon didn't himself see) a little predatory.

*   *   *

Vivien, now dressed, and with her glasses on, was pushing a pin into her hair and had another in her mouth when her husband came back into the bedroom.

'Right,' he said. 'On with the dance.'

Round the pin, she answered: 'I'll be down in a minute.'

'Take your time, my dear.'

This exchange, or something like it, was their usual one at these moments. Even after nearly five years of marriage, his telling her to take her time still had the effect of making her ever so slightly flustered. She didn't want to 'take time'. After all, what with? She couldn't help inferring that he wanted her to be engaged in a more elaborate toilette—one involving make-up, and petticoats and a light but sophisticated French scent.

She pushed her feet into her black, thick-soled shoes. Then she opened wide the window. A rustle, and a darting movement just above her head, reminded her that the first swallows had returned, bearing a flicker of southern sun on their wings. Each year she took pleasure in them: their homing instinct, their loyalty, the thought that in whatever Mediterranean place they had spent the winter the eaves of this grey English house had remained as a single, fine, background note, calling them home.

9

She braced her hands on the sill and leaned out, like a figurehead on the prow of a ship. At this time of the year, before the leaves on the churchyard trees had grown too thick, you could still just see the green hill to the east of the village. It put her in mind of the arched neck of a horse, with a dark mane of trees along the top of the ridge.

It was not yet nine o'clock and the sun struck the top of the church tower, turning the slates to silver. Vivien had an ambivalent relationship with St Catherine's. She was not a true Christian in the doctrinal sense; there was much she did not and could not believe though she stood there on Sundays and mouthed the creed for Saxon's sake. On the other hand she was fond of the building itself, the core of which had stood on this spot for nearly six hundred years and which was Saxon's place of work and their livelihood. She was not the only one; others felt the same. Over the past four years people had 'turned to the church' in a quite literal sense, wanting to find there some reassurance in fear and comfort in loss. So many families had lost their men—excited young men, proud, stubborn older ones, baby-soft boys whose lies were greedily accepted, heroes, opportunists, cowards, fools, leaders and foot-draggers. They had set out as individuals, distinct and particular, and become The Fallen, a human mulch for other Springs, in other places. The memorial was still with the monumental mason in the local market town of Bridgeford, (just in case—one lad was still in hospital in London, very poorly), but it would be put in place soon, and a service of dedication held in honour of those it commemorated.

10

With these thoughts running through her head it wasn't surprising that Vivien was startled to see a man standing down in the churchyard with a haversack on the ground next to him. Could this be one of those sons of Eadenford, a late returner from the war? There was something unusually assured in his manner. He was smartly dressed, in a dark jacket, collar and tie, and was gazing about him, feet apart and hands in pockets, like a prospective buyer weighing up a purchase. She took a small step back, and he must have noticed the movement because he lifted his head and looked directly up at her. Embarrassed, she retreated swiftly from the window, but not before she had registered something very strange about his face.

*   *   *

Susan Clay was the oldest child in her family, but also in a way the youngest, because she was simple. At thirty-two Susan had the mind of a seven-year-old. Her face was young, too, round and bland, and her body had matured without that tingle of womanly awareness, so it was lumpy and slack. She liked decoration as a little girl does, and her thin hair bristled with bows and colourful tin slides which she put in herself, carefully, with her chubby fingers. She hadn't a mean bone in her body, everyone liked her. The Clays were nice people; Ted, the blacksmith, had added bicycle and even car repairs to his repertoire; not many in the village at present, but they would come. His wife, Edith, was a big, strong, no-nonsense woman who ran a tight ship at home and was well able to help in the forge when necessary, holding the heads of the great shires, or putting her shoulder to their stubborn backsides. Susan's younger sisters were both married; one lived in the next village and one here in Eadenford. Of her two brothers one had been killed early on in the war. Jamie, the youngest, lived at home like Susan, and worked with his father in the smithy.

Susan may have been simple but she was not idle, Edith saw to that. She was quite able to help out with domestic chores and to perform straightforward errands. Friends and neighbours willingly cooperated out of affection and respect for the family. On this particular morning Susan was on her way to the vicarage with a note for the reverend. This was a commission which suited everyone—Susan because Mrs Mariner was very pretty and nice and let her stay as long as she liked, and Edith because her daughter would be safely and happily occupied till at least midday.

Depending on her destination, Susan followed various prescribed routes around the village— Edith's encouraging of her independence wisely did not extend to the exercise of too much initiative. The walk to the vicarage took her along Back Street, which ran east-west parallel with High Street. At the end of Back Street, before the Jug and Bottle, she turned right, and joined High Street near Moon's the bakers. If Mr Moon was in a good mood and not too busy he'd jerk his head to invite her in and give her a bag of 'bits' still warm from the oven. Today was not one of those occasions, though Susan dawdled past and gazed hopefully in Mr Moon's direction. There were several people at the counter and he wore an irritable expression. Edith often expressed her bafflement at why people like Arthur Moon went into the retail business when they didn't care for the customers, but there it was.

About fifty yards further along the High Street curved to the northwest, and the buildings petered out, leaving the road to continue to climb its winding way up Fort Hill. On the far, outer side of the bend stood the church, and just beyond it the vicarage. Both of these buildings Susan found rather forbidding, the first because she was occasionally dragged along there for what seemed hours of sitting still, keeping quiet and paying attention, the second because Mr Mariner, architect of her misery in church, lived there, and she sensed (there was nothing the matter with her woman's intuition) that he was not generally liked. Also the vicarage, a much more recent building than St Catherine's, was a tall, frowning house made of gloomy grey brick. The front door seemed to crouch in darkness behind its pillared porch, but mercifully Susan didn't have to use that. Her route took her through the churchyard and the iron kissing-gate into the vicarage garden and hence to the back door, which was perfectly ordinary and led into the province of Hilda, and the nice and smiling Mrs Mariner.

Susan was utterly dependable. Given a task, she carried it out to the letter. From the moment her mother said 'Here's a note for Mr Mariner,' she carried in her head the picture of herself placing the note into Mrs Mariner's hands (she rarely saw the vicar) and that became her whole focus until the picture coincided with reality, when she would relax and give herself into Mrs Mariner's keeping until she in her turn said: 'Better get along home now'—when she would set off along the way she'd come with the picture of her mother's kitchen in her head all the way until she got there.

So it was a surprise when, as she came round the corner of the church, a voice said:

'Morning.'

*   *   *

Ashe had seen the woman watching him from the vicarage window—he assumed from its position that it was the vicarage. She might have been a maid, or the lady of the house, hard to tell. He was aware of the impression he made and was amused at how rapidly she disappeared when he caught her looking. Just like the girl earlier on. People spying thought they had the advantage over you, but if you let them know you were on to them, then quick as a flash it was they who were at a disadvantage.

That wasn't going to happen to him. He'd sat down in a sunny position in the angle between the vestry door and one of the stone buttresses. If anyone walked through the churchyard he'd see them before they saw him. Like this one, stumping along and humming to herself, in a world of her own. Perfect.

*   *   *

Susan didn't for a moment think anyone could be addressing her, so she ignored the greeting. But next thing she knew a dark figure reared up beside the church, and she heard the voice again:

'Hallo!'

14

She paused, but didn't look round, and kept her eyes fixed on the gate, now only a few yards away. The man came right up to her and bent his head sideways to look at her. His eyes were dark and bright, adding to the birdlike impression, but she avoided looking directly into them, both from shyness and because there was something frightening about him.

'What's the hurry?' he asked. His voice was soft and friendly and he seemed to be smiling. Susan, who tended to reflect whatever came her way, smiled too, but kept her eyes on the gate.

'That's better . . .' He straightened up. 'So where are you off to?'

She nodded in the direction of the house. 'To the vicarage.'

'Do you live there?'

She shook her head. 'I'm taking a note.'

'A note for the vicar, eh?'

'For Mrs Mariner.'

'I see.'

Susan started once more walking towards the gate, but he took a long stride and a turn so that he was walking backwards in front of her, and she stopped, confused. He leaned forward again, getting his face where she could see it. She stared, unhappily. It was a strange face, some of it the same as other people's, some of it not, but he was still smiling and she was beguiled, and stopped again.

'That's better. What's your name?'

'Susan Clay.'

'All right, Susan, would you like to sit down and have some cake with me?'

With the scent of Moon's still in her nostrils, it

was as if he'd read her mind. Still she hesitated, mindful of her mother's injunctions not to speak to strangers. But it was sunny here, and she was only a stone's throw from her destination.

'What sort of cake?'

'Come and see.' He walked away from her, back to the corner of the church wall, where a canvas bag lay on the grass. He didn't look to see if she was following, but crouched down, opened the bag, and took out something wrapped in a checked cloth like the ones Susan's mother used in the kitchen. He untied the corners, and lowered his face, sniffing with his eyes closed.

'Mmm . . .'

Cautiously, she advanced.

Ashe was almost ashamed of himself for practising on such an easy subject. He spread the cloth on the ground and stood what remained of the simnel cake upright in the centre, repositioning a couple of the marzipan balls which had come askew. He did all this with eyes downcast in apparent concentration, reeling the girl in. When he'd finished she was there, standing next to him. It was good to know his gift hadn't deserted him.

Still without looking up, he said: 'Sit down, make yourself comfortable.'

She only hesitated for a second. Till now there'd been no sign of the note, but as she sat down he saw it, pinned inside her skirt pocket. He studied her covertly as he felt in his pocket for a penknife. Simple she might be, but she was not neglected. Though her fat legs covered in downy hair stuck out in front of her, apart, like a doll's, there was no smell and her hair and clothes were clean. It was impossible to judge her age except that she was no

16

child; she carried her ungainly breasts awkwardly, like a bolster strapped to her chest. None of this prevented Ashe's usual reaction of revulsion.

He cut off a small piece of the cake and popped it in his mouth, conscious of the girl's eyes glued to his every movement.

'It's good . . . Want some?'

'Yes please.' She was polite, too.

He cut off another, larger piece, topped it with a piece of marzipan, and held it out to her on the flat of his hand. She took it carefully and held it in her own cupped hand, gazing with obvious longing first at the cake, then at him beneath her sparse, pale lashes. He realised that she was being well brought up, waiting for him to begin eating again. He popped in another mouthful and she did the same, tucking in with gusto, and continuing in silence until her slice was all gone. Then she dusted busily at her lap, and flapped her floral cotton skirt, shaking crumbs in all directions.

'Food for the birds,' said Ashe.

'Yes.' She nodded, her moon-face illuminated by a sweet smile.

*   *   *

He was a nice man, and Susan had enjoyed the cake. A couple of sparrows hopped about in the grass nearby, feasting on the crumbs. Susan peered over her shoulder, checking that the vicarage was still there, and no one was getting cross, but all was tranquil.

Her new friend leaned his head back against the church wall and closed his eyes in the sun.

'So what's the vicar like, then?'

17

Susan had never before spoken to anyone she did not know, or who did not know her, so a question of this sort was unprecedented and she had to give it serious thought.

'He's very clever.'

'Is he now.'

*   *   *

Ashe, self-trained to detect verbal nuances, heard someone else talking through the girl. Whoever looked after her so well, kept her clean and smart and sent her on errands, had no great opinion of the vicar. The best thing you could say of a man of the cloth was that he was good; or kind, perhaps; patient, generous, understanding . . . But clever? The words 'by half' hung in the air. Ashe experienced a prickle of curiosity.

'What about Mrs Mariner, is she clever?'

She shook her head and said, as if the two qualities were mutually exclusive: 'She's nice. She lets me stay and help.'

'Make yourself useful, do you, Susan?'

She nodded, beaming.

'Well . . .' Ashe stood up and stretched. 'I mustn't keep you, then.'

Awkwardly, she leaned forward and got on to all fours. Her tongue stuck out slightly. Ashe stifled his disgust, and extended a hand.

'Here,' he said, 'allow me.'

He hauled her up, legs braced—she was no light weight. The effort turned her own face pink. As soon as he let go her hand, she felt for the note in her pocket.

'Thank you.'

18

He nodded.

'And thank you for the cake.'

' 'Bye Susan.'

Ashe watched her as she waddled away towards the gate. All very informative.

*   *   *

Saxon was in his study at the front of the house, but the tenor of the voices floating up from the kitchen told him that the Clay girl had arrived, doubtless bringing the bill for her father's work on the car. The envelope would be addressed to him, delivered to his wife. He suspected the Clays of presuming on Vivien's good nature, as they could always rely on her to keep the girl amused for hours. He was well aware of how fortunate he was in Vivien. Those aspects of the ministry which came hard to him—social intercourse at every level, little acts of everyday charity involving humour, patience and forbearance—were as natural as breathing to her. His belief was crystal-clear, his faith firm, but they manifested themselves in his relationship with the Almighty rather than with his fellow man.

Saxon had been acutely asthmatic as a child, and was still mildly so now. It was that as much as his vocation which had prevented him from joining up. As a young man he had been an editor of scholarly works on the world religions, among which were several exhaustive commentaries on the Bible and lively interpretations of Christian teaching. Till then he had been a churchgoer for broadly cultural reasons—he found the music and language of the Anglican liturgy inspiring—but his reading of these works had excited his intellect. To begin with he had seen taking orders as a way of perfecting his faith through study, but experience had shown this to be a naïve expectation. Here in Eadenford his role was not so much priestly as social, and if it weren't for Vivien he would quite frankly have failed in it. He admired and appreciated her ability to do what was increasingly beyond him—to love his neighbour.

He heard Hilda come up and begin clattering in the dining room. He closed his eyes; the world was too much with him.

*   *   *

Once the purse-lipped Hilda had gone—she was ambivalent about the Clays' daft lump of a girl—Susan began laboriously to unpin the note from her pocket. Vivien watched but knew better than to intervene or offer help. At last it was placed in her hand.

'Thank you. Is that for me?'

'For Mr Mariner.'

'Let me see . . .'

She knew perfectly well what it was, but to please Susan she opened the still slightly warm envelope, spread the page on the kitchen table and studied the bill, written in Ted Clay's round, deliberate hand.

'Good—I'll give this to Mr Mariner in a moment.' She refolded it and replaced it in the envelope. 'Can I get you something, Susan? A drink or a biscuit?'

Susan shook her head, hesitantly. 'I had some cake.'

'Ah . . .' Vivien smiled. 'Did Mr Moon have something for you?'

'No—the man out there.' Susan pointed in the direction of the churchyard.

With a little pulse of anxiety, Vivien remembered the stranger she'd seen from the window earlier. 'What man was that?'

'We had a picnic.'

'Did you? Did you really?' Susan nodded. Vivien took her hand. 'Let's see if he's still there.'

She opened the back door and they walked, still hand in hand, across the corner of the lawn to the kissing gate.

'Where was he?'

'There.' Susan pointed again. 'He's gone now.'

Viven stepped through the gate and took a look around. There was certainly no sign of anyone. She turned back, took Susan once more by the hand, and they returned to the house. Once inside she took her other hand as well, and faced her squarely.

'Listen, Susan. You really shouldn't talk to strangers. You know your mother and father say the same.'

Susan blushed guiltily. 'He liked me.'

'I daresay he did—of course he did, everyone likes you, but—it's just not a good idea.' She put her arm round Susan's plump shoulders and gave them a squeeze. 'Promise me you won't do it again. Hm?'

'I promise.'

'That's that, then. I shan't mention it to anyone. Now, I've got lots of things to sort out for Eaden Place, will you help me do that?'

'Yes, please.'

Saxon, deep in his writing, stifled his annoyance at the discreet tap on the door.

'Come.'

It was Vivien, with a note in her hand. He caught a glimpse of the Clay girl standing behind her in the hall.

'Saxon, I'm sorry to disturb you—it's Mr Clay's bill.'

'Thank you.' He took the envelope and laid it unopened on the desk. 'I do sometimes wonder if it's a good idea sending business documents by means of—' he nodded at the door'—that particular Ganymede.'

'Oh for heaven's sake!' Vivien gave a snuffling, contained laugh. 'Susan's safe as houses.' She paused, reflecting on a recent exchange and added, a little too emphatically: 'None safer!'

She touched her fingers to the back of his neck, and left the room. Saxon reproached himself with having been grumpy, but knew that his wife, if she had noticed at all, would have forgiven him.

*   *   *

Eaden Place was currently given over by its owners, the Delamaynes, to war-convalescents. Every room except their private quarters was packed with beds and on fine days the terrace, overlooking the broad walk and vista designed by Capability Brown, held rows of wheelchairs and truckle beds, while on the broad walk itself those patients who were able perambulated slowly up and down, on their own, in pairs, or aided by the nursing staff. The magnificent dining hall with its French wallpaper and engraved windows was crowded with unlovely metal-framed tables and folding canvas chairs, and the curtains smelt of overcooked vegetables and Bisto. But great work was done there. Since it had opened two years ago Vivien had organised regular collections of clothes, linen, blankets and bedding, and a couple of times a year, spring and autumn, the station van would carry a load up Fort Hill to the big house.

The trouble was that not everyone was scrupulous about what they gave. It was essential to sort through the donations in order to filter out items with holes or ineradicable stains, and make a separate pile of those that would simply benefit from laundering. When things were brought to the back door they were put in the little back sitting room which served as a general boxroom, and also as Vivien's retreat.

She took Susan there now. The sash window was raised a chink, but the first thing she did was to open it wider.

'Phew! Musty!'

'Oh look, puss!'

A sulky-looking tabby lay on top of a pile of blankets, narrowing its eyes and stretching its legs crossly at being disturbed. Susan scooped it up but it struggled free and disappeared through the window. The cat did not belong at the vicarage, and in fact Vivien had no idea to whom it did belong. She liked the cat and felt sorry for it, but its hairs, drifting through the house, made Saxon wheeze, so she tended to keep quiet about the surreptitious saucers of milk and fish-skin that she put down outside the window.

Susan went to the window and stared wistfully out. 'He's gone.'

'I'm afraid so,' said Vivien. 'He's not much of a pet. I suspect he only comes here to escape being made a fuss of somewhere else. But he'll be back, don't you worry.'

She felt in her pocket for her cigarettes and matches, and lit one. 'That's better . . . When I've had this, we'll make a start.'

* * *

Ashe took himself on a little tour of the village. The few locals that were about he avoided, looking away or crossing over the road so as not to ruin their day. For the rest, he liked what he saw: a high street with a baker and a butcher; a doctor's house; a forge and repair shop; a post office; and, most importantly for his present purposes, a couple of decent public houses, the Jug and Bottle and the Waggoner's Arms. Of these the latter looked the more respectable, and at twelve o'clock he went in and bought a pint of the local beer at the bar, and established there was a room to be had for the night.

'Passing through?' enquired the publican, with studied casualness. He was a professional, of course, used to dealing with all sorts; only his pallor gave him away.

'Might be,' said Ashe, 'Might not. If there's any work about, I might stay.'

'Oh, there'll be work all right.' The man leaned his beefy folded forearms on the bar. One of them bore a mermaid tattoo. Strong man—Ashe

24

wondered how long it would be before he made a comment.

'Perhaps you could give me a few tips.'

'I dare say I could . . .' The implication was that this depended on several things. 'Mind if I ask you a question?'

Ashe nodded.

'Nothing rude, but what happened to you?'

MESOPOTAMIA, 1916

They do nothing but complain. I can hear them now, whining and grumbling, pretending it's a bit of a joke, that they're Tommies and this is what's expected of them, but I don't think it's funny. What did they expect for Christ's sake—clean sheets, home comforts, a hot dinner on the table? They're all scared shitless, of course, that's why they're pissing in the wind: it's a hell of a lot easier to focus on food and filth than on having your brains blown out by the Infidel.

You won't catch me complaining. I like it here. Don't get me wrong, I hate dirt more than most people, had enough of it to last me a lifetime, but there's nothing I miss about Civvy Street, or England—and my view of 'home' is none too rosy, either. What you haven't had, you don't miss. My whole life so far's been a training in opportunism and Basra's an opportunist's heaven. Every single bloke here, officers and men, is after something, and if you can provide even a little bit of what it is they're after you'll be quids in. Not that I ever ask for payment. It'll come round, given time. And even if it doesn't, there'll be an opportunity to take it and no questions asked, because they know you're owed. With the officers, a bit of an obligation goes a long way, they like to pay up. They probably call it honour, but it's just they don't like owing anything to a member of the lower orders.

My three are pretty typical. Lieutenants Cornwall and Morrish, and Captain Jarvis,

Queen's Own. He's the senior officer, the boss, I don't do for the others till I've done him. Does justice to the uniform, I'll say that: long legs, straight back, beer-bottle shoulders—time spent on his turnout is never wasted: 'Ashe,' he says, 'appearances are important and don't let anyone tell you different.'

'Yes sir,' I say. 'Johnny Turk'll see his own reflection in these buttons. And if he scares himself half as much as he scares the rest of us we won't see him for dust.'

From time to time I play the colourful character; they love it. Jarvis isn't daft—he knows there's a bit of play-acting going on, but not how much. The trick is to flatter people by stealth, to feed them a few clues so they think they've arrived at some great insight all on their own, whereas it's only what you allow them and want them to know and not a fraction more. He thinks he knows me, but he doesn't. Nobody does.

He's an educated man, and a cultured one, I'll give him that. Taken the worst that public school and Sandhurst could throw at him and still come out halfway decent. When he found out I like to read he started lending me books. They don't like this climate, the pages get all spotted with mould if you're not careful, but if you rub the covers with a bit of dubbin you can keep them looking all right on the outside.

'Ashe, you're one of the few people I don't mind lending books to,' he said. 'They come back quickly and looking better than when they left.'

'Maybe,' I said, 'I should have been a librarian, sir.' That made him laugh.

I think he's a bit embarrassed at how well we get

27

on. He's not one to pull rank, likes to think he can get along with anyone, but in the army the leaders of men are supposed to be out in front and several rungs up the social ladder. I accept that, hierarchy's fine with me. Gives you something to work with. So Jarvis's attempts to get matey don't work with me. I never drop a 'sir' and I never take advantage. I keep that gap in place. It's more fun that way.

Well. I say fun—when there's sweet Fanny Adams to do, you have to make your own amusement. And the whole army—regulars, volunteers, Sikhs, top brass, cavalry, infantry, sappers, grafters and idlers—are hanging about in Basra waiting for the Call to Arms. No one's got any idea what that will involve when it does come. I mean there's not likely to be some glorious charge, we don't know what we're dealing with, and the terrain, from what we can tell, is pretty fair old hell. The Buddhoos (our name for the Bedouin) are at the gate, galloping about and firing the odd shot, showing off while they decide whose side they'd most like to be on. Perfectly understandable—we're in their country and when the show's over they'll naturally want to be alongside the top dogs.

At any rate, Jarvis and I and the other two are pretty comfortable in one of the requisitioned houses. Enough to eat, a roof over our heads, and only the number of creatures you'd expect at this latitude: mosquitoes, lizards, the odd little snake. That's not counting the flies, there are millions of them. Anything that stays still, they settle on, especially if it's dead. If you live on a swamp, you have to expect them. Like the Buddhoos, we're on

28

their territory.

Jarvis comes back from company HQ this morning relaying the master plan of some bright spark.

'A competition, Ashe,' he says. 'First prize to the man who catches most flies over the next week.'

I can't tell if he's joking, so I stay deadpan. 'Sir.'

'You have to have the corpses to prove it. To which end—' He produces a fly-swatter and a length of fly-paper, but he's still straight-faced. 'The tools for the job.'

'Thank you sir,' I say, 'I'll see what I can do.'

He hands them over. 'For the honour of the regiment, Ashe.'

'Sir!' I snap to attention.

*   *   *

It turns out it's not a joke. The idea is to stop men getting used to the little buggers and eating too much flyblown food—to encourage them to lay about them with the swat instead. But do they think that flies have a nine-month gestation period or something? For every one of the bastards that winds up on our fly-paper, there has to be another thousand hatching out every five seconds and getting on with the job.

Still, a competition is a competition and there's more than one way to play it. It turns out the prize is a bottle of rum. A lot of people might be desperate for that, but not me; I scarcely drink, and Jarvis and co have plenty of booze. So I set up a fly trap with an empty pilchard tin, grow enough bacteria to start a farm, and when it's seething with them I pop a sieve over the top, slip out the tin and get on with catching the next crop while the first ones die a lingering death. Makes me retch, but it works a treat.

After only one day I'm selling corpses by the handful, for cash. Everyone's got the idea that cash is useless. But when everyone has an idea, that's the moment to buy cheap as the market traders say.

'Come on then,' I say, raking in the lolly, 'I'll take it off your hands, you never know.'

There's an amazing number of simpletons about in the British Army. Or maybe it's one of the qualifications, a requirement laid down in Queen's Regulations as per:

1. *Must be easily led*
2. *Must not be critical of leaders*
3. *Must grouse about conditions*
4. *Must not grouse about hail of bullets . . .*

These men bellyache about everything from hard tack to mosquitoes, but line them up behind some smoothy-chops from officer training and they'll follow him to hell and back, no questions asked. Some chap who's practically in tears about the *gharri* horses in the street will boast of slitting open another human being, liver and lights, and stepping on his head to get to the next one.

I'm on my way out for a bit of a forage. I can cook, and the army cooks let me work round them as long as I don't get in the way. It's worth it, to provide my little gang with something a bit different, and a damn sight nicer, though I say it myself.

I have to stop for a second when I step outside.

30

The heat's solid, a smack in the face, like being too close when you open the oven door. Before, when I heard the phrase 'break out in a sweat' I didn't know what it meant. Now though—every last pore opens its little gasping mouth and the sweat runs down all over me. It's like losing a skin. And the stink! It made me gag to begin with, but now I'm used to it it's like the character of the place—the smell of adventure. Do or be done. The blokes from India say it's nothing to Calcutta but I take that with a pinch of salt. Another saying of the British fighting man: *It is not half as rough as the last place.*

Basra. See it on a postcard and it's the mysterious East; the gateway to Mesopotamia, where the Tigris and Euphrates meet; land of the Bible as they keep telling us (I never read it before but since we've been here I've taken a look at the regulation issue for research purposes). Estuary's called the Shatt-el-Arab—you can guess what the men do with that name. The only motor vehicles here are ours and not many of those; the rest of the traffic is carts and wagons and *gharris*, donkeys and horses, all in a terrible state. The way they treat their animals! Let's just say they don't share the British attitude to God's creatures. I'm not sentimental about animals: this is just plain wasteful. If a donkey's your means of transport, your livelihood, surely it makes economic sense to feed it from time to time, and not flog it to within an inch of its life when it's already carrying five times its own bodyweight in temperatures like a blast furnace? But what do I know, they have their ways. There are a few dogs and cats, feral, not pets. All the dogs, which I call Mr Dog, look the same:

31

pointed face and curly tail, always on the lookout. They're scavengers, but whoever gets the loot first guards it tooth and nail. You come across them dead in the gutter, all the time, torn apart by others of their kind. Dog eat dog. More food for the flies.

Did I say gutter? It was just an expression; there are no *gutters* where I'm going, through the back streets to the *soukh*. Everything, I mean everything, just runs down the middle of the street. You hop over or wade through; the little kids paddle in it and the dogs drink—pardon me, I get this gagging reflex when I think about it. Their standards of hygiene do leave a lot to be desired. Perhaps that's why the people don't age well: the drains and the climate. They're handsome to begin with, the children are the best-looking crooks you ever saw, and the women, you can imagine. But somewhere halfway along they start losing teeth and hair and gaining wrinkles, their hands turn into chicken-claws and in no time at all they're ugly as sin.

We're similar in one way, them and me. We're all opportunists. An Arab will say anything to get the result he wants at that precise moment. Whatever he thinks you want to hear, he'll say it, and at the time he'll mean every word. He's completely self-interested. Once you appreciate that, you can deal with him. You just have to be more self-interested than him. The phrase 'gentleman's agreement' doesn't exist in Arabic. A lot of the Tommies still think because our host's biddable, that means he'll do your bidding and come back. Dear, oh dear . . . These are the marsh Arabs, of course. Jarvis says the nomads out in the

32

desert, the Buddhoos, are a very different kettle of fish, code of honour, sacred laws of hospitality, loyalty and so on. I don't know how he squares that with all the sniping that goes on around the edge of this city every evening. They're superb horsemen and don't they know it! Charging up and down waving their fire-pieces, just so they can turn and stop on a sixpence. Nothing the matter with *those* horses, dripping with silver and silk, fed on Turkish delight and washed in asses' milk I shouldn't wonder.

Another thing, the Arab doesn't like to be known. He doesn't want to be read, or understood, he wants everything on his terms and if that means duplicity, what we'd call treachery, fine. It's the one thing about him I *can* understand—I don't like to be known either. Keep something back, and you hold the cards.

From where I am now you get a view down to the river. Across the end of the alleyway it's like a magic lantern show with the little boats going to and fro—the canoe-shaped ones, *bellums* they're called, and the bigger ones that are like gondolas, with swan-necks, the *mashoofs*. Pretty as a picture, with the palms on the far bank . . .

I stop to admire and the moment I do there's a little hand like a feather on my trouser pocket and I catch it, without even looking down, and nip the soft skin between my fingernails. He doesn't even yelp, just runs away like a shadow. It's all part of the game.

I can hear the noise, now, getting louder, and in a few minutes I come into the market place. It's huge, with dust rising from it like a smoking cauldron. There must be a hundred stalls and a thousand people. On the far side, come in from the desert, the Buddhoos sit on rugs with their camels and horses behind them, selling dates, and fruit, and carvings and jewellery. The tack on those horses alone would fetch a fortune in Bond Street, and the horses themselves—beautiful. As I walk over, the men watch me through their pipe smoke. Which of them was firing at us last night, I wonder? We don't trust each other, but then I don't trust anyone. Best way to be.

*   *   *

That evening I make them goat stew with some dates and onions and rice, and then yoghurt with honey.

'Ashe,' says Jarvis, 'you're a treasure.'

'Sir.'

The other two laugh, and Mellish says: 'And you're not going to give away your secrets!'

'No, sir.'

Later on they go to the officers' mess in one of the big houses by the river, and I lie on the roof and look at the stars. All around the city's seething but up here you can lose yourself. As it happens there's a thin crescent moon like a scimitar up there.

I never felt more peaceful.

CHAPTER TWO

The room at the Waggoner's was comfortable, and Ashe slept well. The next morning he got up early, washed, and shaved carefully. One of several advantages about the bad side of his face was that no hair grew there; which saved time, but you had to be careful, when going round the edge of the raised scar tissue, not to inflict painful nicks.

He dressed smartly (having scrubbed his shirt collar and cuffs the night before) and went down to breakfast feeling crisp and ready for anything. The girl who served him his bacon and eggs must have been primed by the landlord what to expect; Ashe could detect no blenching, or else she managed to conceal it by scarcely looking at him at all. As he was drinking his second cup of tea the landlord himself came in, ostensibly to stocktake behind the bar, but actually to find out a bit more about his only guest.

'Off out looking for work then?'

'That's right.'

'As I say—the forge, the farms, the station. All worth a try.'

'Thanks.'

Ashe wondered how he'd been spoken of in the bar last night after he'd gone up. He'd kept his answers as sparing as was consistent with politeness, but there would have been plenty of speculation in a little place like this. The landlord asked, casually:

'Be staying another night, you reckon?'

'I expect so.' Ashe glanced around. 'If there's

room.'

The landlord chortled. 'Very humorous! I think we can fit you in.'

Shortly after that Ashe went out, reflecting as he did so that the sooner he found a room of his own, the better.

*　　　*　　　*

Though it was no longer a new experience, Saxon never failed to be delighted by the first copy of a poetry collection. The freshness of the paper, its texture and smell—the *purity* of it all. The poems themselves were still at this stage pristine; they bore the fingerprints (both literal and metaphorical) of no one but himself, the printer, and his editor, George Lownes. If he could be said to have 'a readership', Saxon was ambivalent about it. He quite liked the minor celebrity that his writing afforded him, but only from the privacy of his own study: he shrank from the hurly-burly of the open market. After all, his 'readers' that George spoke about, who were they? Even in the rarefied literary world in which Saxon operated there were bound to be those who didn't care for his work, who found it difficult or obscure or who (worst of all) took refuge from their own ignorance by laughing at it. The mere thought of public ridicule horrified him. Saxon took himself seriously, as both priest and poet, and expected others to do the same.

He had unwrapped the little parcel at the breakfast table—Vivien had overslept—but now, almost furtively, he put it back in its brown paper and headed for his study to relish the moment in private and at leisure.

'Saxon! Is that what I think it is? Is it the book?'

She came running down the stairs, pulling on one of her terrible old cardigans, the brown one with pink felt flowers appliquéd over the holes. Saxon felt the usual pang of despairing tenderness. How could a woman so passionate, so intuitive and alluring when naked between the sheets be so completely lacking in style or self-respect when conducting her normal life fully clothed? It was a mystery to him, but one that he acknowledged lent something to their marriage since her other self was known only to him.

'Let me see!'

He held the book out to her and she took it almost reverently, turning it over in her hands, flipping back the dustjacket to admire the binding, glancing at the publisher's encomium, riffling the pages as if the book itself, and not its contents, were the thing to be approved and admired. For Saxon, her reaction was the right one at this early stage—it hadn't taken her long to realise that the actual reading of the poems must come later, when he himself had done so, several times. He appreciated his wife's quick sensibilities in these matters.

'It looks so elegant,' she said, handing it back. 'But have they done you justice? Are you pleased?'

'I am. Of course I need to . . . I shall write to George when I've looked through the book.'

'And reminded yourself what a wonderful writer you are!'

He knew the last thing she intended was to allude to the hint of vanity in his nature, but unfortunately that was the effect. 'Scarcely,' he muttered.

'No, Saxon, you are—everyone says so.' With this she kissed him.

He had already opened the study door when he turned back and asked, more to dispel his uncomfortable feelings than out of any real interest: 'What does the day hold for you?'

'Flower ladies this morning. And this afternoon I'm going into the village. It's my day for the school and I really should drop in on Mr Proudie.'

'That's very noble of you.'

'I like to!' She pulled an amusing little face. 'The school, anyway.'

Mystifying though it was, Saxon knew she meant it.

He went into the study and closed the door. Sitting down at the desk he once more unveiled the book and dropped the wrapping into the waste-paper basket.

Beyond Self by S.J. Mariner

He opened the book at random and glanced down at the right-hand page almost sideways, hoping to catch the poem unawares, to come at it as a stranger might, reading it for the first time. The words that caught his eye made him hot with the memory of their inspiration—so personal, on this cool, printed page!

> *. . . unknowable darkness; an angry pleasure*
> *And a sweet defeat . . .*

Almost superstitiously, before he could be disappointed, he closed the book again and sat still for a moment, with his heart pounding.

Ashe did not immediately take up the landlord's advice, but called instead at the post office.

'Excuse me—the big house, a couple of miles to the west of here—do you know what it's called?'

The postmistress was extraordinarily busy shuffling bits of paper. Her hands trembled; she cleared her throat. Ashe waited patiently for her to collect herself. This was why he wore a collar and tie, and spoke nicely: to help people feel comfortable. In the end she managed to answer.

'Eaden Place.'

He smiled, snapped his fingers. 'Ask a silly question . . . Who lives there?'

'The Delamaynes. Sir Sidney and Lady Felicity.'

'Of course.' Ashe scanned the shelves and pointed to a jar of treacle toffees. 'I'll have a quarter of those if I may.'

'Yes, certainly you may . . .'

Mrs Jeeps, glad of something to do and somewhere else to look, busied herself getting down the jar and weighing out the toffees. Ashe was used to providing people with these breathing spaces. This woman had probably been told about him, but hearing was one thing and seeing for oneself quite another.

'So . . .' he said casually, as she slid the toffees on to a sheet of paper and spun it twice to twist the top, 'a house like that must be a good employer. Does anyone from the village work up there?'

'One or two, yes . . . girl from Low Farm's in service there . . . that'll be a penny halfpenny, thank you, thank you . . .' She dropped the coins in the till and for the first time was sufficiently

39

collected to bring her postmistressly skills to bear on him. 'If you're thinking of looking for work they're not taking on any more at the moment, the place is given over to convalescents. More like a hospital at Eaden Place just now.'

'I see. Well, never mind.'

Mrs Jeeps gave him a sideways look. Now that she was herself again Ashe sensed a crafty, sagacious personality worthy of his mettle.

'Another thing,' he said. 'I'm after a room in the village.'

'I'll keep my ear to the ground, then.'

He favoured her with a smile. 'I'm not as bad as I look. But then I couldn't be, could I?'

'You poor thing,' said Mrs Jeeps, rather flattered to be taken into this stranger's confidence. 'It's not your fault. War, was it?'

'That's right.'

'It's an honourable scar!' she declared. 'Nothing to be ashamed of.'

Ashe forbore, on this occasion, to point out that he was not in the least ashamed, and went to the door. 'Let me know if you hear of anything.'

'I will!' she called cheerily. But her eyes, following him out into the street, held a gleam of speculation. She had a spare room.

*　　　*　　　*

Lady Felicity Delamayne—'Please, Lady D will do!'—was undoubtedly church flower arranger-in-chief, but liked to see herself as one of a team, a mere toiler in the vineyard under the supervision of Vivien Mariner. This set up an exquisite tension, because the fact remained that almost all

40

the blooms and greenery used came from Eaden Place, and arrived with their owner in the back of Felicity Delamayne's car before being sorted, subjugated and advantageously displayed by their mistress.

Eaden Place had once had its own chapel, dating from before the Reformation, but it had long since fallen into desuetude. The Delamaynes now had a family pew at St Catherine's and contributed generously to the upkeep of the parish church. The north wall of the chancel was thickly clad with plaques of brass, copper, stone and marble in memory of Delamaynes past who had lived and died with various degrees of distinction in parts of the world as diverse as China and Tennessee. In the churchyard stood a cluster of lichen-scabbed tombstones marking the last resting place of assorted Victorian Delamaynes, amongst them Sir Ranulph, who, when the original Norman church tower collapsed in a storm in 1852, had replaced it with the present whimsical tiled turret. His name was engraved on the single remaining bell, tolled by Saxon himself on Sunday mornings. It was the sole way in which he chose to show himself as a man of the people, not realising that his thin, corded arms, sweat-bedewed face and silent, masochistic absorption served only to make his flock feel appropriately sheepish as they sidled past him in the south porch. Felicity Delamayne never felt sheepish, but she considered it just as well his wife was waiting in the doorway with a warm smile and a hymn book to make the parishioners welcome, or they might have been tempted to slink away again.

Vivien did not dislike Lady Delamayne, but she

was wary of her. She certainly couldn't bring herself to use the 'Lady D' appellation (she would have preferred Felicity, but that was not on offer), and so tended to use nothing at all. On arriving at St Catherine's this morning, she found her already there and well under way. The other member of today's team, Mrs Spall, had not yet arrived.

'Hallo, hallo!' carolled Felicity from her stepladder by the pulpit, where she was threading forsythia through the seventeenth-century carving of birds and beasts. 'I thought this would look rather pretty!'

'It does,' agreed Vivien.

'I've given the lion a lovely fancy mane, what do you think?'

'Oh yes . . .' Vivien drew closer to admire the effect. 'What a clever idea. The children will love it.'

'That's what I thought. Hang on—steady the Buffs—' Lady Felicity came down the steps and stood back. 'It'll do.' She fixed Vivien with her terrifying smile, lips drawn back from an implausible number of strong, yellowish teeth, eyes narrowed in a way probably intended to convey a teasing jollity, but which Vivien thought more like someone looking through the sights of a gun. She was a handsome woman, smart and tough as the riding boots she wore so well. She usually spurned the chauffeur in favour of driving herself, often at speeds of over thirty miles an hour, drank American bourbon and was frightened of nothing and nobody. At some time in her early (it was said, misspent) youth, she had learned to tap-dance and had been known to do so both off and on the table at Eaden Place. It was generally felt that her husband Sir Sidney had much to contend with, but had known very well what he was taking on.

'Interesting woollie,' she said now to Vivien. 'Did you put the roses on yourself?'

Vivien was quite sure the term 'woollie' was not one Delamayne commonly used, but she was saved from having to reply by the arrival of Mrs Spall. Mr Spall was the butcher, but his wife was thin and pale as if years of proximity to fresh red meat and ripe game had sucked the blood from her. Still, she was of a no-nonsense cast of mind and Vivien was grateful for the diversion.

'Morning, Molly, how are you? Look what Lady Delamayne's done with the pulpit.'

'A poor thing but my own,' said Felicity.

'It's very nice your Ladyship.' Molly Spall's tone was merely polite, but Felicity Delamayne didn't need, or even notice, the approbation of others. Her *amour propre* was enough to keep her blazing away on all cylinders.

'*Now*,' she said, 'to *what* shall I turn my hand next?'

'I think I'll look at the font,' said Vivien, making for the back of the church where lay sheaves of early bronze and white chrysanthemums, daffodils, narcissi, primroses, more forsythia and a great heap of greenery. Molly Spall went first to the cupboard for vases and then, with cadaverous aptness, to decorate the old wooden bier that stood inside the north door.

'Look at us!' cried Lady Delamayne from her position beside the altar. 'You in your small corners and I in mine!'

For the next half an hour the three women worked away contentedly. The font was an easy option, which was why Vivien, lacking Felicity's firm hand with flowers, had chosen it. It didn't take long to fill it with daffodils and primroses and to arrange some of the spindlier greenery to trail down the sides. When she'd finished the other two were still occupied and she bundled up her cut stems and sodden leaves in a sheet of newspaper to take them outside.

It was another day of perfect spring sunshine. Lady Delamayne's motor, maroon and black with gleaming silver headlamps, stood in the road near the neatly prepared site for the war memorial. Vivien wondered whether, if she were to go home at lunchtime, she could persuade her husband to come out for a walk. A poet needed, surely, to be exposed to the beauties of nature. She sometimes worried that Saxon's undoubted talent might wither away for lack of light and air, but perhaps it didn't work like that.

She went to the far corner of the churchyard to dump her rubbish. When she'd done so she rolled up the damp newspaper, pushed it into the pocket of her skirt, and removed her cardigan, beneath which she was wearing one of Saxon's old shirts with the sleeves cut and hemmed just above elbow length. It was wonderfully comfortable, and she'd rescued a couple more that he was about to throw away.

It was as she came back round the corner to the main entrance that she saw the man, hanging about in the road by the car, and recognised him by his manner, which was almost proprietorial. He was walking round the car slowly, hands in pockets, stopping now and again to draw his head back and admire the whole, or lean forward to inspect some

44

detail. Vivien was unsure whether to say something; after all he didn't look or behave like a man who was about to do any damage, let alone jump in and drive the car away. But still—

'Superb machine.'

It was he who'd spoken to her, and who had caught her staring for the second time. She did hope, as she walked over, that he would not recognise her from that first occasion.

'I don't know much about cars, I'm afraid.'

'Take my word for it.' He remained in profile, gazing at the car. Vivien could not place him on the social scale; he was well spoken and did not sound like a labourer, but neither did he look quite like a professional man. His tone was even and civil, a tone used between equals.

'Yours?' he asked.

'No. My husband owns a car but I don't drive it. This belongs to Lady Delamayne,' she said and added, because for some reason she wished to make it clear that she was not alone, 'She's in the church.'

'Delamayne . . . From Eaden Place, then?'

'Yes.'

'Whoever polishes this for her does a good job,' he said, bending forward. 'You can see your face in this.'

Afterwards, Vivien thought that he was giving her a veiled warning, because when he straightened up and turned towards her it was the first time she'd seen him full face and at close quarters, and she could not help herself.

'Oh my God!' Instinctively, she removed her glasses and put her hand to her eyes.

'John Ashe,' he said, as if correcting her.

'I do apologise . . . I'm *so* sorry. Mr Ashe . . .' Covered in confusion she replaced her glasses but was literally unable to know where to look. But his expression, on that half of his face which could express anything, was mild.

'You have the advantage of me,' he said imperturbably.

'Vivien Mariner.' She was still struggling to collect herself. 'I really can't apologise enough for that silly, thoughtless reaction.'

'Don't worry,' he said. 'I'm used to it. It's other people I feel sorry for.'

'How dreadful.' Vivien shook her head. 'The war? I feel so awful.'

He ignored this. 'Mrs Mariner—you live at the vicarage.'

It was a statement. She realised that hers was the second name he had successfully identified and placed.

'Yes. Yes—we're in there doing the flowers.'

'You and Lady Delamayne.'

'There are three of us.'

'I'd better let you get on,' he said and would have walked away then and there.

'Excuse me, Mr Ashe.'

With studied politeness, he paused.

'Mr Ashe, I must ask—only we haven't met before and I thought I knew most—do you live in Eadenford?'

'Let's see . . .' he said, gazing for a moment at the ground. When he looked back up Vivien didn't flinch, and congratulated herself on her small victory.

'I do now,' he said.

Felicity Delamayne appeared in the south door as she returned.

'There you are, we wondered where you'd got to . . .' She peered over Vivien's shoulder. 'Who's that, I wonder?'

Vivien felt an impulse to protect her new acquaintance from Felicity's suspicion.

'A Mr John Ashe. He's new to the village and he was admiring your car.'

'I could see that.' Felicity was if anything even more suspicious. 'Why on earth would anyone new come to Eadenford? The streets are hardly paved with gold. Oh well, there's no accounting for taste . . . As long as you caught him at it.'

'Honestly, you had nothing to worry about,' said Vivien. 'He was a—' She hesitated, the word 'gentleman' not being quite accurate. 'He's just a motor-car enthusiast.'

'I dare say.' Felicity stretched her neck and settled her fine shoulders in a horse-like movement. 'I'm glad you spotted him.'

They went into the church together. Molly Spall was putting a cushion of primroses in moss on one of the south windowsills. She stepped carefully off the pew.

'I saw him yesterday,' she said. 'That man, in the street. Yesterday and again this morning.'

'Did you, Molly?' Vivien was glad to have found an ally to bear out her view that Ashe was harmless. 'Awful, isn't it, what's happened to his face.'

'What's the matter with his face?' asked Felicity.

'Nasty,' agreed Molly, which to Vivien's

47

practised ear seemed to imply neither pity nor sympathy, but a suggestion that disfigurement was a sign of moral turpitude.

'Enlighten me,' said Felicity, looking from one to another.

Mrs Spall waved a hand. 'You wouldn't want to know, your Ladyship.'

'The whole point is that I *would*.'

Vivien wondered how on earth to describe the terrible twist of the features, the gnarled shiny skin and the gash of a mouth. 'He's very badly scarred,' she said lamely. 'Only on one side, but it is frightening when you see it for the first time—isn't it Molly?'

Mrs Spall twitched, and said again: 'Nasty.'

'I feel so sorry for him having to live his life behind that—having to suffer other people's reactions all the time. I'm afraid mine was simply appalling, it gave me such a shock—I was positively rude.'

'I wouldn't give it another thought.' Felicity patted her arm confidingly. 'He probably enjoys it. You'd be surprised,' she sighed with a world-weary air, 'at the things men get pleasure from.'

This was one of those exchanges, freighted with a complex cargo of social nuance, where Felicity might say pretty much what she liked but it would have been entirely inappropriate for Vivien to respond in kind. No matter how much she wanted to reply that no, she wouldn't be in the least surprised, such an answer would have been unthinkable. Instead, she busied herself with the tidying up, and ten minutes later they left the church.

'Would you like to come in for a cold drink? Or

some coffee?' she asked.

Mrs Spall said thank you but she must be getting back, but Felicity proclaimed an agony of indecision.

'Well, I shouldn't . . . no, I mustn't . . . On the other hand, why not?' Vivien stood silently by during this soliloquy. 'Yes—you've persuaded me.'

Vivien declared herself delighted. 'I'm afraid I must take you in at the back door, I don't have my key.' She hoped to be forgiven for this white lie; the front door was not locked, but she didn't want to expose Saxon to the possibility of interruption

'For heaven's sake!' said Felicity, following her across the grass to the kissing-gate. 'Is that clever husband of yours at home?'

'Working in his study,' said Vivien and couldn't resist adding: 'He got the first copy of his new poetry collection this morning.'

'Oh! How *simply* wonderful. I'm in complete awe. And he's so modest, he hides his light under a bushel. I don't imagine there's more than half a dozen people in the village know that their vicar's a famous poet.'

Vivien opened the back door. 'I'm not sure he'd accept "famous". "Distinguished", perhaps.'

'All right, all right, what do I know? I'm the first to admit I'm not a poetry reader, or novels either. Not much of a reader, in fact. But I still think it might wake the congregation up a bit if they knew what he gets up to!'

*   *   *

Saxon heard the unmistakable tones of Felicity Delamayne and held himself quite rigid for a

49

moment until he was sure Vivien had taken her into the drawing room. He trusted his wife implicitly not to breach his privacy, but that woman was a force of nature, and might do anything.

He sometimes felt himself completely surrounded by women. There were activities which another man might have undertaken to remedy this—sports, shooting, the public house (though that particular recourse was hardly open to a man of the cloth), a club in town—but none of them appealed to his solitary nature. If there were just someone, some other male presence, to restore the balance . . . He and Vivien had been married for some years now and though they never discussed it he was beginning to accept that there would be no children. He would have liked a son, if only for simple reasons of male vanity, the continuance of the Mariner line, the signs of his genetic legacy in another. But when his thoughts strayed to the dark and mysterious details of pregnancy, birth and infancy he shied away from them, so perhaps it was just as well that parenthood was not to be.

In one of those subversive, uncalled-for shifts of the imagination he found himself entertaining a picture of Vivien, gleaming and fecund, a baby at her breast, one hand cradling its head, the other guiding her nipple into its rosebud mouth . . .

Saxon shifted in his chair and banished the picture. Even through two doors he could hear the Delamayne woman's voice.

There was a tap on the door. 'Yes?'

'It's me, sir, Hilda.'

'What is it, Hilda?'

'Mrs Mariner wondered if you'd like a cup of coffee.'

'Um, let's see . . .'

' 'I've got one here, sir.'

'Very well then, thank you.'

Hilda came to the desk and set the coffee down at his elbow. It always seemed to him that she moved with maddening, deliberate slowness. By the time she was out of the room and the door had closed behind her, Saxon's teeth were clenched.

He picked up *Beyond Self* again. The gloss of newness had already gone from it and he was beginning to notice infelicities in the production and, worse, the writing.

*   *   *

Seeing that car had given Ashe an idea. After eating a pie at the other pub in the village, the Jug and Bottle, he went back to his room, entering the bar quietly and slipping up the stairs so as not to attract attention.

He certainly wouldn't want to work at Eaden Place, with all that would entail in terms of hierarchy and claustrophobic 'below stairs' power politics—it had been all right in the army but he never wanted to do it again—but he'd learned to drive before the war, and was good at it. He knew how cars worked, too. He wondered how many people there were in Eadenford who could afford a car; those were the ones to be with.

He also thought about Mrs Mariner, with her strange clothes and untidy hair. The spectacles which gave her a schoolgirlish air . . . She was definitely the one he'd seen at the window. A woman with a direct manner, but who could still blush. Not, he'd have thought, your usual clergy

51

wife. What would the man who was married to such a woman be like—the vicar? They'd repay investigation.

The vicarage, of course, had a garage.

*   *   *

That afternoon, Vivien saved the puppies till last, her reward for visiting Sam Proudie in his disgusting cottage. To fortify herself she dropped in at the school first. Saxon went once a week to take morning assembly, which both he and his audience found a high trial and were hugely relieved to get out of the way. Her visits were by way of salving his reputation, but they were also an indulgence. She liked children, and was happy reading to the younger pupils or playing games on the small field at the back with the older ones. They in their turn were entranced by a grown woman who would grab up her skirt in one hand in order to race after the ball or between the wickets, her face pink and her hair falling out of its pins.

'Go on, Mrs Mariner!' they yelled. 'Get it, Mrs Mariner, run!'

After this, half an hour in Sam Proudie's noisome company was just about supportable. She reminded herself that he was stricken in years, had no family, and that cleanliness was only next to godliness if keeping clean was something you could manage for yourself. Worse even than the reek of unwashed clothes, dirty bedding and furniture and mouldy food was Sam's ghastly flirtatiousness, all rheumy, rolling eyes and toothless smirks. When she came out she walked quickly down the alley between the cottages, leaned on the wall and smoked a cigarette rapidly and furtively, like a naughty child.

Clays' Forge was round the back of their house, its entrance on to the lane at the rear, but there was no missing its hiss and clatter, and the singeing reek of iron and horses' hooves. Ted Clay had once told Vivien that horses liked being shod and even the flightiest of them would stand quiet, heads low, while it happened. 'The way some women like having their hair done so I'm told,' he added, which meant little to Vivien.

Edith Clay opened the door to her, and the moment she was over the threshold sniffed, and said: 'Proudie's?'

'Oh dear, you can tell.'

'You're doing the Lord's work there, Mrs Mariner.'

'I'm just sorry I brought it with me.'

'Don't you worry. Now then, you want to see our puppies.'

'I do—if Bramble won't mind.'

'No, no, she hasn't got a mean bone in her body.'

The puppies, five of them, were in a corner of the small kitchen on a folded blanket, a row of them no bigger than guinea pigs burrowing into their mother's flank. Bramble, a black collie-cross, looked up at the women with an expression of patient, slightly anxious, pride.

'Oh, Edith, they're simply adorable . . .' Vivien sank to her knees. 'May I touch?'

'Yes, but better not to pick up while they're feeding.'

'No, I wouldn't dream of it.' Vivien stroked one of the velvet backs with her finger; it was fine, soft and warm, the bones beneath it delicate as a bird's, palpitating as the puppy sucked. She was enchanted. 'I can't believe how tiny . . . how old are they?'

'Two weeks.'

'When will they be able to leave her?'

'Another four, or thereabouts.'

'Will you be able to find homes for them all?'

'I hope so. Ted says we can keep one, that'll make Susan happy.'

'Yes.' Vivien sat back on her heels. 'Where is Susan?'

'Gone to see her sister and the children.'

'She's a good girl.'

'Hm.' Edith pursed her lips. 'She'd better be. So what do you think, Mrs Mariner, you'd like one? There's three dogs and two bitches, if you got any preference.'

'I would, I really, really would . . . I'm just not sure about my husband.'

'I expect the vicar'd like a dog. A man likes a dog about the place.'

'Maybe . . . I certainly think he should get out in the fresh air more than he does. He works too hard,' she added, in case this had sounded like a complaint.

'There you are then. You got to walk a dog.'

'On the other hand,' said Vivien, to herself as much as to Edith, 'for all practical purposes it would be my dog. I *know* I want one, and I'd be the one looking after it.'

'Once it's there,' said Edith comfortably, 'it'll be one of the family in no time.'

Though this was only a form of words, Vivien couldn't help thinking: *But we're not a family*.

She got to her feet. 'I'll have a word with Saxon and let you know.' She gave a little laugh of pleasure. 'They are the sweetest thing.'

'They are now, but remember they'll grow big. Bramble's a good size, and the father was that big old yellow thing from Low Farm.'

'That's good! I don't want a yappy little lap dog. And we have lots of room at the vicarage. If we do want one, when would I be able to choose?'

'Leave it till four weeks,' said Edith. 'They'll be proper little characters then, showing their markings, different sizes and what have you.'

'I'll come back then.'

Edith came with her to the door. 'And if you hear of anyone else that might like a nice pup, I'd be glad if you'd let me know.'

'I will. I'd hate to think of them not finding good homes.'

This time, when Vivien stepped out on to the street, she felt revived and excited. They might not be a family now, but perhaps their dog would make them into one.

*   *   *

John Ashe was approaching Clays when he saw Mrs Mariner come out. A big woman in a pinafore held the door for her and said goodbye on the step. He waited, pretending to look at his watch, until Mrs Mariner had gone, and then went to knock on the front door. He knew the workshop was round the back, but preferred to be a little more formal.

The same woman he'd just seen answered the door. Her sleeves were rolled up to the elbows, revealing forearms like a navvy. If she was shocked, she didn't show it. Word was getting round.

'Yes?'

'Mrs Clay?'

'Yes.'

'My name's John Ashe. I'm looking for work in this area and I was wondering if I could have a word with your husband.'

He stood placidly beneath her scrutiny. Unlike Mrs Jeeps, this was a straightforward woman who considered she had every right to size him up and made no bones about doing so. Eventually, she seemed to find in his favour.

'He's working out the back.'

'Do you think he'd mind if I went round there?'

'Don't worry,' she pulled her chin in and her mouth down in a grimace, but a not unfriendly one, 'he'll soon enough tell you if he does. Here'—she opened the door and stood aside—'might as well come through this way.'

He followed her down a short passage and through the kitchen to the back door. Everything was spotless. By the stove on a blanket lay a black bitch with a row of puppies suckling. The bitch's upper lip quivered warningly as he passed; a single white tooth gleamed.

'There you are.' Mrs Clay leaned out and shouted in to the din: 'Ted! Visitor for you!'

It wasn't the first time Ashe had seen the forge; he'd taken a look at it on one of his walks, yesterday after supper. Being evening then, it hadn't been open. Now, quite apart from Clay himself, and a chap in his twenties who looked like his son, there were two gargantuan horses, one tied up at the side, the other being shod. The horses

56

were shiny and coal black as steam engines except for a white blaze on their faces and the long white feathers over their hooves. The upturned hoof that rested on the blacksmith's leather-clad lap was the size and density of a large cannon ball. In spite of the fearsome force with which the nails were going in, the animal's face was calm, almost torpid, with drooping lids and the big soft lower lip hanging slightly. The other horse must already have been shod, because the younger man was busy putting a finish on its hooves, rubbing in linseed oil and then running a cloth back and forth in two hands to create a high gloss, like the shoeshine at Waterloo Station. Ashe's only experience of horses had been in the war, where there was no time for niceties like hoof-polishing. It surprised him now to see such a fuss made of working animals. His likening them to steam engines wasn't so fanciful, after all—these creatures were, to all intents and purposes, machines. They needed oiling and maintaining. The Arabs could've taken a leaf out of Clay's book . . . A real machine, a van, stood on blocks on the far side of the workshop. Some day the horses would be history. Roll on the engine, in his opinion.

Both the men were completely absorbed in their work and didn't notice him standing there until Ted Clay, his task completed, set down the enormous hoof and straightened up. He was built on much the same scale as the horses but after a quick look, first pitying, then shrewd, he was readier to smile than his wife.

'Hallo there!' He came over. Calluses rasped as he wiped hands like shovels on the leather apron. 'What can I do for you?'

'Mr Clay, I'm sorry to disturb you. Your wife said you wouldn't mind.'

'She did, did she?'

'I'm looking for work. On the motor side, perhaps? I can drive and I know a bit about cars.'

'I don't know . . .' Clay blew out his cheeks and shook his head slowly. 'Not many around here, I'm afraid. Not yet. And what there is we can take care of, along with the horses. These here are Nero and Nancy.'

Ashe held up a hand. 'Not much good with horses, and they don't like me either. Can't think why,' he added drily. It was a joke of sorts, intended to get over any difficulty, but Clay seemed intent on ignoring both.

'You've no need to worry.' He slapped the great kettledrum of a rump that loomed at his left shoulder. 'They're gentle giants.'

'I'll take your word for it.'

'Doug!' Clay called to the hoof-polisher. 'You can have this one when you're ready.'

The younger man, fair-haired and a tad taller and slighter than his father, flicked the cloth over his shoulder and stood up. Neither so steady nor so worldly as his father, he blinked on seeing Ashe and then coloured in confusion.

'Whoa!' He seemed to address his own consternation as if it were a nervous horse. 'Sorry chum, but . . . whoa!'

'Give over,' said Clay affably. 'I don't see him frightening the horses.'

'Not a pretty sight, I know,' said Ashe.

'War, was it?' asked Clay, giving Douglas time to compose himself.

'In a way. Accident.'

58

'I've seen worse.'

'I'm very glad to hear it. I wish more people had.'

'This is Mr Ashe,' said Clay, 'he's looking to work with motor cars.'

'How do you do.' Douglas held out his hand and stared fiercely down at Ashe's as he shook it.

Ashe adopted a philosophical tone. 'Not much going I understand.'

Perhaps Douglas had a conscience about his earlier reaction, or perhaps he simply wished to get rid of this grinning horror. At any rate, what he said was:

'You could try the vicarage.'

MESOPOTAMIA

Unloading is what we're doing, and it's taking for ever. What I don't understand is why the enemy doesn't come down like the Assyrian in that book of Jarvis's—like the wolf on the fold, and wipe us out while we're doing it. Are they waiting for us to finish so we can all have a nice fair fight? Unlikely. I'd say there are no flies on them, except that would sound like a bad joke.

What I'm trying to say is that it's them that put us in this situation, so it's surprising they haven't taken advantage of it. The entrance to the Shatt is pretty wide, but shallow; there are lots of shoals and sandbanks, and any decent-sized vessel practically drags along the bottom—the one we came in on had to creep through it as if we were negotiating a minefield. But what they did was this: before the supply ships started to arrive they scuttled a few boats in the mouth of the estuary, so now it's the hulks as well as the sandbanks making life difficult. Our ships moor out beyond all these obstacles, and our boys have to go in and out in the little Arab boats, lifeboats, anything they can lay their hands on, unloading the stuff piecemeal and piling it up on the docks, then going back and so on and so on. If you think that sounds like a cumbersome procedure, you're right. And because it's slow we have to post guards on the quayside to make sure that everything that gets unloaded goes to the right place afterwards. It only takes a couple of Arab 'helpers' with quick wits and light fingers and you're stuffed. They're the slickest thieves in the world and they do it all with a smile so you don't realise till it's too late.

It's all hands to the pumps. I'm on unloading fatigues like everyone else. I don't mind, to begin with it made a change. But what I didn't bargain for was the mules.

I never had any experience of mules, but one thing I assumed was that being a cross between a donkey and a horse they'd take after whichever one was smaller; in other words I thought they'd be donkey-sized. They're not, take my word for it. They're fucking enormous, with the worst qualities of both parents as far as I can see. God knows what getting a mule on to a boat is like; getting them off is— let's just say I haven't had so much fun since the old Queen died. We go out in a *mashoof*— nothing like the man for the job, but beggars can't be choosers—and the trick is to have the boat right up against the side of the ship so they can lower the mules down in a sling. When they arrive, it's our job to keep hold of several hundredweight of pack-animal in a paddy, with teeth like meat cleavers and a lethal weapon on the end of each leg. On a little wooden boat. Out at sea. In temperatures the wrong side of a hundred degrees. We have to secure it first, with ropes on either side; then get the sling off so they can pull it up and lower the next one. Each one that comes down it gets a lot more difficult, there's more angry mule and less space.

I never signed up for this. But the Turks would be having a good laugh if they could see us. A few more days of mule-disembarkation and they'll have the BEF on its knees.

Jarvis laughs like a drain when I tell him my

adventures. It's a good story anyway and I improve on it. My salt-of-the-earth number never fails to please. I don't mind him, but he's like the man in the moon, shiny bright and a long way away. I can't imagine what it must be like to be born so fortunate. Nice family, nice house, good education, good money, so much certainty. The thing is he doesn't even know that he *has* certainty, because he's never known anything else. He takes it all for granted. He talks about his life quite freely to me, mentions it anyway, and you can build up quite a big picture from the crumbs from a rich man's table. I know that his father was in the army, too, and that his mother had her portrait painted by an artist called Sargent in New York. She's very beautiful, apparently. I might have guessed that anyway, but he's got a photograph of her and he's not lying: 'She had a handspan waist and eyes a man could drown in,' he says. Fancy being able to say something like that about your mother. They have a house in Norfolk called Kersney Lee. That's the address—Kersney Lee, near Sheringham, Norfolk. The bigger the house, the smaller the address.

He's also told me he's engaged to be married. Amanda—I've seen her photograph too. She's not in the same league as the mother; I'm no connoisseur but I'd call her pretty. She doesn't have that regal quality beautiful women seem to have, that air of looking down their noses at lesser mortals. But very charming. Jarvis calls her his angel. They plan to marry next time he's on leave, but it won't be the big society affair they originally had in mind.

I don't know why he talks to me the way he

does, except he's not entirely comfortable with rank. You'd have thought someone who's known nothing but the top drawer and the silver spoon would be, but no. I'm sure he'd like to know a lot more about me, but he's never going to. For one thing, he's too polite to ask and for another he'd be shocked. All he knows is that I'm from London and I don't have any brothers or sisters. He's an only child too—about the one thing we have in common.

He's a funny mixture, Jarvis. Very clever—no, cultured, knows his books, his paintings and his music, and can talk about them. But a bit of an innocent. It's hard to say what he'll be like under fire. The one thing we haven't discussed is death. It's interesting; on the face of it he's got a lot more to live for, but he'd probably say that as an officer and a gentleman his life is forfeit. I have absolutely nothing waiting for me in England, but I still want to get back to it. I want to come out of this, alive, and I'll do whatever it takes to make sure I do.

I work hard for Jarvis. Perform small miracles, he says. I'm what he calls 'a good man'. Let him think what he likes, so long as it keeps him happy. In the meantime, there's more mules waiting. Bastards.

CHAPTER THREE

Saxon was strict with himself about observances. He might not be able to offer up very much by way of a congregation, let alone converts, to God, but he could at least ensure that he maintained a regular presence in God's house. To this end he crossed the churchyard, twice a day where possible, to say matins and evensong, or sometimes simply to pray. He tried hard to be humble, to thank God for his great blessings—his wife, his poetry, his modest success, the beautiful surroundings in which he lived—and to confess his manifold sins, chiefly those of pride and vanity. He prayed for greater understanding and tolerance. He hoped he was heard. He knew that to doubt for even a moment showed a sorry lack of faith, but there had always been a part of him which asked uncomfortable questions such as: Why should God, who had so many more pressing calls on his time and attention, heed the petitioning of a self-centred country parson who was not doing a particularly good job?

Still, Saxon persisted. He might lack natural gifts, but he could be dogged. He referred often to Luke, 18, verses 1 to 8, the parable of the persistent widow. His prayers, murmured in the deep seclusion of St Catherine's, Eadenford, were like the steady drip of water on rock. They would make a difference in the end.

This morning, the day after the first edition had arrived, Saxon had a lot on his mind. In the end, rather than write, he had at great expense telephoned his editor, and the conversation had been unsatisfactory in a way that he found hard to pin down. George Lownes was a big, smooth, handsome man of the sort Saxon had avoided at school and at Oxford, but with whom in later life it was as well to get on, since they were almost guaranteed to wield power and influence in the world. Saxon was far from being unworldly himself (another thing he mentioned to God), but he lacked George's suave bonhomie, his ability to wrongfoot an interlocutor by simply swamping him with charm. Which was what had happened on the telephone.

'Saxon!' he'd cried. 'Congratulations! I hope you're pleased, because we're all absolutely delighted. And I do hope you feel we've done justice to your work which quite simply gets more and more interesting. Tremendously impressive, and so—' here George seemed to struggle to find *le mot juste* for Saxon's writing, eventually coming up with two which Saxon felt sure had been put in place for just this occasion some time earlier '—so *finely wrought*, so simple yet so complex. Oh dear, am I allowing my enthusiasm to run away with me?' George laughed genially. It was another of his tricks always to introduce, early on, a disarming and pre-emptive note of self-deprecation.

Any response of Saxon's was bound to sound a little lukewarm after such a torrent of approval.

'I am pleased, of course. Vivien commented on how elegant it—'

'Vivien—how is she? It's much too long since you brought that charming wife of yours up to London. We must have a little celebration and my only condition is that Vivien accompanies you.'

65

'Thank you. I will, of course. George, there are one or two things I wanted to discuss. About the book.'

'*Beyond Self,*' said George, enunciating the words as though the very title were a source of wonder to him.

'Yes. For instance, I was a little disappointed in the paper quality. And on page twenty-one, 'Standing Souls', there is a misprint which alters the sense of the whole line. I proof-read minutely, as you know, and it's disappointing when something like this . . . as a matter of fact it's not the only one, on page seventeen—'

'Hang on, hang on!' George was laughing—*laughing*. Saxon was not a choleric man, but he was extremely glad they weren't in the room together, because he might well have done something he would later regret. 'Let's not take all the gilt off the gingerbread!'

'I beg your pardon?'

'Let's revel in publication of your masterpiece for at least one day!'

Saxon, whose touchy literary skin already felt flayed, could hardly fail to notice the pinprick of sarcasm in the use—the *wrong* use—of that word 'masterpiece'.

'It is not a masterpiece,' he said icily.

'Now then, no false modesty.'

'A collection cannot properly be called a masterpiece.'

'My dear chap, call it what you like. These are wonderful poems. Yours is a small but discriminating readership. The odd tiny imperfection in the production process is not going to affect their pleasure one way or the other.'

'You misunderstand me,' said Saxon, knowing he sounded pedantic but unable to help himself. 'It is I who am affected.'

'Well, I'm sorry about that, Saxon, I really am.' George allowed a second to elapse, and went on as if that dealt with that. 'When can you come up and wet the book's head—with Vivien of course?'

'I don't know. I'll have to look in my diary.'

Unusually, there was no suggestion from George's end that he look now, so that a date could be arranged.

'Good, but don't be too long, d'you hear? It'd be nice to celebrate while the book is still, as it were, in flight. Congratulations again. I'll look forward to hearing from you.'

Saxon had replaced the receiver with a burning sense of grievance.

*   *   *

At this moment, kneeling in his place at the end of the choir stalls, Saxon experienced that unpleasant feeling again. *Masterpiece . . . small but discriminating . . . while the book's still, as it were, in flight* . . . There was no doubt whatever that George was deflecting Saxon's wholly justifiable concerns by reminding him, none too gently, that the aforementioned flight would be brief, and that his slim volume was unlikely to trouble the bestseller lists. S.J. Mariner (the J stood for Julius) was a well-regarded, but minor poet, whom if push came to shove Lownes and Peart could easily do without. But Saxon Mariner, it was clearly implied, could not do without *them*. His clasped hands showed white knuckles. Dear God! he thought, and then, in a different vein: *Dear God, forgive me my pride and temper, and help me towards greater forgiveness and humility.*

He repeated this, or something like it, several times until his heartbeat slowed and his fingers unclenched. The power of prayer was something he believed in, at least where it affected himself.

After this he sat quietly, eyes closed, and tried to make his mind a blank, a receptacle for God. But inner peace eluded him and in no time at all he began fretting about this issue of the dog, which Vivien had raised at breakfast. In retrospect he was surprised she hadn't chosen an earlier time when he would have been literally unmanned and prepared to agree to more or less anything. He attributed her timing to an innate sense of fair play—another quality he respected in her.

Qua dog, it was not the animal itself so much as the disruption he dreaded. Saxon liked calm, and order, and a dog about the place—a puppy, for heaven's sake, as it would be to begin with—was as he understood it inimical to both. Also, the puppy in question could grow to be of enormous size and uncertain temperament; you never knew with these casual couplings what the result would be. He liked the Clays, but they were a rough and ready village family and any puppies of theirs would be the same.

'Just think,' Vivien had said, waving her slice of toast excitedly, 'what fun it will be taking it for walks!'

'We can go for walks now, whenever we want.'

'Yes, but we don't. At least you don't—or hardly ever.'

'I manage perfectly well without.'

'Saxon! It would do you good.'

'All right,' he said testily, 'so this dog will need walking—in all weathers, remember. Is that a reason in itself for getting one?'

'And it will be *fun*, too!' She leaned forward, smiling her sweet, wide smile that came from some unfathomable source in her, some deep natural wellspring of pleasure and enthusiasm. 'Company—it will lie by the fire, and welcome us when we've been out, and run around after sticks in the garden. It will keep me amused!'

It was a sort of joke, but he had heard something else, just as he'd heard the sarcasm in George's compliment. 'Don't I do that?' he asked childishly.

'You do when you have the time, of course you do, my darling, but you're so busy, and sometimes I just need to—' she smiled and shrugged, mock-sheepishly—'to *play*.'

'What about Hilda?'

'What about her?'

'Unless I'm an even worse judge of character than I thought, Hilda is not a playful woman, and dogs create dirt.'

'Let me worry about Hilda. She'll be fine!' Vivien lowered her voice to a more circumspect level. 'And anyway, the dog will be ours, and any mess that it makes will be ours too, in our house. QED,' she concluded triumphantly.

'We don't want to lose her.'

'We won't. I promise, she'll learn to love it.'

Saxon tried hard to remember how they had left the matter. He had a strong sense that though no hard and fast decision had been reached there was an underlying assumption on Vivien's part that they would be getting the dog. She was going back to look at the puppies again and would probably have chosen one by the time she returned.

Once more, he closed his eyes and prayed, this time for an open mind, and for forbearance. Vivien would care for the dog. It might, as she said, be fun, but Saxon had never been quite sure what constituted 'fun' in that sense. There were pleasures in life, great and small—his car, his writing, his married life, the church—but they couldn't be said to be 'fun' in the way he knew Vivien meant. Fun was a closed book to him. He was already aware of another, far more shameful, reaction to the proposed dog: jealousy. He could picture the scene all too clearly: he would be sitting in his study, head bowed over his work, while his wife and the dog larked about outside in the sunshine, 'playing'.

Appalled, he addressed himself once more to God. This was one of those occasions when he envied the Roman Catholics their recourse to the confessional. How comforting and cleansing to declare your sins and to receive, along with a small and undemanding penance, absolution. A sensible transaction. He knew, of course, that God was listening to his prayers, but there was no absolute certainty of forgiveness, no answering voice, no matter what he said to his congregation on Sundays. All was a matter of faith.

He remained on his knees for another few minutes, trying to focus on others in the parish who needed his prayers—the old, the sick, the unbelievers, the bereaved, of which the last remained by far the largest group. Then he said the Lord's Prayer, as being the one which

70

summarised and encapsulated all the others, and stood up. His knees were getting stiff, so maybe Vivien was right about the walking.

The ladies had done their stuff; the church looked lovely. One could not fail to be moved by people's hidden talents. Or, in the case of Felicity Delamayne, not so hidden. He took a turn, up to the altar rail, and back past the pulpit and down the north aisle. The air was full of the delicate scent of jonquils. Someone had arranged primroses in moss so they seemed to be growing on the grey stone windowsills. Another pleasure, this ancient place . . . Saxon actually preferred the building when it was empty, a place of seclusion and contemplation. Perhaps, he thought, I should have been a monk. But then there would have been no Vivien, without whom life would be quite simply insupportable.

Propelled by a warm rush of feeling for his wife—she should have her dog!—he left the church by the south porch and strode quickly down the path, through the lych-gate and into the vicarage drive. He was uncomfortable using the back door because the kitchen beyond it was Hilda's territory, where he was conspicuously out of place. He had no wish to be there any more than he wanted others in his study.

Perhaps due to his thinking about the dog, he did not go in at once, but paused in the drive. It was spring; very soon the garden would undergo a tremendous surge of growth, and they'd need to contact the lad from the village to come and cut the grass once a week. Vivien did a lot of the work in the garden herself, but like her its appearance was always slightly out of control. When the lawn

71

at the rear of the house was short and dry enough, the badminton set would emerge from hibernation in the greenhouse, and they'd have the occasional game. It was the only form of outdoor exercise that Saxon enjoyed. He was less energetic than his wife, but had a better eye, and very often won. Afterwards he always wanted, urgently, to take her to bed.

He walked now to the side of the house, to the wooden garage he'd had built to house his car. With summer on the horizon, he looked forward to doing more motoring. He took his keys from his pocket and undid the padlock, opening the doors and pulling back first one, then the other, over the thin gravel with that rasping, crunching sound which never failed to fill him with anticipation.

There it stood, waiting for him, massive and refulgent like a sacred object in its shrine: a car that was a touch too smart for a country vicar and which in consequence he didn't drive as much as he would have liked. The maintenance alone was an indulgence—Clay's bill would have to wait for a week or two. Saxon walked round the car, running his hand fondly over the forest-green paintwork, the shining headlamps and handles. It was a thing of beauty in which design, form and function were perfectly combined. He chastised himself, though only mildly, because he felt much happier now, for being grudging about the dog, which would cost a lot less than this, and repay a hundredfold in terms of Vivien's happiness. After all, if there were to be no children, a dog was the next best thing.

As he closed the padlock on the garage doors, he felt greatly cheered, and resolved to write to George Lownes—not apologising, for he had nothing for which to apologise, but in a friendly manner—and suggest a date for their meeting in London.

*   *   *

The station van arrived at midday to transport the clothes and blankets up to Eaden Place. This was the last port of call and the van was already half full by the time it reached the vicarage. The driver was the station porter, Higgins, a man of few words. The two of them, with Hilda's help, lugged the bundles out of the back door and round the side of the house to the van. This was to avoid too much cat hair floating about indoors and making Saxon wheeze.

When that was done Vivien went into the back room, and thought how nice it looked without the piles of bedding and clothes which had been accumulating in the corner for the past two months. The cat prowled about with its tail twitching angrily, looking for somewhere to nest.

All to the good if it didn't get too comfortable. She shooed it out of the window. When the puppy arrived, everything would change.

*   *   *

An unwritten rule at the vicarage decreed that daytime callers would always be passed by first Hilda, then Vivien, as through a sieve, so that only the most important or deserving got through to the vicar himself. There were hours, between four and six p.m., Monday, Wednesday and Thursday at which Saxon was at home to his parishioners. So when half an hour later the front doorbell rang Vivien looked up from her book, but on hearing Hilda's footsteps allowed her to answer it.

A very brief and muted exchange followed. Then there was a tap on her own door and Hilda stepped inside at once, with a distinctly flustered appearance, flushed, pop-eyed and slightly short of breath.

'Mrs Mariner—there's a man here!'

'Did he say what about?'

'No. I don't know, but he's—he doesn't look right to me.'

This could have meant any number of things, but there was no doubting Hilda's consternation.

'I didn't like to disturb Mr Mariner, but maybe—'

'No, no, Hilda, don't do that. You were absolutely right. I'll come.'

She closed her book and came to the door, where Hilda was dithering and puffing most uncharacteristically.

'Mrs Mariner, he doesn't look very nice.'

'Never mind, Hilda, looks aren't everything.'

'Just as well, dear oh dear . . .'

'You get on,' said Vivien soothingly. 'I'll see to it.'

By the time she opened the front door (which Hilda, in her panic, had closed in the visitor's face), it had dawned on Vivien who this visitor might be, and she had taken the precaution of removing her glasses.

'Mr Ashe! Hallo again.'

'Good morning, Mrs Mariner. I'm sorry about your housekeeper.'

'Please—what can I do for you?'

74

'I wondered whether I might have a word with your husband?'

'He's working at the moment.' Vivien lowered her voice pointedly. 'Can I help?'

*   *   *

Ashe knew at once that this was a more sensitive encounter than the one he'd had with Mrs Clay on her doorstep. Mrs Clay had not been in the business of protecting her husband, so the tenor of the exchange had been pretty straightforward. Though polite and welcoming, Mrs Mariner was a very different proposition.

'I hope you won't think this impertinent,' he said, 'but I wondered if there might be a job for me here.'

'What?' She seemed genuinely astonished, putting her hand to her breast and almost laughing. 'You mean work?'

'Work, yes.'

'Look, why don't you come in?' She led the way into a large and, he guessed, seldom used room to the left of the front door. 'What sort of work?'

'Well, for instance . . .' He smiled and looked round, making an expansive gesture. 'This is a big place. You might need help with the garden, the outside of the house, cooking.'

'Cooking?' She gave another of her puzzled laughs.

'Nothing funny in that, Mrs Mariner.' He kept his tone as light as he could. 'I can cook. I used to do it in the army. No one ever complained.'

'No, no . . . it's not that.' She put her hand, in which she held her glasses, over her eyes for a moment as if to clear her mind, and when she took it down she looked composed. 'Not at all, Mr Ashe. But we have a cook.'

'Very well. What about a car? I understand the vicar has a nice car.'

'He does.'

'I like cars. I can drive, and I know what goes on under the bonnet, too.'

'I'm sure you do,' she said, in a way that acknowledged his self-confidence if not his qualifications. 'I'm sure you do, Mr Ashe, but we really are not in a position to employ anyone else. Hilda does very well for us.'

'Hilda—was it Hilda who opened the door just now?'

'Yes . . .' She sounded wary.

'Can she drive a car?'

Mrs Mariner burst out laughing again. 'Certainly not! Hilda? No!' She shook her head helplessly; he'd never known anyone so ready to laugh, as if all the laughter was piled up in there waiting, needing to be used. It was incomprehensible to him. 'What a thought!'

This, he realised, was the moment to back off. 'Anyway, I'm taking up your time. Sorry to have troubled you, Mrs Mariner. If you do hear of anything, I'd be grateful if you could let me know, I'm moving to Mrs Jeeps's tomorrow.'

'Of course I will, Mr Ashe, I'm sorry I can't be more help.'

She showed him out. His hat was back on his head and he was halfway down the steps when he heard another voice, the husband's, saying: 'What on earth's going on?'

'Nothing, really.'

76

'Who's that?'

Ashe, his hackles prickling, kept walking, but was still close enough to hear Mrs Mariner say his name. He could picture the vicar's reaction. Still, he had planted the seed and sensed that he could leave it alone to germinate.

*   *   *

Saxon was firm. This was a situation where he was clear that a man must be master of his own house.

'I hope you said no.'

'Of course . . .' said Vivien, but the wake of her laughter was still on her face, as though she were keeping a secret from him.

'What's so amusing?'

'Oh, just something he said. About Hilda.'

'I don't see what opinion he could possibly have about her—he's a complete stranger.'

'It wasn't his opinion. He asked—' she giggled, and stifled it—'he asked if she could drive. And it was such a funny picture, so improbable, I couldn't help . . .'

Saxon ignored the laughter. 'Why did he ask?'

'Because he *can* drive, and knows about cars, apparently. So that would be a possible line of work for him.'

'But not here,' said Saxon. Irritably, he opened the front door and looked out; the drive and the road beyond it were empty. 'He shouldn't be knocking on the front door like that, and bothering you.'

'It was no bother.' Vivien dipped to glance at herself in the hall mirror, poking her fingers into her disarranged hair; she could see Saxon's frowning reflection over her shoulder. 'He was very polite.'

'I'm sure he was. He'd have wanted to ingratiate himself.'

'Actually,' she straightened up and faced him, 'he has to behave pleasantly because something terrible happened to his face, during the war. It's quite shocking. Every day of his life he must have to put up with other people's reactions, not all of them particularly kind, I imagine.'

'Well, I'm sorry about that. But others of them,' Saxon pointed out sceptically, 'those of the tender-hearted like yourself, extremely sympathetic.'

'I suppose.'

'He's a good deal more fortunate than many,' said Saxon. He didn't intend to be harsh, simply to protect his wife from importuning strangers on the doorstep. 'Many young men came back without arms and legs, unable to work at all.'

'I know that.'

'There are still dozens of them up at Eaden Place, facing an extremely uncertain future.'

'I know that, too.' His wife's face had become closed, and he felt suddenly that his well-intentioned warnings had stifled something in her.

'Vivien, don't misunderstand me. I just don't like the thought of some complete stranger taking advantage of your good nature.'

He had put his hand on her arm, and she touched it lightly with her fingers, acknowledging his apology.

'I know, I know . . . But he wasn't. He asked to speak to you but I said as I always do that you were working.'

'That was quite right. As long as you never

78

hesitate to call me if you—if you feel in the least uncomfortable.'

'I won't.'

'So we understand each other,' he said.

*   *   *

On her way downstairs to reassure Hilda, Vivien thought that no, Saxon did not understand her. Her reaction to Mr Ashe had not been, as he put it, 'tender-hearted'—but disconcertingly strong. Her heart felt not tender but—she sought the right word to describe it—alert. Unpredictable, and alert.

'He was perfectly pleasant,' she said in answer to Hilda's question. 'Poor fellow, imagine having that effect on everyone you meet for the first time.'

'What did he want?'

'He's looking for work. Like so many others.'

'There's nothing for him here, ma'am,' said Hilda. The 'I hope' was left unspoken.

'No, unfortunately, it seems you're right. A pity, it would have been nice to be able to help, but there we are . . .'

Hilda felt no compunction, only relief. She was as one with her employer the vicar, but for different reasons. She gave a shiver of revulsion; she could think of nothing worse than having to put up with that every day.

*   *   *

Back at his desk, Saxon remembered his wife stooping to look at her reflection, her hand straying, however ineffectually, to her hair . . . An

79

instance of small, feminine vanity so unusual that it had stayed in his mind. That, at least, was pleasing.

*   *   *

Ashe was prepared to bide his time on the vicarage, but in the meantime he needed work, both for the money and more importantly for reasons of reputation. Moving in over the post office in Mrs Jeeps's back room was a step in the right direction. The room was nothing much and she was a terrible cook, but she was a lot cheaper than the Waggoner's. If there was or ever had been a Mr Jeeps he was not in evidence, and Ashe sensed in his landlady an excellent source of and disseminator of village gossip.

He had no desire to remain a stranger in Eadenford, an ugly, unemployed, unknown quantity hanging about and providing easy meat for gossips. Work of the sort he wanted would be much more likely to come his way if he was gainfully occupied and accepted in the village. Clay's forge and workshop would have been ideal, suited to his abilities and tucked away round the back. But since there was nothing doing there, he preferred to be a little less central. He had seen the carrier's van with Higgins in his porter's uniform at the wheel, leaving the vicarage as he arrived there, and the next day he set out to walk the two miles to the station.

He was in luck. The stationmaster, Alf Trodd, was friendly and phlegmatic, and in need of an extra pair of hands now that Sam Higgins was 'driving about the countryside on charitable work' for a day or more a week. He stated plainly—no offence intended nor taken—that he thought it best if Ashe were not on the platform or in the ticket office dealing with the passengers face to face, so to speak, at least to begin with.

'In fact,' said Trodd, 'you could do the driving, the fetching and carrying and so on, and Mr Higgins can resume his normal duties down here.'

Higgins looked so crestfallen that Ashe, mindful of the need to stay on good terms with the village, suggested they take turn and turn about.

'Let me start with the driving and after a couple of weeks we can swap over. If that's satisfactory to you.'

The stationmaster professed himself perfectly happy so long as the work got done, and mentioned a going rate which would cover his room without much to spare. Still, this situation was only temporary; with a following wind something else was going to come up soon.

The very next day he took the wheel of the van to deliver packages off the London train to Eaden Place. Just sitting up there, feeling the throb of the engine and the road unwinding beneath the wheels, was exhilarating. Freedom. When people said that's what they'd been fighting for he'd remained unconvinced—most of the men doing the fighting had about as much freedom back home as the average pet rat. Such a luxury was enjoyed by people with money. Money bought you choice, and the power to exercise it. But this, this wonderful mobility, was a little taste of freedom. He could so easily—though he wasn't about to—have simply gone on driving, gone wherever he chose until the petrol ran out. He felt no particular gratitude to Trodd, let alone Higgins, for this

81

opportunity; he was using them, and they were lucky to have him.

As he began the ascent of the long hill towards Eaden Place he reflected on Mrs Mariner, taking his small store of observations out and turning them over in his mind like a boy with a couple of bird's eggs.

Starting with his own mother, Ashe had never cared for women: their smell, their essential slipperiness, their peculiar and disobliging mix of dependency and power. Events over the past few yeas had only served to harden this view. Religions that considered women unclean were right—the female of the species was rank. When in need of relief, he'd only ever used prostitutes; there was no point in pretending that it was anything other than a dirty, necessary exchange.

While conceding Mrs Mariner's unusual qualities, Ashe did not believe that on a fundamental level she would be different to all the others. That laugh . . . She might even prove a trickier customer than most. An assiduous student of human nature, he had learned to trust his judgement. One thing was certain. Provided the husband was right, the vicarage was perfect.

*   *   *

What with the driving, the weather, and the relishing of his plans, Ashe was in high good humour by the time he arrived. The parcels had to be delivered at the back door, and who should meet him there but the girl he'd seen on the river bank the morning he arrived. She let out another little shriek, but at least this time he had the van and the parcels to show he was respectable, and she calmed down even though she couldn't look at him properly.

'Sorry about that,' he said. 'I was just taking a dip.'

'You startled me, you really did!'

'I startle everyone, I'm afraid.' He saw the beginnings of a smile in her face and added: 'And I ate your cake, too.'

She giggled. 'I hope you enjoyed it.'

'My compliments to the cook.'

She led him through the back corridors to the foot of the stairs leading to the Delamaynes' private quarters, and instructed him to leave the parcels on the table.

'Let me know when you have another cake,' he said, and she giggled as she scuttled off.

Ashe took his time. When he'd dumped the parcels he couldn't resist taking a look around. He was unimpressed by the owners' philanthropic gesture in giving over the stately pile to convalescents. Who needed a place this size? And what exactly had Lord and Lady Muck been doing while these poor bastards were losing bits of themselves in the desert and dying of disgusting diseases in the swamps? Just the same, curiosity led him towards the south side of the house where he'd seen the terrace with its fleet of wheelchairs. He was surprised by how many of them there still were, and God knows how many more indoors. Some of them looked pretty chipper, but most were pale and withdrawn, and a few were shaking, and muttering, like a bunch of derelicts, old before their time.

A middle-aged nurse wearing a cap that looked

like a brace of seagulls perched on the back of her head strode briskly up to him—without, he noticed, a flicker of anxiety, but then she must have seen most things in her time.

'May I help you?'

'No thank you,' he said. 'Just taking a look.'

'Are you looking for someone in particular?'

'No.' It was clear she thought some explanation was necessary, so he added: 'I was in the war myself.'

'I guessed as much.'

'Any here from Mesopotamia?'

She shook her head. 'I'm afraid I couldn't tell you. They're all just our patients to us. Anyway, if there's nothing I can do . . .' She held out her arm in an ushering gesture.

'Look after them,' he said, as if that was what she meant.

'That goes without saying,' she replied frostily. 'Now if you don't mind, it's only visitors and staff allowed here and I have to get on. I must ask you to leave.'

She took a step, but when he didn't move she paused and added pointedly, 'Can you find your own way out?'

'I believe so.'

This time, under the nurse's suspicious stare, he turned, and left. As he walked down the corridor he saw a tall woman come down the stairs and study the parcels on the table. She looked up briefly from the labels as he approached, then with a swift double take looked again.

'Oh—good morning.' Everything about her proclaimed her the lady of the house.

'Good morning.' He wasn't going to use 'your

ladyship' until it became unavoidable.

'How are you today?'

'Very well, thank you.' He nodded at the pacels. 'I just delivered those.'

'Thank you. Ah!' She raised an index finger. 'I see!' Her eyes narrowed and the index finger, which had been pointing at the ceiling, angled in his direction.

'I think I know who you are.'

He couldn't resist it. 'Then you've got the advantage of me, madam.'

'My apologies—Lady Delamayne. And you must be Mr Ashe.'

'Correct, your ladyship.'

'I believe you showed an interest in my car the other day, when it was parked outside the church.' It was not so much a question as a challenge. Her eyelids snapped at him like twin terriers.

'Outside the . . . ?' He pretended to search his memory. 'Oh yes. Nice car, that.'

'I'm glad you think so!' She bridled, censorious but amused in spite of herself. 'You know about cars, I assume?'

'I've had a bit to do with them, your ladyship. I can appreciate a good motor when it's in front of me.'

'I take it you brought these up in the station van. How does that score?'

'About—' he pursed his lips—'four out of ten. Serviceable, willing—not exciting, but then it's not supposed to be.'

She laughed, a fruity chortle, the edges roughened by cigarettes. He didn't laugh with her, and he was right not to, because the next moment she waved a hand at the parcels and said: 'Since

85

you're here, would you be kind enough to bring these up for me, to the flat?'

There was no mistaking the order disguised as a request. Lady Delamayne didn't wait for his reply, but set off up the stairs. Ashe picked up the parcels and followed, her broad, firm bottom in county tailoring and strong, rounded, silk-clad calves bobbing upwards at eye level. She was a supremely confident woman who knew what she was doing, all right. But she had picked the wrong man; his imperviousness to Lady Delamayne's backside gave Ashe considerable satisfaction.

'This is us,' she said. 'Holed up in the attic, all in a good cause.'

The 'attic' was a section of the first storey big enough, from what he could see, to house at least three village families. Lady Delamayne led him into a drawing room lined in apple-green brocade. A small brown and white dog lay on a plaid rug which had been thrown over one of the green and pink sofas. As soon as they entered it jumped down and began barking noisily at Ashe.

'Be quiet! Be quiet! Bad dog, Monty! Quiet! Go back!'

After this brief and noisy exchange of fire Monty, vanquished, retreated to the sofa. Ashe stood holding the parcels with slightly exaggerated patience. Lady Delamayne waggled a big hand with three handsome diamonds.

'Over there, that'll do.' He put the parcels on the other sofa. Monty growled, the rumble thinning into an unpleasant snarl.

'Stop that! Bad dog! Don't worry, he's like this with everyone.' She went to a desk in the corner and opened a drawer, returning with something in

86

her hand. 'He's the only one allowed inside and he thinks he owns the place. It drives my husband insane with rage.' She held out a sixpence. 'Thank you.'

For a couple of seconds Ashe just looked at the coin, lying on her palm. She was no fool, she'd get the message: he'd take her sixpence, eventually, and the offence that went with it.

'Your ladyship.'

'Good!' This had the air of an announcement, as though sealing some pact or understanding between them, which irritated Ashe, as perhaps it was meant to. Now, she showed him to the door.

'Thank you.'

He let that hang—it had not been his pleasure— and was halfway down the stairs before he heard the door close behind him.

MESOPOTAMIA

A desert and a quagmire—seems like a contradiction, but then there's contradictions everywhere you look here. Two great big rivers but precious little to drink that won't poison you—the estuary's salt, and the shallows are so full of filth you might as well drink out of a privy. Every kind of waste floating around. Corpses, too: donkeys, dogs, even people, I shouldn't be surprised, I get the impression life is cheap even without a war. No wonder the flies are the only ones that grow fat. And it's a lucky man who hasn't got the shits. We like to think we're the hygienic ones around here, but when your innards are pretty much turned to sewer water, what's a man to do? There are precious few latrines, and finding somewhere private to dig a hole takes a lot more time than you've got.

This army runs on tea. You boil the water and make a brew from just about anything—grass, leaves, even tea leaves if you can get them. We keep on hearing that supplies have arrived, rations a-plenty, but they're all sitting in the Shatt, being unloaded by two men with a teaspoon and a rowing boat . . . When the stuff's on land that's only the start. It's got to get from A to B on wagons pulled by those blasted mules, and sand or sludge, either way, the wheels sink. There are teams of fighting men spending their time just laying duckboards and corduroy roads so the wagons can roll. It's not the best use of soldiers at the front, and it's not quick, either. One thing we're getting expert at is waiting.

We had a bit of a run-out against the Turk the other day, and experienced the difficulties for ourselves. It was all quite exciting to begin with. You get sick of hanging around, being bored makes you jumpy, especially with the Buddhoos up to their tricks after dark, galloping about, wailing like banshees, firing randomly—showing off mostly, the only damage is on the nerves, but that doesn't make for a peaceful night.

Jarvis is in charge of our lot, 'D' Company. He's well liked. Sometimes I feel a sort of pride, as if I'm responsible for him, his superior, instead of the other way round. Silly really. I can see him as captain of cricket at his school, firm but fair, an encouraging word for everyone, leading from the front. Untested in battle conditions as far as I know, just like the rest of us. Anyway, we set off in pretty good order at o-fuck-hundred hours; about five a.m. to be precise. Objective was a small forward group of Turks well dug in at a disused factory building ten miles up river. We're given to understand that we have the advantage in numbers, but they have a well-defended position. The general feeling is: let's get at them.

The first few miles aren't bad, the sun's not up and the ground's load-bearing. There's even a sort of track, a stony unmade road that we can follow, nice easy marching. But as the sun rises everything else starts to go downhill. The track peters out. We're coming into a marshy area, one of the nastiest terrains it's ever been my misfortune to encounter—a thin, baked crust on top of treacherous slop, like ruddy rice pudding. The crust's got these great cracks all over it, and every so often it'll give way and you're up to your knees in slime. There's a kind of long, sharp grass growing all over it, something like rushes, and we're finding out why they call them 'blades': the edges can cut you to ribbons.

We keep on marching, but getting slower. By seven o'clock the sun's well and truly up and we've got four miles to go. It's flat as pancake, lots of nothing in all directions. We keep on thinking we can see the factory, but it's a mirage. We can't get used to them. The horizon shimmering and creating shapes that aren't there. Sometimes it looks like the entire Turkish army bearing down on us. And then it dissolves, and there's nothing. I don't know what's worse, the apparitions or the emptiness. The heat's indescribable, everyone's gone quiet. The pace has slowed to a crawl, the column has to keep stopping so the stragglers and the gun carriages can keep up. Stopping seems like a good idea till you do it, and then you realise that where the desert sun's concerned you're better presenting a moving target. When you stand still it's like the sun's actually pressing down on you. And then when you start marching again every bite and blister and stiff muscle and corner of chafed skin hurts like hell.

The man next to me is Stan Maidment, from Nottingham. He's one of those big, weak men—tall and broad, but soft. They say the human body's three-quarters water, and with him I believe it. He's suffering. I can almost hear him drying out. During one of our stops I glance at him and he's got that look I'm beginning to recognise. Like a dog. I saw a greyhound once, came off the track and died of a burst heart. Just before it went, this was the look it had: eyes red, not seeing, mouth open, like its brain had switched off and its body was panicking, fighting the inevitable. I'm not saying Stan's about to drop dead just yet, but he has the look. He doesn't care any more where we're going, what we're going to do, whether he's going to get shot or not. He's punch-drunk. The next step's quite enough of a challenge. As we trudge on again and I'm listening to his thin, dry breathing, I wonder what Jarvis will say in the letter to his mother. 'Died in the service of his country'? One thing she'll be pleased about, he's stopped biting his nails.

Now it seems to be more stopping than starting, and when we do move it's a snail's pace. Trudging, not marching. The sky's not blue, it's off-white, like a duck egg, and the sun's bright white in the middle of it. All around us is the dust we're sending up, and further away the whole horizon's a mirage. I hope someone up in front's got a map, because we don't know where we're going. Communications are terrible, a couple of little planes rattle to and fro doing recces, and the worrying thing is, we rely on them. If they get it wrong we could find ourselves attacking an empty building while the enemy comes round from the back, laughing their heads off. The blokes in the planes draw maps, freehand. An officer goes round and says: 'Anyone here nifty with a pencil?' and the first artistic types to put their hands up land themselves a cushy number. Jarvis says it's one hell of a responsibility and he wouldn't want it. I find myself wondering if they embellish things a bit— put in figures in turbans, palm trees, a camel or two . . . Must be a temptation.

Right now I don't care as long as the main features are all there and in the right place. We could be going round in circles for all we know. Right then one of the planes flies over, and a man just in front of us waves. A sort of reflex I suppose, like waving at trains. What do we look like to those men, up there? A huge dusty centipede crawling through the desert. Pity they can't tell us whether we're on course, 'left hand down a bit', that kind of thing. I suppose if we were heading in the wrong direction they'd find some way of letting us know, heading us off at the pass—if there was a pass.

We stop again. This time the order comes along from the front, so it's not for stragglers. Looking back I can just make out the mules pulling the gun carriages, about three-quarters of a mile away. The only reason I can see them is because they're not immediately behind, but over to the left as I stand facing this way; to the east, in other words.

So we must have turned a corner. What corner? What for?

Stan lists a bit in my direction. I put up a hand to steady him so he doesn't fall on top of me—even in his sorry state he could crush a few ribs.

'All right Stan?'

He mumbles something.

'What's that?'

'I'm not going to make it.'

What am I supposed to say? Might as well be realistic.

'None of us are, chum.'

'I can't go on . . .'

He means it, and I believe him. Anyway, given that 'making it' and 'going on' mean our first proper scrap with the Turks, why worry? It's a choice of two evils.

'Then don't,' I say. 'Stay here. The wagons'll be along in due course.'

Hark at me, like a guard on a railway platform. And I'm taking a liberty making out there'll be more than one wagon. There won't be, and the MO won't be pitching his tent, either, till we're within striking distance of the objective. Leaving Stan here's going to be the equivalent of burying him up to his neck in sand and playing a blowtorch over him. He'd be better off catching a nice clean bullet and knowing no more, as they say.

I prop him up with both hands and hold him upright till he feels steady and I can let go, like balancing a telegraph pole on its end. There's a mutter coming down from the front end of the column, like the spark running along a fuse. The man just in front of me turns round.

'Can you credit it?'

'What's up?'

'Ditch. Empty,' he adds. 'Not full of Turks.'

It turns out it's a big drainage ditch. Another sign of the madness of this place; when it's not cooking it's awash. The water comes down from the mountains up there to the north and the whole place is flooded. Noah was from round here.

The trouble is there are no stones, and no trees. Nothing solid underfoot no matter how far you dig, and no materials to shore up the ditch, or to build a bridge with, and men and horses are getting stuck. It'll be ten times worse for the big guns and the other wagons and they haven't even got there yet.

We're bogged down, in a desert. Tommy, as ever, is philosophical in adversity and in some cases even begins to make tea.

Captain Jarvis comes riding down the line. There's dollops of yellowy scum all over his horse and its nostrils are gaping, but Jarvis himself looks very brisk as if he's out for a turn in Rotten Row.

'We're having to make an earthwork, men,' he announces. 'Take this opportunity for a rest, we can't say when the next one will be.' And on he goes.

I give Stan Maidment a little downward push on the shoulder, that's all it takes. He slithers down in a heap. I take off his neckerchief, sprinkle a bit of water on it out of his canteen and put it over his eyes and forehead, with his pith helmet balanced over that to keep the moisture in for a couple of minutes.

I stay standing. We're already a sitting target, without adding to it. A wagon, a real bone-shaker, trundles past from the rear with some men riding on the back, presumably engineers or sappers off to help with the earthwork. It's hard to imagine. I went to Margate once with my father, and sand's the most useless stuff there is. It slithers and slides, it's got no substance. Even when you get it wet and manage to make a castle, one finger-touch and the whole thing collapses. And our brave boys are going to make a bridge out of it? A bridge big enough and strong enough to support nearly a thousand men, fifty horses and mules and half a dozen wagons?

They do it by simply filling in a fifty-yard stretch of the ditch, an area between two bends so the sand can't so easily fall away at the sides. This heroic exercise (and I'm not joking, it is heroic) takes an hour, which is pretty good going, but all that time our numbers are going down as men fall over with heatstroke, and doubtless the Turks now know we're on our way and are lined up with guns primed to greet us.

By the time the order comes down to fall in and start marching, Stan's too far gone. Out cold I'd say if that didn't sound like a bad joke. Nothing we can do but leave him there with another sprinkle of water on the handkerchief. I don't expect to see him again. At least he's not alone—there's dozens of casualties sprinkled along the route, like litter thrown out of a train. I wonder where the Buddhoos are, they've got a reputation for looting, scavenging and ripping open bodies, not always those of the dead.

We march on for about a mile, and then another halt's called, this time so that the guns can be brought up and got over the ditch first. They have to line up their sights on the target, and that can take a while. Will the Turks play cricket and wait for us all to get into position before letting us have it, is the question . . .

We'll never know the answer because we never get that far. The gun carriages rumble past in a cloud of dust and grit, and an hour after that we hear that the second one's sunk in the earthwork, which has collapsed under its weight. The mules floundering about are only making things worse, so they have to be unharnessed and dragged out separately—I had my share of mules in the harbour at Basra and don't envy the poor bastards who have to deal with them now.

Realising we're having our difficulties, the Turks send out a raiding party, assisted by fifty or so Buddhoos who were probably the ones who alerted them in the first place. The gunners and the rest who are held up in the collapsed trench are stuck, poor bastards, the rest of us are told to make an orderly withdrawal. Which we do, during the hottest part of the day, sniped at from both sides and passing the men fallen along the way. I don't spot Stan, I can't tell him from all the others, but the MO's outfit is on its way, travelling against the flow of traffic, so maybe he'll make it.

People say what a terrible waste of life war is, meaning all those young men dying in battle. At least they're doing what they signed up for—having a go at the enemy. Today we marched eight miles into the desert, stopped, started again, got bogged down and marched back, sustaining over a hundred casualties and at least as many dead in the process, many of them from heatstroke, finished off by the Buddhoos. Now that's what I call waste.

Jarvis is shaken. He makes no bones about it.

'It was a fiasco, Ashe,' he says. 'A bloody fiasco.'

'Yes sir,' I say. 'Better luck next time.'

CHAPTER FOUR

Felicity Delamayne cornered Vivien after evensong the following Sunday.

'He was up at the house,' she announced. 'That rather strange creature—your Mr Ashe.'

'Poor man,' said Vivien carefully. 'You see what I mean—about his face.'

'But he's doing fine!' Lady Delamayne seemed not to have been in the least perturbed by Ashe's appearance. 'He delivered some shooting kit Sidney ordered from Waring and Gillow.'

'So he's found work?'

'Driving the station van.'

'Yes, he said he could drive . . .'

'There you are then. When did he tell you that?'

Vivien glanced across from their position near the font at Saxon, who was bidding farewell to the small congregation. 'He called a few days ago looking for work.'

'How extraordinary. And what did your husband make of *that*, I wonder?'

'Saxon was working, I didn't bother him with it. We did discuss it afterwards, and there's nothing for him at the moment.'

'I should think not.'

'If there was,' said Vivien firmly but with her voice still lowered because she feared she might be traducing Saxon, 'we would definitely consider him. He's very personable, in spite of—in spite of everything.'

'Hm.' Felicity raised an eyebrow and delivered herself of a damning judgement. 'Well, I don't care for people who go around knocking on doors. It smacks of begging.'

Returning to the vicarage, Vivien weighed up this remark, which contained a grain of truth but which did not, she considered, apply to Mr Ashe. He had made an offer of his services; which she had been unable to accept. His manner had been neither servile nor ingratiating and had not, on either of their two meetings, contained the smallest trace of self-pity. In fact, for someone so badly disfigured, he appeared surprisingly confident and sanguine, as though the outcome of their exchange had been Vivien's loss. She couldn't help feeling bitterly disappointed that Ashe had found work elsewhere.

*   *   *

Sunday supper chez Mariner was an informal affair, but that wasn't to say that Vivien didn't take some trouble over it. Tonight it was omelettes Arnold Bennett, a particular favourite of Saxon's and now a speciality of his wife's. They could not have managed without Hilda, but her absence brought a sense of freedom.

Saxon loved to see Vivien cooking, and without Hilda in the kitchen he would venture down into this female stronghold and keep her company. The delicious smell of poached haddock made his mouth water. And his wife . . . Vivien was like a Dutch painting, standing now at the table, now at the stove, with her smooth, flushed cheeks and downcast eyes, her hair tied back in a frayed silk scarf from which one long wavy strand emerged. From time to time she blew at the stray hair, or swiped at it ineffectually with the back of her wrist. At times like these Saxon forgot his irritable wish to see her in smart clothes, coiffed and soignée; she was alluring just as she was, and part of that allure was that she wore it lightly. If she had been armoured in expensive chic she might have attracted admiring glances, (mainly from other women he suspected) but not the senses—or not in the same way.

Saxon, standing behind her, took it upon himself to catch the lock of hair in his finger and thumb and tuck it back beneath the edge of the scarf.

She thanked him. She was at a delicate stage in the omelette-preparation, spreading the flaked haddock onto the half-cooked egg mixture. This did not prevent Saxon placing his hands on her waist. He loved the feel of her, both the soft indentation of the waist itself, and the sense of her body's balanced swell above and below. As he touched her she smiled, still concentrating on the task, drawing the edges of the omelette in from the side of the pan.

'I hope you're ready,' she said.

'I am,' he replied, meaning something different.

Sighing, he slid his hands up to her breasts, which had always seemed to fill his cupped palms perfectly, to have been waiting for them.

'Come upstairs,' he whispered. 'There's time.'

'The omelette will spoil,' she said, but as she did so she released the handle of the wooden spatula and pushed the pan off the hot plate. Her hands came up to cover his and her head tilted back on to his shoulder.

'Then we can make another.'

'We?' She turned now, into his embrace, letting

her arms hang by her sides, in an attitude of what Saxon took to be calculated compliance. She knew instinctively how to excite him to distraction.

'I don't care,' he muttered brokenly. 'I'll do anything . . .'

*　　*　　*

They were not alone. Standing in the dusk, not ten yards from the kitchen window, John Ashe watched as the vicar untied his wife's apron, pulling with urgent, scrabbling fingers at the knot behind her back. He noticed how she stood quite still with her forehead bowed into the angle of her husband's neck in an attitude of curiously knowing passivity, both the foil and spur to his urgency. What was she thinking? Confident that they were too absorbed, and too secure in their supposed privacy ever to see him, he advanced a little closer. The apron finally yielded to Mariner's fumblings and was thrown aside. He kissed her, not prettily but greedily, his knees bending to enable him to clasp her buttocks, she leaning backwards as a counterbalance, both of them staggering slightly. For a moment Ashe thought they would copulate there and then in the kitchen, standing up, dangerously close to the hot stove, and the still-smoking pan but then, to his surprise, Mariner picked his wife up and carried her to the door. He was a slightly built man and she was tall, but he only staggered a little beneath her weight. Ashe was impressed by the unexpectedness of the scene. Especially that when Mrs Mariner's head fell back over her husband's arm, her eyes remained resolutely open.

100

After they'd gone, he remained in the garden until a lamp came on in the upstairs window, the same one where he had caught her looking at him on his first morning in the village, then moved swiftly away.

*   *   *

In the very heat of the moment, just as he cried out, Saxon registered, blurrily, that his wife was staring at him, or at some point beyond his shoulder.

He rolled away from her and raised an arm to cover his face, a barrier behind which to collect his thoughts. It was not the fact that her eyes had been open that disturbed him, but the expression in them: something quizzical and objective, as if she were seeing him for the first time.

A minute later, lying on his side, facing towards her, he said: 'I adore you.' It was the simple truth, but also on this occasion a test, or experiment, for the results of which he scrutinised her profile.

Vivien did not answer, but smiled dreamily, and closed her eyes in a long blink of acknowledgement. Saxon's world shifted minutely on its axis. They lay side by side, gazing upwards. He could smell the aroma of the half-cooked omelette, but his appetite was gone.

*   *   *

George Lownes made no bones about the fact that he thought the Mariners an extraordinarily odd couple. How, he asked himself, and anyone else he happened to be with when the subject came up,

101

had Saxon Mariner managed to snare the delightful Vivien? Mariner was a gifted poet and might well (though George was a lifelong atheist without the least knowledge of these things) be an exemplary parish priest, but he was a dry stick; and a prickly one, too. Whereas his wife . . . George shook his head and smiled to himself as he alighted from a cab in Jasper Place, W1, outside Rosa's restaurant. To know her was to love her, he thought fondly. Why on earth would a woman like that choose to be the helpmeet of a country parson? What the devil did she do with herself all day? How many good works could there be in a place the size of Eadenford? George had visited them there once, and it had been more than enough. He had never experienced such gratitude and relief as when he was on the train back to London and his urbane Fitzrovian life. People spoke of the joys of country living, of natural beauty and the sturdy virtues of village folk, but nothing George had seen chez Mariner had altered his view that it was a living death. Rural life may have suited Saxon, who was after all a writer and a man of the cloth, but what possible attraction could it hold for a vivacious young woman?

Currently, George had three preferred locations for the entertaining of clients. The first was his club off Piccadilly, one of the oldest and grandest in London. The food was sound and wholesome, but unexceptional, it was the grandeur you paid for; that and the exclusivity—the waiting list was longer than Eton's. For obvious reasons, this option was not available if there were to be ladies present. For mixed company he used the Savoy grill (impeccable), or Rosa's (bohemian). Today, he'd chosen the latter, mainly for Vivien's benefit. It would be more to her taste than her husband's, but George took the view that the poor girl needed spoiling a little.

He was greeted by Gianni, the head waiter and shown to his usual table on the far side of the room against the wall, a position that was both discreet and perfect for seeing and being seen. The room was crowded and noisy and the kitchen, occasionally visible through flapping swing doors at the back, appeared suitably hellish, the chefs conducting their business in a swirling vapour, clashing and shouting like men on a battlefield. The emergence of perfectly decent food at regular intervals seemed incidental to the ongoing drama, and Rosa's clientele, an eclectic crowd in any case, took their tone from the kitchen: they spoke loudly, gestured extravagantly, smoked like dragons and generally projected as if trying to upstage one another in an elaborate theatrical piece of ensemble playing. It pleased George to imagine that the shade of the eponymous Rosa, said to have been the madam of a brothel on this same site, hovered over the whole enterprise, imbuing it with a raffish glamour.

At this moment he was completely happy. He liked to feel that his job in publishing qualified him to be a member of the artistic *beau monde*, and was sure he would appear so to the pleasant but provincial Mariners.

And here they were, being escorted between the tables by Gianni. George rose to greet them, shook first Vivien, then Saxon, by the hand—the latter gesture accompanied by a manly squeeze of the elbow by way of congratulations.

103

'I thought this place might amuse you,' he said, as Gianni drew back the chair for Vivien. 'It's absolutely full of people who would like you to think they are somebody.'

'And are they?' she asked, looking round.

'Mostly not—but nil desperandum. Just occasionally a real luminary sneaks in.'

'Then I shall have to keep my eyes peeled.'

'You'd better,' said Saxon. 'Because I shouldn't recognise them anyway.'

'Ah, writers . . .' George, who was sitting between them, beamed fondly at his client, but inclined his head towards Vivien to align himself with her. 'Writers! They truly are in a world of their own.'

*　　　*　　　*

Vivien saw exactly what George Lownes thought about the two of them, and it enraged her. He was one of those maddening people who fancied themselves students of human nature and who allowed a hint of their supposed 'insight' to seep into their manner and conversation, to let you know how clever and intuitive, but also how discreet, they were.

In these circumstances she felt oddly protective towards Saxon. For all his prodigious intellect and outward composure, pride and an air of stiffness made him vulnerable to a particular kind of covert ridicule. She also wished—for that moment only—that she had it in her to be more fashionable. Wearing smart, expensive clothing, with elegant shoes and bag and a chic hat perched on curled hair, she might have been better able to redress the balance. She would not have appeared so much the sort of simple soul whom George Lownes could invite into his sniggery collusion.

Unfortunately, that recourse was simply not available to her. She could not do it. Not because of lack of funds; Saxon often suggested she 'buy something nice', and had once or twice even ventured to buy her something himself (she winced at the memory). It was simply that she lacked both judgement and inclination. She wouldn't have known where to start, and so chose not to.

On the other hand, she could see that she was not too out of place in here. Rosa's was a restaurant with artistic pretensions, and the appearance of the diners was in keeping with this conceit. Long scarves, peasant shirts, dramatic jewellery and arresting hats were much in evidence. If anything, she though despairingly, she had made the mistake of trying *too* hard. Instead of her one respectable jacket and skirt, and rather prim pre-war blouse she would have been better off in Saxon's old shirt and one of her 'interesting woollies'. She had been wearing a hat she liked, in jaunty tweed with a feather, rather Tyrolean, but had taken it off before she sat down. Her hair, floppy as usual, felt as if it were about to descend all over her shoulders. Her left stocking had snagged on torn upholstery in the train. She was hot. The two of them were being patronised by this sleek, smiling tomcat of a man and she badly wanted to let him know that she, at least, was on to his game and did not take kindly to it.

Champagne arrived, ordered by George without reference to his guests. Vivien knew that Saxon didn't much care for the stuff, and would be looking forward to a nice claret with his fillet of beef. But the champagne lent an air of instant celebration to the proceedings, and they clinked glasses.

'To the book!' cried George heartily.

'To the book,' murmured Saxon. *'Beyond Self . . .'* he added, almost warily, as if the words were so much a product of another place and time they had become strange to him.

Vivien lifted her glass higher and said in a forced tone: 'Success!'

They drank, thinking in their different ways about *Beyond Self*. George was first to end what threatened to be an awkward pause.

'I'm looking forward to some splendid reviews. Edward Jacob at Phaeton has already been in touch, he's a tremendous admirer of yours.'

'Is he?' said Saxon.

'He particularly likes the fact that these are not poems about the war. He feels there may have been enough of that, that people are ready for something different.'

'Good.' Saxon wasn't sure whether it was or not. As a man of God had he perhaps been remiss in not writing (again, his last volume had dealt with it) about this overwhelmingly important subject?

'What I'd really like,' went on George, wagging a finger, 'and I'm not the only one, would be for you to do a reading. Some time in the month after publication. For readers, and potential readers, nothing beats hearing the work read by the poet himself.'

'You think so?'

'I know so.' George turned to Vivien. 'Mrs Mariner, what do you think of the idea?'

106

She considered before replying, not to George but to Saxon: 'I think it would only work if you wanted to do it—if your heart was in it. You're a poet, after all, not a performer.'

Unfortunately Saxon wasn't quite quick enough, and George cut in.

'But he is! You are, Saxon—every Sunday you get up in that pulpit and preach to the multitude. Or however many are there,' he added, in response to Vivien's incredulous expression. 'At any rate you're a practised speaker. And no one can ever render poetry as truthfully and sensitively as the writer himself. All I ask is that you consider it, Saxon. Go home and think, discuss it between yourselves. We need to introduce you more fully to your public. Ah, the roast beef of old England . . .' He leaned back, rubbing his hands, as their plates were put in front of them. 'Now then, I want to hear about the parish and all its doings . . .'

He didn't, of course, and Vivien could hardly bear to hear Saxon dutifully outlining his schedule of humdrum meetings and poorly attended services. Her husband was a brilliant and unusual man, but beneath the pretence of admiration Lownes was subtly subverting the occasion, obliging him to recite in detail the essential dullness from which Lownes and Peart had the power to lift him.

When pudding arrived, she took the opportunity to break into Saxon's analysis of church finances.

'I know what *I* think. I think you *should* do a reading.'

George's eyebrows rose high in his round, pink face. 'Bravo, Mrs Mariner.'

'Perhaps more than one, around the country.

You could organise that, couldn't you, George?'

'Of course.'

Saxon smiled thinly. His high cheekbones were a little flushed—with the wine, perhaps, or with embarrassment. 'Vivien, don't let's get ahead of ourselves. This idea has only just been mooted.'

'I simply wanted to say that I think it's a good idea. You're too modest, Saxon.'

'Hear hear,' said George. He looked from one to the other as if umpiring a tennis match. 'Well said!'

*   *   *

Saxon would have been more flattered by this observation if he'd known it to be true. Whatever his faults, complacency was not among them. Not knowing how to acknowledge the compliment, he ignored it.

'I couldn't possibly travel about the country like some itinerant entertainer.'

'Like Charles Dickens?' suggested Vivien, not looking at him, running her forefinger along the edge of the cloth. She continued to feel angry and out of sorts, not only because of George.

Who now, annoyingly, tapped his finger to his mouth, eyes narrowed. 'A palpable hit, I think.'

'I couldn't leave the parish to go swanning off. Eadenford is where my real work is. I'm needed there.'

'Don't they have'—George cudgelled his brains—'curates? Aren't curates supposed to step in when the incumbent is away? I'm sure I've read it in Trollope.'

'No . . .' said Saxon. 'No.'

Vivien realised that her spirited call to arms on Saxon's behalf was being traduced, and all her good intentions in danger of backfiring. The likelihood of his undertaking one poetry reading, let alone a tour, was becoming more remote by the second.

'Of course,' she said humbly, 'the parish must come first. I wasn't taking that into account—I let my enthusiasm run away with me.'

Saxon nodded austerely, but George was enjoying himself.

'And a lovely thing it was to see, if I may say so. If you ever tire of parish duties, Mrs Mariner, you could always find a place in the world of publishing. That sort of unalloyed delight in another's work is rare. It cannot be feigned.'

'I'm glad to hear it,' said Saxon, but the mild sarcasm was lost on George, who slapped his midriff contentedly and asked who wanted cheese.

*   *   *

Saxon held his peace in the cab, paid for by Lownes, but once they were aboard the train, facing each other in window seats in an otherwise empty compartment, he felt obliged to say, as gently as possible:

'I know you meant well, but on the whole it's best if we talk about these things privately before voicing an opinion. Arguing—or appearing to argue—in public only muddies the water. And it's such bad form.'

Vivien, who had been staring out at the low grey ramparts of London drifting past behind rags of smoke, turned to face him. Her eyes were big and bright.

'Bad form?'

'A silly expression.' He flicked his fingers, dismissing it. 'Ill-mannered, then.'

'If I was rude, I apologise.'

'You weren't intentionally so, but the effect—'

'I'm sorry, Saxon. Truly.'

Her words may have been contrite, but her tone was sharp; he almost wished he hadn't spoken. 'It doesn't matter.'

Looking out of the window she said, in the same voice:

'I don't like the way he treats us.'

'Lownes? What's the matter with him?' Saxon knew the answer to this perfectly well, but for some reason did not wish to hear it articulated by his wife.

'He's horrible.'

'He just entertained us royally.'

'I don't care, he's a vile man.'

'I must say I think that's rather a harsh judgement. He's—of a certain type, certainly. But, forgive the cliché, life would be a dull thing if we were all the same.'

'No!' Vivien sat back, slapping her hands down on her knees as if that did it. 'No, Saxon, I won't forgive the cliché. Not from you; you're only doing it now to excuse that awful man.'

'Very well,' said Saxon. 'In what way is he awful?' He found himself hoping, somewhat cravenly, that the ways in which Vivien thought George Lownes awful would not correspond with his own views, so he would be able honestly to disagree with her.

'Let me see.' She began counting off on her

110

fingers. 'He's patronising, and smug, and insincere. He pretends to admire your work—'

'Vivien!' He was sharp, she had touched a nerve. 'I'm sorry—are you saying that he's *lying*?'

'Not exactly.' She paused, not wanting to hurt him. 'I think he doesn't care. It's all just business to him. We come up to London with straws in our hair and we're supposed to be pathetically grateful for that expensive lunch. You're a *poet*, Saxon. I wonder, does he know how lucky he is to have you?'

'Whether he does or not, I'm lucky to have him, too. I'm sure there are many hundreds of excellent writers, unsung and unknown, who are never paid the compliment of being published.'

'You see?' she cried vehemently. 'Compliment! He's not complimenting you when he prints your wonderful words, he's engaging in a business transaction.'

'In that case,' said Saxon drily, 'he lacks acumen. I don't imagine my books swell the publisher's coffers by as much as a brass farthing.'

Vivien gave a short, impatient sigh with eyes closed, composing herself to return to the fray.

'There are other kinds of value. Your value to them is as an adornment. Your presence tells everyone they are discriminating and thoughtful, that they have taste. They can show you off in the places where these things matter.'

Reflecting on this, Saxon gazed out of the window. They were leaving the outskirts of town now. On a school games field, boys were playing rugby, for perhaps the last time that season. Saxon shivered at the thought of the school's roll of honour, swelled by hundreds over the past four years. Perhaps, though, the terrible slaughter of their predecessors would at least have paid for the freedom and safety of these lads, running and shouting in the spring sunshine. He wished fervently that he had written a poem along these lines . . .

'Well?' asked Vivien.

'I'm afraid,' he said in a chastened tone, 'that "these things" as you put it don't matter at all.'

'Not to *you*, Saxon, I realise that. To *them*.'

'You may be right.'

'I am.' She settled back, quite flushed. Saxon was wary of Vivien in this mood. He was warmed by her strength of feeling, but sensed a rather less attractive lack of control. With hindsight, perhaps they had all got off lightly at lunchtime.

*　　　*　　　*

The Mariners changed trains at Salisbury on to the branch line, and reached Eadenford at half past six, the only passengers to alight there. As the train huffed and snorted away, the smoke floating and dissipating in its wake, the peace of evening seemed to settle around them. The station was a little way from the village; they could hear the soft, dying fall of a wood pigeon, and the sporadic barking of a dog in the distance. Beneath the trees at the top of the far embankment the ground was misted with violets. On the rough grass lower down a scattering of rabbits, accustomed to both trains and passengers, hopped and nibbled.

Saxon took his wife's hand. 'We're lucky, Vivien, in so many ways.'

She didn't reply, but briefly squeezed his hand

before releasing it. He wondered if she had understood him correctly or whether she suspected his remark to have pointed up, by leaving deliberately unspoken, the ways in which they were *not* lucky. Women were prone to such misunderstandings.

'Evening Reverend! Mrs Mariner.'

Mr Trodd, flag in hand, came down the platform. 'How was the big city?'

'Noisy and dirty as ever,' said Saxon. He took their tickets from his pocket and handed them over. 'It's nice to be back.'

'East west home's best,' said Mr Trodd, unlike Saxon no stranger to the comforting cliché. 'You wait till you see your car, Reverend.'

'Why is that?'

'You just wait.'

Saxon, who didn't care for surprises, walked if anything more slowly; Vivien, who did, hurried ahead of him through the gate into the station yard.

'Oh my goodness!'

To say that Saxon's car had been cleaned would have been a sorry understatement. It was gleaming, burnished, coruscating in the evening sun.

Vivien, her old self again, laughed delightedly, running her hand over the car's satiny surfaces. 'It's a chariot of fire!'

Saxon surveyed the car from a safe distance, and turned to Mr Trodd.

'Who's responsible for this?' He heard how this sounded, and added more emolliently: 'Whoever it was made an excellent job of it.'

'You can tell him yourself, Reverend.'

Saxon looked in the direction of Trodd's nodding head. A dark-haired man was tinkering beneath the bonnet of the station van, parked in the far corner of the yard. Aware perhaps of being the focus of attention he looked up. His face wore an odd, grinning expression.

'It's Mr Ashe,' said Vivien. 'Saxon, do you remember, he came round looking for work.'

'And appears to have found it.'

Mr Trodd leaned confidingly towards Saxon and spoke *sotto voce*. 'He may be no daisy but he's a good worker, and a wonder with motors.'

'Well I should certainly have a word with him.'

Saxon set off across the yard. At least on this occasion Vivien didn't rush ahead but observed the proprieties and stayed at his side. The man came round the bonnet of the van, wiping his hands on an oily cloth. Saxon had prepared himself, and flattered himself that he betrayed not a hint of shock.

'Mr Ashe?'

'Mr Mariner.'

Saxon told himself that he should not be put out by a form of words. 'Mr Trodd tells me you were kind enough to polish my car.'

'She's a beautiful machine.'

'Even better now, thanks to all your hard work.'

'Thank you, sir.'

Saxon felt in his pocket. 'You must let me give you something . . .'

'No need.'

'But I must. For your time.'

'It's my own. Once I've done what needs doing.'

The two men stared at each other. Saxon felt that he was being challenged to accept, and be

114

grateful for, the favour. Irritating though this was, he decided it wasn't worth making an issue over.

'Very well. Thank you. The car looks splendid.'

Ashe inclined his head in acknowledgement, a gesture which Saxon could not be sure wasn't impertinent.

Vivien, however, was unreservedly enthusiastic. 'Such a lovely surprise. It quite restores our faith in human nature, Mr Ashe.'

'Thought you'd be pleased, Mrs Mariner,' said Trodd, anxious to identify himself with any credit that was going, especially from the reverend's wife.

'Best get back, next train's due. Good night, Reverend.'

'Good night.'

They moved to get into the car. Ashe was quicker than Saxon, and held the door open for Vivien. He then watched as Saxon fitted the crank-start, and just as he was about to turn it, said:

'I tuned her up a bit as well. She should start like a bird.'

'Thank you.'

The engine caught on the second turn, and Saxon dropped the crank-start in the driver's footwell and took his place behind the wheel. He found his audience of one irksome but could think of no way to tell Ashe not to watch that would not sound simply petulant. He was enormously relieved when they were out of the station yard and bowling down the lane towards the village.

'The car's positively gliding along,' said Vivien. 'Wasn't that nice of him?'

Saxon took the question to be rhetorical, and didn't answer.

At the vicarage Hilda, as instructed, had left a cold supper under covers on the dining-room sideboard. As soon as they got in Saxon went over to the church to say evensong, and Vivien walked out into the garden. There was no ill-feeling behind this separation, but still each of them breathed a little more freely. It was not often that they spent long hours together, especially in company, and afterwards it was their habit to go in different directions, as if they needed a space apart to restore the delicate balance of their shared life. So much of that life depended on if not exactly secrecy, then at least a sort of mutual discretion; an allowance made on the part of each for the other's privacy and distinctness.

The dew was beginning to fall and the grass, still in its lush, uncut spurt of springtime growth, was damp. An early honeysuckle, tempted into flower by the fine weather, crawled up the side of the garden shed and over the roof, its fine tendrils like wayward curls of hair. The few small, freckled flowers, like cupped hands, gave off a wave of sweetness as Vivien tugged opened the warped wooden door.

The smell inside the shed was dank and musty. She sensed the scuttle of spiders, and something larger, a mouse perhaps, as she stepped inside. Earthenware pots of all sizes, the smaller ones stacked in uneven towers, stood on a trestle table. Facing her against the back wall, slumbering beneath its mould- and oil-spotted green tarpaulin, was the mighty lawnmower. On the wall opposite the trestle hung garden tools: a rake for soil and another for leaves; a hoe; spades of different lengths; a trowel and small fork; long-handled secateurs for pruning. Beneath these, on the ground, was a cluster of buckets and watering cans, a trug full of desiccated bulbs and a black hose coiled in a heap like a sleeping snake. In the far corner between the cans and the mower were the apple boxes. Every year Vivien picked the apples from the vicarage's two ancient trees, wrapping each one separately and laying them carefully in rows in slatted wooden boxes; and every year the apples, an almost luminous golden-brown local variety whose name was lost to history, turned woolly and soft. The windfalls, though, and any that she picked and put directly into the fruit bowl, were fragrant and crisp with a distinctive sharp flavour. She'd come to think of them as wild apples, not suited to domesticity, but they were so good that she continued to squirrel away a few boxfuls in the increasingly forlorn hope that some would survive.

She took one now from the top box and unwrapped it. On the piece of paper the words 'England rejoices' in large letters appeared dimly through the grey wrinkles of newsprint. The apple in her hand was also wrinkled, and felt slightly spongy. A rank, cidery odour rose from the boxes. Vivien told herself she really had to stop engaging in what was a futile exercise.

There was a sudden explosive scrabbling behind the mower and a large rat darted from under the tarpaulin and scampered across the floor and out of the door, its naked whip of tail wriggling behind it. Vivien felt a prickle of shock, but the incident was so brief—barely two seconds—that she neither moved nor screamed.

The unpleasant realisation that the rat had been there all along and that its quick, furtive footsteps were what she'd heard on entering made her disinclined to linger. She left the useless apples to him and his kind, and for another day, collected what she'd come for, and left hurriedly, shooting the bolt behind her.

*　　　*　　　*

'Lighten our darkness, we beseech thee, O Lord; and by thy great mercy defend us from all perils and dangers of this night . . .'

Saxon did not, as a rule, take this prayer literally. Night in Eadenford was not perilous, and those dangers against which he needed defending were largely within himself. This evening, his conscience was troubled and he did not need to search it very far to find the cause. On this of all days, he had not behaved as he would have liked. The composure and dignity he sought had eluded him, he had been tetchy and awkward with George Lownes, grumpy with Vivien, and downright uncharitable towards the man Ashe.

He thought about Ashe. A terrifying appearance, the sort to give children nightmares. Saxon had needed all his self-control not to recoil, but the man himself conveyed neither shame nor self-consciousness. Indeed—Saxon's shoulders twitched uncomfortably—he had been all composure, a very model of self-possession.

'Almighty God, who hast given us grace at this time with one accord to make our common supplication unto thee . . . Fulfil now, O Lord, the

desires and petitions of thy servant, as may be most expedient for them . . .'

Saxon clenched his clasped hands until the knuckles whitened. What would be expedient?

MESOPOTAMIA

Jarvis tells me Qurna's the site of the Garden of Eden. All I can say is, I'm prepared to take his word for it, but a lot can happen in a few thousand years. This may have been a nice area then, but it's gone downhill.

This is what I'm thinking on church parade. It's eight o'clock on a Sunday morning, and already hotter than hell. We're at morning prayer, those of us who aren't Sikhs or Muslims. I wouldn't go so far as to call us Christians, we're just a bunch of so-called C of E's with something serious to pray for at last.

'Dear God, let me get out of here alive. Don't let this stinking swamp be the last place I see on earth. Let me get back to—' Where? Lewisham, Barnsley, Ipswich, Yeovil, Hull? I bet the daggy provincial towns of old England never looked so appealing as they do now, inside these men's heads, bathed in a rosy glow of homesickness and last-minute religiosity.

Anyway, 'Dear God, just let me get back and I'll lead a good and blameless life, work hard, support the wife and children and be a pillar of the community!' As if you could do a deal with God— as if you'd *want* the sort of God who'd do a deal with you. Even I can see that if it were that easy it wouldn't be worth bothering with. And if it was worth the paper it's written on we wouldn't be here anyway, hats off in the heat, being bitten to bits in the name of the Lord. I'm only here to please Jarvis.

Now it's time to sing, God help us (and I mean that). Dog-eared hymn sheets at the ready. They've gone all spotty in this climate, I wonder how far they've travelled in their time. Ah, here we go, Padre's striking up:

'Christian, dost thou see them, on the holy ground,
How the hosts of Mideon prowl and prowl around?'

An old favourite, and very apt. Chosen to make us feel we're part of a crusade. Plenty of prowling going on, Buddhoos on one side and Turks just across the river. Us in the middle, in the Garden of Eden.

'Christian, up and smite them!' Well, we can but try. Let's get there first.

I don't sing. It's madness. A couple of hundred lost souls in the middle of a desert, surrounded by the enemy, advertising their whereabouts by bellowing platitudes.

' . . . counting gain but loss'. I beg your pardon? It's bad to win, then? And anyway, I thought it was the other way round, a good thing to die because then you were up there at His right hand, snug as you like. They get you coming and going.

The padre, Mills, is off his rocker. No joke. He's got a little white scar below his right eye from duelling when he was in Heidelberg in the eighteen-nineties. His eyes are pale china-blue like a doll's and just about as friendly. Mouth like a parrot—beaky, turned down. When he speaks it's like he's pecking at you, sharp, tap-tap. There's no shortage of material for sermons here, the trouble

121

being that this is the land of the Old Testament, all blood and guts and vengeance and an eye for an eye. There's a devil of a lot of contradiction in the good book. This place was tearing itself apart before gentle Jesus was even a twinkle in God's eye.

There's a bush that grows around here called Eve's Tears. The flowers are supposed to look like the tears she shed when they were thrown out, her and Adam. And about half a mile inland, to the east of the river, there's a strip of land that's all green and fertile: date palms, and flowers and grass underfoot, good soil you can grow things in. It's not Kent or anything, but in a desert, every oasis is paradise. Perhaps that's where the idea came from.

Ted Wellbeloved and me went to walk over there one evening when it was quiet, hoped to pick some fruit, perhaps do some trading with the locals. But it was further away than we thought; we were bitten to bits by the mozzies, and then he nearly trod on a snake. A serpent, I said, there you are! It was only a littl'un, it would have broken its fangs on our puttees, but he was still shaken up. He said some snakes can jump for your throat, like rats.

On the way back we met this young girl. Well, I say met—she'd been doing her business in the ditch by the side of the path, no doubt about it, and came scrambling out pulling down her skirt, uncovered. A brunette, all over, what a surprise. What did surprise me was what she did next. Catching us looking at her, two soldiers of a foreign army, you'd have thought she'd have been embarrassed; scared, even. Not a bit of it. Instead of covering herself and clearing off double quick, she pulled the skirt right up and pushed her hips forward, with her legs bent. With the other hand she's pulling open her fanny. I don't know about the snake, but for two pins this young lady would have jumped for our throats.

'Is she trying to tell us something?' asked Wellbeloved. Poor chap, he thought this was an invitation.

'Look at her face,' I said, keeping my voice down in case she understood.

'That's a pretty tall order under the circumstances.'

'Try.'

She might have been pretty, it was hard to tell. This was no invitation, this was contempt and hatred, pure and simple, like a cat putting its back up at a couple of big dogs. She hissed something at us, spat at our feet, and then she was off—running, but not hurriedly, her long clothes rippling and flapping, disappearing into a mirage. Back to the burned-out village of Muzareh.

'Well!' said Wellbeloved. 'Bugger me. What are we supposed to make of that?'

'We should be insulted,' I said. 'She doesn't like us.'

There was a pause. We began walking again. I could feel the sweat crawling grittily over my skin, in fact I could suddenly feel every inch of my sweating, sore, stinking body and it was like carting an extra load that I didn't want and had no use for. That girl had reminded me of a whole pile of things I was never going to forget. I wanted to be sick.

'Blimey . . .' Wellbeloved was still disappointed.

'She had a funny way of showing it.'

*   *   *

Now we're on about being lost sheep. Apparently we've 'followed too much the devices and desires of our own hearts'. Oh, really? At this moment I can't think of a single man with the opportunity for that around here; apart from the odd spot of self-abuse, excusable under the circumstances.

We're all standing with heads bent, droning away, our hands folded over our private parts, but with the dog-eared bits of paper sticking up so we can follow what the hell's going on and what we're supposed to be saying. We're standing in a box shape, with the officers along the side. I sneak a look at Jarvis. His eyes are closed, he knows all the words and he means them. He looks handsome and smart. Looking at him you get an inkling, just a glimpse, of why some people think soldiering is a noble profession. Jarvis would have signed up for the Round Table before you could say knife. Dragon-slaying, maiden-saving, right up his alley. Whatever he says, he believes we're doing the right thing. I'm not saying he thinks about it all that much. He just believes it, like he believes in all this God guff. I don't know whether to envy him or feel sorry for him. In one way it must make life a lot easier if you're not kicking at the traces. But he's not stupid, far from it, so what's going on in that head of his?

Neither of us minds being here. But our reasons aren't the same.

*   *   *

He's got his own Bible, don't suppose he'd leave home without it. When we get back from the service I get out the regulation issue.

'Undergone a road to Damascus, Ashe?' he says, twinkle in his eye. 'I must tell the padre.'

'Just want to look up a couple of things, sir.'

'I shall leave you in peace, then.'

I want to see what it says about the Garden of Eden. Here it is . . . Our ancestors got their marching orders from a flaming sword. Yes—I can feel it now, burning my arm where it's out of the shade, uncovered. I shift a bit to avoid it. My skin's pale, I burn in seconds. There's no mention of a river, though. Where we are now, there's rivers on two sides—the one I can see from here is the Euphrates, about the size of the Thames, choppy and swollen at the moment and yellow as mustard. If you watch for long enough you'll see the odd dead animal bobbing down, on its way to the Shatt. Over to the left it's the River Tigris. That's not so wide and a lot more sluggish. On the far side there's a big plantation of date palms, and beyond that Muzareh. The smoke's still rising. Maybe Eve was like that angry Arab girl.

Jarvis comes along. 'How's the Good Book going?'

'Interesting, sir.'

'Bit hard to imagine, isn't it?'

'Sir.'

I wait, with my finger on the page. Sometimes I get the impression that given half a chance Jarvis would unburden himself to me but I don't want that. I like things just the way they are, with us both playing our parts.

125

'I'll let you get on with your reading.'

'Sir.'

I pretend to get on while I watch him from the corner of my eye. He looks almost crestfallen. How can an intelligent, educated man like that let himself be dictated to by someone like me?

Either he's not as clever as I thought, or I'm a lot cleverer.

CHAPTER FIVE

The following Sunday, Ashe went to church. He arrived at St Catherine's a few minutes early, and it was raining, but even so he hung about outside the porch till he heard the organist playing the introduction to the opening hymn. Only then did he open the door, turning the big iron ring very gently so as not to make a noise. Of course some do-gooder looked over her shoulder, did a double take and managed to beam welcomingly. She came bustling out of her pew to give him a service book, but he was too quick for her, took a book for himself and sat down in a place off the side aisle, at the back.

The hymn rang some sort of bell from his army days, but he didn't join in. The remnants of a choir stood out front: two old men, four sturdy women and half a dozen small boys to make up the numbers, who were no more singing than he was. One of them spotted him and there was a bit of nudging and staring until a female chorister intervened with a sharp prod. The congregation, about thirty of them, sang along apathetically.

Ashe thought perhaps they were taking their tone from the vicar. The Reverend Mariner held his book in front of him at chin height, but his eyes were fixed, quite literally, on higher things, somewhere around the apex of the north wall and the roof, and his lips moved desultorily as if he were talking to himself, not singing.

The hymn had a lot of verses. The organist liked to finish each one with a *rallentando*, as if that—

was—the—end . . . but no! On and on it trudged. Ashe saw Mrs Mariner sitting in the middle of a pew, several rows from the front. She was wearing a tweed hat with a feather, the whole thing a bit askew, as though it had fluttered down and perched there. Her hair at the back looked none too secure either; a couple of long strands had already come loose. Lady Delamayne, on the other hand—front row, opposite side—was smart as paint, encased in a well cut, fitted green suit with a round, buttoned collar, and a green and black cloche; no hair showing. When her head turned slightly Ashe caught a flash of red lipstick. He pictured her shoes, black, with tall, thick heels and a strap across the instep. Next to her was a man who must have been her husband, big, pear-shaped and florid with a shock of greying curls that started well back on his freckled dome. He was a loud but inexpert singer; Ashe could hear his slightly off-key rendition from here.

There were one or two others he recognised—the Clays, Spall the butcher and his wife, the woman who worked at the vicarage, his landlady Mrs Jeeps (he hadn't told her he was off to the same place), and a few others he knew only by sight.

The hymn ended. Mariner began to speak—not his own words, but those laid down in the service. He held the book, a different one, but did not consult it. The archaic English rolled out of him like scarves out of a conjurer's mouth. His voice wasn't his own either, but one assumed for the occasion, highly enunciated and full of odd, unresolved cadences. Ashe thought you could almost feel the boredom through the backs of people's heads. No, not boredom: disappointment. There was something here for the taking, but Mariner wasn't the man for the job. The mad army padre Mills had been the same. What was it about these men? A brush salesman could have made a better fist of it.

The service went on, with more stuff from the book, prayers, another hymn, then the sermon. Mariner rose slowly to the pulpit, put his notes on the lectern, and rested his hands on either side of it. Some of the heads tilted hopefully in his direction, but most remained staring straight ahead, or at the floor.

'I take as my text those words from the epistle for the day.' Mariner looked down, as if reading. '"This is thankworthy, if a man for conscience toward God endure grief, suffering wrongfully."' Now he looked up, repeating the words slowly and with greater emphasis. '"If a man for conscience toward God endure grief, suffering wrongfully."'

Ah, thought Ashe, martyrdom. Always a good one, especially in the shadow of war. It transpired, however, that Mariner was making his point on a more domestic level—it was time the parishioners of Eadenford turned out and came to church on a Sunday. 'Conscience toward God' was a matter of standing up to be counted. What, asked Mariner, would a stranger passing through Eadenford think of the spiritual life of this beautiful village? That the inhabitants were people of faith and constancy, behaving according to a strong moral law? Or a bunch of shifty backsliders? (These last words were Ashe's private interpretation of what Mariner said.) He couldn't be sure if the vicar had seen him. His position away from the rest of the

129

congregation might have made him more rather than less conspicuous. But Mariner's preaching style was lofty and old-fashioned, addressed not to individuals, but to a space somewhere above and over their heads, most of which were now sheepishly bowed. Lady Delamayne gazed straight ahead and unblinking at the altar, confident that she herself was not among the castigated. Her husband sat with arms folded high on his chest, jowls resting pensively on his Sunday collar, his thoughts almost certainly elsewhere—lining up on some wretched pheasant or pursuing a fox to its death. Only Mrs Mariner seemed to be looking up at her husband with complete attention. An aqueous grey-green light fell from a window on to her face, which was still and serious beneath the rakish hat. As Mariner continued to berate those present for the shortcomings of those who weren't, Ashe studied his wife. When, after about twenty minutes, Mariner drew the sermon to a close in the name of the Father and of the Son and of the Holy Ghost, outlining a swift cross on his front, Mrs Mariner glanced Ashe's way and widened her eyes in a welcoming half-smile, which he did not return. All he'd wanted was for her to register his presence. He had achieved his objective.

The last hymn was 'Bread of Heaven', rousing but brief. Ashe planned to slip away just before the end, but during the last verse the choir, followed by Mariner, processed down the aisle and effectively cut him off at the pass. Then everyone sank to their knees while another short prayer was murmured, inaudibly, at the back. He sat impatiently on the edge of the pew; the moment the final 'Amen' was muttered, he got to his feet and left, keeping his eyes on the ground, and pulling the door to behind him.

It was good to be outside, with the soft hiss of the rain, the smell of greenness and growth from the unmown churchyard, the muted chirrup of birds sheltering in the shaggy black boughs of the yew tree. Ashe breathed deeply as he headed for the lych-gate. In the lane outside stood the Delamaynes' car.

'Mr Ashe! Wait!'

He stopped and looked over his shoulder. It was Mrs Mariner, hurrying down the path with her hat in her hand. Below the hem of her skirt sturdy, brown laced shoes, splashed through the puddles.

'Oh—Mr Ashe!' She reached his side, panting. 'I'm so glad I caught you.'

'Good morning, Mrs Mariner.'

'How nice to see you in church. I didn't somehow think'—she frowned, smiled, then waved her hand—'I don't know what I thought, but anyway it was nice to see you.'

There was something excitable in her manner. He stood quietly, not helping her. The rain sifted gently down. In the dark doorway of the church stood the white figure of Mariner in his surplice. One or two other people were beginning to emerge, pausing in the porch to button coats and put up umbrellas. Their voices, less than thirty yards away, seemed distant.

'I just wanted to thank you again,' she said animatedly, 'for cleaning the car for us that day we went to London.'

'That's all right,' he said. It had occurred to him that she liked speaking to him, and to be seen speaking to him.

'I don't know—it seems to go better when it's clean!'

He nodded.

'Not that *I* drive,' she added. 'But that's what my husband says.'

He was sure her husband said no such thing; the observation had been entirely hers, and made on the spur of the moment.

People were beginning to come down the path. She looked up into the rain, blinking, then pulled her hat on.

'You could learn,' he said.

'What?'

'To drive. Your husband could teach you.'

'Heavens!' She seemed always ready to laugh, and did so again now. 'I can't imagine that!'

He didn't join in her laughter, but waited politely for her to finish.

'Oh well . . . Goodbye, Mr Ashe.'

'Good morning, Mrs Mariner.'

He walked quickly away, conscious of her watching him for a moment, before being sucked into the group of departing worshippers, the Delamaynes among them; he could hear Lady Delamayne's resonant tones cutting through the rest.

He was exhilarated. Church had done him good after all.

*   *   *

The rain intensified during the afternoon. The badminton set which Vivien had taken out a couple of days earlier was still in its canvas bag, propped against the side of the shed. The temperature in the vicarage—not a warm house at the best of times—dropped sharply, and Vivien, swathed in her largest cardigan, lit a fire in the drawing room, and curled up in an armchair beneath a lamp, with her book and a cigarette.

Saxon was restless. Having gone into his study after lunch, Vivien could hear him moving about in there, and then the door opened and his footsteps sounded in the hall, on the stairs, across the landing, down again . . . pacing about in irritable boredom.

Familiar with this mood, she didn't look up when he came into the drawing room, but kept her eyes, self-protectively, on the page. The rain thrummed and streamed on the window. The chimney didn't draw well in this weather and the fire was no more than a dull red glow, smoking sullenly. She leaned forward and threw her cigarette end on to the coals.

'I wish you wouldn't do that,' said Saxon, referring to the habit rather than the action.

'I'm sorry.'

'You're not yourself, somehow, with a cigarette in your hand.'

'But I am.' She laid the book face down on the arm of the chair. 'Just not a side of me that you like.'

'No.'

'Not ladylike.'

'That doesn't—' He hesitated, and then said firmly: 'No.'

She gave a brief sigh of exasperation, and changed the subject.

'Did you see Mr Ashe in church?'

'I did.'

133

'I thought that was rather surprising. I wouldn't have taken him for a churchgoer.'

'I'm quite sure he's not,' said Saxon thinly.

She laced her fingers behind her head. 'He doesn't think much of me.'

Saxon frowned. 'It's of no possible concern to me what he thinks of either of us.'

'Of course not.' There was a lengthening pause, during which the only movement in the room was the tip of Saxon's index finger tapping a rapid and uneven rhythm on the arm of his chair. She wished he would stop.

'I wonder,' she said, 'if I should learn how to drive . . .'

'By all means if you'd like to,' he replied, as if she had asked his permission. 'Where did this idea come from?'

'I've been thinking about it recently. So many women can now, because of the war and so on. It would be useful, wouldn't it?'

'I suppose so.'

'If I did want to, would you teach me?' Until then she hadn't wanted to look at him, but now she did, the better to gauge his reaction.

'I'm not sure that would be a good idea.'

'Why ever not?'

'I'd make a very poor teacher. I'm not sure I have the patience. We should argue.'

'I promise not to.'

Saxon rose from his chair. 'Well?' she asked, 'what do you think?'

'I don't know.' He began to move towards the door, driven out by her questions. At the door he said, over his shoulder, 'I'd be no use at all to you. But there must be someone else who could teach

134

you.'

He left, and in a moment she heard the study door close, this time followed by silence.

*   *   *

Two days later Ashe was loading the station van with trunks for Eaden Place—there were still patients arriving, even now—when Mrs Mariner cycled into the station yard.

Her appearance was nothing short of bizarre. She was wearing a pair of over-large moleskin trousers held up with a belt, and her hair was tucked up in a cap. The bicycle's seat was set a little high for her. He pretended not see as she stopped, hopping awkwardly with one foot on the pedal and the other on the ground, then dismounted and leaned the bicycle against the wall. Mr Trodd appeared and greeted her; they exchanged a few words and he pointed towards Ashe. Ashe kept working as she came over.

'Good morning, Mr Ashe.'

'Mrs Mariner. Morning.'

'I'm sorry to disturb you.'

He tossed the case he was holding into the van. 'You're not.'

'There's something I wanted to ask you. After our conversation the other day.'

'What was that?'

'You know—about learning to drive.'

'I remember.'

'I was discussing it with my husband—' she began, and then must have seen something in his face because she glanced down at herself and said, 'By the way I apologise for my appearance, these

135

are so much more practical for cycling.'

He shrugged. 'I can see that.'

'Anyway, Mr Ashe,' she went on briskly: 'I mustn't waste your time. I wondered if you could teach me to drive?'

'I could,' he replied, an emphasis on the second word implying reservations.

'Then—would you? I'd be so grateful.'

'I work full time here,' he pointed out.

'I realise that, and I don't want to impose. But perhaps, say, an hour a week? I'd pay you, of course.'

Ashe took his time. 'What does Mr Mariner think about this?'

'As a matter of fact it was his idea.'

'He doesn't want to teach you himself?' Ashe pushed the bounds of propriety a bit, to see what he could get away with.

'No.' She didn't even seem to notice. 'He's much too busy, and anyway he doesn't think it would work. He thinks we might . . .' She hesitated. 'I agree with him, actually.'

Ashe picked up another suitcase. He kept his movements slow because his brain was racing. 'I don't mind.'

'Splendid.' She sounded businesslike, but she was a lot more pleased than she was letting on. 'When shall we start?'

'The evenings are getting lighter.' He slung the case into the van and dusted his palms. 'What about six o'clock on Friday?'

'Perfect. Will you come to call?'

'I'll wait by the garage.'

'Yes, but if I'm not there do come and ring the doorbell. The front doorbell,' she added.

He inclined his head.

'I'll see you soon then.'

'Afternoon, Mrs Mariner.'

She collected her bicycle and stood astride it before first scooting unsteadily, then pedalling away. Trodd, quivering with curiosity, came out of the station office and walked over crabwise, his head slewed round to watch her retreating back view.

'What was all that about?'

'Nothing much.'

'Get yourself invited to the vicarage tea party did you?'

Ashe made no comment, and closed the back of the van. 'I'll take this lot then.'

'Yes, yes, on your way.' Trodd waved an arm in the direction of the road. 'Watch out for lady cyclists!'

*   *   *

Edith Clay needed to get shot of the puppies, or at least to know that she would definitely be shot of them soon. Whatever disagreements went on behind closed doors at the vicarage were no concern of hers.

'So will you be wanting one, then?' she asked, standing over Mrs Mariner as she knelt on the floor.

'Oh yes, I think so.' She glanced up at Edith. 'May I pick one up?'

'Course you may.'

'Let me see . . .' Mrs Mariner deliberated, and settled on one of the dogs, black with white feet. 'Hallo, hallo . . . Aren't you handsome?' She held

137

the pup up in front of her face. It stretched its front legs towards her, paws turned up, with splayed toes. 'What does that mean?'

'He'd be a good choice,' said Edith firmly. 'Biggest of the litter, and the strongest. He'd look after you.'

'Would he really?' Mrs Mariner laughed. 'Would you?'

'Men like a dog about the place,' offered Edith. 'Dog more than a bitch,' she explained, 'suits them better, somehow.'

'Is that so?' Vivien peered closely at the puppy. 'Does he have a name?'

'That's up to you. If you want that one and you're going to pick him up a couple of weeks from now, we can start calling him whatever you like. Get him used to it.'

This was one of the means by which Edith hoped to pin Mrs Mariner down. Once she'd named a pup it would be that much harder for her to change her mind.

The strategy seemed to have worked. Vivien returned the puppy to its siblings and stood up. 'Boots,' she said. 'I think we should call him Boots.'

'That's it then. Nice and simple. Boots it is.'

Edith went to the calendar that stood on the mantelpiece. She picked up the stub of pencil that lay next to it, and marked a large cross, and the letter 'M' on a date two weeks hence.

'He'll be ready for you.'

'I *shall* look forward to it.' Vivien bent to pat the puppy. 'Goodbye for now, Boots.'

Susan came into the kitchen and plumped down heavily on a wooden chair. In her hands was a rag doll with a mop of string hair, which she began plaiting. As she did so her tongue protruded slightly, and she sent a shy, sideways smile at Vivien from beneath the hank of hair that had escaped its armoury of coloured slides.

'Susan, on your feet, say hallo to Mrs Mariner.'

'Don't worry. Hallo, Susan.'

Susan stood up, the doll dangling by its half-finished plait. 'Hallo.'

'I do love your puppies,' said Vivien. 'Guess which one I've chosen.'

'No,' said Susan. To Vivien's horror, the girl's eyes had filled with tears, and her mouth puckered. 'I don't want to. No thank you.'

Vivien realised that she had touched a nerve. 'Susan, I'm so sorry, I didn't mean to upset you.'

'Daft girl.' Edith sucked her teeth. 'That's quite enough of that, I told you they have to go to new homes, we can't keep them here all their lives, how would we feed them? And who'd look after them all, I'd like to know?'

In response Susan began to sob, her plump shoulders quivering. She pressed her hands to her eyes and the doll with its fixed, stitched grin fell to the floor. Vivien darted forward to pick it up, and put her arm round Susan, making an anguished face at Edith over her daughter's head.

'I feel terrible,' she whispered. 'She must love them so much.'

'Sooner they're gone the better,' said Edith. 'Out of sight, out of mind.'

This abrasive comment, though no doubt true, was no comfort to Susan, whose sobs came even more thick and fast. She sank back down on to the chair, and covered her head with her skirt,

139

revealing large, serviceable pink knickers almost to the knee. Halfway between elastic and hip was a patch pocket from which protruded an incongruously dainty white handkerchief, the letter 'S' embroidered on the corner. Edith sprang forward, pulled the hankie out and the skirt down in one more or less seamless movement.

'There now, that's enough, girl, blow your nose.'

Edith was not a harsh parent, far from it, but she was plainly mortified by this display of her daughter's, especially when it might jeopardise a sale. Vivien pulled another chair close to Susan's, cudgelling her brains for something to say which would reassure both of them.

'I tell you what—Susan, I'm going to need some help. The puppies know you. Will you come and visit every day, and tell me if I'm doing things right?' She put her arm round Susan's still-heaving shoulders, and gave them a squeeze. 'Hm? Will you? It would be such a comfort, to me and to Boots. That's another thing, perhaps you could make sure to call him by his name every day so that he gets used to it.'

'That's a good idea,' said Edith. 'That's a very good idea, Susan. You could make yourself useful, tell Mrs Mariner where she's going wrong.'

Vivien took the remark in the spirit of encouragement in which it was obviously intended. 'Perhaps,' she said, warming to her theme, 'you'd come round some time soon, before he arrives, and tell me where the best place would be for his bed, and everything. I've never owned a dog before.'

During this exchange the snuffling and snorting had gradually subsided. Vivien replaced the rag doll gently on Susan's rather damp lap.

'How does that sound?' she asked. 'Could you come tomorrow?' She glanced at Edith. 'If that's all right.'

'It's very kind of you,' said Edith. 'Say thank you.'

'Thank you, Mrs Mariner.'

'No, no, it's I who should be grateful. I'll look forward to it. Come in the morning, and we'll get everything organised, won't we.'

Susan beamed blotchily. 'Yes!'

Edith saw Vivien to the door.

'Sorry about that carry-on, Mrs Mariner. I've told her a dozen times the puppies have to go.'

'Poor Susan, I can imagine how horrid it must be for her.'

'You've been very understanding.'

'Please, Mrs Clay . . .' Vivien held up her hands. 'I'll see her tomorrow morning.'

*   *   *

Saxon, looking out of his study window, saw his wife return, cornering out of the road at speed and coming to an ungainly halt beside the front door. She looked up briefly, caught his eye and waved. He raised his pen in reply; she looked flushed and pleased with herself. Saxon knew she had been to the Clays' house. So any day now there would be a dog about the place—correction, a puppy—chewing and barking and making messes . . . He closed his eyes, tapping the pen against his lower teeth. What he must do, he decided, was to accept the fact that the dog was hers, Vivien's, her pet and therefore her responsibility. They would both be happier, and life easier, if this was clearly

141

acknowledged, than if he were restlessly, irritably and in all probability ineffectually attempting to intervene in the animal's training and care.

He heard her come in, and clump swiftly down the hall in her heavy shoes to the back of the house. He could only hope that her puppy-related tasks included telling Hilda, whose reaction he did not care to imagine.

But the arrival of the puppy exercised Saxon a lot less than his wife's impending driving lesson. He should not have been surprised that she'd gone to the station and asked the man Ashe—after all, he had declined to teach her himself and had even suggested that someone else might be able to—but he was nonetheless more than a little shocked. It had all happened rather too quickly, as if she'd known he would refuse and had the next step already planned. Hadn't she been rather forward in putting her request? Her impulsive and open nature could so easily be misconstrued.

Then there was Ashe himself, and that face. Saxon would have liked to feel some ordinary Christian pity, but it was impossible. The man had an inherently superior manner which was irritating, when as far as anyone could see he had absolutely nothing to be superior about. Who was he, after all? A complete stranger about whom nothing was known, who'd been reduced to going from door to door like a tramp in search of work, and who was now no more than the station van driver. How would the vicar's wife's choice of driving instructor look to other people? There again—Saxon sighed—did that matter? Wasn't it his own reaction that troubled him most?

There was also the question of the fellow going

out in his, Saxon's, car: his most prized possession! Vivien had clearly not considered this to be an issue, and the arrangement had gone by on the nod. He grimaced in annoyance. He should have undertaken the lessons himself! It was not too late. And yet he had the feeling that he had been overtaken by events, that Vivien was actually looking forward to going out with this—this gargoyle.

Saxon put down his pen, and clasped his hands on his open sermon-book. For a full minute he sat very still, eyes not closed, but fixed on his thoughts, in a state suspended uncomfortably somewhere between prayer and furious agitation.

*　　　*　　　*

'What'll I do with it when I'm working?' asked Hilda.

'Nothing,' replied Vivien, '*you* don't have to do anything at all.'

'It'll be underfoot.'

'No, he won't, he'll be good as gold.' Vivien was determined to attribute both gender and personality to her pet. 'I'll see to that.'

'What about its business? I can't be responsible.'

'Hilda, you're not responsible!' Vivien's voice had risen slightly and she brought it back under control. 'Please don't worry. I'm going to house-train him at once. Susan's coming up to help me, she knows all about puppies.'

Hilda sucked in her cheeks. 'Whatever you say, Mrs Mariner.'

'He's lovely, Hilda,' said Vivien. 'A month from now we'll wonder what we did without him.'

'She was perfectly all right about it,' Vivien told Saxon over lunch. 'All that worried her was whether she'd be able to get on with her work, and I soon reassured her about that.'

'Good,' said Saxon, 'We're very fortunate in Hilda, I'd hate to lose her.'

'Not half as much as I would! Imagine me in sole charge of this place, it doesn't bear thinking about!'

'That's true,' he said. This made her laugh, as she was always more than ready to appreciate a joke against herself.

Taking advantage of this moment of light-hearted mutuality, Saxon asked casually: 'Is it your driving lesson tomorrow?'

'Yes. Mr Ashe is coming here at six o'clock.'

'Then I shall make sure the car is out on the drive for you.'

'There's no need, Saxon. The whole point is that he's a competent driver.'

'That may be so, but I'd prefer to. It would be very awkward for all of us if he sustained a bump first time out; I'd like to spare him the possibility.'

Vivien looked at him for a moment. She seemed to be making a decision. Then she got up and walked round the table. She embraced him, and held his head to her breast.

'Thank you,' she said. 'For being so good to me.'

He raised his hand and placed it gently beneath her right breast, feeling the soft weight of it in his palm. At once, as always, he was overtaken with desire for her. He let his hand slide down to the join at the top of her legs. His other arm crept round her, encircling her bottom. He heard her breath quicken into a sigh. It never failed to astonish him, that she seemed to desire him as much as he desired her. Everything in his upbringing, and in the attitudes of other men and women, especially those of married couples, had led him to believe that most women (except those of easy virtue) simply put up with physical love; that they did their conjugal duty as the price they had to pay for the affection and fidelity of their husbands. When Vivien had accepted him he had scarcely dared believe that his feelings would be so fully and gloriously reciprocated. He knew it was not a sin, but a gift from God, and yet to have access, always, to such overwhelming pleasure seemed almost sinful, as if his pleasure were at the expense of others'.

She turned slightly and sat down on his knee, her arms about his neck, her head hanging languidly. He was enveloped by her. In a sort of ecstasy, he fondled her. It was as he imagined it must be to play some large and beautiful musical instrument: the responsiveness to his touch, the sweet, soaring, transcendent excitement . . .

She rose, with a sort of heavy, sliding reluctance, from his lap, her fingers trailing from his mouth to his hand.

'Come along.'

*   *   *

Half an hour later, when the bell still had not rung, Hilda came up the stairs and peered from the end of the hall, to see how the land lay. The dining

145

room door stood wide open. The remains of lunch, the used plates and half-full water glasses, were on the table. Near Mrs Mariner's chair, a napkin lay on the floor; Mr Mariner's was dropped anyhow on his used plate. His chair was pushed well back from the table and the cloth at his end was pulled all to one side. Hilda sucked her teeth—the whole lot could have gone for six.

She went in and began clearing up. The small sounds she made only emphasised the extreme stillness of the house. As she scraped the leftovers on to one plate, she supposed that once they got this dog, it would be able to eat scraps. Whatever Mrs Mariner said, Hilda was not convinced that it wouldn't be a nuisance. At times like these, for instance . . . When they were having what she thought of as their private moments. The marital bedroom was no place for a dog, it would be left to her to look after it. And apparently—she clattered the knives and forks into the potato dish—Susan Clay would be calling even more often. The Clays were a nice family, and Hilda didn't mind Susan, in moderation, but Mrs Mariner was always asking if she could stay 'for a bite of lunch' or 'a slice of cake', and the girl had an insatiable appetite.

Hilda knew she was well off with her job at the vicarage; the Mariners might have been an odd couple, but they were fair, and not fussy, and let her get on with her work with the minimum of intervention. But there were limits to her tolerance, and not every employee would be as discreet and understanding as she knew herself to be.

With the tray stacked to capacity, she set off back to the kitchen. A dog underfoot now, she thought grimly, and there'd be a disaster.

*   *   *

Saxon stroked Vivien's hair; such beautiful hair, soft as a cloud, fluid as water, sifting and stirring under his fingers. This was the moment, he thought, when he might say exactly what he wanted, and be heard.

'It's not too late to put off Mr Ashe, you know.'

'What?'

'I've been thinking. I should like to teach you to drive. It was simply that you startled me rather when you first asked, I'm a creature of habit as you know. Anyway,' he finished, somewhat lamely. 'There it is.'

She said nothing, but he seemed to feel her stiffen.

'I believe,' he went on, 'that I made some foolish remark to the effect that we'd argue, but with good will on both sides there's no reason on earth why that should happen.'

She was still silent, and he had nothing else to say. Except, of course: 'So perhaps you could tell Mr Ashe he won't be needed.'

Those silences had given him his answer. But he had said his piece and now, unhappily, had no choice but to hear her out.

'Saxon, I can't. Not after agreeing, after approaching him. Quite apart from the fact that it's work for him, work he needs, what will he think? He'll guess that we've been discussing him. And don't say that it doesn't matter, because it matters to me. That poor man has so much to contend with every day of his life, every time he walks out of his door in the morning, I'd so hate us, of all people, to add to his unhappiness for the sake of a few hours out in the car.'

With an enormous effort of will—she could not know or imagine how great—Saxon thrust aside the angry, wounded, wounding things he most wished to say, in favour of a direct appeal to her loving nature.

'I had thought that you might genuinely prefer to learn with me.'

Unfortunately this sounded merely petulant, but it was too late to take it back.

'Do you know . . .' She reached up her hand to touch his cheek. 'Do you know, Saxon, I wouldn't.'

He felt turned to stone. 'Why's that?'

'Because I thought about it too—what you said, and I think that you were right. You have so much to do, and I don't suppose I'll be a particularly apt pupil. It will be so much better to pay someone— someone who really needs the money—to put up with me.'

'Quite right,' he said. 'Let sleeping dogs lie. I should never have mentioned it.'

He swung his legs out of the bed and began pulling on his dressing gown, suddenly ashamed of his nakedness. Not wanting to see Vivien, either, he kept his back to her. Guilt and resentment flooded him. This was not what a parish priest should be doing at two o'clock in the afternoon; desire had made him vulnerable and stupid and he had got what he deserved. The disobliging feelings he was experiencing were no one's fault but his own.

'We should get up,' he said.

He went into the dressing room and closed the

door. As he did so he was acutely aware that his wife had not moved, but was lying with her head averted, gazing out of the window, her hair spread around her on the pillow.

*   *   *

It would have surprised Saxon to learn that Vivien, too, was examining her conscience. For almost the first time she was aware of having exploited the peculiar chemistry of their marriage. She had manipulated her husband's pride, and his conscience, to her own advantage—though what advantage precisely she was unable or unwilling to admit, even to herself.

When she heard his footsteps on the stairs, she got out of bed and dressed quickly.

*   *   *

Susan set off for the vicarage next morning carrying another note, this time a list, laboriously compiled with her mother's help, of preparations Mrs Mariner could make for the puppy's arrival. The list was long, and included among other things a box or spare drawer with an old blanket for Boots to sleep in; a clock to wrap up and tuck next to him to remind him of his mother; a large box of porridge oats, because he wouldn't yet be on to meat; a collar and lead; and plenty of newspaper to put down while he was still being house-trained. Susan hoped she'd be able to remember everything and explain it sensibly to Mrs Mariner. Her mother had been stern on the subject of silly behaviour, and bursting into tears: there was to be no more of

149

it. Boots was as good as Mrs Mariner's now, she said, and it wasn't polite to make a fuss.

Susan was sure that this time she'd be all right. For a start, the puppies wouldn't be there, so she wouldn't be reminded of their soft coats and paws and their sweet, snuffling noses . . . And for another, Mrs Mariner always made her welcome at the vicarage and told her what a good girl she was.

She was at the end of the High Street when a van pulled up next to her, and a man leaned across to speak to her.

'Hallo, Susan.'

'Hallo.' It was the man with the funny face, who had given her the cake.

'Off to the vicarage again?'

'Yes.'

'Want a lift?'

She took a step back. 'No, thank you.'

'Good girl.' It was peculiar when he smiled because one side of his face was already grinning, so the other side just seemed to catch up with it. 'Cheerio.'

'Goodbye.'

*   *   *

As Ashe drove past the vicarage gate he caught a glimpse of the Reverend Mariner, sitting at his desk in the study window. Not working though; just staring into space.

MESOPOTAMIA

Years later if I heard some officer type say he'd 'been at Ctesiphon' I'd think, if I were him I'd keep quiet about it.

The night before a battle you're supposed to have serious thoughts—say a prayer, think of home, write a letter to be opened if you 'don't come back'. Plenty of people do, for the same reason they turn up at church parade—because they're scared shitless and they want to build up a bit of credit. Not me. The night before Ctesiphon I sit and clean Jarvis's kit.

'That's it, Ashe,' he says approvingly, 'there's a lot of comfort in ritual.'

'Perhaps you're right, sir.'

He smiles, he likes the way I speak; it amuses him. Early on I realised that the right kind of voice can get you a long way. I listened, and copied, and taught myself to speak like an educated man. Not plummy, not like that, just properly. Another thing: lower your voice and people have to listen. And when in doubt, keep *schtum* as they say in the East End. No one ever got into trouble by keeping their mouth shut.

I'm only cleaning the kit for something to do, whatever Jarvis says. The last thing I ever want to think about is where I lived as a kid—I couldn't call it 'home', that woman my mother made sure it was never that. That said, I've got a lot to thank her for. She made me what I am today: devious, cunning, secretive. I get a lot of quiet pleasure from how much she'd hate my gratitude.

People often say only children are spoiled. Well, I was an only child, and there are two meanings of the word 'spoiled': one of them is 'overindulged', and that's not me, the other is 'damaged'.

I'm sure my parents only did it the once and that was enough for both of them. My father Gerald was nice but useless—it was my mother who ruled the roost. She was always a bully, cold and cruel. She had one of those sneering mouths, with lines that ran all the way from the corners of her nose down to her jaw like a wooden puppet. Her name was Audrey. Sounds like the creak of a prison door.

She had never been a beauty, but in old photographs she looked thin and bright-eyed, and smart as paint. Even I remember she had a way with words, she used them like weapons, so perhaps she was an amusing, witty woman before she became bitter and disappointed, and that was what attracted my father.

He wore a collar and tie to work but he was a dogsbody just the same, shat on by the bosses and despised by the workers, you could just tell. Before I started to despise him too, I felt sorry for him because he hadn't always been a dull, weak-tea man. He could play the banjo, and sing, do a bit of soft-shoe. He was good-looking, with crinkly hair and dark eyes, but the day he married my mother her first job as a wife was to set about killing his spirit. I can just remember when there was a little bit of it left; days when he'd catch my eye and pull a face as much as to say 'Hark at her!' and for a moment we were two blokes together, under the thumb.

But it wasn't a joke, and he was dying right there

in front of me. I used to wake in the night and hear them in their room—hear her, attacking him in a low, vicious whisper, hissing and spitting. Once or twice I heard him crying, and that was worse. That made me want to be sick. To hear my own father, a grown man, sobbing and choking and pleading. For what? For mercy? For sex, is what I think now. Why he didn't walk out and get what he wanted somewhere else, I'll never know, it's easy enough. But the crying, on and on . . . That turned over my whole world, as well as my stomach.

She won, of course. He seemed to shrink, and get paler. His crinkly hair got thin and his face sagged so that the bottom of his eyes showed a wet, red crescent. Even his lips and fingernails became bluish, like a corpse's. He became of no consequence in the house, just going to work and coming back, a nothing, a ghost. I took my tone from my mother. What was I supposed to do, I was what, nine years old? At that age it's like the Buddhoos, you'll stick with whoever's winning. For a while we held it there—him coming and going, us taking no notice, no respect and affection between any of us, but going through the motions. We were very respectable. I was doing well at school and she liked that. She used to taunt him with how different I was from him and little Judas that I was I let her do it, and never caught his eye any more.

But she had to feed off something, and gradually, because there was nothing left of Gerald, she turned on me.

'John,' she said one day. 'I want a word with you.'

We were just finishing tea. Gerald was still eating his, but she got up.

153

'Not here,' she said.

He was so defeated by then that he didn't even look up from his plate as we left the room. Over the years I've kept that picture in my mind of him sitting there, gazing down at his lamb chop, chewing, swallowing, his Adam's apple jerking, letting us go . . . I've kept it because it was the end of the beginning. From then on everything changed. He must have had some idea, but he was just a thing by then, or so I thought.

What she hadn't wanted from him, what she had spurned and spat at him for all those long, awful nights, she wanted from me. Or at least, she wanted to take it from me because I didn't want to give it. Didn't even know how. I hadn't even had a wet dream yet, but she got hold of me and said it was time she taught me something. I was horrified. Shocked. To lose control like that is bad enough. But to be made to do it by her . . . I didn't know where I was. No matter how horrible she was, or what she'd said or done to my father to make him blub like a child, she was my mother, the only one I had, and so I *had* to believe it was all right. Perhaps all mothers did it. It felt exciting but nasty at the same time, and she seemed to think so too—carried away, but immediately afterwards she'd be cold and cross and clean us both up roughly with a disgusted look on her face. But I couldn't talk about it, so I had no way of knowing just how disgusting it was.

The only certainty was that it was a secret. She told me there were some things it was wicked to tell other people, and this was one of them. That wasn't a problem. As I say, who would I have told?

It was always very quick, and very quiet. And

154

always when my father was in the house, that must have been part of the thrill for her, knowing he was only a few feet away. Whether he had any idea, I don't know. He'd got so uninterested, so detached from his surroundings, that he probably didn't. Unless she told him—I wouldn't have put it past her. The only time her mouth lost its sneer was when she was doing that to me. It got loose, so I could see her tongue and the spit on her teeth. Her cheekbones went pink.

The minute I was respectable again she'd shoo me away. 'Go on!' she'd snap, sharp as a pair of scissors, her eyes all small and flinty, 'Go on! Go and see what your father's up to!'

Till then I'd been doing all right at school, but my work soon went downhill. I'd never had a big gang of friends, but now I let go of the one or two I had. I felt tired, and guilty, and my body didn't seem to belong to me, but became like something I dragged around and couldn't escape from.

With all this, you'd have thought I'd mature early, but I didn't. Some instinct—fear probably—held me back. I was thirteen before I began to look at girls in a different way, and that was when I began to realise just how bad what I did with my mother was. What happened to me with her was what happened to me when I thought about girls. Only she was my mother. She was old (all of thirty-five), and rough and nasty. I was scared of her and disgusted with myself.

One Sunday afternoon when I was fourteen, I was clearing away the dinner dishes with my father. My mother had left the room, but not asked me to go with her for once. My father and I didn't talk much—not a lot of talking went on in our house in those days—except once, to pat me on the back and ask how I was getting on at school. I told him fine, which was a lie.

'Got a girl?'

I was appalled. I think I blushed; I didn't want him thinking about these things. If he'd been wondering about that, then what else? I didn't want to be in his head at all, ever.

'No,' I muttered, dead surly.

'Never mind,' he said. 'Plenty of time for all that.'

I didn't answer, but he wouldn't let it go. After years of silence he had what amounted to verbal diarrhoea.

'If there's anything you want to know, lad, you only have to ask.'

A couple of years before it might have been possible. But now the idea was ghastly. It made my flesh creep.

And then my mother called. 'John! John—can you come up here a moment?'

For once I didn't mind. No price was too high to pay to get away from my father at that moment.

But this time it was different. She was sitting on the edge of the bed, in her petticoat, and the covers were turned down.

'Over here, John,' she said. 'Quickly now.'

*　　　*　　　*

For another year, I did as I was told. I couldn't look at a girl, and I truanted from school. I looked awful, I was beginning to look like my father: the walking dead. I was pale, I had spots, my hair was greasy and my eyes were fish-eyes, dull and flat. I had impetigo as well, the scurfy patches of peeling skin painted with gentian violet to make them even more noticeable. I was a leper, a pariah—unclean, inside and out. God knows why my mother kept on with what she did. Perhaps the state of me gave her a perverse pleasure; after all, it was sort of punishment for being male.

And then my father—I can't say 'dropped the bombshell' because it was more like thistledown, or a little piece of paper that floated in through the window.

I was walking back from school and to my horror he was standing on the corner of our road, waiting for me. I pretended I hadn't seen him, but there was no escape. He raised his arm and crossed the road.

'Hallo, son.'

'What are you doing here?' I said.

'Came to meet you. There's something I've been wanting to say and I thought, no time like the present.'

I didn't ask him what, I just kept walking. He was panting like an old dog trying to keep up.

'Steady on, you're too quick for me.'

I stopped dead. 'What is it?'

'Come in the park, let's sit down for a minute.'

'The park' as he called it was a gritty little garden with black iron railings and a cinder path. We went in and he sat down on a bench. He sat in the middle of it; I hovered, not wanting to be too close. I never wanted to be physically close to anyone, ever again.

'Sit down, why don't you,' he said, patting the seat, and moving to one side a bit so there was more room.

Gingerly, I sat down, pressed up against the arm at the opposite end.

'Don't worry,' he said, with a flash of his old, knowing spark, 'this won't take long.'

'Go on then—what?'

'But I want you to hear me out.' When I didn't reply he cocked his head to peer at me. 'All right?'

I shrugged.

There was a grey squirrel scampering about on the balding patch of grass in front of us and he watched it as he spoke, following it closely with his eyes, as if what he had to say just had to be spat out and got over with, without too much fuss.

'You don't need to put up with anything you don't like around the place. At home, I mean—you know that, don't you, John?' His use of my name, instead of the usual 'son' was a shock. It put the whole exchange on a different footing. I felt cold, and my stomach bubbled nervously.

'Your mother,' he went on. 'It pains me to say it, but she's not the woman I married. She's changed, and not for the better. I've put up with a lot, over the years, as I'm sure you're well aware. You're a bright boy. The only reason I haven't gone long ago is because of you. But you're growing up, and I may not stay much longer.' I wasn't looking at him, but he must have known I'd be terrified, because I felt him glance my way. At least he had the sense—or the sensitivity—not to touch me.

'Don't worry,' he looked away again. 'I won't go till you do.'

The squirrel darted up the wide trunk of a tree and stopped dead, spreadeagled, as if someone had pinned it there with an arrow. Stopped dead was how I felt.

It wasn't so much what he'd said, which wasn't a lot after all, but what lay behind it. Was he really telling me that he'd known, all this time, what was going on? And more importantly that he knew it wasn't something my mother and I got up to together, but that it was her fault? I'd always suspected that she might have told him, as part of the special torture she handed out to him, but she certainly wouldn't have taken responsibility—it would have been me that was the dirty, unnatural little beast. But if he'd known that much, why hadn't he stepped in, done something about it, behaved like the man of the house?

'How did you know?' I asked. I whispered it, and my head was turned away from him.

'I know your mother.'

That was all he said.

I could have forgiven him, just, for being defeated and wretched, a nobody around the place. But for this—for knowing, all these years, and doing nothing—I knew I never could. My mother was wicked, sadistic; perhaps even a little mad. My father had no such excuse. He had decent instincts, was holding down a job, providing for us, paying the rent on the house where I was subjected to that, eating the food cooked by her hands, closing his mind and his conscience to my thousand private, sickening humiliations. Before today, I'd merely despised and discounted him as pathetic, a defeated man, but at least there was a part of me that identified with him; we had both suffered at her hands. Now, when he spoke to me so calmly of my not needing to 'put up with anything', of his leaving, but not until I did, I wanted to kill him! Not dispose of him cleanly but

159

to tear at his flesh with my nails and teeth, to hear him scream! All those days when he had sat there at the dining table or in his chair in the front room, eating or reading, with meek, downcast eyes, and he had *known*. In my eyes at that moment he was as much her accomplice as if he'd been in the room with us.

That was when I learned you couldn't trust anyone. It's lies, not love, that make the world go round, and you're a lot safer acknowledging that and acting accordingly. No one says what they mean. And what they do isn't what they think. No one's feelings are clean, or straightforward. There are very few honestly good people, the ones who seem good are just better at concealment. Bigger liars, in other words.

I got up and left my father in the park, and I never saw him again. I called his bluff; he was free to go then, but I don't know if he did and I don't care. I went straight home, and luckily my mother was out at the shops. I went to my room, put some things in a pillowcase and set off up the road, like Dick Whittington.

I only slept rough for a week. Every day I went to the Gents in Holborn and washed and made myself respectable. Then I got a job as an office boy on a little newspaper in the East End, the *Bethnal Green Bugle*, and a room—cupboard, really—with the man in charge of the personal ads, Mr Hawkins. 'Call me Philip'. He was bent as a butcher's hook, but kind. Never took advantage, but liked to give the impression to his friends that we might be together, as you might say. Lies again. We understood each other.

I was good at the job—I was even offered a

promotion, thanks to Hawkins, as a clerk in the ads department. But I needed to move on. The moment I felt people were beginning to know me, I had this urge to get out. When Hawkins implied that maybe I should be a little bit grateful, I was gone.

And that's how it was with me, for years, till I went in the army. I never had any trouble finding work, I could always parlay my way into a job, and do it pretty well, too. Wherever I was, I kept my eyes wide open and my mouth shut, and didn't mix. The first sign of someone getting chummy and you couldn't see me for dust.

I learned a lot, though, as you do if you're not wasting energy on other people. In a restaurant, I picked up a few basic techniques. You don't need to learn the recipe for lobster thermidor, you need to know how to make a sauce. I worked as a bootboy in a big house off Piccadilly and the chauffeur showed me how to drive (the first time I sat behind the wheel of a vehicle I'd never actually driven one of the things in my life, but I winged it). I watched the people I worked for, and saw how it was done. You don't have to be quality to act it. That's why I taught myself to speak properly.

I joined the army at the start of the war, and it suited me down to the ground. A big institution's a great place for a loner. When the show started I was in my element. All bets were off. The world had gone mad, and I was the only sane person in it.

*   *   *

And now it's the night before Ctesiphon. I've done Jarvis's kit and I'm throwing dice for a chicken. I'm

161

going to win.

Half an hour later the scrawny bird's skewered on a stick over a fire and I'm the bee's knees.

'Ashe,' says Jarvis, 'that smells ambrosian. You'll make some woman a wonderful husband.'

'Maybe sir,' I say, 'but I wouldn't marry any woman who'd have me.'

He roars. Probably thinks I can walk on water, but for now the chicken will do.

CHAPTER SIX

Saxon, standing in the drawing room window at five to six, saw John Ashe walk up the drive and take up a position next to the car. He stood with his hands in his pockets, gazing back the way he'd come, presenting his damaged profile to Saxon, who frowned with distaste. Thankfully his wife, during the course of her lesson, would be in the driving seat, and therefore not exposed to the dreadful spectacle.

He heard her quick footsteps in the hall, and a moment later she appeared in the drawing room doorway. She was respectably dressed, thank God, in a jacket and skirt, but had spoiled the effect somewhat by wearing what he thought of as her errand-boy cap, tied on with a scarf.

'There you are,' she said. 'We'll be off in a minute.'

Saxon turned back to the window. 'He's out there now.'

'Then I must dash!'

'No need for that,' said Saxon testily. 'He's only just arrived. Anyway, I shall come out with you and see you off.'

'Thank you!' Impulsively she flew to his side and kissed his cheek. He felt he had been thrown a sop.

Outside, Saxon deliberately slowed his pace; it was a kind of experiment, to see whether Vivien would remain at his side, or be unable to prevent herself from rushing enthusiastically forward.

To his great satisfaction, she stayed with him, even putting her hand in the crook of his arm, though he suspected the gesture might be in the nature of a self-imposed restraint. It would have been too much to expect her not to call out, and of course she did so.

'Mr Ashe! Good evening!'

He took his hands from his pockets. 'Good evening, Mrs Mariner. Reverend.'

'Good evening.'

'I'm glad to have seen you, Mr Mariner. I was in two minds whether to knock on your door.'

Saxon felt himself slightly on the back foot. From where he'd been standing two minutes ago, Ashe had certainly not looked like a man in two minds.

Not waiting for an answer, he went on in his quiet, unassuming way: 'I hope you're quite happy with this arrangement.'

'Of course he is,' said Vivien, 'I told you. You are, aren't you, Saxon?'

She was putting him on the spot. Ashe's level gaze hadn't left his face.

'I trust you to look after the car, naturally,' said Saxon.

'Naturally,' said Ashe. 'And Mrs Mariner, too.'

'That goes without saying,' said Saxon, irritated at this appearance of being prompted on a matter of form.

'Do let's start,' said Vivien impatiently. 'And Saxon, you're not to watch.'

'Let me see you safely out of the drive, at least.'

'I'd be grateful if you would,' said Ashe.

Saxon stood looking on, without comment, as Ashe started the engine, took his place next to Vivien, and took her through the controls. It was frustrating not to be able to hear what was being

164

said, but the man's manner was reassuringly calm and workmanlike. By the time the car turned, a little jerkily, out into the road with Vivien at the wheel, Saxon was some way to being mollified. Apart from that one remark, to which he had responded oversensitively, Ashe had been a model of calm civility, if not exactly of deference. There had even been the implication that the two of them should agree, man to man, before the lesson could take place.

Saxon returned to the house, and his book. But he couldn't concentrate, and ten minutes later set the book aside and went out of the back door into the garden. Once outside, he wasn't sure what to do. This was not his domain: he did no gardening, and only spent time here with Vivien and at her instigation. It wasn't quite warm enough to sit, and besides he hadn't brought his book with him. What, he wondered, gazing about him, did people do? They strolled, perhaps. Saxon wasn't one of nature's strollers, being more accustomed, and inclined, to short, brisk journeys with a clear end in view. However, since he was here, he began a somewhat self-conscious perambulation around the edge of the vicarage's quarter of an acre, glad that Hilda had been given the evening off.

He walked with long, slow strides, his hands behind his back. He didn't know the names of plants, but it was impossible not to notice the surge of uncontrolled growth that was taking place. The apple trees next the shed were already in bud. Great rafts and tuffets and fountains of greenery swelled on every side. The 'lawn'—even Saxon mentally placed inverted commas round the word—was sprinkled with the white dots of early daisies, now closing demurely for the night, and patched with archipelagos of moss. A mole had been busy, the fresh brown eruptions of a new fortress dotted the grass furthest from the house. Saxon, largely indifferent to what went on in the garden, didn't much mind, but knew that the catcher would have to be got in. With the evenings drawing out and the weather improving, visitors to the vicarage would be more likely to see the garden. Molehills all over the place created a slovenly impression.

He noticed the badminton set, still in its canvas bag, propped up in the angle between the side of the shed and the water butt. With summer ahead, Vivien must have taken it out. Another reason to see off the moles. Maybe this was something he could do to while away the hour. He loosened the drawstring and pulled open the top of the bag, but after peering in glumly at the jumble of racquets, iron rods and string he concluded that it was definitely a job better undertaken by two. He moved on. Croquet was a good game, and one he'd showed an aptitude for on the occasions he'd had to play—notably up with the Delamaynes, one day last summer. Vivien had enjoyed herself (he smiled at the memory) but had lacked the killer instinct. In any event, the agricultural surface of the vicarage lawn was hopeless for the purpose. Perhaps a large roller—he believed the cricket team had one, but how would one get it here from their field on the other side of the village . . . ?

Saxon reached the end of the garden some hundred feet from the house, in his opinion the most attractive area, though it was terribly overgrown. Here the snaggle-toothed fence, scabbed with lichen, rambled across part of a small wood. The stately trunks of mature chestnut, elm and beech trees gave the place a churchlike air, and layers of leaf mould muffled his footsteps. In January there was the odd snowdrop, and this evening he could see one or two plucky primroses shining through the undergrowth. Saxon's faith was largely cerebral, the product of reasoned thought and wide and intensive reading, but here he could fully acknowledge that God was manifest in natural beauty, and that the phrase 'God's own cathedral' (often used facetiously by Sidney Delamayne to justify a Sunday morning's shooting) was appropriate.

A huge branch had split away from one of the elms during a winter storm, and collapsed, dipping, then extending a beseeching, horizontal arm, before sagging finally to the ground. Already the sharp, white scar between branch and trunk had been colonised by thick plates of orange speckled fungi. Gingerly, Saxon lowered himself on to the natural seat of the branch, testing it carefully with his weight. It barely moved. He sat, looking back at the house. It was interesting to observe it from this angle, which provided a more intimate, domestic view than that from the front, and one which in some small way altered his perception of himself. He again pictured Vivien and the puppy running about, enjoying themselves, only this time he also pictured himself, if not running about with them, then sitting here beneath the trees, looking on indulgently as a father might do with two high-spirited children. Then there was the badminton to look forward to with its attendant frisson, and Hilda's home-made lemonade . . .

A single swallow swooped down from high above the trees, with a sound in the stillness like the whistling flight of an arrow. At lightning speed it described a long, low inverted arc from the treetops to its nest beneath the bedroom gable and once there seemed to melt, in an instant, into the stone. Vivien was right—he should try to be out of doors more. Nature refreshed the soul and fed the imagination.

Like one of the fresh green spears at his feet, a line of poetry popped into Saxon's head:

If I am quiet, it is to hear your music

The line, as always, came as a surprise, breaking into his thoughts spontaneously; fragile, but nonetheless demanding his attention. At once he was filled with the thrilling anticipation that preceded a poem.

He got up from his tree-seat and began walking back across the rough grass to the house, slowly and deliberately because to hurry might be to douse the frail, enchanted spark of inspiration.

*　　　*　　　*

Vivien's prediction had been incorrect: she *was* an apt pupil. In no time at all, under Ashe's tutelage, she had mastered the controls and had to be restrained from going too fast. Rather than attempt Fort Hill, with its steep gradient and bends, they had driven down the High Street and continued some way along the road beyond the village, in the direction of Bridgeford. Several people stared as they went by, and then waved or smiled when they saw it was Mrs Mariner at the wheel.

She was exhilarated. After half an hour, Ashe suggested they stop at the next farm gateway, and she managed that quite well, too.

'If we could change places for a moment, Mrs Mariner,' he said, 'I can turn her round.'

'Can't I do that?'

'Next time, perhaps.'

She climbed out of the car, a little wobbly on her land legs, and watched as he performed the manoeuvre. When it was done he turned the engine off and jumped down.

'Might as well take a little break.'

She said: 'I can't remember when I last enjoyed myself so much!'

'You're doing well.'

He leaned his forearms on the gate, looking away from her, over the field. There was something attractive in his studied detachment; a consciousness of the rules that could be broken.

'You're a good teacher.'

He lifted his chin—maybe, maybe not.

'Would you mind if I had a cigarette?'

'Not at all.'

He took a box of matches from his pocket, waited, and lit the cigarette for her. She joined him at the gate, leaning her back against it.

'I hope you don't think this is unladylike,' she said. 'My smoking.'

'That's not my business.'

She realised as he said this that she wanted to make it his business—to elicit an opinion, any kind of response, from him.

'Have you taught anyone to drive before?' she

asked and, when he shook his head, added: 'Because you're a good teacher.'

'It's not hard.'

All this time he had stayed in the same position, looking out across the field. Now suddenly he turned to face her and she felt again the shock of his damaged face, the calm way the rest of him looked from behind it, as if wearing a mask. A bird twittered its spring song; otherwise the early evening was quiet. She thought: *These feelings are wrong, but I wanted to feel them. I made this happen, I wanted to be here.*

Ashe opened the driver's door and stood waiting for her.

'Better get back,' he said. 'We don't want Mr Mariner worrying.'

*   *   *

Saxon heard the car in the road, and looked up, slightly tranced, from the sheet of paper where there were now some eight lines in black ink, busy with crossings-out and corrections. The car turned into the drive, but the mood of the poem still held him in its spell; he watched without great attention as Vivien got down from the driver's seat, and Ashe took her place to manoeuvre the car into the garage. They exchanged a few words, after which Ashe left, and Vivien walked back to the house. Saxon did notice her expression, which was oddly concentrated and inward-looking. Perhaps, he thought, with an unworthy lurch of hope, it had not gone well.

But when she came into the study she was her usual self, and full of her success.

170

'That was marvellous,' she declared, pulling off her hat and with it most of the pins from her hair. 'Bother. Anyway, Saxon, I can drive! I enjoyed it, and you may not believe this but we never had a nervous moment . . .' As she spoke she was picking up the hairpins, which she then put on his desk where they lay higgledy-piggledy, like stray pine needles from a Christmas tree.

'I'm very glad to hear it.' Absently, using the side of his hand, he clustered the pins together and laid them the right way round.

'I hope you didn't spend your time fretting about us. Or about the car. I was safe as houses, I promise.'

'No,' he said truthfully. 'I didn't fret at all.'

'Mind you,' she went on as if he hadn't spoken, 'I was in good hands. Mr Ashe is a first-class teacher.'

'I'm sure he is.'

How perverse, he thought. I'm longing for her to go, so that I can continue writing about her.

'How have you been?' She went to the window and stood with her back to him. 'Have you been all right?'

'Perfectly. I went out in the garden for a while.'

'Saxon!' She feigned exaggerated surprise. 'The garden?'

'Yes. Not like me, you're thinking. But it was very pleasant. And then I came in here to do a little writing.'

He half hoped she might ask what he was writing, but no.

'Shall we have supper then? It's waiting for us.'

Eating was the last thing he wanted to do, and he very nearly said that he simply wasn't hungry.

171

But the contrast between these thoughts, and those that had inspired the lines of poetry that lay before him, shamed him. He got up, stiffly, scraped the hairpins into his cupped hand and handed them to her.

'Yours, I think.'

*   *   *

Very late that night, Saxon woke up. He woke suddenly and cleanly, and was instantly alert, as if someone had tapped him on the shoulder. He peered at the clock on his bedside chest: half past twelve. What had woken him? He was a sound sleeper and rarely even dreamed. He glanced down at Vivien. She was curled tight as an ammonite with her back to him, her hands bunched beneath her chin, her hair pushed up, folded, on to the pillow like the loop of a bow. Her lips trembled on a long breath: she was far away.

He got out of bed and went to the window. An almost full moon had bleached the garden of colour; it was a place of shadow and pallor like a faded photograph. He could see the pale canvas of the badminton set, the livid scar of the broken branch, the inky-black blobs of the mole fortress on the fog-grey grass. He fancied he could see himself, sitting down there, gazing back at him—the other Saxon, who had been inspired to write those tender, confessional lines. The notion made him suddenly anxious, because he did not wish to lose either.

His bare feet felt cold and he returned to bed, reaching for Vivien and scooping her, just as she was, into his arms. Still deeply asleep, she settled

172

her back against him, and murmured something, a single word, which he couldn't make out.

* * *

'Come on Sunday,' Mrs Mariner had said during their second outing in the car, 'when we're in church. It's one of Hilda's Sundays on, so make sure she doesn't get a fright—a man in the garden, I mean.'

Ashe had known very well what she meant, and didn't hold it against her. And now that he was here, he intended to present himself to Hilda anyway. A good housekeeper's standing in the household and her value to it could never be underestimated, and after his poor showing on the front doorstep a couple of weeks ago he was anxious to secure a place in her good books. That meant behaving with a good deal more deference to Hilda than to her employers.

He knocked on the back door and waited until the moment Hilda opened it to remove his hat respectfully.

'Oh,' she said, looking away, 'it's you.'

'Good morning. Mrs Mariner asked me to put the badminton up for her.'

'Yes, she told me.'

'Thought I'd better let you know I was here, just in case.'

'She did warn me.'

Ashe took no offence. 'They're in church, I believe.'

'That's right.'

'Mr Mariner's busy day I suppose.'

'That's right.'

173

'I'll be getting on with it, then.' She was itching for him to go, but he had one more card up his sleeve and paused, sniffing. 'Something smells good.'

'It's silverside of beef.'

'Wonderful. Silverside! Food for the gods.'

Hilda unbent a little. 'It's the reverend's favourite.'

'And your speciality, I bet . . .' He smiled.

'I'm a good plain cook,' she conceded.

'Oh well . . .' He sighed, as if tearing himself away. 'Mustn't keep you from it.'

As he walked away he was conscious of her looking after him for a few seconds before she closed the door. He considered that it had gone pretty well.

It didn't take Ashe long to set up the badminton. The slowest part was disentangling the components, the rods, net, pegs and guy ropes, and laying them out in order on the ground. Once he'd done that it was the work of minutes to see to the rest. He left the racquets and shuttlecocks in the canvas bag and put them just inside the shed, noticing as he did so the mower standing beneath its tarpaulin. He hesitated, hand on the door. The grass was badly in need of a cut, probably hadn't been touched since last year, and the moles had been having a field day.

He glanced first at his watch—only twenty-five past eleven—then up at the sky. It was nice enough at the moment, but cloudy and uncertain. Definitely not set fair. And at this time of year a fall of rain would render this lot too soggy to mow for days.

He weighed up the pros and cons. They couldn't

but be pleased to have it done. He'd do a good job, and there'd be no need of payment—it would be off his own bat. No question but Mrs Mariner would be delighted. Her husband would have reservations, but wouldn't (if Ashe had read things correctly) want to voice them in front of him.

On balance, Ashe reckoned he'd go ahead.

*　　　　*　　　　*

At the end of the service Vivien got talking animatedly to the Delamaynes about her driving, so that in the end Saxon was waiting for her in the porch, his surplice over his arm long after the sidesmen had left.

'High time!' remarked Sir Sidney approvingly on his way out. 'A young woman these days should be able to get about a bit.'

'And very charitable of you,' added Felicity pointedly, 'to give the job to that strange chap with the face.'

Vivien sensed that Saxon had been about to deny any charity, but had thought better of it.

'He seems very competent,' was what he said instead. 'And he knows about cars.'

'What a useful fellow he is,' commented Felicity. 'I do like a man who can turn his hand to things.'

As Saxon and Vivien walked together across the churchyard a few spots of rain began to fall. Approaching the gate, they heard the rapid, uneven snicker of the lawnmower bouncing over the bumpy ground. He was still here; Vivien caught her breath.

'What's going on?' Saxon asked, moving ahead of her into the garden.

'I have an idea it's Mr Ashe.'

'Ashe?' Saxon frowned, taking in the assembled badminton net and the neatly tramlined grass. 'Good heavens.'

She said, as if excusing all this industry: 'I only asked him if he'd put up the net.'

'I must say . . . Yes, I suppose—I don't know what to say.'

Vivien left her husband and walked towards Ashe, who was turning at the far end of the lawn, to execute what would be the final run. She noticed that he had stamped down the molehills and mown over them.

'Mr Ashe!'

He raised a finger in a gesture that might generously have been interpreted as forelock-tipping or, more realistically, as an indication that she should stay where she was until he had finished. Saxon, with a slight lifting of the chin, elected to choose the former interpretation, Vivien the latter. Just the same both waited, like dignitaries at a march-past, as Ashe completed his run.

He left the mower near the house and came over to them.

'Good morning. I hope you don't mind, Reverend. Mrs Mariner asked me to put up the net, and I thought you might like to play some time soon, so I had a go at the grass.'

'Mind?' began Vivien, but Saxon cut in.

'The mower needs some oil, it hasn't been used since last year.'

'I found some in the garage. She's rolling along nicely now.'

'It's like a park,' said Vivien, walking into the

176

middle of the grass and performing a slow pirouette of inspection. 'We shan't know ourselves.'

'Right you are,' Ashe pulled down his sleeves and began buttoning the cuffs. 'If there's nothing else I can do, I'll cut along.'

'Can we get you a drink after your labours?' asked Vivien.

'I'm all right, thank you, Mrs Mariner. Hilda was good enough to bring me some lemonade.'

'Did she?' exclaimed Vivien and, glancing at the kitchen, lowered her voice: 'Goodness, you did make a hit.'

'And very nice it was too.'

Saxon cleared his throat. 'Mr Ashe, what do we owe you?'

'The net only took me a few minutes, Reverend. The price of a drink's fine, no hurry.'

'But'—Saxon made a jerky gesture—'what about—all this?'

'I did it off my own bat. Gave me something to do.'

Saxon, as so often with this man, felt that he had been wrongfooted, and on his own territory.

'As you wish.' The moment he'd said the words he realised they sounded stuffy, but didn't know what else to say. The man had been thanked, had made the case against payment to both his own and Saxon's satisfaction, and there was an end to it.

'I'll be on my way then,' said Ashe. 'I'll be here for your drive on Friday, Mrs Mariner.'

'I'm looking forward to it.'

Ashe sent Saxon a man-to-man glance. 'I shan't be needed for long, Reverend. Your wife's a natural driver. She's taken to it like a duck to water.'

'I'm glad to hear it.'

As he walked away, Saxon sensed Vivien's barely restrained desire to accompany Ashe to the gate, to thank him again, to be friendly beyond what was necessary or appropriate. He himself walked steadily in the direction of the back door, and after a minute she caught up with him.

In the kitchen, a glass and a jug containing dregs of fresh lemonade stood on the table among preparations for lunch. Hilda was in the scullery, scraping carrots at the sink, but as they entered she came over, wiping her hands on her apron.

'That Mr Ashe was here, Reverend.'

'I know,' said Saxon, 'we met him. Excuse me, will you?'

Hilda's eyes followed him as he left the room and then returned to Vivien. 'He was very polite,' she said, as if refuting an unspoken criticism.

'I'm sure he was, Hilda.'

'He went ahead with the mowing, he would do it—I hope that was all right.'

'Of course! For one thing it's not your responsibility to tell him what to do, and for another Mr Mariner and I are delighted. I'll tell young Paul he doesn't need to come for another week or two.'

Hilda appeared genuinely relieved. 'Only I wasn't sure.'

Vivien would have gone, but Hilda hovered.

'I took against him when he called the first time.'

'Who could blame you, Hilda? He does look rather alarming.'

'He can't help that, though, can he?'

'Certainly not.'

'As I say, Mrs Mariner, today he was a perfect gentleman.'

'Good.'

'And the lawn's come up a treat.'

'Never better.'

'Oh well.' Hilda's tone said she could have gone on, only duty called. Vivien saw her opportunity.

'Hilda.'

'Yes, Mrs Mariner?'

'I'm collecting the puppy at the end of next week.'

'Oh, yes.'

'I thought I should let you know.'

'Don't you worry about it,' said Hilda, heading for the sink. 'We'll shake down in no time.'

On her way to join Saxon in the drawing room, Vivien caught sight of herself in the mirror and paused for a moment, examining her reflection closely, as though identifying the face that looked back at her.

*   *   *

The day the puppy was to be collected was the day that Saxon—driven by a sense of duty and against his better judgement—had agreed to go to London to do a reading from *Beyond Self* at a specialist poetry bookshop in the Gray's Inn Road.

George had wanted the reading to take place in the evening but Saxon had refused point blank. It was enough that he had agreed to do it, without the added inconvenience of the last train home or a night in town. Even so he would not arrive home much before seven, and since it was also the day of Vivien's driving lesson Ashe, in his capacity as station employee, was despatched to drive him to the train. However, a potentially uncomfortable experience proved not as bad as Saxon feared. Having asked what was taking Saxon to London, Ashe said:

'I didn't know you were a writer, Mr Mariner. Would I be able to read one of your books?' He seemed to see that this query was open to misinterpretation, and clarified it. 'I mean, could I get hold of one?'

'The works of minor poets are not that widely available, I'm afraid.'

'I like poetry. You can pick up a poem as often as you like and see something new in it every time.'

'That's so, yes.' Saxon could not help but be impressed by the perceptiveness of this observation.

'It must be a comfort,' went on Ashe, 'in your position, to have another life.'

'Yes . . . Yes, I suppose it is.'

'Some men kept diaries, in the war.'

'A worthwhile exercise, I should think.'

'It helped pass the time.'

'Did you keep one yourself?' asked Saxon.

'Me? No.'

They drove for a while in silence, but as they turned into the station Saxon was moved to say: 'I could always lend you one of my collections if you're interested.'

'I'd be very interested, Mr Mariner. Thank you. You wouldn't need to worry, I'm a good borrower—you'll get the book back good as new as soon as I've read it.'

Saxon waved a hand. 'I'm sure I will.'

Once on the train he was immediately assailed by doubts—his poetry was essentially private. That it should be read by strangers, people who didn't know him, was just about bearable, as well as being economically desirable. But did he want Ashe, this oddity who had somehow taken a place in their lives, to form an opinion, perhaps to draw conclusions from it? Too late now, the offer had been made, he could scarcely withdraw it without seeming rude. Perhaps it was a good thing that he had agreed to do this reading (which he had been dreading for days), because it would accustom him to the idea of being seen and identified. Other writers managed, so why not Saxon Mariner?

*　　　*　　　*

He was soon reminded why not. The Phoenix Bookshop was halfway up the Gray's Inn Road, between an Italian barber's and a large, well-frequented pub, the Prince Albert. Given the area's proximity to Bloomsbury, Saxon had pictured the shop as solidly literary, a thoughtful, dignified place reminiscent of a college library. The reality was small, chaotic and almost as bohemian as that frightful restaurant had been. The twenty or so people assembled there seemed to fill all the available space. George was there to greet him, glass of sherry in hand.

'Saxon, there you are! How the devil are you, my dear chap?'

'Not looking forward to this, I'm afraid.'

'Nonsense, you'll be a riot. Let me get you one of these. For VIPs only, the customers get tea.'

'No thank you,' said Saxon. 'It's a little early for me.'

'Calm your nerves.'

'I need to keep a clear head.'

George steered him past the seated audience to the back of the shop. 'Point taken, but I'm going to get you one anyway, so that you can take the odd nip when and if the occasion demands.'

There was no arguing with him. Saxon took the proffered glass and stood with George near the table on which lay a modest display of his books, past and present.

'We don't put out too many on these occasions,' explained George, having mistaken Saxon's wan look for one of disappointment. 'The audience for this kind of event tend to be serious aficionados of the work, not highbrows. In other words they'll probably already have read your backlist. But we'll hope to sell some of the new collection, and of course the value of word of mouth is simply incalculable.'

Saxon glanced nervously at the assembled enthusiasts, a more eclectic group than he'd bargained for: young men in hats, older women with long hair, several characters who, in other circumstances, one might almost have taken for tramps.

'I hope I shan't disappoint them.'

'My dear chap, how could you?'

'I've never attempted anything like this before.'

'But you're the poet himself, the one who knows how your work should sound, so whatever you do will be definitive in their eyes. Besides, you're an old hand at performing—just imagine you're back in that pulpit of yours, and this lot are the faithful, gazing up at you. Which in a way they are!' George chortled at his little conceit.

Another glance at the audience only confirmed Saxon in his view that such a leap of the imagination was quite beyond him.

'I'll do my best.'

'And as I say,' went on George, as if he'd only just said it, 'about ten poems, depending on length—well, none of them are that long—with perhaps a few words from you about the genesis of each one, any difficulties you had . . . You know the sort of thing.'

It was a waste of time Saxon telling George that no, he didn't. A couple more people arrived and sat at the far end of the back row, though there were empty chairs at the front—perhaps these people had more in common with his parishioners than met the eye.

The bookshop owner, a whey-faced little man with Chatterton-esque wavy locks, took one more look up and down the street and then came over to them.

'Mr Mariner,' he said. 'The floor is yours.'

'Enjoy yourself,' whispered George. 'It's going to be a roaring success, and afterwards I shall take you out to lunch!'

*   *   *

At about the same time that her husband was suffering his ordeal at the Phoenix Bookshop, Vivien arrived at the Clays' front door to collect the puppy. She had come on foot, and had with her the small red collar and lead she'd bought in Bridgeford, and payment in cash in a brown envelope.

Edith Clay accepted the envelope with thanks, but cast a sceptical look at the collar and lead.

'You'll not get very far with that I'm afraid, Mrs Mariner.'

'Oh dear. Did I do wrong?'

'It's just that he's not used to it. He's never been on a lead, remember.'

'I wasn't thinking he'd walk all the way back,' said Vivien. 'He's only a baby after all, but—'

Edith shook her head, eyes closed, as if she had failed to make herself clear. 'He's not going to want to go at all, Mrs Mariner, that's the trouble. You'll have to carry him.'

'That's fine, I'll do that then.' Vivien saw Susan appear behind her mother. 'You'll keep me company, won't you, Susan? I could do with some help.'

Edith looked over her shoulder. 'You'd like that, I dare say? Yes, she would, look at her face, all smiles. Come along in and fetch him then.'

The walk home, even with the two of them, became something of a Via Dolorosa. Boots whined and trembled unhappily. When they carried him he struggled, and nipped with tiny pin-sharp teeth. If they put him down he wouldn't move at all but dug his paws into the ground and wriggled so violently that he eventually slipped out of the collar and they had to chase after him.

'Your mother was right,' said Vivien. 'He really doesn't want to come.'

'He's leaving *his* mother,' Susan pointed out. 'And his brothers and sisters. He's sad because of that.'

'Yes, I mustn't forget that for now I'm the brute

that snatched him away from his family. Here, Susan, he's used to you—you take him.'

In the end they swaddled the puppy in Vivien's waistcoat which seemed to calm him by simply stifling movement, and took turns to carry him to the vicarage.

When they arrived, Vivien said, 'I think we should do what your mother suggested and give him something to eat straight away so he knows this is home.'

She left Susan with the puppy in the back room housing his box and blanket, and went to the kitchen.

'I've got some milk warming,' said Hilda.

'Hilda, you think of everything. I'm going to make him some porridge.'

'Can I take a look-see?'

'Go and say hallo, do, he's in the back room with Susan.'

When, a few minutes later, Vivien returned with the porridge, she found Hilda and Susan both sitting on the floor with the puppy scrambling over Hilda's aproned lap.

'Look,' said Susan, 'he's cheered up.'

Hilda turned her face up to Vivien, her cheeks quite pink.

'Mrs Mariner, I think he likes me.'

*   *   *

The bookshop owner professed himself more than satisfied.

'Not many left,' he said, returning the remaining copies to the shelf. 'I may have to order some more.'

185

'You see?' George slapped Saxon on the shoulder. 'It worked. Your public adored you.'

In fact, Saxon was rather pleased, but the habit of caution was hard to shake. 'I can't think why. It seemed very dull to me.'

'Not even the tiniest bit flattered?' George tilted his head roguishly.

'Of course I'm flattered, a little, it's just incomprehensible to me why a group of intelligent people would want to come and sit on hard chairs to hear my rather indifferent rendition of those poems.'

George and the proprietor raised their eyebrows at one another.

'I shall take him to lunch and explain,' said George. 'Are you sure you won't join us?'

'No thank you, this is my busy time. Mr Mariner—Saxon—it was much appreciated. Perhaps you'll consider doing it again?'

'Patience!' George put his hand up. 'The poor fellow's still recovering. Send the order form direct to me, if you would, then I can speed it on its way.'

This time, with no lady present, they went to George's club. Over steak and kidney pudding washed down with a decent claret, Saxon began to relax for the first time that morning. He certainly felt energised, his movements lighter, his head clear, even his palate cleansed . . . Perhaps, he thought, this was the fabled exhilaration experienced by actors and entertainers (a thing which till now he'd found impossible to imagine) which kept them up half the night carousing and unable to contemplate sleep.

'. . . if you'd like me to arrange one or two more,' George was saying. 'But the ball's in your court. Cheers!'

'Your very good health,' said Saxon. 'I shall certainly think about it.'

This he did, on the way home, as the train chuffled and clattered through the south-western suburbs and out into the countryside. In the peace of his window seat, in a compartment containing only one other passenger, an elderly woman knitting, away from George's voluble insistence on how wonderful it had all been he was able to take his own feelings out and examine them at leisure.

He was pleasantly surprised to find that they remained favourable. He had not felt exposed, or not unpleasantly so. The poems had somehow stood for him, and between him and his audience. They had protected him. The small amount he had managed to say about them had not proved too much of a torture and had been well received. One of the tramp-like people, a man of indeterminate age with wild hair and a tweed cloak, had turned out to be himself a distinguished poet, who claimed to have thought highly of Saxon's work for some time. That had been very gratifying. It was after all the approval of one's peers that meant the most to a writer.

What with the success of the reading, and the pleasure of being once more at home after a day in London, he was in good spirits when he alighted from the train at Eadenford. He had ordered the village taxi, and it was there to meet him. When the driver asked him how his day had been he had no hesitation in replying: 'Excellent, thank you.'

When the taxi had driven off he stood for a moment in the vicarage driveway, savouring his homecoming, and the prospect of well-earned rest

187

and recuperation. He had become a new person today—more complete, recognised in a field other than the small one of the parish, and as a consequence more ready to face his parochial tasks. It seemed that George, an unlikely angel in disguise, had been right all along.

He noticed that the garage door was closed, Vivien must be back. Just then he heard her voice from the garden, whooping and laughing; playing with the badminton, he had no doubt, trying to keep the shuttlecock in the air. As he walked round the side of the house he was already smiling in anticipation of seeing his wife on this beautiful evening. He was actually looking forward to her enthusiastic enquiries, and to the answers he would give.

She was not holding a racquet, but running round in circles with a puppy at her heels. Saxon halted. Not a puppy—*the* puppy. In the excitement of his own day he'd forgotten that this was when it was due to arrive. Normally, he would have been rather put out by this oversight, and taken aback by the small piebald interloper scampering and bouncing on his back lawn. But still carried on a warm wave of success, Saxon was enchanted by the sight of his wife and the little dog, so full of life and joy and movement. It was as if his home, in his absence, had undergone a change that reflected his own.

'Well, I never . . .'

'Saxon!' Vivien stopped and bent over, hands on knees, panting and laughing. The puppy rolled, wriggling, on to its back displaying a pink and white tummy.

'Look who's here!'

188

Saxon set down his briefcase. 'Remind me what we call him.'

'Boots.' Vivien picked up the puppy and snuggled him against her shoulder. 'Come and say hallo.'

She walked to meet him and they kissed. As they did so Saxon put one arm round her shoulders and with his other hand touched the puppy's head, feeling with a pang the silky softness of its coat, the delicacy of the skull beneath, the feathery snuffle of its small nose against his palm.

'Welcome, Boots,' he said.

Just then he saw from the corner of his eye a movement on the far side of the garden—a figure with a billhook, hacking with slow movements at the long grass. He withdrew his arm.

'Who's that?'

Vivien glanced over her shoulder. 'Who—oh, it's only Ashe. He offered to clear some of that when we got back, so I thought why not? Saxon, watch this.'

She put the puppy down on the ground and began walking backwards away from him.

'He doesn't know what to make of it when I do this . . .'

Saxon watched as the puppy crept, paused, laid its head on its paws, then bounced forward. But the moment's romantic, sylvan domesticity had become something else—subtly altered by that quiet, industrious dark figure behind him, cutting the grass.

He retrieved his briefcase, and Vivien scooped the puppy up again. 'Poor thing, he's tired. He's only a baby. That's enough.'

She linked her free arm through his. 'Let's go in

189

and you can tell me about your day, I'm dying to hear.'

'I'll do my best,' said Saxon, 'but there isn't that much to tell.'

MESOPOTAMIA

'Are we downhearted?'
　'No!'
'Are we downhearted?'
　'No! No!'
'Are we downhearted?'
　'No! No! No!'
'What are we after?'
'Bags in Baghdad!'
　And who's going to get us there? Our Charlie. General Townshend. For some reason he's got this reputation for getting things right. Talk about blind faith. If these men can believe that, without a shred of evidence and when most of them have never clapped eyes on him, they'll believe anything. No wonder so many of them turn up on church parade.

'Are we downhearted?'
　Not so sure now. It's getting hotter by the second. The shouting's died away. Now it's just the crunch, crunch, crunch of thousands of boots on the gritty sand. Nobody looks at anyone else. Eyes front. Crunch, crunch, crunch.

*　　　　*　　　　*

Time out of mind it's been nothing but battles round here. The longer a place has been civilised, the longer it's been at war. A nice little paradox. You can feel them, just below the surface, all those battles, all those centuries of strife and carry-on. Our army's like a column of ants crawling over the scars—what's our little bit of bother compared to everything that's gone before? Whole civilisations have been, and had their day, and gone in this part of the world; wiped out by people pretty much like us. Cannon Fodder. Enlisted men. Time-servers and mercenaries who knew who the enemy was, but not why. As a matter of fact, they may have had a better idea than us, because of tribes, and territories. We don't even have that. We're not on our patch, and none too clear what our quarrel is with the Turks except that they're pretty good fighting men.

Ctesiphon's a case in point. It doesn't exist any more. But we're getting the idea, because we're two miles away and already we can see the thumping great arch that Jarvis told me used to be the palace gates. It's as high as a city church and as wide as a football pitch, just standing there on its own in the middle of nowhere. All that's left, but it's enough to send shivers up your spine. The arch is rising up out of a mirage, a kind of shimmer . . . Like the cloud of dust raised by all those past armies. The ghosts of all those other men who are dust themselves. Not nice.

We're on the old caravan road. Well, I say road, but it's just a track across the desert wastes. Funny how it winds about for no reason, and we follow it like sheep. If we marched straight we'd be quicker but no, we follow the track. Maybe there were other buildings here once—forts and castles—and that's why the track winds.

It's fucking hot.

As usual, they're waiting for us. They're dug in somewhere to the east of the arch, and behind that as well. So from where they are we're just a cloud of dust too—a sandstorm moving in their direction. But you can bet they're ready. The minute we stop being a cloud, and start being ants, then a millipede, then a column of men, they'll open up on us. We just have to hope the powers that be have a plan.

It's hot. If I so much as think of a glass of cold, clear water I'll go mad. Smelly tepid canteen stuff's what we've got, and not much of it.

'A bold heart is half the battle.' Latin proverb. I saw it once on a gravestone.

We're about to find out what the other half is.

The raw patches on my feet are too far gone to hurt now, but they're going to give me gyp as soon as we stop marching. The sweat's making my eyes sting.

*   *   *

Night, and it's freezing. It's so cold if you poke your nose out of the tent and look around you'd think it was snow, not sand, all around you. Miles and miles of it, grey in the moonlight with a few little bits of scrub sticking up. Icy dust, stones like iron. A frozen, dry desert. And thousands of us lying on it, like maggots. My feet hurt now, but from the cold, not the blisters. Thawing out's going to be fun.

Because it's flat I can make out the arch against the sky, blacker on black. No sign of the enemy, he'll be below ground like any creature with sense. Keeping his head down and his feet warm. I look up. Thousands of stars, some of them close, like lamps, others so many and so far away they make a kind of haze.

I think about Jarvis. Shivering and miserable, or sleeping like a baby? Looking at the stars, like me? Suddenly I've got this picture of the army, the tents, like something out of the Bible, spread out on the eve of battle—and just one or two pale faces like sixpences turned up to the sky . . . All those men, all those thoughts and dreams and nightmares and fears. All those fucking blisters! All freezing and alone.

*   *   *

Next morning there's a kerfuffle. Not till we've got up, mind you, and we've struck the tents, and loaded our kit and got the weight back on our poor bloody feet (and I mean bloody, my socks are matted with the stuff).

Then they tell us there's been a change of plan; and we wait. It's hotter than hell, and we're standing around exactly where we slept. There was a hot drink (tea? who can say) earlier, when it was still cold and dark, and because we're not moving it's gone straight through us, so first piss of the day's happening on the spot. Very nice. Thousands of square miles of desert and the BEF's created an area that smells like the gents' urinals at Piccadilly.

My companion on today's gallant enterprise is Dick Drago, originally from County Cork but serving with our lot. He talks up a storm, I say very little, so we go together pretty well.

'You know what, Johnnie,' he says (I'd lose my rag if anyone else called me that, but I take it from him), 'you know what—any other nation and there'd be a mutiny in the ranks. But you British can stand and wait till the cows come home. It's your greatest talent, you know that?' He's a champion at rhetorical questions, I don't even bother shaking my head. 'How many massacres have been avoided because you knew how to wait your turn? You know what this is?' He waved an arm at the motionless host before and behind. 'It's just a bloody great queue.'

'If it is, you're in it,' I pointed out.

'Dead right I am, Johnnie! What would I do, run off all on my ownsome into the desert? No, when in Rome. I'm staying put where there's a chance of some refreshment and good craic.'

He ranted on, more or less amusingly. At least when he complains he has the good grace to make a joke of it. Better still he doesn't wait for a laugh, I don't have to contribute anything, my attention can wander and no offence taken.

It wanders now . . . About a hundred yards away there's a couple of horses standing with their heads hanging, reins trailing on the ground. Their necks and flanks are already scummy with sweat. The officers are standing in the little bit of shrinking shade on the other side of them. As I watch, one of the horses staggers. Its front hooves go wide apart, its head's swinging from side to side with the tongue protruding, yellow liquid trickling from the side of its mouth. Its knees are buckling now, and as it goes down I can see that one of the officers is Jarvis. He grabs the animal's reins as if he wants to stop it falling, but what can he do? It's three times his size and in the throes of a heart attack, poor bugger. In the end the horse takes Jarvis down too, he stumbles and crashes down on his knees, falling forward awkwardly on to its neck. I can't help it, I want him to get up and not make an exhibition of himself.

He straightens up, but stays on his knees. The horse's legs are sticking straight out, shaking like there's an electric current going through them. I don't mind admitting that what happens next surprises me. Jarvis unbuttons his holster, takes out his pistol, puts it against the horse's head just above the eye and pulls the trigger. There's a muffled bang and then that funny little silence afterwards—'dead' silence, must be where it comes from. Jarvis stands up, looks down at the horse. He's done what needs doing, now it's my turn, and I put my pack down and go over.

'Shame about that, sir.'

'Yes,' he says, looking a bit green about the gills. 'And now we have a problem.'

'Digging fatigues, sir?'

'Good man, Ashe.'

At least when you're moving about you've got a reason to be hot. I don't know why that should make a difference, but it does. Drago comes to help—that's how much he appreciates a good listener—and a sergeant, Sergeant Singer, built like a brick privy, and we take off the saddle and bridle, and get on with it. The ground's like concrete, we're not so much digging as chipping at it. Jesus wept! From frozen solid to baked rock-hard in a few hours. Nothing in between in this place. Madness. The flies are massing already, all over the horse's head and backside, looks like a crawling, buzzing extra skin. The odd few million that can't find a place on the horse settle on us; there's no point in brushing them off, you might as well get used to them. Makes our little competition back in Basra look even more stupid than it was, and that's saying something. I mean, these fat bastards are laying eggs inside the horse while we work. That's how to colonise a place: occupy it, then populate it with your own side in less time than it takes to run the flag up. Come to think of it, that's the only reason I know for letting women in on the show.

We never finish, because the order comes to resume the march, this time up the Baghdad road. Word is we're some sort of decoy: we're supposed to look like the advance guard of some massive push on Baghdad, then we can swing round and deliver a right hook to his position at Ctesiphon. It seems to me that if the Turks are as well dug in as we think they are, all they have to do is sit tight, keep their heads down and see what happens.

Another horse is brought up for Jarvis. We load up again. A minute later we're off. Crunch, crunch, crunch. The sky's white, the sun's the whitest bit, bang in the middle. What were we thinking, trying to bury that fucking horse? It'll be bones by tonight.

*   *   *

At two o'clock they call a halt no more than a couple of hundred yards from the river and we're told we can fill our water bottles. We're a long way upstream here so they must reckon the water's clean.

I've noticed it doesn't take much to turn men into monkeys. One minute it's crunch, crunch, the great fighting force moving as one et cetera, the next everyone's dropped his kit and is charging and barging for the river bank. I won't do that. The first ones are kneeling down and dousing themselves before I've even started moving. And just as well because all of a sudden there's a crack-whoomp! of shellfire and about half a dozen of the men at the front have pitched forward into the water's edge. And again, some more go down, the wounded are thrashing about in the shallows and screaming, others have waded in to pull them out. The puffs of smoke are coming from three-quarters of a mile upriver—our flotilla! No one told them about the change of plan that involved us taking the Baghdad road, so to them we're just a force where no force ought to be and wallop! Blood in the water and brothers-in-arms grabbing the spare water bottles before running for—well, the only cover is the rest of us.

Signals are exchanged and the firing stops. Only a dozen dead and twice that wounded, all in a day's work.

Dick Drago sums it up: 'Good to know it's friendly fire. We'd never have guessed, but.'

CHAPTER SEVEN

It was June, and summer had arrived in all her glory. Not that the puppy knew this. All he was aware of was the sun warm on his back and the smells tickling his nostrils drawing him this way and that over the lush grass. To the puppy, the vicarage garden had its own sensory map, one that shifted and changed according to the weather, the time of day and who was there.

Some features were constant: the dank, musty boards at the base of the shed, where woodlice lurked; the threshold of the back door where food, security and a certain sternness awaited him; the green wilderness at the end of the garden where he sometimes disturbed mice, and even rabbits, and once a grass snake slithering alarmingly between his paws and away down its hole; the fierce, pungent smell near the fence, full of threat, that sent him skittering away, ears back, from whatever padded silently on the other side . . .

Further away and higher up, in a different dimension and one that wasn't so clear, he was beginning to recognise voices. The one he knew best meant play, comfort, caresses, occasionally being whooshed up to where the voice was closer and he was overpowered with scents and sensations, of smooth skin and fluffy hair, the touch of a mouth, the playing of fingers round his ears and ruff. Happiness, insofar as the puppy knew what that meant. Absence of happiness he had experienced—when he had been dragged away from his mother and siblings—but there was nothing to associate that with, and consequently no memory. This was his home now.

There were other voices. In the kitchen, at something of a distance, a background voice that occasionally became louder but no closer, and which meant no harm. In other rooms, on different surfaces, some soft, some slippery, with stranger and less appetising smells, there was a deeper voice and occasionally a tentative hand, patting and feeling him. This was a touch that elicited no particular response; it was cautiously enquiring and that was how the puppy responded, lowering himself on to his stomach and sniffing the black, shiny shoes for clues.

There was one voice which he did not hear often, but which brought with it a sensation of warmth and companionship, and an associated longing for others of his kind. This voice was the slowest and the gentlest, the lap the broadest and most accommodating. The reaction it produced in the puppy was like that of being with his mother. He quickly relaxed, and often slept on this lap, comforted by the faint, familiar smell that was like an extension of himself.

Occasionally the puppy encountered another person, one who rarely spoke, or touched him and had, strangely, almost no smell. And yet the puppy was besotted. When this person arrived, or was nearby, he became at once the centre of the puppy's universe. The puppy, by nature a pack animal, needed order and the authority of a leader to feel secure. And every sense and instinct told him that here was that leader. Of all the people he'd encountered in his new home, this was the one whom the puppy would follow through thick and thin with blind trust and devotion.

* * *

John Ashe worked at the vicarage most evenings now, and very often on a Sunday, too. The days were long and the weather fine, and there was plenty for him to do. He was still doing his job at the station, so his time was full, but that didn't bother him. He had no social life, he preferred to be occupied, and he was saving his money. Mr Trodd's eye was on him, but Ashe was careful not to let his duties at the station slip. There would be no cause for complaint.

Ashe looked after the car, keeping a high gloss on the outside and a knowledgeable eye on the engine. Mrs Mariner no longer needed driving lessons, but the lessons had served their purpose, in more ways than one. All those casual questions, humming with excitement; all those glances that she thought she'd kept hidden; all the little touches, intentional and not so intentional . . . The tension was building, he had only to maintain a distance to keep it taut. Then she could be reeled in.

He was careful always to maintain a veneer of absolute neutrality: there must be no clue, not the smallest hint, of his interest in her. On the contrary, he was scrupulous in referring any queries first to her husband, the one who paid him. He never went into the house unless invited, nor cast a look their way if they came into the garden when he was there—at least not until he was addressed by one of them, when he was a model of restrained civility. It was his experience that once the correct conditions were in place, you rarely lost anything by holding back. Other people, subject to those conditions, would reward your patience by doing the work for you.

Mariner had lent him the book of poems, which he'd read in a single evening. He'd been surprised at how good they were, and how personal; it had been another eye-opener. But perhaps he shouldn't have been so surprised after what he'd seen in the kitchen that night. The vicar of Eadenford was a satyr beneath the skin.

He'd returned the book wrapped in brown paper and with an accompanying note, to which he'd given careful thought.

Dear Mr Mariner

Thank you for lending me this book. I greatly enjoyed reading your poems, some of which reminded me of Ovid, who I read during the war.

I hope the new collection does well, and look forward to reading it.

Yours ever
John Ashe

There had been no answer as yet.

*   *   *

This evening he was engaged in removing the old, rotten outside sill from one of the vicarage's downstairs windows. His workbench and tools were at his side, as he worked.

The window, at the side of the house, nearest the back, belonged to the room used by Mrs

Mariner for various purposes: storage, doing her correspondence, practising dance steps to the gramophone (yes, he'd seen her), or simply listening to music or reading, generally with a cigarette in her hand. Ashe had never seen Mariner in there—it was her domain, just as the study at the front was his. The puppy's cardboard box had been in her room to begin with, but now it had a proper dog basket down in the kitchen, near the stove.

The dog was with Ashe now, snuffling around in the tussocky grass at the side of the path, never straying more than a few yards. From time to time it made a little play for attention, pouncing on his bootlace and giving it a tug, or hurtling furiously after some invisible prey only to skid to a halt, ears askew and tongue hanging out, pretending to have seen off the imaginary interloper.

Ashe ignored it. The more he ignored it the better it liked him. Mrs Mariner pretended to be quite put out.

'I'm his favourite person until you turn up, Ashe,' she'd said only the other day.

'Then all of a sudden I'm cast aside like an old glove. And—I hope you don't mind—but you do *nothing* to deserve it.'

Ashe had shrugged. What could he do about this fatal magnetism?

He did, however, make sure always to have a few broken biscuits in his pocket when he was there, and before leaving he would give one to the puppy as its reward for staying with him. Everyone had his price, and a dog's was next to nothing.

Though to all intents and purposes his eyes and his mind were always on his work, he was learning the rhythm of vicarage life, its comings and goings, its small excitements and its longueurs, the habits of its occupants. He was careful not to display the smallest curiosity with Hilda. There was no point in testing her loyalty and discretion and so running the risk of losing her hard-won friendship.

With young Susan Clay it was different. In some respects she was like the puppy: she had time on her hands, and she liked to hang around with him if Mrs Mariner was busy. Like the puppy, he often ignored her and she didn't mind; indeed, he sensed that she found it relaxing. Sometimes he'd say 'hold this' or 'pass me that' and she'd jump to it, wanting to be useful.

As long as you were careful, you could ask her anything, and get an answer: she was transparently truthful and guileless. But the innocence which told you what you wanted to know would be just as likely to relay your question to someone you'd rather was kept in the dark. And to suggest that something was just between the two of you might lead to another person being told 'it's a secret' and having their suspicions aroused.

His way round this was to start her talking with a statement. He might come out with something like: 'Mr and Mrs Mariner are out today.'

And she'd pick up the cue and say: 'They've gone to London,' or whatever it was.

What he wanted, of course, was something more personal, but that would have to be taken at a snail's pace. This was frustrating when Susan would have told him everything in a minute. All in good time, he reminded himself. More haste, less speed. Because something was easy made it no more safe, but less so.

Susan wasn't here today. But Mrs Mariner was about, he'd been aware of a flicker of movement on the other side of the window. The puppy, getting less roly-poly and more gangling by the week, lay on the grass chewing an old tennis ball, intermittently shaking its head and snapping its jaws in an attempt to spit out the shreds of fluff.

He succeeded in removing the old sill and laid it on the ground alongside the piece of wood he was preparing to take its place. The puppy immediately abandoned the tennis ball, scampered over and began to gnaw on the discarded sill, gagging noisily on splinters and flakes of paint.

'No.' He pushed it away and it flopped down, gazing at him as if awaiting another command.

Ashe picked up the new sill and tested it in its position. As he did so he saw, from the corner of his eye, Mrs Mariner come into the garden from the direction of the back door. She was wearing her glasses and had her arms folded as she looked around her. She spotted him and began walking in his direction but he was careful to give no sign of having seen her.

'Ashe—goodness, you're doing wonders.'

He looked up. 'We're getting there.'

The puppy rolled over, waggling its bottom back and forth. Mrs Mariner crouched down to pet it. She was wearing a threadbare man's shirt with a button missing; it gaped at the neck.

'Faithless beast.'

Ashe removed the new sill, placed it on his workbench, and began planing the side, bending forward to his task with narrowed eyes as though playing billiards. Mrs Mariner stood up and the puppy rolled over on to its front. They were both watching him now.

'I drove all the way up to Eaden Place this morning,' she said. 'By myself.'

'How did you manage on the hill?' he asked, not looking up.

'She laboured a bit, but we didn't have to stop.'

He nodded, and blew the shavings off the sill. 'That's good.'

She rubbed the puppy's chest with her foot. 'I was wondering if you'd like a drink?'

'As a matter of fact I would.'

She hesitated. 'I bought some bottled beer . . . Does that appeal?'

'I'm not a drinking man.'

'Oh . . .' She looked almost crestfallen. 'What then?'

'Cold water's fine. Thank you, Mrs Mariner.'

'Coming up.'

She went. The puppy rose and looked after her. Ashe touched his pocket, and it lay down again, resting its chin on its paws.

*   *   *

'I'm beginning to wonder what we did before he came,' said Vivien at supper.

'He certainly makes himself useful,' agreed Saxon.

The subject of Ashe's usefulness was no longer a source of annoyance to Saxon. The man was undoubtedly an asset, and not just in the practical sense. It might have been coincidence, but Saxon had noticed a greater calm, a harmoniousness about the place since Ashe had been working there. He could not for the life of him have said why this was, though it was true that he liked the man better than he had to begin with. He was quiet, and industrious, he used his initiative and so did not need constant instruction or supervision. Most gratifying of all had been his articulate and perceptive appreciation of Saxon's poems, in which admiration had been tempered with just enough comment to render it respectable. Saxon knew he should not have been surprised, but there it was.

There was also the simple fact of having another male around—two, he reflected, if you included the dog. Though he and Ashe had little to do with one another on a day to day basis, Ashe's response to his poetry as well as the better balance in the household had made Saxon more appreciative of the work done by his new hardyman. Saxon had no real friends, and friendship with an employee would have been unthinkable—but he nonetheless found the mutual respect between them pleasing. A comfort, almost.

'I'm thinking of doing a reading in Bridgeford,' he announced.

'I think you should,' said Vivien.

'I quite enjoyed the one I did in London and it seems a pity not to spread the word, as it were, a little closer to home.'

'Exactly. Think of all the people who'd come. One word to Lady Delamayne and you'd have to hire the town hall.'

Saxon grimaced. 'Vivien, please, I beg you not to say anything in that direction until we've given it some thought.'

'My lips are sealed.'

'You don't think it would seem at all—vain? Inappropriate to a man in my position?'

'No, I don't.' She rose from her place and pulled another chair close to his, sitting with her folded arms leaning on the table. 'I don't, and nor will anyone else. You may be a man of God, but that doesn't mean you can't be a poet too. Look at David, look at the psalmists.'

'Those were songs to God.'

'What about the parable of the talents?' She caught his hesitation. 'You see?'

'You have a point.'

Saxon's hesitation had been only a formality, his mind was already made up, but guilt and self-doubt were endemic to his nature; he was glad to have his wife's approval. Her approach to life was so much easier, so straightforward, one that owed more to God the Son than God the Father. The moral centre, he felt, lay somewhere between her approach and his. There was a button missing on her shirt, he noticed, and her hair was falling down. The smell of the sunny garden rose from her clothes and skin. Saxon was stirred as ever by her warm, wanton untidiness.

'Vivien . . .' He put his arm round her waist, but she slid away, placing a butterfly-light kiss on his mouth in what was unmistakably a tender gesture of withdrawal.

'You must go into Bridgeford soon,' she said, 'and talk to Mr Baynes in the Dane Street Bookshop. If that's the place you were thinking of?'

'Vivien—'

'He's such an admirer of your work.'

'He's always been very polite about it.' Saxon tried unsuccessfully to keep a dejected note out of his voice. The space next to him, where his wife had sat, seemed to have filled with cold air on her departure. But she appeared full of energy.

'Shall we play badminton? I need to have my revenge.'

'I have a meeting with the churchwardens.' He took a small, bitter pleasure in his excuse.

'When?'

He glanced at his watch. 'In half an hour.'

'We could manage a few points.'

'There are one or two things I need to do first.'

'Never mind.' She seemed completely unconcerned, her mind already on other things. 'I shall take Boots for a walk—if I can drag him away from Ashe.'

*   *   *

Ashe had fitted the new sill and was packing up when Mrs Mariner came round the corner, carrying the dog lead, and with a scarf tied round her hair.

'Thank goodness you're going,' she said, 'or he'd probably refuse to come with me.'

'A dog's always ready for a walk.'

'Come on, you.' She clipped on the lead, but did not go. Ashe raked the wood shavings into a pile and began loading them and his tools into the wheelbarrow.

'So what does the evening hold for you, Ashe?' she asked. 'You're a man of mystery.'

'No mystery,' he said. 'I'll walk back to my lodgings, have supper, and go to bed.'

'How is it at Mrs Jeeps's?'

'Passable.'

'Oh dear, no better than that.'

'It's all right.'

'Are you getting to know people in the village? They can seem an insular lot to begin with, but they're good at heart.'

'I wouldn't know. It doesn't bother me.'

'You're not lonely?'

'No.' He shook his head and lifted the shafts of the wheelbarrow. 'Never.'

She shook her head incredulously. 'What a wonderful thing to be able to say—that you are completely, psychologically self-sufficient, when so few people are.' Her eyes became inward-looking. 'My husband's like that.'

Ashe, holding the wheelbarrow, waited politely for a moment. When no answer was forthcoming, she said:

'Oh well . . . Good night, Ashe. Shall we see you tomorrow evening?'

'I'll be along to paint this. Good evening, Mrs Mariner. Enjoy your walk.'

*   *   *

Saxon, awaiting the arrival of the church wardens, saw first his wife with the dog, then John Ashe, walk out of the vicarage drive and set off in opposite directions. Gradually, he was recovering his equilibrium. He had overreacted. His advances had not been rebuffed; his wife had not rejected him; indeed, he reminded himself, it was she who had come to sit next to him, who had been so encouraging about the reading. There had simply been a tiny misunderstanding—no, no, not even that, a brief moment which she had probably not even noticed and so about which she could not

210

possibly have made a judgement.

The two wardens, walking side by side in deep conversation, appeared in to the drive, each carrying a businesslike folder. Hastily, Saxon lowered his eyes to his desk, as if working, and waited for Hilda to answer the door.

*　　　*　　　*

In spirit, what Ashe had told Mrs Mariner about his habits was true. He was a solitary animal, who didn't need company in order to feel comfortable. But he was disposed to watch, and observe, and relished the advantage this gave him. So a couple of evenings a week, when he had finished at the vicarage, he would sit on a stool at the far end of the Waggoner's bar, in the corner between the bar and the taproom door, and see what went on. Now that the locals were used to his appearance they accepted him and he sensed that he had won a certain wary respect for working hard, particularly at the station where he was exposed to public view the whole time. His job at the vicarage did no harm, either. Everyone liked Mrs Mariner and had a somewhat cowed respect for her husband, and Hilda had not had cause to say a bad word about him. His reputation, after a relatively short time, was for moderation, industry and reserve; as a man who preferred to keep himself to himself. Which suited both him, and others, who were content to leave him to it. Live and let live, said the village— and rather prided itself on harbouring in its midst someone of such a terrifying appearance, an emblem of their tolerance.

'Oh yes,' they might say, to a startled visiting

friend or relative, 'that's John Ashe, nothing to worry about, he's not a bad chap . . .'

All this Ashe knew perfectly well. It was the effect he had sought, and he had succeeded in achieving it. As with everything, his position in the village was a question of balance, and he had found the precise equipoise between friendliness and distance which suited him.

On this particular evening, after he left the vicarage, he did make his way to the pub. He'd been careful to time his departure so that he and Mrs Mariner would be no more than a hundred yards apart, and he was prepared to bet she'd cast a glance his way. Not that he'd have checked. You had to trust your judgement.

He had not been around long enough to have his own stool and tankard but increasingly the place where he liked to sit was left vacant, and so it was on this occasion. The place was dim and cool after the sunlit evening outside, and there were only a handful of men in there, three young chaps playing shove ha'penny, and Ted Clay standing at the bar talking to the publican, who greeted him.

'Evening, Ashe.'

'Evening.'

'Usual?'

'Please.'

Ted Clay lifted his chin. 'Evening.'

'Evening.'

There was a silence broken only by the soft 'glug' of the ale from barrel to tankard. Clay left Ashe to take his first long, satisfying swig and wipe the foam from his top lip with the back of his wrist, before asking:

'How's it going up at the vicarage, then?'

'Well, thanks. Plenty to keep me occupied, big place like that.'

'How does the reverend suit you?'

Ashe was far too canny to be drawn on this. 'I seem to suit him, that's the main thing.'

The other two men gave a grunt of amused understanding. The landlord remarked:

'Mrs Mariner's a nice lady, though,' as if someone had cast aspersions on her husband.

'She is,' said Clay. 'She is.'

A pause spread into a perfectly companionable silence, which Clay broke.

'Do you see much of her?'

'She's around,' said Ashe.

'How's the dog doing?'

'Fine. That's a nice dog.'

'From a good bitch,' Clay pointed out, with pride. He tilted his chin again. 'Another reason for our Susan to be going up there.'

Ashe said nothing. The publican chipped in. 'Mrs Mariner makes everyone welcome.'

Clay gave his empty jug a nudge. 'So long as she's not being a nuisance.' When Ashe again said nothing, he added: 'Don't know what the reverend makes of it.'

'He likes her,' said Ashe. 'He's good to her.'

This, being more information than he'd volunteered since walking in, and more than he generally offered in a week, caught their attention.

'Is that right?' said Clay. 'I'm glad to hear it. I've always been of the opinion Edith lets her go to and fro a bit too often. I wouldn't want her taking advantage.'

Ashe sipped his beer and let it rest.

'Your Susan's a lamb. She wouldn't do no harm

213

to anyone,' said the landlord, as if that closed the matter; though Ashe knew it had only just been opened.

*　　*　　*

It was nine o'clock when Vivien began to walk home and the sun was setting. With the tired puppy lolloping alongside she descended from the golden, west-facing hillside into the deep relief of the valley, where the church spire and its surrounding roofs were half bright, half dark, and the river of the High Street below, with its tributary lanes and alleys, lay in deep shadow.

Halfway down the hill she paused. Without the accompanying beat of her footsteps and the vigorous swing of her arms, the utter stillness of evening fell around her like a veil. She was suspended in a pin-drop hush broken neither by sound nor movement. The village where she had lived her married years in an uncomprehending trance seemed no longer prosaic, but mysterious. A place of secrets—alliances, enmities, perhaps of spells. The puppy, a little to one side of her, stood motionless, equally spellbound.

A single swallow sped from left to right, swooped, rose, and dived down again towards the twilit valley. She wondered if it was one of their swallows and, if so, whether it had recognised this woman with whom it shared its house.

MESOPOTAMIA

It took us an hour or so to recover from that spot of bother. Casualties to be retrieved, wounded to be sorted and patched up, then we're told to take a rest, which isn't easy. Knowing your own side's getting trigger-happy is enough to make anyone jumpy. An even trickier one for the telegram. Drago suggests: 'No harm intended'.

Now we're on our way again, night marching. It's pitch black—no moon and overcast as well. Every so often we hit one of these damn drainage ditches, and because we're about halfway back in the column it's turned into a sodding great crater by the time we get to it. On top of that we're coming into an area where there's the ruins of a couple of ancient cities, and most of the foundations are still there, so if you're not hauling yourself out of a ditch you're clambering over piles of old stones. Everyone's feet are giving them gyp. If there's one thing worse than blisters, it's a spot of sand between them and your boots. In the unlikely event that I'm ever in charge of getting an enemy spy to talk I'll stuff his sweaty feet into hard boots with a handful of sand inside and get him to double round a few times—he'll be squealing like a stuck pig in no time.

At least if you're moving you don't feel the cold quite so much. And the great thing is, we're doing what we came for: going on the attack. So morale's not bad, considering, but there's no singing because of the element of surprise. Presumably the Turks had their ear-muffs on when our flotilla

215

opened fire . . .

Some time in the small hours a halt's ordered and we take a break. Now I can really feel the desert stretching out around us in all directions. Miles and miles of miles . . . And somewhere out there the enemy, not that different from us I imagine, waiting and listening. Some blokes light up, little red sparks glowing and fading as they inhale. An officer on horseback trots past, black on black . . . whoof, whoof, whoof, the hoofbeats in the sand and the creak of the harness. There's a kind of magic about it, so many of us stranded out here in the endless dark; thousands of men clumped together and alone. The sky's cleared, and it's beautiful in this place you can really see that we're outnumbered by the stars. Like that other time, up on the roof in Basra, I feel more peaceful than I ever did in England.

'Will you look at us . . .' Dick Drago may be thinking the same thing, but not for the same reason. He treads out his cigarette beneath his boot.

'We could just walk away, Johnnie—shall we do that now, just walk away into the night and never be seen again?'

I shake my head, but of course he can't see me. 'What's that?' he says.

'Count me out.'

'Well, I shan't be going on my own, that's for sure.'

'Sorry to disappoint you.'

'Don't give it another thought. It's tough, so it is, being the only one with a spirit of adventure.'

I smile, but he doesn't see that either.

The order comes down to continue. 'Hey-ho,'

says Drago. 'On with the dance.'

*   *   *

The next time we stop is just before dawn, about four thirty. The landscape's just beginning to show itself, like a photograph in developing fluid—I used to see those when I was on the paper. Our surroundings emerge from the dark, and as that happens our sense of scale returns, and it's no comfort: we're still in the middle of nowhere. We all look terrible: skinny, dirty, unshaven, knackered. Just the lads to attack a well-entrenched enemy.

The arch is colossal, and as the sun comes up it seems to get bigger. There's a moment when the rays catch it bang on the edge, and it looks as if it's on fire. It's so impressive that it takes a minute or two for us to register the barbed-wire entanglements in front of it, like a bloody great thicket of brambles. And between the barbed wire and the arch there's a ruined wall, a lot bigger than the ones we've been scrambling over. Still about half a mile away, but in this terrain things can look closer than they are; the light and the flatness play tricks on you.

It turns out the commander of the other column's a bit keener than ours, and since there's been no sound of attack, his lot's going to swing out and head for the Turkish second line. There's a rumour going up and down that Charlie Townshend's luck has held up, and the Turks have turned yellow, withdrawn, and left the way to Baghdad open. This creates the dangerous expectation among some of us that all we've got to do is keep marching and we'll be painting Baghdad red in no time.

Suddenly we're having a picnic—sun's rising but it's not too hot yet, we've got plenty of fresh water and bully-beef sandwiches all round. One or two of the officers ride up and down, making encouraging noises. Jarvis is one of them, looking like a man who spent the night on a feather mattress, as per.

'Make a good breakfast, men,' he says, 'keep your strength up.'

He spots me and rides over. 'How are you doing, Ashe?'

'Sir!' I snap to attention. Drago gawps. He doesn't know it's all for my own amusement.

'Stand easy, man, eat your breakfast. We don't know what's out there.'

'No indeed, sir.'

'We must hope for the best and prepare for the worst. Good luck.'

'Sir.'

When he's ridden off, Drago makes a blowing sound. 'What does *he* eat? I wouldn't mind some of it.'

Bully beef's like a shot in the arm when you're tired and hungry. Ten minutes later we're looking a lot more like fighting men and when the order comes to get back in line even *I* start on this crazy optimism lark. Baghdad—now there's a place I wouldn't mind doing business in.

*   *   *

I still look back and wonder what was going on in our commanders' heads that morning. Did they think if the Turks were there they'd stand up and wave? We're in open desert, they're snug as you like behind a wall and several miles of barbed wire.

We fix bayonets and advance. We've gone no more than twenty yards when they open fire, big guns and small arms all at the same time. We're surrounded by the whine and crash of the shells and the mean, sharp chatter of the rifles, and the yells of our men getting hit. Dick Drago just disappears. That's what it feels like—whump!—and he's gone. I'm still moving forward and suddenly he's not beside me and my leg's covered in sticky matter: his blood and brains. I'm not going to see him again.

We have to go to ground, and now we're thanking God for all the fucking ditches and ruins we were cursing last night. At least there's somewhere to hide. You have to hand it to the Turks, they've played a waiting game. All this time they've had a bead on us, while we were standing around watching the sun come up, eating breakfast, having a fag and a slash . . . They must have watched us load up and start the advance, and still kept their fingers off the triggers until just the right moment. Till they could smell us, almost. I thought they were supposed to be the hot-blooded ones. It's the English who are meant to be patient and dogged. Talk about beaten at our own game.

It's hellish. Literally, like hell. The sense of helplessness. We're pinned down. It seems like hours before our heavy guns get the range. And with full daylight there's a mirage in the middle distance, so anything could be happening out there. A lot of us got hit in the first round of fire, there are dead men all over the place, and as many again yelling and screaming in pain, an animal sound. Heard a rabbit scream when the stoat catches it? Like that—shrill, panicky agony. Bullets and shrapnel rip men to bits. Less than half an hour ago we were standing around eating and drinking and talking amongst ourselves, our bodies were something we felt safe in. Not now. If I so much as glance to one side or another I can see bodies in tatters, broken and bubbling, torn open, and whatever you call the human bit, the part you can't see, reduced to this awful screaming.

For some reason I don't think I'll get hit. Don't know why that is, it's as though I'm in a cocoon. I've got no idea what we're supposed to be doing, I'm not going anywhere, just lying behind this heap of stones, loading and firing into the quivering, shimmering mirage. I think somewhere I've got the idea that I won't get hit as long as I keep firing. It didn't help any of the other poor sods but once the idea's there it sticks and I just blaze away.

All that stuff that used to be Dick Drago—all the blarney and the bullshit and the bloody terrible jokes—has formed a big crust on my leg. Tenacious in death, then; he always was a relentlessly sociable bastard.

From the direction of the firing it's pretty obvious there's a party of Turks up on the high wall, and that their front-line trench leads off from there to our left, to the west. In breaks in the smoke I can see in the distance a hillock which gives them another vantage point. They're laughing. We can only hope someone in charge has a bright idea because it's not looking good.

They've had an idea. The order comes to 'advance at right angles to present line of attack'. So we're going to leave what cover we've got, and cross open country, in full view of the Turkish front line. I'm not afraid. What's the point? It's all so straightforward—they have the advantage, we'll be alternately scampering like rabbits or crawling like lizards. We'll be a moving target but a bloody easy one for marksmen as good as the Turks.

We're off!

The Battle of Ctesiphon. Like shooting fish in a barrel.

CHAPTER EIGHT

Midsummer, and it was hot, they said in the village. Eighty degrees, and only June! It boded well for the harvest, though people weren't as well disposed as they had been to one or two of the farmers, who'd been coining it in during the war years, growing fat while young men got cut down.

To Ashe, this wasn't hot, and the people who said it was didn't know they were born. This was pleasant, English weather at its best. You got some warning—a long, red sunset . . . a slow, hazy dawn . . . a sun that slid indolently up into the sky, taking its time so you could grow accustomed to the temperature. And there was always the green, enfolding English countryside to shield you, always shade, and water and grass beneath your feet.

As to the profiteering farmers, he had no feelings about them one way or the other. War was bound to be exploited by someone. The other harvest, though, that was a genuine grievance. In Eadenford, a village of about three hundred souls, thirty men had been killed or lost. There was scarcely a family left unaffected. The vicarage was one of the few households which had not experienced the dread and agony of the postmistress's call, the bicycle against the wall and the tap on the door. Mrs Jeeps, through no fault of her own, had become the harbinger of tragedy, accustomed to keep her features tight and her eyes down as she handed over the mean little brown envelopes. One family had lost two sons in France and a daughter in a Zeppelin raid in the Midlands where she had been visiting relatives. Every day, all over the country, these small, stifled explosions of tragedy had been happening, too many griefs to be acknowledged, wounds imploding, leaving a land that still bled internally.

Almost none of the bereaved knew where the bodies where. It had been decreed that the task of bringing the war-dead home was simply too vast, costly and complicated, and that they would therefore be buried—or commemorated—where they had fallen. A photographer from the local paper had showed considerable enterprise in travelling to certain areas on the Franco-Belgian border and taking pictures of rudimentary war cemeteries that were being initiated in the wake of the government's decision. The parents of the girl bombed in Wolverhampton were accounted lucky because they had been able to bring back what remained of her and give her a decent burial. Talk of them had been tainted by real jealousy. Ashe was well aware that his face acted as an outward and visible expression of all the savage, bitter loss which the village had hidden away in bedroom drawers, and understairs cupboards and on high shelves . . . out of sight but far from out of mind.

*   *   *

The official memorial arrived. Due to the dearth of able-bodied young men about the place, and because he was working more and more for the vicar these days, Ashe had been released from his station duties to join the work party: they cemented the stone cross into its plinth on the corner of the churchyard, facing down the High

223

Street. Seedlings had been nurtured on warm windowsills and in greenhouses since early spring and were now planted around the base of the plinth. The ceremony of blessing and remembrance was set to replace matins on Sunday. Two Eadenford men who had returned would take pride of place at the ceremony. Neither of them was from Mesopotamia.

*   *   *

This was Saturday morning, the day before the ceremony. With Mr Mariner's approval Ashe had set himself the task of mowing the grass in the churchyard and giving the place a general sprucing-up. There were three relatively new graves, one of which was that of Amy Paget, the bomb victim, another that of her mother, Dorothy: 'Beloved wife and mother, died of a broken heart. Rest where the angels sing.'

Before he started mowing, Ashe went round all the graves with shears, and weeded the plots where necessary. He dead-headed the old-fashioned roses that lined the church path, and cut some narrow turfs from the far corner at the back of the churchyard, to fill in the raw patches around the memorial. By the time he got hold of the mower he was sweating, and took off his neckerchief to mop his face.

His first visitor was Lady Delamayne, her car loaded with flowers for the church. She had brought with her one of the gardener's boys from Eaden Place, and the lad staggered self-consciously up the path in her wake, loaded down with rhododendron, chrysanthemums and roses with their stems bundled in newspaper. Spotting Ashe, she paused to speak to him.

'Good morning!' She motioned the boy to put the flowers down in the porch. 'Let's hope we have this weather tomorrow!'

Ashe halted the mower. 'Yes indeed, m'lady.'

'But just in case I thought I'd make sure we put on a good show inside as well as out—we don't want the church looking neglected on such an important day, do we?'

'Certainly not.'

She came over the grass towards him in her high heels, gazing about her imperiously as she did so. Her grand but rather flirtatious personality, edged (as so often, he'd noticed, with the upper classes) with a certain coarseness, preceded her like a force field, but Ashe was proof against it. From the corner of his eye he saw the boy emerge from the porch, brushing at his shirtfront, and stand leaning against the wall.

'The memorial looks very splendid,' observed Lady Delamayne. 'Though I suppose it's shocking that in such a small place we should need to have one at all.'

Ashe didn't answer, but gazed, like her, at the stone cross glinting in the sunshine. He felt the moment when her eyes turned to rest on him, but didn't alter his stance one iota.

'All this must bring back many memories,' she said.

'One or two,' he agreed.

'But of course no two persons' experiences will be the same.'

'Very true.'

The lad by the church door bent down to pull a

225

grass stem, and put it between his lips but Lady Delamayne, intent on her interrogation, was impervious to his boredom, if she had even noticed it.

'Were you in France, Mr Ashe?'

He shook his head. 'In the Middle East.'

'Ah . . .' She bestowed her vulpine smile. 'So these temperatures are nothing to you.'

'Not really.' He took hold of the mower handle again. 'Nice working conditions as a matter of fact.'

'And I mustn't hold you up any longer . . .' She glanced at the boy, who pulled the grass from his mouth and stood to attention. 'Tony! You might as well take those in—and get rid of the newspaper!' She turned back to Ashe. 'We must both get on.' But she still didn't go, and added, as he took a first step forward, 'Do excuse my vulgar curiosity, Mr Ashe, but was it in the East that you received your injury?'

'That's right.'

'In battle?'

'Not exactly.' Ashe sensed her excitement, which he fully intended to fuel. Leaning down to pull some weed-fibre from the blades of the mower he added tersely: 'I'd prefer not to talk about it, your ladyship. If it's all right with you.'

'But of course!' It was the use of her title that nailed her, as he knew it would, reminding her of their relative positions and the importunate nature of her question. 'What was I thinking of? I do apologise.'

'No need.' She'd get no more 'ladyships' out of him and they both knew it.

'There we are. Better get on.'

He was on his way at once, leaning into his task as she began to walk back to the church. Five minutes later he saw Mrs Mariner arrive via the vicarage's garden gate, wearing a straw hat and a striped sundress, and with some sort of canvas haversack slung round her, from which protruded handles and string. She gave him a wave before disappearing into the church. He heard the dog bark excitedly a couple of times on the far side of the gate.

Ashe mowed on, moving around the eastern end of the church beneath the Lilies of the Field stained glass window. Ten minutes of concentrated work later he was on the north side, the door in which was kept locked. The building was between him and the road and he had a clear view of the vicarage garden gate. Scenting him, the dog was still standing there, ears pricked expectantly; when it saw him it began to wag and wriggle, squeaking and scratching at the bars. Ashe raised an admonitory forefinger and it sat down, shifting from foot to foot and panting.

He glanced at the house. Hilda came in late on a Saturday, but he had no idea where Mariner himself was. Best to play safe. Accordingly, Ashe slipped the full grass-bucket off the mower and carried it with him over to the gate. The dog stood to greet him, and he lifted his finger again.

'Stay.'

With his free hand he opened the gate. The dog was through in an instant, circling his legs but keeping low to the ground in a display of respectful adoration. Ashe pushed the gate without fully closing it, and patted his thigh, near his pocket.

'Here.' The dog stood at his side, quivering in

anticipation, and followed him as he walked across the churchyard in the direction of the compost heap he'd begun at the edge of the wood.

A couple of minutes later Ashe returned, clipped the now-empty container back on to the mower, and resumed his careful, arcing progress between the graves. As he came round the west end who should appear but Susan Clay, at almost precisely the same point where he had first met her on his arrival in the village nearly three months before. She was one of the few people whom he was in the habit of addressing before they addressed him.

'Morning, Susan.'

'Hallo.'

She was empty-handed, and had a pink bow in her hair instead of the usual slides.

'You look pretty.'

Beaming, she touched the bow. 'Ma put it in.'

'Very nice. Looking for Mrs Mariner?' She nodded. 'I'm afraid she's not there at the moment.'

This was truthful, if misleading. Susan looked crestfallen, her shoulders slumped and her lower lip pouted in disappointment.

'But Mr Mariner's in, and he's all on his own. I expect he'd like to see you.'

'What?' She looked baffled; he could see this was going to take a bit of doing.

'I said why don't you go and call on Mr Mariner?'

'I'm not allowed.'

'Who says?'

'Ma told me.'

'I see.' Ashe wiped his face. 'Of course you mustn't be a nuisance if he's busy. But you never know, there might be something you could do for him. Walk the dog or something . . .'

He watched this idea take root. That was enough for the time being.

' 'Bye Susan.'

He pushed the mower forward. She hung about hesitantly for a minute or two but he ignored her, and in the end she pottered off quite purposefully in the direction of the vicarage.

*   *   *

Saxon was preparing the few but important words he must say the next day. He was acutely aware that this was an occasion when he would have a large crowd and their undivided attention. Every eye would be upon him, every ear attuned to what he would say. He wanted, fervently, to get this right. He must strike a note that was decently sympathetic, respectful and dignified . . . which acknowledged the horrors of war and also its sublime sacrifices . . . which looked forward to a long peace won by those sacrifices. Mourning must be given its due, but be placed in the service of building a better and more peaceful future.

He rubbed his eyes with both hands. These things did not come easily to him. He was happier with interpreting points of doctrine and how they applied to human behaviour. He preferred careful, scriptural preaching to the capturing and expression of a mood. He was not a man of the people.

One thing he had decided upon was a roll of honour: each name from the memorial to be read out, simply and straightforwardly, not by him but

229

by a carefully chosen lay individual whom the village held in high regard. There need be no personal details, the memories of the bereaved would supply those. No one would be omitted, all would be equal.

Saxon might be no orator, but he was not without a sense of theatre and already, in his mind's ear, he could hear the steady, dignified recital of names, sonorous and melancholy as a funeral drum. Unfortunately, there was a hitch. One of the two war survivors was unable to read and almost pathologically shy, the other, having accepted the task some two weeks ago, had called at the vicarage last night and cried off, overcome by the prospect of standing up there in front of everyone and mentioning all those dead men. When Saxon's powers of persuasion failed he had been as understanding as possible, but there was no denying how awkward this was. If the worst came to the worst he would, of necessity, step into the breach, but he felt most strongly that this was not a role for him, that it should be filled by someone who had been in the war.

Frustrated by this impasse, he rose from his desk; a turn in the sunshine might assist the decision-making process. Preparations for tomorrow were well in hand; he would go over to the church, show an interest, compliment those involved on their work. Now he came to think of it, one of them might well have ideas about a suitable reader.

Saxon was about to leave via the front door when he sensed someone hovering at the back of the hall and saw that it was Susan Clay, presumably looking for his wife. He found the girl something

230

of a trial with her driftings in and out, her animal-like devotion to Vivien and her childishness, disconcertingly housed as it was in a bulky, woman's body. In his present mood however he was disposed to be welcoming.

'Good morning, Susan. How are you?'

Blushing furiously she mumbled something ending in ' . . . thank you.'

'I'm afraid Mrs Mariner's not here.'

'Can I do something?'

This enquiry, apparently simple, was so open-ended as to leave Saxon baffled.

'Um . . . I beg your pardon, Susan?'

'Please can I do something for you?'

Now Saxon understood. Vivien wasn't in and the girl wanted to be given some small task to perform. It was commendable that she liked to be useful—but he couldn't for the life of him think of anything suitable.

'I'm sorry, I can't think—perhaps another time.'

'Can I take Boots for a walk?'

'Boots?'

'Please?' she added as if he had prompted her. Of course, the dog.

'Have you done that before?' She nodded vigorously. 'Then you may—for no more than half an hour, though, just up the hill and back, perhaps?' Another nod. 'I don't know where he is, you'll have to find him.'

'I'll look for him in the garden.'

'Excellent.' She blushed again and Saxon felt suddenly quite remorseful about his habitual mild irritation with her. She was good-hearted, as the simple often were. And what was it Our Lord had said about suffering the little children?

231

'And Susan, thank you. It's very kind of you to offer.'

Quite overcome by the exchange, she stumped hurriedly away down the back stairs and Saxon, as if in reward for his good deed, had a bright idea.

*   *   *

'Morning, Reverend,' said Ashe in response to Saxon's greeting. 'Just finished.'

'So I see. Splendid.'

As usual, the man stood politely, waiting with slightly studied patience for whatever he might say next.

'Ashe . . . I have a suggestion to make. A proposal.'

Ashe still seemed to be waiting, so Saxon pressed on.

'Tomorrow as you know is the ceremony of dedication. What all your hard work has been for. I want there to be a roll-call of the fallen, a roll of honour, read out during the service, so that each man on the memorial is personally named.'

'That seems only right.'

'I don't wish to do this myself. I feel such a contribution would come best from someone who served in the war—I mean not as we all did, even those of us on the home front, but who actually took part in battle. Who can be said to have shared the terrible experiences of those who didn't come back. The question is, who?'

Ashe said in a matter-of-fact voice:

'One of the men from the village.'

'That was my initial thought, but one wasn't able and the other has decided at the last minute that he'd rather not. Which of course I understand. So I wondered,' he pressed on, 'whether you yourself would consider helping out?'

There was a pause, during which Ashe's face remained quite inscrutable. Then he said: 'I'm afraid not. Reverend.'

'Now then, I had predicted you might initially refuse, but let me try and—'

'No.'

'But why? Consider—'

'I'm an outsider.'

'Mr Ashe, you've been here, what, several months now. You're a member of our village community, and an extremely useful one, if I may say so. You are a young man. You bear—pardon me for mentioning this—you bear on your face the scars of conflict. I can think of no one better qualified for the job.'

'No.' The word was repeated with slightly greater emphasis, stark, plain and irrefutable. Saxon had no alternative but to accept defeat.

'Well, I must say I'm sorry, but I entirely respect your decision, and your reasons . . .' With an effort, he found a lighter tone: 'You will be coming tomorrow, though?'

'I'll be there,' said Ashe.

'I'm glad to hear it.' Saxon hastened to change the subject. 'By the way, I don't suppose you've seen that dog of ours? Young Susan Clay wants to take him for a walk.'

'He was by the gate earlier, when your wife came through. I haven't seen him since. Must be in the garden somewhere.'

'I expect you're right.'

'He could have dug his way out. They do that.'

'But if he had, then you'd have seen him, surely,' said Saxon. 'His main object in life seems to be to seek you out and stay as close to you as possible.'

'There's no accounting for taste.' Ashe gave the faintest hint of a smile. 'Anyway, I'll keep an eye out for him, Mr Mariner.'

In the church, Saxon found his wife sweeping up stray greenery and twigs from the flagstones around the font. Lady Delamayne and Mrs Spall were deployed in the chancel and the north aisle respectively. When he told Vivien, *sotto voce*, about his exchange with Ashe she pulled a grimace of dismay.

'Saxon, you didn't!'

'Why not? He'd have been an admirable choice, and would have made a good job of it too. He's a surprisingly articulate, well-read fellow. Anyway, this is all academic, because he declined.'

'Of course he did.'

'I don't see that there's any "of course" about it.'

'He's very sensitive to his position here—I mean in Eadenford—he would never in a million years agree to stand up in front of everyone else and do something like that.'

'You obviously know him much better than I do,' said Saxon, a little peevishly. 'I thought it a perfectly reasonable request, and a rather flattering one as a matter of fact.'

Vivien ignored this. 'Here's Lady Delamayne, let's ask her.'

'Good morning, Vicar!' Too late to demur. Felicity Delamayne was striding down the aisle with her horticultural debris in a large canvas holdall designed for the purpose. 'All set for tomorrow?'

234

'Pretty well,' said Saxon cautiously, but Vivien appeared to have the bit between her teeth.

'Not quite,' she said, 'there's no one to read out the roll of honour. I don't suppose you've got any suggestions?'

'Let's see now.' Felicity put her burden down on a pew near the door, the better to think. 'Of course Sidney would always be willing, but he might not be quite what you're after—no, no, I know it's nothing personal, simply a question of what would seem right . . .'

She frowned, cudgelling her brain. Saxon wished, oh how he wished, that Vivien had not brought this woman into it. She was quite bossy and interfering enough without encouragement.

'I've got it!' she exclaimed now, holding up a forefinger at head height as if to still the masses. 'Why don't I ask one of our young men from Eaden Place?' She sent a quick, bright, interrogative glance back and forth between the Mariners. 'Hm? What about that? There are several nice young fellows who are back on their feet and a bit bored, and I'm sure any one of them would consider it an honour. I could take the list of names back with me now, and we could bring the volunteer down with us when we come tomorrow.'

She stared again, head cocked, but thrust forward a little—aggressively, in Saxon's opinion. Vivien was also looking at him and he could tell from her expression that she considered the problem solved.

'What do you think?' Felicity asked again.

'If that's not going to cause unnecessary complications to you and Sir Sidney . . .' he muttered, 'what can I say?'

'You can say yes, Saxon, and leave it to us. You know you can trust our judgement, we see these poor chaps every day.'

'Then thank you,' said Saxon, though he felt distinctly rebellious. He couldn't help feeling that he had become the victim of some 'women-know-best' conspiracy. In the case of his wife he was prepared to recognise that in certain areas this was generally true. But Felicity Delamayne was a trying woman at the best of times, and to have her so obviously riding to the rescue was most irritating. Because these were uncharitable thoughts, not fitting for a man of the cloth, he added:

'It's very good of you, Lady Delamayne. If you could contrive to arrive a little early tomorrow then I can have a word with whoever is to be the reader—about timing, and so on. Because of course the roll of honour doesn't feature in the printed sheet,' he explained.

'Why don't we report to you at the vicarage half an hour in advance? Then Sidney and I can make ourselves scarce while you two have an O-group.'

'Yes—yes, absolutely.'

'So that's that, now tell us what you think of the church.'

For the first time, Saxon looked around him. Despite his irritation, he was moved by what he saw. The church looked lovely—sombre greens, lit here and there by pale blooms, many of them wild flowers: campion, Queen Anne's lace, foxgloves and dog roses. He observed that not only the font, Vivien's responsibility, but also the altar and lectern arrangements showed great imagination and a sensible understanding of the meaning of tomorrow's occasion. What he aspired to in words had here been achieved in the frail medium of flowers and foliage, and much of it by Felicity Delamayne towards whom just now he had felt both grudging and resentful.

'Not bad for a bunch of amateurs, eh?'

'No indeed.' He cleared his throat, and raised his voice to include Mrs Spall, on the far side of the nave. 'It's quite beautiful. Thank you all.'

*   *   *

A few minutes later they all four emerged into the brilliant, hot sunshine, fragrant with the smell of new-mown grass. Ashe had gone, and they took a moment to admire his handiwork.

'He's done us proud, Reverend,' said Mrs Spall. 'I can't remember when the churchyard looked so nice.'

When she'd gone, Lady Delamayne tapped Saxon's wrist. 'He's wasted driving that station van about the place. If I were in your shoes, Vicar, I'd take him on.'

'How do you mean?'

'Employ him full time. There's plainly nothing the man can't turn his hand to.'

Saxon felt his wife's eyes upon him, as if this was a suggestion she had forborne to make herself, but with which she wished to align herself. For this reason, he answered carefully.

'It hardly seems necessary. He already seems to spend most of his time here.'

'Precisely!' Lady Delamayne clearly considered her point proved.

'And I have to say he seems more than happy with the present arrangement.'

'Think about it.' She turned to Vivien. 'Both of you.'

*   *   *

The Mariners walked back to the vicarage in silence. As they came through the back gate they were greeted by the unusual sight of Hilda out in the garden, still in her hat and with no apron on. Susan Clay was with her and they were holding hands, or at least Hilda was holding Susan's hand, for the latter was red-faced and in tears. The moment Saxon and Vivien appeared, Hilda hailed them with a mixture of relief and perturbation.

'Mr Mariner, Mrs Mariner, there you are—we were just about to come and find you!'

Saxon's heart sank somewhat, but Vivien hurried over and put her arm round Susan's shoulders.

'What's the matter?'

'It's the dog,' said Hilda, 'we can't find him anywhere.'

'Oh, is that all. Don't worry, Susan, he'll be around somewhere.'

'We've looked all over,' declared Hilda.

'He'll come back when he's hungry,' suggested Saxon, who seemed to have heard this said of both dogs and children who had strayed from home.

'Exactly,' agreed Vivien, casting him a grateful look. 'And when he does we shall be sure to let you know.'

'I was—I was going to take him for a walk!' Susan was still sobbing and choking inconsolably. 'I wanted to take him for a walk!'

Saxon could see that as the other party in this

arrangement he would have to take some responsibility in the matter, and tried manfully to adjust his expression and tone to suit the circumstances.

'Yes, you were going to, and it was very kind of you to offer, Susan. But if he can't be found he can't be found. Run along home now, and as Mrs Mariner says, when he turns up you will be the first to know.'

'There,' said Hilda, 'hear that? Off you go now. Dry your eyes, here—'she offered a corner of her apron—'your mother'll be wondering what we've been doing to you!'

A moment later the still-snuffling Susan went on her way and Hilda returned to the kitchen. Only now did Vivien express her own anxiety.

'Where on earth can he have got to?'

'We'll find him. Maybe he's shut in somewhere.'

'He'd be barking and scratching—we'd be able to hear him.'

Saxon couldn't help being annoyed at this, yet another distraction in what had already proved a somewhat trying day.

'Let's have lunch, and then conduct a thorough search. We could ask around the village, too. He may well be sitting in someone else's kitchen, happily tucking in.'

'They'd know whose dog he is, surely . . .'

'Not necessarily. Anyway, it would be worth enquiring.'

Vivien continued to look unhappy. 'Yes, you're right I suppose. I just can't bear to think—'

'Then don't,' said Saxon firmly. 'We shall find him. If you'll excuse me a moment, I think I left something in the church.'

He was slightly ashamed that he found it necessary to make an excuse to return and say a prayer. Or why he needed to do so alone. After all, he could have said 'Let us go back and pray'; they could have gone together. It would have been companionable and very possibly a comfort, especially to Vivien. Alas, he knew himself all too well. His solitary prayer would indeed be for the speedy safe return of the dog, but less for the dog's sake than his own; so that he might not have to endure much of the minor upheaval contingent on its disappearance. Of course he did not like to see Vivien distressed, but mainly he longed for the status quo to be restored.

But once in the church his surroundings exerted their usual benign influence and he felt sufficiently humbled to ask, more or less selflessly, that the missing one be found unhurt, and before too long. He tried hard to think of the dog as an individual—Boots, as Vivien had named it: the pointed black and white face, eyes bright and alert, ears pricked, fronded tail waving, an animal which, whatever one's views on dogs in general, was certainly full of fun and always good-natured. Innocent, too, he reminded himself, as animals were.

Saxon concentrated hard for some minutes, then said aloud: 'Amen.'

*   *   *

But by that evening his prayers, and Vivien's less formal but more desperate ones, had not been answered. They had scoured the house and garden, the cellar, sheds and garage. They had

240

walked round the village, circulating his description and asking people if they'd seen the dog (no one had) and if they would kindly keep an eye out for him. Not wanting to upset Susan, they did not call on the Clays, but knew it would be only a matter of time before they heard. Everyone had been most kind and concerned—almost too much so, Saxon thought. He hoped the dog's disappearance was not assuming too great an importance, especially in view of the next day's solemn proceedings.

It was this uncomfortable sense of disproportion that led Saxon to abandon the search first, and return to the vicarage at about eight, leaving Vivien to call on one or two more houses and walk back via the river-bank path in the hope that the dog might be wandering somewhere there. (He made a small addendum to his earlier prayers: that his wife would not come across her pet, floating, dead, in the water.) Every effort had been made. Enough was enough.

By the entrance to the churchyard he paused to admire again the memorial, in all its simple dignity. He would rise early tomorrow and complete and polish his sermon. In the absence of Lady Delamayne and her irritating manner it was possible to feel more genuine gratitude for her contribution. As to the choice of reader, whatever the Delamaynes' faults they were experienced in the matter of public occasions and Saxon had no option but to trust their combined judgements.

*   *   *

Some time later, when it was almost dark, John

Ashe left Mrs Jeeps's house and went for a walk. With his small haversack over his shoulder he turned right out of his lodgings and set off along the High Street in a westerly direction, but after a hundred yards or so he turned right again down one of the alleys that led to Back Street, and walked the opposite way, in the direction of the vicarage.

It was a perfect late summer's evening, the sky a deepening shade of violet, through which the whole panoply of constellations were softly beginning to appear, a pinprick at a time. The dappled tracery on the pale, luminous face of the moon seemed clear and close enough to touch. The darkening hill beyond the village, with its black crest of trees, was large and mysterious. Walking past the backs of the houses, their small lights and small lives, he felt a scornful pride. Not for him!

Just as he passed the Clays' yard their back door opened and he quickened his stride. At the end of Back Street he turned right for a third time, emerging on to the High Street with the church opposite, about twenty yards to his left. He crossed the road and walked swiftly across the new-mown grass between the graves. In the gathering dusk they reminded him of kneeling people, lining his route. Once on the north side of the church he cut across the churchyard at an angle, heading for the far corner where the smooth short grass disappeared into a tangle of brambles beyond which lay the wood, the same that bordered the vicarage garden. Ashe negotiated the hedge of thorns with giant strides, legs lifted high, but even so his forearms and ankles were scratched by the time he'd reached the other side.

Here, amongst the trees and swamped by the tangle of long-dead twigs and branches were a handful of ancient, neglected graves. He doubted whether the Mariners, or even their very keenest parishioner, knew or cared that they were here— the area had reverted to nature. He himself had only come across them in the course of fairly determined exploration. The furthest one, and the most densely covered, was in the form of a stone coffin or sarcophagus, the lid of which tilted at a very slight angle, allowing an aperture of about half an inch.

This was the one which Ashe approached. He laid his haversack on the ground and grasped the heavy lid with both hands.

MESOPOTAMIA

I'm in a shell-hole in the desert. My back's against the side, so it's like sitting in an armchair. Everything's very quiet. The sky's full of stars. The air's cold and clear, my breath's smoking. The only place my skin is broken is these fucking blisters.

My companions are two dead men, and one as near as makes no difference. One of the corpses fell into the hole headfirst, he looks like he's trying to tunnel to Australia. The other one landed across my legs and when I pushed him off he settled on to his side as if asleep. He's a Sikh, I can see where his long black hair's neatly combed up at the back of his head, below his turban. The third bloke's sitting opposite me, we're looking at each other over the heads of the others; so he's company of a sort—but there's nothing in the way of conversation. The only sound he makes is a sticky, crackling noise when he takes a breath, which is about once every five seconds; I counted. His face is shiny in the moonlight, like a waxwork, and his eyes are open, but they're dull and fishy; if he can see me at all he doesn't care.

Just as well. I'm thinking I ought to do something, but to be honest it's the first peace I've had all day. I was thrown in here by shell-blast, and must have been out cold for quite a while. One of my ears feels as if it's had cement poured in, but a bit of deafness never hurt anyone. I turn my head so my good ear's against the bank; that way I pick up less of that nasty gargling from over the way.

It's odd to think that around me here in this

hole in the desert two—nearly three—tragedies have occurred. Several families will never be the same. How ironic. My parents don't even know where I am, and wouldn't care if they did, and I'm alive, never more so. These three probably have mothers and fathers who love them. Maybe wives and children, too. They're out there in Surbiton, or Simla, or wherever, worrying about these men, but they don't know what's happened. Not yet. But I do. Twenty years from now, in who knows what sort of world, they still won't know much except that this person was killed in the war. They won't know about the desert, or the shell-hole, or the great big fucking shambles that led to this moment. And they won't know about me, John Ashe, the survivor who sat here with them tonight under the stars . . .

A bit late in the day I'm doing it—having serious battle-thoughts; getting philosophical. And suddenly I realise that while I've been having them, the gargling's stopped.

I'm alone now, and I need to get moving. I turn over on to all fours and everything screams with pain. I may have escaped the shrapnel and the bullets but I was thrown through the air like a human cannonball. And it's freezing! While I was lying still I was numb, but now everything hurts. I put my hand up to my deaf ear to check it hasn't fallen off. It feels like a piece of meat that's been grafted on to the side of my head. My movement's caused a minor disturbance among the other occupants and one after another they change position. The Sikh flops on to his back, the tunneller slithers down to join him, causing a minor landslide of sand and stones. His collapse

245

nudges the gargler who slips gently to one side like a drunk at a party. They're all in a heap now, every mother's son: a load of battle rubbish. To help me clamber out I brace my foot against the pile of bodies—it's surprisingly stiff already.

I remind myself to be careful. It's a clear night and if memory serves the Turkish vantage point is no more than a few hundred yards away. So I pull myself over the lip of the crater on my belly and lie there, looking around. A lizard's-eye view.

It's extraordinary. What I can see is hundreds, thousands, of other human lizards scattered over the desert in the moonlight. Some perfectly still, some crawling, others, like me, lying with heads raised, staring about in disbelief. In the shell-hole I'd been insulated by the walls and my partial deafness, the insistent, intimate rattle of that dying man's breathing. Up here I can hear, and the air's full of sighing and moaning, like the wind, though it's completely still. In the middle distance a scream goes up, then turns into a feral howling and yelping . . . Some poor bugger can't stand it, but doesn't want to go.

Seems it's been carnage. And now I'm beginning to get my bearings, I can see the Arch up ahead, and the hillocks, the Turkish redoubts, black on softer black, the first slow seepage of dawn; it must be between four and five. So our lines are behind me. I'm in no-man's land, me and God knows how many others, of both sides by the look of it.

We're not all lizards out here. I can just make out figures moving quietly among the bodies, medical orderlies, leaning down to give what help they can. No idea if they're Turkish or ours, but it's good to know someone's getting help. I can't just stay here, I'm going to start moving back. The sand's cold and clammy. I'm thirsty. I begin moving round the shell-hole, hand over hand, one leg dragging after another in a kind of swimming motion. I don't feel particularly strong, so by the time I'm on the far side of the hole I'm panting and light-headed and I've no idea how far I've got to go. I seriously consider going back in the hole and watching the stars fade and the sun come up . . . The trouble is, once that happens it'll be hotter than hell and if I'm thirsty now—

I keep going. It's like negotiating a graveyard, one where the bodies have been dug up and left lying on the surface with holes and ditches in between. I don't know which is worse, the dead bodies or the ones that look dead and aren't. I crawl through patches of slimy matter, which clogs the sand and trails stickily through my fingers. Blood, viscera, vomit, faeces—the effluent of the battlefield. Faces look at me as I slither by, some of them with unlit eyes: gone, dead. Others twist and gape and croak, asking for something that I can't give. One man roars and lurches violently, his arm falls heavily across me and I have to struggle to escape. I'm terrified that he'll give me away and I'll get blasted.

A hundred yards feels like a mile when you're on your stomach, but I get used to it. After a couple of hundred yards I don't care about the sights and sounds and the stuff underneath me, I just keep going. I'm black and filthy and single-minded, a creeping thing. But when I hear a voice I recognise, it stops me in my tracks.

'Ashe! Over here! Ashe!'

I turn my head this way and that. There's a man

247

to my right with a bundle of chewed, clotted rags where his leg used to be, but it's not him . . .

'Ashe! For pity's sake . . .'

I look the other way and suddenly I can see him—Jarvis. He doesn't seem to be injured, he's scrabbling his way towards me, his face is twisted, almost unrecognisable, so that if it wasn't for the voice I wouldn't have known it was him.

'Sir—are you all right, sir?'

'They're coming, Ashe.'

'Who's coming, sir?'

'Arabs—behind you!'

I sneak a glance over my shoulder and now, of course, it's obvious. Those ministering angels of mercy are the Buddhoos going about their business. That's not water they're carrying, it's knives. And when they bend down it's slice, chop, rummage. They're having a field day. If they want a ring, they take a finger.

The nearest one's about fifty yards away.

'We're sitting ducks, Ashe!' moans Jarvis. He's got a hold of me now, his fingers dig into my arm. It's funny but what gets me the most isn't the knife-wielding Arab looters getting closer by the second, but the sight of Jarvis so reduced. I don't care if he's a coward—who isn't?—but I don't want to have to see it. He's broken the invisible barrier, and with it the rules of the game. I can see that what bothers him is our helplessness. It bothers me, too. We're neither of us armed. We can only lie here and hope we're not the unlucky ones.

'Quiet, sir,' I say. It's an order and he takes it as one. 'Lie face down keep your ring hidden.' He's got a nice signet ring with a green jade stone. He presses his face into the sand. I don't have anything

248

worth taking.

Now the nearest Buddhoo is close enough that we can hear what he's doing. Jarvis whimpers and I push him roughly; he turns on to his face with his arms bent up under him, so he looks dead. There isn't time for me to move as well.

That knife will either have our number on, or it won't.

CHAPTER NINE

On the morning of this most solemn occasion Vivien could think of little but her lost dog. Though Saxon was far from unsympathetic, he could hardly be expected to demonstrate much concern, preoccupied as he was with the forthcoming day's events. She tried hard to put the matter in its proper place, but her thoughts kept wandering, obsessively, to where the animal might be and how he might be suffering—hungry, thirsty, perhaps injured, certainly pining for the people and places he knew. Ashe, for instance, wouldn't he miss Ashe? The dog was like her familiar, following Ashe when she couldn't, displaying feelings she herself had to hide. With the dog's absence that link had been severed! She was distraught.

Without drawing attention to herself, she went out after breakfast and took another look round, calling his name quietly. Once she thought she heard an answering sound but it was indistinct and not repeated and she was obliged, reluctantly, to put it down to hopeful imagination.

Returning, wretched, from this fruitless expedition she heard clearly, from the front of the house, the sound of voices other than her husband's, chief among them Felicity Delamayne's. Of course—the introduction of the officer who was to read the roll of honour! Joining them all in the drawing room in her present state was out of the question. And she wasn't even changed! She was already weeping as she flew upstairs, and once in the bedroom she cried as she hadn't done since she was a child. Where was he?

Where was Ashe?

She heard the Delamaynes leave, and went downstairs, slipping first into the dining room. From this window she could see people were already beginning to assemble near the memorial, a clump of respectably clad dark figures in the brilliant sunshine. A small boy kicked a stone; another charged to kick it back and was pursued and restrained, caught by his mother's hand on his sleeve. A cuff was administered to both boys. A group of old men stood together doggedly, some leaning on sticks.

A lone figure entered the picture and stood apart, between the graves at the edge of the churchyard.

Almost faint with relief, she stepped back from the window. At the same moment the voices from the far side of the hall became louder as Saxon and his guest emerged from the drawing room. Her head was still swimming as she went out to meet them.

'Vivien—I wasn't sure where you were.'

'I was getting ready.' To her own ears her voice sounded brittle and forced, but he appeared not to notice anything. 'And here I am.'

*   *   *

Ashe remained where he was, well away from everyone else. He had long ago acquired the animal skill of assumed invisibility, and was by now a past master. If you kept perfectly still and perfectly silent people didn't notice you. Or if they did they received the unspoken message that you did not wish to be noticed, and behaved accordingly. In this, his threatening appearance was an asset; everyone was quite happy to let sleeping dogs lie.

Mrs Mariner came out of the vicarage drive, and went to stand with the others. She looked pale, her eyes puffy. Ashe touched the biscuit in his jacket pocket. Saxon and the captain waited for a couple of minutes once Vivien had gone. Then, each in their uniforms, they walked side by side out of the vicarage gate and to take their places beside the memorial.

'It's very good of you to do this,' said Saxon quietly.

'It's a pleasure, Padre. Honestly, a privilege.'

With this tall young man by his side Saxon was suddenly vouched an insight, only the merest glimpse, into the pride and pleasure that might go with having a son. And with it another, still more poignant one, which he prayed would remain with him and inform all he was about to say and do.

The village, he noticed, still tended to congregate according to unwritten rules of class and social distinction. At the front of the loosely assembled congregation Saxon saw Vivien, at the end of the row, near the Clay family, and the Delamaynes, dead centre. On his own, in the churchyard, stood John Ashe.

Saxon stepped forward. All faces were tilted expectantly upward, but now, at last he felt calm, and confident of his ability to fulfil those expectations. When he began to speak his voice was clear and resonant, with an unusually warm timbre for which he had not striven.

'We are gathered here, on this beautiful morning, with three purposes. To dedicate, to commemorate, and to celebrate. Yes, celebrate . . .'

In the summery air, fragrant with roses and new-mown grass, nothing stirred as Saxon spoke. There was no sound—no car, no train, no animal, no bird, not so much as the hum of a bee, or the flicker of a butterfly.

'. . . himself a survivor of one of the recent conflict's most testing campaigns, to read aloud the names of every one of those from this village who did not return, and whom we hold in our thoughts today. Eadenford's roll of honour.'

The captain stepped forward and removed his cap. Snapped to attention, the cap held in the crook of his arm.

*   *   *

'Thomas Abel . . . Henry Axelrod . . . Percy Beem . . . Edward Egerton . . . Samuel Clay . . . Arthur Clay . . . Daniel Firth . . .'

*   *   *

As the names were spoken, Ashe gathered the surrounding stillness around him so that his invisibility became complete.

*   *   *

'Horace Hillier . . . Malcolm Jeffs . . . Peter Lodd . . .'

*   *   *

253

This much was certain: Jarvis hadn't lost his touch. He stood before the people of Eadenford like a prince, or an ambassador, representing in an idealised form all the men who had been robbed of their lives. Ashe could feel—as Jarvis himself surely must—the powerful wave of gratitude that rushed from the congregation toward him as he stood there on the rising ground next to the sparkling stone cross.

In less than two minutes it was over. A long silence followed, broken only by the odd muffled sob. Jarvis remained at attention, his gaze fixed on a point in the middle distance, his face a patrician mask, stoical and noble. All eyes were upon him, except for when, here and there, a handkerchief moved, a hymn sheet fluttered, a hand was lifted to a face, a head leaned on a neighbouring shoulder.

Now he stepped back, and Mariner took his place.

'Let us pray.'

All heads bowed, except Ashe's. He continued to observe, more intently now that he could do so without being observed himself. Mariner had a piece of paper inside his open prayer book from which he read the words he had composed. Jarvis still stood to attention, cap in the crook of his arm, but with his eyes on the ground, in the manner of a guard at a ceremonial lying-in-state. Assuming he had been selected from among the residents at Eaden Place, Ashe wondered what his injury had been. He appeared unmarked—no limp, no stick, no sling, no scars. How typical of Jarvis to emerge with his looks intact.

Ashe's gaze travelled over the rest of the

congregation. The Delamaynes were bang in the middle, her Ladyship armoured in that tight suit of hers and a black hat with a cockerel feather that curled like a billhook, casting its sharp crescent-shaped shadow on her cheek. Next to her Sir Sidney looked hot and bothered, his jowls folding over his collar, his forehead gleaming. On the far side of the gathering were the Clays, solemn and uncomfortable in their Sunday best. For once Susan looked the most at ease in her printed cotton frock with its full skirt, and a straw hat like an inverted pudding basin. Her hands were pressed together childishly beneath her chin as she prayed. The hat shielded her face so he couldn't see her expression.

Beside them was Mrs Mariner, whose mind wasn't on higher things. She stood with an appearance of devoutness but her attention was wandering. Now she removed her glasses, polished and replaced them as if that might help her concentration. She looked up and caught his eye; her face changed, but his didn't, he returned her stare boldly and she gave way.

His attention returned to Jarvis. Praying like a trouper, as you might expect.

After the muted rumble of 'Amens', Saxon announced a hymn. 'O Valiant Hearts' would be sung unaccompanied with the assistance of members of the choir, who were invited to stand forward for the purpose and face the rest of the congregation. After a tentative start, the voices swelled. There was a palpable sense of relief at this legitimate unleashing of shared emotion. From where he was standing Ashe fancied he could hear Jarvis's pleasing public-school baritone soaring, confident and clear, above the rest.

He himself had no hymn sheet, and did not know the words. Anyway, he would not have joined in. Valiant hearts? Glory? It was an insult, and Jarvis's presence compounded the offence. Only Ashe's curiosity kept him there.

The hymn ended. In the ensuing hush a swallow swooped over the heads of the gathering as if in aerial salute. Children pointed, haggard faces smiled to see it. People were so *easy*, thought Ashe—so easily moved, so easily pleased, so unquestioning, so readily duped. So pleased by the swallow, and by the brave captain.

Mariner lifted his hand to say the blessing. As the holy trinity was invoked, Ashe moved quietly away. By the time Vivien opened her eyes, he was gone.

*   *   *

'I only hope it didn't matter that I wasn't a local man,' said Jarvis over sherry in the vicarage drawing room. 'I'd hate anyone to feel I'd been foisted on them.'

'Foisted?' cried Felicity Delamayne before anyone else could speak. 'Hardly. You were perfect.'

'You were,' said Vivien. 'Thank you.'

'We only just caught him, you know,' went on Felicity, 'he's flying the nest very soon.'

'Actually,' said Jarvis, pulling a charmingly diffident face, 'I feel as if I've been malingering for the past week.'

'No, no, doctor's orders!'

Saxon, who had been looking on attentively

during this exchange, asked: 'When you leave, what are your plans?'

'To return to his charming wife, I sincerely hope!' said Felicity.

Jarvis smiled. 'We're going to stay with my parents in Norfolk, but we want to buy a house in London.'

Sir Sidney scowled humorously. 'Why on earth would anyone from the country want to do that?'

'To seek my fortune,' said Jarvis in the same vein, and then added: 'I adore art but I've no talent for it myself, so I'd like to encourage talent in others.'

'You'll be a *patron*,' said Felicity.

'Dealer, more like,' said her husband.

Saxon stepped in. 'What do you have in mind?'

'To open a gallery. I have a little capital, and a good eye—I think.'

Vivien asked politely: 'Is your wife interested in paintings, too?'

'Amanda?' Jarvis considered this. 'Not especially, but she's interested in me.'

This, as intended, provoked general laughter, and Vivien stood up, because she felt she could no longer breathe in there.

'I know, shall we take our glasses into the garden and sit under the tree in the shade?'

*   *   *

Ashe, returning across the churchyard, heard voices in the garden, including Jarvis's, animated and boyish. There was laughter; he seemed to be keeping them all amused.

Continuing on his way, he paused by the

257

memorial, which already seemed always to have been there, like an inn sign or the weathervane on the church tower. Very soon, though, he was prepared to bet people would stop noticing it, or reading the names so neatly and carefully inscribed. The names and the cross that bore them would become part of the furniture. He put his hand to his face, running his fingers over the ugly furrows and ridges. In the garden, Jarvis's laugh rang out.

MESOPOTAMIA

We just have to lie still and pray like hell. Something tells me we'll attract less attention if we're face down, so I shuffle alongside Jarvis in the same position and we lie there like a couple of sardines in a tin. I can feel him shuddering and I know it isn't just the cold. I'm scared too, but he's a hospital case.

There are these two different beats, then, that I can feel right through my body. The quaking and shaking that's coming in waves from Jarvis next to me. And the soft, uneven crunch of the nearest Buddhoo's footsteps as he gets closer. One thing in our favour, night's ending and we're among the furthest back. Soon the bloodthirsty buggers will be clearly visible to our gunners at the back and they aren't going to hang around for that. I'm pretty sure they're getting less systematic.

Funny what you think about when there's every chance you'll be murdered in the next few seconds. An old South Africa hand told me the Zulus cut open the dead on the battlefield so their souls can fly to heaven. I'm just praying the Arabs don't have the same idea, or playing dead could prove a bad idea.

He's quite close now. My eyes are sealed shut, but from his footsteps I reckon he's about five or six yards away and to our left—at about eleven o'clock. He's near enough for me to hear the rest of what he's doing—the rustle as he looks in pockets . . . the click of a buckle . . . the clink of metal . . . a little grunt and a few words to himself in Arabic . . .

Then there's the bit I've not been looking forward to. First of all the material goes, a long, snickering, tearing sound like a snarl. Then the other part. It's much quieter, and uneven. If I didn't know what it was, God help me, I don't think I'd be able to guess. Sawing soft plywood? Pulling apart old velvet? And it's followed by a sort of sigh, a breathing-out. It'd be nice to think that was the soul flitting off to heaven, but in all the circumstances I reckon it's a heap of hot, fresh human lights falling out on to the sand. Another one dealt with, and he'll be looking around. Jarvis's signet ring with the green stone that was on his right hand—well hidden I hope. Jesus, I hope so.

Then there's a shout. A great big, excited shout, not from our bloke, from one of his oppos a little further away. Jarvis gives a whimper of shock and then goes still for the first time, so perhaps he's passed out. The shout, in Arabic, sounded like 'Over here!', and now our man calls back, and gets a reply, same words.

He goes! I can hardly believe it. Whatever it is his mate's come across, it's a lot more interesting or valuable than anything our chap can see over here. I don't move a muscle, I'm taking nothing for granted. But he's gone.

No footsteps. No shuddering. Suddenly I want a piss so badly I seriously consider letting it go, but the proprieties rule, even when you've just missed being slit from stem to stern, and I hang on to it.

Besides, someone might think I'd wet myself not out of relief, but fear. And it's not me that's done that.

*   *   *

Once the sun gets up it's business as usual. To begin with there's some sniping from the other side but you only have to look around to see there are as many of them as there are of us lying out here, and after a while some agreement's reached and the clearing-up operation begins.

It turns out Jarvis does have something to complain about; he got a shot in the leg, just above the ankle, not much more than a scratch really, but quite painful I should think. Not that he does complain about it, he's quite the little stoic as we hobble back to the bivouac beneath the ridge. I sense he's trying to make up lost ground, in every sense. Maybe he's hoping I'll forget how he was during the night, the state he was in. If he thinks that he's not the clever chap I took him for. I'll never forget. Much too valuable. And now I've seen that handy little wound in the leg I've got more food for thought.

*   *   *

When we reach the outskirts of the bivouac it's so bloody horrible I fully expect him to crack, but no. However he got that injury, we've stumbled more than half a mile through the bodies and the heat to get here and it must be giving him gyp. I haven't got a scratch, but I'm done in. There's something squalid and depressing to see what's left of an army all sat about, bedraggled and bleeding with that half-dead look in their eyes.

They're loading the injured on to a fleet of

261

native *gharries*—mule-driven commissariat carts, with iron-tyred wheels, and no springs or any sort of cover. The moans and screams are shocking. I'm not surprised when Jarvis says to let someone worse off than him ride, he'll walk for as long as he can. That's not selfless heroism, that's looking after number one.

Everyone who can walk is being ordered to march back to a place called Laji, on the river. Most of us haven't got the remotest where this Laji is, but when we ask one of the cart drivers he shouts something back and points, and then holds up the fingers of one hand, twice. Just as well because we can't hear a word he's saying over the racket being made by the passengers. Ten miles! Poor sods. The 'ATs'—Animal Transports—aren't meant to be a cushy ride for anyone, let alone the sick and wounded. They're just for lugging stores and equipment around. You can tell that the drivers have given up on going slowly, and are hell-bent on getting their load delivered as quick as possible.

Even so carts and walking wounded are going at about the same pace. Or at any rate covering the same ground in the time. This is because every time we reach one of the dried-up irrigation ditches the mules spook at all the noise and confusion. I suppose they're used to going along in a nice orderly column, but all this screaming and struggling's another matter. First time it happened the nearest driver got those of us who could walk unaided to pull the mules' heads, but they just dug their heels in and wouldn't budge. It was like having a tug of war with a double-decker bus. These mules aren't like donkeys—they're the same size as shire horses and not nearly so polite. My hands got skinned raw, and one of them kicked me in the thigh—it was worse than the battle. The whole exercise only made things more difficult because once we gave up and let go they reared up and skittered about more than ever; some of the wounded got pitched off—not a pretty sight, and getting them back on wasn't nice for us or for them.

The next time we catch up with the ATs they've reached another ditch and it's chaos. Mules may be stubborn, but they're not stupid: they remember the last time. One wagon's already lying in the bottom, one of the mules has broken its leg and the others are thrashing about treading on the injured men. It's a pity Jarvis hasn't got his revolver, he could have waded in and done his stuff like the time he did with his own horse. As it is, he's white as a sheet and has to sit down. Looks as if he might throw up, so I stand back a bit.

'Look at us, Ashe,' he says. 'We're done for.'

'I doubt it, sir,' I say. 'Just a temporary setback.'

He pulls a wan smile. 'You sound almost like an officer.'

I pretend I don't know what he means. 'Thank you, sir.'

I go and put my shoulder to the wheel. Literally—me and a sergeant from the West Kents and a few others get under the rear wheels of the collapsed wagon and another lot get between the shafts, and somehow we manhandle it up the far bank. The Indian drivers make one hell of a song and dance about rounding up the three uninjured mules, hooting and yelling and laying about them with their sticks until the wretched beasts are mad-

263

eyed and lathered white by the time they're in harness again. We lug the wounded men up the bank, not gently but fast, and get them back on board. No point in using our imaginations—it's muscle that's needed, not sympathy.

Then it's the turn of the next wagon and the driver decides to rush the ditch, not give the animals a chance to think about it. It's not a bad idea, and it works; he gets over, but the screams are terrible. It's bad enough for the blokes on board rattling along over the rocky ground, on the level, but to career hell for leather through a ditch, crashing down this side and rocking and jerking up the other must be agony.

Jarvis can scarcely walk, and he won't ride. And there's still seven miles to go. All this to get out of fighting.

CHAPTER TEN

The week following the ceremony remained unbearably hot. In the vicarage garden the soil was bone dry and cracked, the lawn bleached brown, the plants limp and gasping. Even the weeds had given up.

Vivien had abandoned all hope of the dog. It had been gone too long; how could it survive in this terrible heat? And she scarcely saw Ashe, since there was nothing for him to do but watering, which he did late in the evening when it was almost dark. He came and went like a ghost, and she sometimes felt she was becoming a ghost, too, half-dead with unhappiness and longing.

The next Sunday only a handful of people appeared at matins; Saxon hoped more might come to evensong, when it would be cooler. They had a simple cold lunch together and afterwards, from custom, went up to the bedroom and lay facing one another, not covered by so much as a sheet. Outside the afternoon shimmered, breathlessly, disturbed only by the occasional small rush and flutter of the swallows under the eaves. They did not, to begin with, touch, for which Vivien was grateful. Each, preoccupied, sensed the other's preoccupation. After a while, Saxon placed his hand on his wife's shoulder, smoothing the skin with his thumb.

'I hoped there might be more people,' he said. 'After last week. Everyone seemed so affected.'

She was tired of hearing about it, and didn't reply, but this was a favourite theme of Saxon's at the moment, and he went on. 'I'm not deluding myself am I, Vivien? It did go well.'

She replied, listlessly, that it had.

'I was worried, as you know.'

'You had no need to be.' She was worn out, unable to share in his interminable pleasure in the occasion. She thought of Ashe.

'I did my best, of course,' Saxon was saying, 'but I think it was Captain Jarvis who made all the difference.'

'He seemed nice enough.'

'More than that—a very dignified and impressive young man, I thought.'

She was silent, and he withdrew his hand.

'I hope he achieves his ambitions in the art world, I believe that—'

'Saxon.'

'What is it?'

'I'm so tired. Is it all right if we don't talk?'

'Of course. I'm sorry, Vivien.'

She felt his eyes move over her face, examining her in a way that made her profoundly uncomfortable.

'I'm so sad about the dog,' she said. She knew he would believe this small, foolish part of the truth.

'Naturally.' He stroked her hair. 'You'll feel better in time . . . Ssh . . .'

He rolled away from her and was asleep almost at once. She lay with her hands beneath her cheek, letting the tears roll quietly over her face to soak her hair and pillow.

*   *   *

Ashe helped himself to a slice of the bread, and the

266

hard cheese that was always available beneath the net in Mrs Jeeps's larder. Then he set off for a walk, cutting through the heat with long, fast strides.

There was no one about in the High Street, except Susan Clay, who was sitting on the doorstep of her house, playing with her doll's hair. She heard him coming and looked up, but he said nothing—it was a little test.

'Hallo,' she said. That was good.

'Hallo, Susan.'

She stretched her plump legs out in front of her; the doll lay on her lap, staring madly up at the blue sky. 'What are you doing?'

'Going for a walk.'

'Can I come?'

'No.' Her face crumpled with disappointment. 'It's too hot,' he explained, 'and I'm going too far.'

'Where?'

'Not sure—I'll know when I get there.'

She smiled, diverted by this idea.

'I saw you last week,' he said. 'You looked very pretty in your hat.'

She blushed, and he added: 'Mr Mariner noticed you.'

The blush deepened. 'You ought to go up and see them. Mrs Mariner's still sad about her dog.'

'Boots is lost!'

'I'm afraid he is. But we don't want Mr and Mrs Mariner missing you as well. That would make them lonely.'

Susan picked up the doll and kissed its blank face absent-mindedly. At that moment the girl's mother appeared in the open doorway behind her. Checking up, no doubt.

'Mr Ashe—it's you.'

'We were just passing the time of day, weren't we Susan?'

'Can I go to the vicarage?'

'Not now, girl. They've had a busy day,' she added in the sceptical tone of a woman who really knew what a busy day was. 'They need a bit of peace and quiet.'

'They haven't found Boots.'

'Never mind about that,' said Edith Clay, plainly sick of hearing about it. 'These things happen.'

Ashe bade them good afternoon and went on his way.

At the foot of the memorial, butterflies flickered and trembled over the simple wreaths and bunches of flowers which had long since wilted. He went over to the corner where the old graves were and fought his way through. Lifting the stone lid made him break out in a sweat. Quickly, he did what he had to do. All still well at the moment—just. As always he checked carefully that no one was around before scrambling back out and emerging from the trees. Then he dusted himself down and smoothed his hair.

The vicarage had a slumbering appearance as he walked round it. There was no one in the garden and no voices to be heard. The study window was closed but the long window on the turn of the staircase stood ajar (Ashe had made it his business to acquaint himself with the geography of the house). Now he walked down the side furthest from the church, between the garage and the window where he had replaced the rotten sill. In front of him now he saw the shed, a lot less ramshackle now with the window cleaned, the boards shored up, and a coat of dark green paint. He had put away all but two of the chairs where they'd been sitting out the week before, but the harsh sunlight revealed a few cigarette ends still lying on the sparse, desiccated grass. With an expression of distaste, he picked them up and shied them into the undergrowth. The blossom on the apple trees, he noticed, had been replaced by small green apples. As Ashe plucked the dead heads off the climbing roses, he reflected that it was a pity he wouldn't be here come late autumn, when the apple trees would need pruning; no one else would do it and they'd never fruit better till it happened . . .

A narrow border edged the foot of the back wall, beneath the kitchen window, and he crouched to prise out a couple of wizened, hardy weeds. Straightening up, he looked into the kitchen—dark and tidy, apart from a couple of used plates and their accompanying cutlery on the table in the centre.

He took a couple of steps back and looked up towards the Mariners' bedroom window. It was a bay, that hung out slightly like the bridge of a ship. Every panel had been thrown open carelessly, without so much as a latch fastened. He could have thrown a stone straight into that room and be gone before they had a chance to look out. As he looked, one of the swallows appeared from its nest under the gable and hesitated for a second before launching itself on its lightning arc towards the trees.

Softly, Ashe tried the kitchen door. It was not locked and he entered. Inside the air was deliciously cool. Drops of sweat trickled

269

refreshingly over his skin. He moved through the kitchen like a ghost, touching nothing, placing each foot with a rolling motion, padding like a cat.

In the hall he paused, and looked up the stairs. On the wall at the top of the first flight an oblong shaft of sunlight slanted from the open window at the front of the house. He felt completely in command, as if he could see through walls and ceilings, as though he himself were invisible and could be surprised by nothing. He did not need to open doors, to snoop—he knew more about this house than its owners did. Watching was his greatest talent. Watching and observing. All the time he was working here, repairing windows, refreshing paint and woodwork, tidying the garden, collecting and carrying, he kept his eyes wide open and his mouth shut. The satisfying thought occurred to him that he had the measure of this place, and the people who lived here.

Stealthily, almost drifting, he ascended the stairs. By the open window he paused. A bee had come in and was buzzing and stumbling against the glass, unaware of how easy escape was. Ashe pulled the window shut and continued to the first floor.

The door of their bedroom was not completely closed. From the landing at the head of the stairs he could see the end of the bed and one pale foot. As he watched, the foot moved, and turned the other way, the toes flexing slightly as it did so. The movement was accompanied by the metallic clicking of the bed frame and a sigh, very slightly vocalised—Mrs Mariner was awake.

He moved along the landing banister rail to where he could see directly into the room. The

Mariners lay naked, back to back. He was certainly asleep, with one leg and one arm bent, as if about to bowl a cricket ball. She lay with two pillows beneath her head, and her hands tucked beneath them. Her glasses lay open on the table next to the bed. The hair around her face looked wet. She was staring out of the window. If Ashe had thrown that stone, he might have hit her in the face.

She withdrew her right hand from beneath the pillow and tucked it between her thighs. She cleared her throat and swallowed. He sensed that her mind was working, strenuously. She was fully awake, not even relaxed, and might at any moment decide to get up.

He withdrew, taking the first few steps backwards as if by retracing his footsteps exactly he could avoid making any sound. Then he turned and went back down the stairs, stepping over and between the loose boards as though negotiating stepping stones. Inside the window the bee lay buzzing feebly, legs twitching, with no strength left to escape. He pushed the window open, exactly as he had found it.

Once out of the kitchen door he returned via the same route to the front of the house, and there to his surprise was Susan Clay, hovering uncertainly in the gateway.

*　　　*　　　*

Unlike Ashe, Susan wasn't surprised by his sudden appearance—she took people as she found them, and was pleased to see her friend. The sight of his funny face coming towards her made her feel safe. He always understood her and was never cross or

271

shouty. She was never intentionally disobedient, but this time her attention had wandered and she'd wandered with it. Now she found herself at the entrance to the vicarage drive without really knowing how she got there. Her head had been full of Mr and Mrs Mariner and how lonely they were, and she had been drawn to them. She held her doll beneath her arm, so it was slightly damp with sweat.

'You decided to come then.'

She nodded. 'Yes.'

'You go along in then, the kitchen door'll be open.'

'Will you come?'

'No, I'm off on that walk I told you about. It'll be cooler in an hour or so.'

He began walking away from her, whistling a little tune. She watched him, torn. He glanced over his shoulder and winked with his good eye.

'Give my best to Mr Mariner.'

Obediently—for she was by nature an obedient girl—she did as she was told.

*   *   *

Ashe went up the hill fast and steadily, swinging his arms as if he were on a route march. He was bursting with energy in spite of the heat and he pushed himself hard. He enjoyed the pain in his legs as the incline steepened, and when the sweat began to run into his eyes he undid his kerchief and tied it round his head like a gypsy.

He entered the cool of the woods and kept going, through the muffling dappled shadow and down the other side towards the next valley where

272

the little river widened and there was that flat, shimmering ford where he'd bathed. He was retracing his steps just as he had in the vicarage an hour ago, rewinding a spool of film. The walk had become a ritual, with a ritual's prescribed moves and unquestioned rhythm. Though tempted, he did not run down the hill but maintained a steady, military pace which made his thigh muscles and knees complain. The trees on either side of him stood like a guard of honour. Once or twice a sharp scrabbling and rustling sounded as some small creature fled his advancing footsteps. A flurry of wood pigeons took off from the branches; the clattering fusillade of wing-beats made his scalp prickle.

At the bottom of the hill he paused to get his bearings. When he looked up to where he'd come from he was surprised at how steep the incline was. No wonder his legs hurt. With the wood rising up behind him, rank on rank, he felt at last cut off from the village. And now he could hear the thin, silvery ripple of the river to his right, and made his way towards it.

He reached the bank a little above the ford. Even here the Eaden at its centre was no more than eighteen inches deep, but the bustling current carved the surface into thick, silky ropes. Sitting down on the grass he pulled off his boots and socks and waded in. The water was icy, and tugged strongly at his ankles, but he didn't allow himself to be hurried by it as he moved downstream to the ford. He was pleased by the notion of the river slipping round him, touching him, and continuing on its way to the village. He might be out of sight, but he was still in touch.

In the space of a few yards the river widened and became not just shallower but paler, changing from green to amber as the shingle grew closer to the surface. Ashe's feet looked very white. Here and there fine green waterweed streamed and fluttered like hair. In the centre of the ford he stopped and turned a slow, full circle on the spot. This was where the girl had been when she saw him. Ahead was the broad, shallow step over which the river slipped like an unfurling bolt of silk, and over there at the side the deep water from which he'd emerged to give the girl the fright of her life. To be fair he'd been pretty surprised himself to discover that round-eyed, white-faced audience of one, petrified by shock in mid-river. But his recovery had taken only a split second, and then there had been the exhilaration of watching her flee. Ashe was not by nature an exhibitionist, but that little incident had given him an insight into the exhibitionist's power and pleasure. Those pathetic specimens who got their excitement through displaying their private parts to strange females . . . He'd been amused to discover, and to remember, that the girl's terrified reaction and her headlong flight had given him an erection.

He tugged off his clothes and threw them on to the bank before wading across, and then sitting, arms extended, in the freezing water, pushing his heels into the gravel to anchor himself. He felt the need to urinate and did so, glorying in the way the fluid was snatched away by the current—another message to Eadenford, the more satisfying for being secret.

This time no one disturbed him. After a couple of minutes he was almost numb and got out. He dressed carefully and set off on his return journey, now following the longer, but easier, route along the river bank.

*   *   *

As usual, Saxon was dressed and downstairs first, to find Susan Clay sitting patiently in the kitchen. She gave him a fright. He had no idea how long she had been there, it was slightly disturbing to think of it. She was so passive, so phlegmatic, in many ways more dogged than their own dog had been. When he asked what she was doing there, her answer had been devastatingly plain:

'Waiting for you.'

'But Susan . . .' He heard the exasperation leak into his voice and made a determined effort to eliminate it. 'Susan, it's Sunday afternoon. Do your parents know that you're here?'

'I asked,' she said, with a worried look.

'They don't, do they?'

She shook her head. 'Then you really mustn't come wandering up, and into the house whenever you feel like it. They will be worried. We shall worry—Mrs Mariner and I. You don't want to upset people, do you?'

'No . . .' To his horror he saw tears well up in her eyes. 'I want to help.'

'Now, now, you mustn't cry.' To his great relief, Saxon heard Vivien coming down. Awkwardly, he put his arm across Susan's shoulders. This was a good girl, he told himself—well behaved and well brought up, a strangely affectionate girl. He patted her back, and this was how Vivien found them when she came in.

'Susan was here,' he said. 'I've no idea for how long.'

*   *   *

Gentle interrogation revealed that all Susan had done was to sit down in the kitchen and wait, in the hope of making herself useful, so when five minutes later Edith Clay knocked on the front door, Saxon (left holding the baby, Vivien having disappeared) felt obliged to come to her daughter's defence.

'She shouldn't have wandered off without permission,' he said, 'but she's done nothing else wrong. In fact it was a very generous impulse, which it would be wrong to punish.'

'We'll see about that,' said Edith.

Saxon knew that she was right to be protective, but the look of utter misery on Susan's face prompted him to say: 'Now that you know she's here, and all's well, why don't you let her stay for a little while? I'm sure we can find something for her to do, and I promise we'll see her safely home.'

'I don't know, Reverend . . .' Edith's brow was still stormy. Saxon was still enjoying the warm glow from his success the previous Sunday. He laid his hand on Susan's shoulder.

'We're very fond of Susan.'

'Well.' Edith leaned forward and wagged a finger in her daughter's face. 'You be good, you hear? And don't you ever do this again!'

Vivien was in her room at the back, and anyway Saxon knew that she was not herself. So it fell to him to occupy the girl.

Interestingly,   he   found   her   to   be   an

exceptionally amenable and agreeable assistant. Preparing the church for evensong was not a complicated or arduous task—hardly a task at all, really, since the church warden always left things ready after morning service—but he made more of it than was necessary to satisfy the girl's desire to help.

Once given an instruction, Susan carried it out at once, and to the letter. No detail escaped her. For instance, he could say, demonstrating with his hands: 'I want the hymn books laid this way round, and this far apart,' and that was precisely what would happen. She would actually place her hands so, as he had done, to make sure she got it right. There was something soothing in this perfect, assiduous obedience—to have simple tasks performed well for their own sake. Or—he considered this—for him, because he had asked it. In Susan's obedience he perceived a kind of metaphor for his own priestly role: 'Who sweeps a floor for thy name's sake . . .' and so on.

Nor, once employed, was she any trouble. She did not talk, she made neither comment nor complaint. She was *content*. Even as he framed the word Saxon realised what an agreeable and obliging quality that was, not only for the contented person but for those around them. The small, gentle sounds of Susan going about her business were music to his ears. He was beginning to appreciate why Vivien always welcomed her so readily. Here was a person who longed to be useful and was entirely without self-interest. Susan did not affect humility, she *was* humble.

As he laid his sermon on the lectern in the pulpit he was able to look down on her as she

277

arranged the hassocks, so that each hung from its hook on the back of the pew with its embroidery (courtesy of the Mothers' Union) facing outwards. These small things pleased him. Order was not only desirable of itself, it was conducive to prayer, and serious thought. He decided to suggest to Vivien—and to the church wardens who would need a little more persuading—that Susan should be placed on the church cleaning roster. It would be so good for the girl herself, and she would be an undoubted asset.

Now that she'd finished with the hassocks she sat down quietly in the front pew and waited for him to descend to her. Which, when he was ready, he did.

*   *   *

'She's been a very good girl and a great help,' he told Mrs Clay when he took Susan home.

'I'm glad to hear it, Reverend.'

Edith spoke sternly, but Saxon could tell that she had calmed down. 'I'd very much like it if she could help with the church cleaning from time to time, would you like to do that, Susan?'

Susan nodded vigorously.

'Very well, if you say so,' said Edith. 'No harm in giving it a try.'

'In that case I shall arrange it. Goodbye, Susan.'

'Say goodbye to the vicar!'

Susan beamed. ' 'Bye, vicar.'

*   *   *

Saxon permitted himself a little quiet self-congratulation on having handled a difficult situation well, and to everyone's advantage. He only wished he could cheer his wife as easily.

*   *   *

Vivien attended evensong, because Saxon had almost insisted that she should. He did not, in so many words, say that she should put herself in God's hands, but that was the clear implication. She had never before minded going to church for Saxon's sake, but this evening it seemed intolerable.

When the service was over, she could not bear to talk to anyone, and went straight outside. Her head ached fiercely and she stood with her fists pressed to her temples, her eyes tight shut.

'Mrs Mariner.'

She opened her eyes.

Across the sunlit grass, through the lengthening shadow of the church tower, came John Ashe, walking slowly, with something in his arms.

MESOPOTAMIA

I do a lot of thinking as we stumble along. It occurs to me that there are different ways of losing people. For instance, a lot of families in England lost someone only a few hours ago at the so-called Battle of Ctesiphon—but they don't even know it yet. That's the best way, the cleanest way.

The worst way is what happened with my parents. As far as I know I never loved them, but I took them for granted like kids do; we were a family, not story-book stuff, but no worse than most and a bit better than some. There was food on the table, and clean clothes, and I was doing all right at school.

From the time my mother started doing what she did it was as though we were all being slowly poisoned, rotting away. But we didn't die. I'm out here, so I suppose I'm likely to go first. As far as I know they're still out there somewhere. If I cop one, I wonder if they'll ever hear about it, and if they do, I wonder what they'll think? Anyway, the point is that I lost them, but I'm worse than an orphan; my mother infected me with something I'll never be cured of. The parents who get the telegram at least have their happy memories to keep them company.

And now there's Jarvis . . . We stop so I can get round the other side of him, give this shoulder a rest. It's a balancing act, he's a lot taller than me and his head's lolling about; I don't want him to keel over, I'm not sure I'd ever get him up again. Not sure either of us would.

Hup! Done it.

'You're a good man, Ashe,' he croaks.

He's polite again now, and it takes an effort to be civil under these circumstances. I used to admire him in a way for that keeping-up of standards. I could see it was a real talent even if it was a pointless one.

It won't do him any good now, not with me anyway. Now I know what he's really made of. Don't get me wrong, I like to feel I've got the edge, and now I have.

But I'm sorry to have lost the old Jarvis. He brightened up the day.

CHAPTER ELEVEN

Ashe waved away their thanks and made little of his triumph.

'I was pretty sure we'd come across him sooner or later. He's only a youngster, he wouldn't have gone far. Got stuck down a hole over the back there. No harm done.'

'But he must be starving,' whispered Vivien, stroking the puppy's head. 'He's a bag of bones.'

'He'll be fine in no time,' said Ashe. 'But don't feed him too much at once, his belly won't take it. Only slops tonight.'

'I will . . .' She looked up. 'Ashe, you have no idea how happy you've made me.'

He nodded. 'My pleasure.'

*   *   *

Saxon walked with him to the end of the drive. 'We owe you a considerable debt. My wife has been wretched, absolutely wretched about this.'

'You don't owe me a thing.'

'You found him, Mr Ashe.'

'One of us was bound to.'

From habit, Saxon put his hand in his pocket and fingered his change, calculating what would be a suitable amount. Only in the nick of time did he stop himself making that error of judgement again, and clasped his hands together prayerfully.

'As long as you appreciate how grateful we are.'

'Glad to help. See you tomorrow, Reverend.'

Ashe began to walk away.

'Mr Ashe.'

Ashe stopped and turned with an air of studied patience. Saxon covered the space between them. 'There's something I've been thinking about for a little while.' This wasn't true, the thought had only just occurred to him, but now it seemed so obvious he did in fact wonder why it hadn't done so before. 'If we were able to match your present wages, do you think you might be able to work here full time? At the vicarage?'

He was about to run on about the sort of work that could be done, how useful it would be and so forth, but realised from the look on Ashe's face that these explanations weren't necessary. In fact, it was almost as if the invitation had been expected.

'Thank you for the offer, Reverend. I'll think about it if I may.'

'Of course . . . Of course. Take your time.'

'Oh, I shan't be long.'

*   *   *

After supper, Vivien returned to the dog. At ten o'clock Saxon went in to her and announced that he was going to bed.

'I'm sure you needn't worry about him,' he said. 'He's going to enjoy the best night's sleep he's ever had.'

Vivien frowned. 'I don't know . . . He's still trembling.'

'He's probably dreaming of chasing rabbits.'

'Or having a nightmare, about whatever awful things he's been through. Think of being trapped in the dark, so that no one can hear you.'

283

'Someone did hear him,' pointed out Saxon a little testily. 'Ashe heard him.'

'That's true.'

Inexplicably, she was almost in tears again. Saxon would have liked to say he understood, but he did not. He considered mentioning his conversation with Ashe, but since he was waiting for the man's decision . . .

'Vivien. Stop torturing yourself, please. The dog is found. He's here.'

'You're right, I know.' She turned to kiss him, and pressed her face into his neck for a moment. But it was only a show of contrition, because then she said: 'I'll just stay down here for a moment, if that's all right.'

'As you wish.' He moved towards the door. 'I'll see you shortly, then.'

But she was once again kneeling down by the dog's basket, and didn't answer.

*   *   *

Vivien stroked Boots until, gradually, he stopped shivering. Two of the wooden kitchen chairs had threadbare cushions, which she took to make a more comfortable seat for herself on the floor.

She knew she should feel sorry that she had, in a sense, sent Saxon away, but his presence had irritated and stifled her, and his mention of Ashe . . . It had hurt and offended her, with its implication that she, of all people, did not appreciate what Ashe had done.

She had been the first to reach him. He carried the thin dog easily in his pale, sinewy arms, and as she approached he had stopped and held out the

284

sagging body towards her. But as she'd held out her own arms she had looked not at the dog but into Ashe's face. Because of its disfigurement it was a hard face to read, but the eyes had burned with a fierce, cold command. Remembering it, she shivered.

'There you are,' he'd said. 'Told you I'd find him for you.'

As she had taken the dog from him, awkwardly, clutching and grabbing, his own arms had lowered slowly to his side and hung there, the fingers slightly flexed. She noticed then that they were cross-hatched with fine scratches, some of them bleeding. She'd had to look away, but not from pity.

She had not met his eyes again after that one, brief exchange. The moment had been swallowed up in a clamour of welcome and celebration. But she sensed—no, she was sure—that she had entered into a contract with John Ashe.

*   *   *

Not only did Ashe not give his answer to Saxon at once, he did not present himself at the door of the vicarage for the next couple of days. In his experience nothing was ever lost by holding back a little, especially when one was in a position of strength. He was careful to run through a mental inventory of the place to confirm to his own satisfaction that there was nothing outstanding to be done; he must be seen to be conscientious. The fence near the churchyard gate was sagging slightly and would need shoring up soon. There would be little point in his having painstakingly engineered the dog's disappearance and rescue if the silly animal escaped a second time with who knew what unforeseen consequences, this time beyond his control . . .

Just in case, he went round at twilight on the Monday evening with some heavy-duty twine, and did a makeshift job on the loose uprights from the churchyard side. While he was there, Mrs Mariner came out into the garden. He kept his head down and stayed still; she wouldn't see what she wasn't expecting. He had a good view of her however, and it was interesting. She had the air of having simply risen from her chair, left whatever she was doing, and come outside to be alone with her thoughts. Her glasses were pushed up into her hair, which was loose, and she'd pulled the sleeves of her cardigan down over her hands, and folded her arms, the effect rather like that of a straitjacket. She walked to the middle of the lawn, near the badminton net, and stood looking up at the sky. There was already a half-moon in the dark blue, but Ashe could tell it was whatever was in her mind's eye that she was looking at. He could take a guess.

Still looking at the sky she turned slowly, on the spot. Her glasses slid off and fell to the ground but she ignored them. Then she stretched her arms above her head, letting the baggy sleeves of her cardigan slip back below the elbow. She swayed, shifting her weight from foot to foot. In the gathering dusk, she looked like a fury or an eccentric priestess officiating in some arcane rite. Ashe had the feeling that if he entered the garden and went over to Mrs Mariner right now, he could have done whatever he liked. But when something

286

seemed easy, that was usually not the moment to do it.

After a few seconds of the swaying she seemed to recollect herself. She peered shortsightedly around on the dark grass for her glasses, located them and slipped them into her skirt pocket. Then she took hold of her hair with both hands, twisted it into a makeshift plait and tucked it inside her collar. After this she went briskly inside and closed the back door after her.

Ashe tested the fence before slipping away.

*　　　*　　　*

On the Tuesday at midday Trodd told him to pick up some men and their luggage from Eaden Place, in time for the London train.

'Another bunch cured,' Trodd said sceptically; he took a dim view of the post-war world. 'Poor blighters, they won't know what hit them.'

It was another hot day. The station wagon laboured up the hill and Ashe had to stop on the way to top up the water.

These days he knew the score. When he arrived at the house he drove round to the front, circled on the gravel and pulled up just to the right of the main door, facing the way he'd come. He got out and opened the back of the wagon for the trunks. Then he rang the bell. One of the young nurses answered, but she'd seen him before and didn't flinch.

'Oh, hallo. Yes—I'll go and see if they're ready.'

'If you show me where the luggage is, I'll start loading.'

'That's it, over there'. She nodded in the

direction of the back of the hall. 'Do you need any help with it?'

'No thanks.'

He felt the flick of her curious glance as she walked away. By the time he was stowing the last of the four trunks, the men appeared. Jarvis was among them.

They were accompanied by Matron and Lady Delamayne, who was wearing riding clothes. She was talking and laughing with Jarvis, and the rest of them were smiling at whatever was being said. Ashe climbed into the driver's cab. Behind him, he felt the springs lurch as each man got aboard. They made quite a load, just as well it was all downhill to the station. One of them had seen him; he was conscious of the brief silence that denoted polite, whispered warnings. He imagined Jarvis's face, wondering if . . . could it be? Kept his own face to the front.

Matron, very upright and detached, stood in the doorway with her hands clasped over her crisp white apron. Uniform apart, you'd have taken her for the chatelaine, thought Ashe, whereas Lady Delamayne was full of beans, with her 'Boys!' this and 'Boys!' that and blowing kisses and hoping to see them again. It was as well that on this occasion she had other fish to fry and so paid him no attention, but simply tapped the roof of the wagon when she was ready and called: 'Off you go! Safe journey! Don't forget to write to us!'

She stood in the centre of the drive, waving as they drove away. Three of the officers began to talk among themselves, about where they were going, their families and plans. Jarvis said very little to begin with, but after a couple of minutes

288

when there was a lull, he announced quietly that as far as he was concerned, his real life was about to begin. Ashe's mouth curled.

'Wasn't the war real enough for you then?' asked one of the others.

'I mean do what I always wanted to do.'

'What's that?'

'Be an artist!' said a third, who sounded a lot younger. 'You could be, you're bloody good at it.'

'Not nearly good enough. But I do have an eye. I'd like to work *with* artists.'

'For at least ten per cent of the takings!' exclaimed the teasing young man, and they all laughed: men who could choose what to do; who could do whatever they liked.

The conversation became general again, with the others voicing a commonly held opinion that artists weren't painting anything you could recognise any more, so what was the point? Ashe could picture Jarvis's charming smile, his easy, pleasant air of taking the joke with a good grace while not accepting its premise. He'd always been a man whom it was hard not to like.

They swung into the station yard and Sam Higgins wheeled over the trolley to transport the trunks and cases up to the end of the platform where the goods van would stop. Ashe kept the engine running and when everything was offloaded, Jarvis came to the window on the passenger side of the cab and handed in a tip.

'Thanks for a smooth ride, driver.'

Ashe took the money and turned to face him. 'Thank you, sir.'

It was a sweet, powerful moment, seeing the shock spread across Jarvis's face like a subterranean explosion.

'Good God! Ashe—is that you?'

'Sir.'

'I had no idea—I don't know what to say.'

'You look well, sir.'

'Yes—yes—I am. Thank you, Ashe.'

'Off to London now.'

'Yes, indeed. Then home—Ashe, I'm sorry, this is so extraordinary . . .'

Ashe watched impassively as Jarvis struggled to regain his composure, to find something appropriate to say. Time to put him out of his misery, for the time being anyway.

'Safe journey, sir.'

'Thank you.' Jarvis frowned, both anxious and puzzled. 'Goodbye Ashe. Good luck.'

'And yourself, sir.'

He revved the engine and pulled slowly forward. Once the van was parked he took a long, hard look in the rear-view mirror. The men were buying their tickets, with Jarvis at the back of the queue, lighting a cigarette as he waited his turn. It took him a while, because his hand was shaking, Ashe was prepared to bet. When it was lit he raised his head and stared, through a long exhalation of smoke, in the direction of the van. Ashe stared back, into the mirror. Then one of the others tapped Jarvis on the shoulder and he disappeared into the ticket office.

Good luck! Ashe made a sound of disgust in the back of his throat, rolled down the window and spat like an Arab into the lush green hedgerow.

*   *   *

290

That evening he handed in his notice at the station. He had only to work the week out. Mr Trodd professed himself sorry, but not surprised.

'A good man's always in demand. Can I ask where you're going?'

'Not sure yet,' said Ashe.

Now Trodd's eyebrows did rise slightly. 'You're taking a risk, if I may say so. These are hard times.'

'Something'll come up.'

'Maybe, maybe . . .' Trodd shook his head and blew his cheeks out. 'Staying in the village?'

'For the time being.'

'Well, if you need a reference I'll be happy to give you one.'

'Thank you.' Ashe turned to go.

'Ashe—' He stopped. 'Wouldn't be the vicarage, would it?'

'Might be,' said Ashe. 'I'll have to see.'

Mr Trodd stared at the closed door with a baffled but respectful expression, tapping and turning his pencil on the desktop. There was a cool customer. Walks into Eadenford less than six months ago, out of nowhere, casual as you like, face—let's not mince our words—like an open-cast mine—and what happens? First of all he, Alf Trodd, gives him a job pretty much out of the kindness of his heart. Next thing you know the fellow's made himself indispensable to the reverend and his missus and is all set to be sitting pretty at the vicarage.

What impressed Trodd most of all were those words: 'I'll have to see.' As if it was all a matter of his say-so. As if he could pick and choose, and turn down what didn't take his fancy! He shook his head again. There was something not right about that, as if Ashe knew something that the rest of them didn't, and could call on it whenever he wanted. It wasn't natural.

Trodd shook his head again, this time not in bafflement but decisively. You didn't want that in an employee. Perhaps after all he wasn't sorry to be losing John Ashe. The vicar was welcome to him.

*   *   *

Hilda could offer no explanation. 'I don't know where he's got to, Mrs Mariner. I saw Alf Trodd, and he's been down at the station as usual.'

'I hope he hasn't taken against us . . .' murmured Vivien.

She knew at once that she had said the wrong thing. Hilda had the vices of her virtues, and on the other side of her liking for Ashe lay a warm professional jealousy

'Why would he do that, for goodness' sake?'

'No reason at all, but he's a good worker and I'd hate to think we'd lost him.'

'There's others,' said Hilda, and added, when her employer didn't answer: 'If he's the sort to go off without a word, then it'd be good riddance.'

'I suppose you're right.'

Saxon to begin with affected a lofty indifference, which Vivien was not prepared to accept.

'He's not ill, or anything, Hilda says he's been doing his other work—you didn't say anything that might have offended him, did you?'

'Of course not!'

'There might have been something you weren't even aware of—'

292

'I told you, Vivien, no.' They were in Saxon's study, he at the desk, she standing with her back to the window, arms folded.

'Well,' she said, 'I think I should find him and have a word with him.'

'No.' He'd spoken quite sharply, and regretted it. 'No, he'll be in touch soon. I asked him if he'd like to work here full time and he wanted time to think about it.' Saxon was a little embarrassed at being kept waiting by Ashe, and this was not how he wanted the information to come out, but he was compensated by Vivien's obvious delight. It was as though he had given her a present.

'Saxon! Why didn't you tell me?'

'I was going to, of course.'

'I thought you were against the idea.'

'I never said that.'

'You didn't have to.' She came over and put her arms round his neck, the first time she had done so in weeks. Saxon felt bathed in her—her scent, silky floating hair, the summery warmth of her skin, the softness of her rumpled clothes . . .

'Maybe not, but I knew.' She let go, and leaned back on the edge of the desk. 'What made you change your mind?'

Infected by her happiness, he opted for the simple truth.

'I suppose it was seeing your face when he brought the dog back. I also wished it had been me.' He blurted out the words—in for a penny in for a pound, but when she answered she was matter-of-fact.

'How can you say such a thing? He was fortunate, that's all.'

'Extremely fortunate,' said Saxon somewhat

wanly. 'Anyway . . . I thought he deserved some sort of reward, and he won't take money. So as he's made himself invaluable about the place, I feel sure we could fill his time profitably.'

Vivien looked down at him; her expression was puzzled, as if there was something she couldn't understand. Saxon longed for another embrace, but at that moment she moved away.

*   *   *

The following morning the front doorbell rang when the Mariners were still at breakfast. Vivien, who had finished her toast, left the table and forestalled Hilda in the hall.

'That's all right, Hilda, I'll answer it.'

Ashe was on the doorstep, hatless, facing in the other direction. He turned a fraction more slowly than was respectful. She remembered the contract.

'Mr Ashe.'

'Good morning, Mrs Mariner.'

'We wondered where you'd got to,' she said, but he ignored this.

'I hope I'm not disturbing you.'

'No, no—we were just having—you're not disturbing us.'

'I wonder if I could have a word with Mr Mariner.'

'I'll see. Come in.'

He stepped past her into the hall, in silence, and watched her as she closed the door. She looked up once, quickly, into his face.

'Wait there, I shan't be a moment.'

He nodded.

She went back into the dining room. Saxon, who

was reading the newspaper, didn't look up.

'Who is that?'

'John Ashe.'

'Ah.' Saxon folded the paper with one snap, then again. 'Right.' He pushed his chair back. 'What's the matter?'

'Nothing.'

'Sit down and have some more coffee—with sugar perhaps.'

Saxon went out, closing the door behind him. Trembling, Vivien returned to her chair and poured some black coffee into her cup. She swallowed it down quickly, like medicine, and poured another, the cold, tarry dregs this time which she sipped with distaste. Her nerves began to steady; her hand had almost stopped shaking.

The front door opened and closed. There was a pause. Then Saxon's footsteps approached, and he came in.

'All settled,' he said. 'He'll start here full-time on Monday morning—' He looked at her more closely. 'Vivien?'

'I heard. Good.' She put down her cup. It rattled slightly on the saucer. 'I wonder, would you mind if I took the car out?'

She had no idea where she would go, only that she needed to be out of the vicarage. There was no one to whom she could talk; no woman friend in whom to confide even the partial truth of what she was feeling.

In a mood of desperation, she turned east, and pointed the car up Fort Hill, in the direction of Eaden Place.

*   *   *

Saxon had a parish council meeting later that day and once Vivien had left and he was in his study he took from his desk drawer the agenda, the minutes of the last meeting and papers concerning various matters arising. But it was dry stuff and he found it hard to concentrate. Sitting there staring dully at the handwritten sheets he heard the desultory clicking of the dog's paws on the hall floor, and it occurred to him that at last he had a perfectly respectable pretext for leaving his desk and going out of the house, alone.

*   *   *

Lady Delamayne was about to go out herself when the Mariners' car pulled into the drive. But her outing wasn't urgent—a visit to the outfitter's in Bridgford to buy socks and vests for Sidney—and she replaced her hat and gloves on the hall table and went to welcome her visitor.

'Vivien, my dear, how nice. Is this a philanthropic call, or a social one?'

'I don't know—a bit of both, I suppose.'

Felicity noted first the girl's pallor, then the scuffed shoes, the frayed cuff, the disarrayed hair—the lack, in fact, of any of the toilette which would in her own book precede the making of a call. On the other hand, she reflected, in Vivien Mariner's case one need not read too much into this *laissez-faire*.

'Would you care for some coffee? I can assure you I'm gasping for one.'

'No, no thank you.'

'A cold drink? Lemon barley?'

296

'That would be nice.'

'I'm going to suggest we hide from the sun just this once. We've had so much of it I think we can afford to behave like foreigners and take it for granted.'

She led the way to that part of the house which for the time being constituted their private apartments. In the 'small drawing room' (twice the size of the one at the vicarage) she rang the bell for their drinks.

'Sit down, do.'

Vivien lowered herself on to a pink brocade armchair, but almost at once got up again and stood by the fireplace, presently filled by a huge arrangement of tea roses in a Josiah Wedgwood urn. She was still wearing her glasses, and it didn't seem to bother her. Felicity, who herself wore glasses for reading these days, nonetheless regarded them as the symbol of a shameful weakness and would never have dreamed of keeping them on a moment longer than was necessary. Still, she knew that Vivien's poor sight was congenital rather than the concomitant of advancing years, so perhaps she should be given the benefit of the doubt . . .

'How are you?' she asked in her blunt, keen way, narrowing her eyes as if the answer would be visible, whatever the reply.

'Oh—you know.'

'No, I don't. Or I shouldn't ask.'

Now Vivien did take the glasses off, but only so that she could rub her eyes and face vigorously and then replace them.

'I'm awfully tired at the moment. And so . . . restless.'

Here was something with which Felicity could thoroughly identify, but the tray arrived and she waited until it was set down and the butler had withdrawn before responding.

'You poor thing. That is terribly trying.'

'I expect it sounds pretty silly to you.'

'Not at all . . .' Felicity poured lemon barley for Vivien and coffee for herself. 'I've been restless my entire life, my entire married life, but fortunately I've always had a good deal of room, and latitude, in which to operate, so it hasn't been too uncomfortable for me or anyone else.'

'How is Saxon?' Felicity went on, stirring sugar into her own cup. 'We both think he's been in particularly good sermonising form recently.'

'He has been.'

'Sad to say,' observed Felicity, 'I don't think most of the village appreciates how fortunate we are to have him.' She sipped, looking at Vivien over the rim of her cup. 'How is his latest book doing?'

'Pretty well, I think. He went up to London to do a reading, his publisher persuaded him—'

'No! We had no idea. How simply splendid, we'd have gone if we'd known.'

'He said there were quite a few there—readers, of course. And other writers. Poets.'

'Mm . . . Probably better not to have people one knows, first time out.' The language of the turf came naturally to Felicity. 'Cigarette?' She proffered the silver box and Vivien took one. She put her own in an ivory holder, and held the lighter for both of them before settling back. Smoking conveyed an air of greater equality between the two women; the possibility, Felicity hoped, of an exchange of confidences.

'He should do more,' she said. 'In Bridgeford, for instance, the locals would adore it, I'm sure.'

'He is thinking about that. I'll tell him what you said.'

'Excellent.' Felicity put down her cup and cocked her head slightly, like a gun dog awaiting instruction. 'So what are we going to do—about this restlessness of yours?'

'I don't know.'

'You could start by sitting down, my dear.'

'I'm sorry.' Vivien sank down once more on to the plump, pink brocade, but remained poised nervously on the edge of the seat, puffing on her cigarette like a working man.

Felicity, on the other hand, leaned back in her chair as if there were all the time in the world.

'Don't be.' She tapped ash into the glass ashtray and crossed her fine, strong legs with a whisper of silk. 'As I say, I've been fortunate in having the right circumstances. I don't mind admitting that yours would have driven me stark, staring mad.'

'Really?' Now she had got Vivien's undivided attention. 'Why?'

'Oh for heaven's sake, where to start? Being a clergy wife, living in that gloomy place, having to consider village opinion the entire time—I should *simply* loathe it. And don't think I don't know how difficult it must be to be married to a clever, discontented man—' she heard Vivien's hissed intake of breath—'because of course he is, though not with you, my dear. But a man like that shouldn't be stuck away in Eadenford. He's a poet. A scholar. The constraints must be appalling.'

'You may be right about that,' said Vivien in a

small, humble voice.

'So all things considered,' Felicity gave her short, barking laugh, 'you both do terrifically well.'

'Thank you.'

'But that doesn't solve the problem, does it?'

'No.'

There followed a long silence during which Felicity did not take her eyes off Vivien. She sensed that there was more to say, and that a little frankness on her part had gone a long way to create an opening. But as far as she herself was concerned nosiness was by far the greater part of philanthropy, and nosiness won out.

'We're so pleased that you have your dog back.'

'How did you hear about that?'

'My dear, the whole village rejoiced! How wonderful that Mr Ashe found him.'

'Yes—yes, it was.'

Felicity's antennae detected something there. Ah! 'He's rather a remarkable chap, isn't he? Breezes in from nowhere and makes his presence felt in no time.'

'Yes. Actually—'

'Mm?'

'He's coming to work for us full time. Starting on Monday. Saxon asked him,' she added, as if that needed saying.

'He took my advice!' declared Felicity, 'good show!'

'Why do you say that?' asked Vivien defensively.

'Only that if you hadn't taken him on I probably would have done.'

'I see.'

'Because *I* believe,' said Felicity, leaning forward confidingly, 'that you and I know he is

300

someone it's good to have on one's side!'

MESOPOTAMIA

At Laji I'm lucky getting a place on one of the two hospital ships. Too lucky, according to some of the other blokes who make their feelings plain as I help Jarvis up the gangplank. They think I'm swinging the lead. The truth is, Jarvis has got feverish and can hardly walk, and we benefit from being among the last to arrive on the quay: they're filling up the corners, they see an officer in a bad way, and a chap in a position to help out, and they wave us on. There's a second wave arriving from Ctesiphon, worse off than us, and they're having to cram them aboard whatever boats and barges they can lay their hands on. Some of these boats are having cargo and animals taken off so the wounded can be piled on in their place—no preparations of any sort.

So at the time, yes, it feels lucky. We've already spent the night on the outskirts of Laji and the last couple of hours on the quayside, and it's mayhem, what with the backwash of the battle and several hundred stinking, jabbering, shoving locals like jackals round a kill. I'm glad I've got Jarvis draped over me for a bit of protection. This isn't something I'd say often but if my hands were free and my head was up I'd be tempted to take a swing. I swear I hate these people more than I hate the Turks. My opinion for what it's worth is: the Turks are just the opposition; these bastards are the enemy.

As I say, we're among the last. It's absolutely jam-packed on board, but I manage to push through a little way, and then stand between Jarvis and the rail, so he can slither down on to the deck without getting trampled.

I crouch down for a moment. 'How's it going, sir?'

His mouth's all dry and cracked and I have to bend over and put my ear up against it before I can hear him say: 'Thirsty.' Now there's a surprise.

'I'll see what I can do, sir. Once we're under way.'

He nods. No fuss. He's a patient patient.

The fact is I've got a little water left in my bottle, but it's going to be like gold dust on this trip and there will be plenty of men on board this tub a lot more desperate than Jarvis. An opportunity to do favours never does any harm. Canny does it, Ashe.

When we cast off—that's a good moment, a real relief. When the big old rope falls into the water, I can't hear the splash because of the hubbub, but the ripples spread out and we can feel the boat come to life; the engine starting to drone, the plates creaking, the swell of the murky river underneath us. The last thing I notice on that crowded quay is an Arab wearing a Sam Browne round his middle over his *djellaba*, and holding a pith helmet upside down in the crook of his arm. I don't suppose he can see me, not separately, we're one big floating audience to him, but as we're pulling away he hawks and spits into the helmet, a great big gob. Then he holds the helmet up above his head like a trophy—him and his pals think that's very funny, they're cackling fit to bust, and he offers it round so the toe-rags can all can have a good spit.

What I don't know is that leaving Laji is going to be the best thing about our river cruise, by a long chalk. Less than an hour later and I'm thinking come back, Laji, all is forgiven. Give me a go at that spittoon.

*   *   *

If I ever thought I was fortunate getting on to this floating midden, I don't now. Those blokes who were barracking earlier would be laughing like drains if they could see this lot.

I don't know who was doing the sums, but they got them wrong, as usual. They threw thousands of us at the Turks, but they never reckoned on the Turks being any good. This all goes to show how wrong they were. Ours is the second boat, so it's probably the worst crowded. I hope so, or the other one—let alone all the small craft—doesn't bear thinking about.

They must have started by putting the really bad cases below decks, and run out of room. Just glancing round where we are, aside from what you might call the regulation stuff, I can see a man with his guts on show, one with the top of his head missing like a soft-boiled egg, and another with a leg that's just pulp from the knee down. There's no cover up here, it's white-hot, the flies are feasting. The stench is enough to make you vomit now, plenty of men are. And the rest. With no room to move, the poor sods have to get rid of whatever it is exactly where they are. All that stuff that comes out of us, that usually stays hidden . . . Jarvis is a fastidious bloke, and there's nothing to lie on. I weaken, and give him a mouthful of water, but

304

hiding it as best I can.

It's like a tonic, he comes round almost at once, and says: 'Help me up, Ashe, can you?'

'Sir.'

I get an arm under his armpit and he staggers to his feet, using his other hand to prop him up on the rails. He's green at the gills, but he steadies.

'Thank you,' he says. Always such a gent. Does he remember what happened out on that desert? I can't tell. It'll be our little secret for now.

I decide to make conversation. Besides, there's something I need to know.

'How far to Basra, sir—any idea?'

'Let's see . . .' He closes his eyes. His eyelids are white as a woman's, so white they're nearly transparent.

When he opens them, though, there's a glint there. Even he can see the joke.

'Not that far, Ashe. About four hundred miles.'

*   *   *

Word comes round that the trip's going to take five days or thereabouts. It finishes up being twice that and seems like three times.

The first night on board ship we get the first rains of the season—solid, like being under a waterfall. We, that's a couple of the medical orderlies and me, manage to rig up a few awnings out of old tents and what have you, but five minutes of Mesopotamian rain and they're flattened, or the rain's collected on the canvas and starts pouring through. One thing, it rains so hard that the water gets down between the bodies and washes some of the filth away, but it doesn't do sick and wounded men any good getting soaking wet, and by the morning when the rain eases a bit the situation's worse than ever. The few men who still give a tinker's fuck about the niceties, and who can scramble that far, stick their heads or their arses through the railings and pollute the water supply for our Arab friends. The railing's soon crusted with the stuff, and we're right next to it. But if we move, we'll be in the thick of it, with even less air.

'Better the devil you know,' says Jarvis, with a grim little smile. By the standards of the other passengers he's in clover. His foot's not looking too bad, I've kept it clean and poured a bit of rum on it.

'You'd make a lovely nurse, Ashe,' he says. 'Don't worry about me, you make yourself useful.'

I do what I can, with some advice here and there from the orderlies. They tell me there's six of them, and three doctors. For what—five hundred or more of us? They don't care who helps, if you've got the use of your legs and hands you can do something. A lot of the dressings are alive with maggots, but it's a fine judgement who gets their dressing changed. Is it worth it, for a start? And if it is, are there any dressings? To my knowledge most of the men near us never got their wounds looked at, let alone changed, for the whole ten days. Besides, I'm no Florence Nightingale, it turns me up after a while and I go back to Jarvis, who's sitting down again, bunched up sideways against the rail like a monkey in a zoo.

'Not good, eh?' he asks. Or rather says.

'No, sir.'

There's nothing to eat, either, or nothing that I

can find, and almost no water, which is worse. Plenty of the men on the deck are delirious. On the second night it gets a lot noisier before it gets quieter. We put in at Kut the following day to offload the corpses, and take on another load of wounded so the small craft can go back for more. More! It beggars belief. More screaming and yelling, more insults from the docks, but one of the orderlies and I brave the crowd and go in search of some water. We come back with two oil cans full that's been stashed away for the military vehicles. It should be boiled, but we'll cross that bridge when we come to it.

Off we set again, and I'm not feeling too chipper myself now. I've got the runs and my arms, legs and head hurt like hell. What it must be like to have this and half your stomach missing I don't know . . . better, perhaps.

Another thirty-six hours and we're past caring, all of us. I don't give a tinker's about anyone, not Jarvis and certainly not the others. I don't care very much about myself, I just want to get by. Just let the bloody boat keep going, let's get there before we die, or so we can die in a clean bed.

I won't go into it.

But no—there's some sort of hoo-ha with Arabs in a boat, a lot of shouting and gesturing. Why don't they fuck off and let us get on with it? No, we turn round and head back the way we've come. Three thousand Buddhoos, apparently, though don't quote me, waiting round the bend to tear us limb from limb.

In Kut—again—there's a bit of a clean-up operation, and a bit more water comes on board. Some sacks of rice! I don't know which is worse, knowing there's fuck all food on board, or knowing there's *some*, and wondering if you'll get a bit. Jarvis is worse off than me; being tall and gently reared, his body's used to better things. I find myself wondering, cool as a cucumber, if he'll make it.

Both of us do, God knows how. Downriver it's so shallow the ship keeps foundering on the mud banks and we lie there sweltering till the tide or any bunch of passing locals floats us off. I don't like to think how many dead there are lying about, the flies are starting to outnumber us.

Never mind, we'll be in Basra by Christmas.

CHAPTER TWELVE

Ashe was working on the end of the vicarage garden, in the wooded area. No-one had asked him to, he'd set himself the task. With her approval, of course. He'd brought her up here and outlined his ideas, which she had understood at once.

'You're going to make a Garden of Eadenford.'

'We'll see.'

'*I* can see it already.'

'Perhaps I'd better have a word with the vicar about it,' he said flatly.

'There's no need. He trusts me. And I—' Here she looked away for a second. 'I trust you.'

Ashe knew what she meant, and it wasn't trust. She had not found the right word. Or more likely she had found the right word but found herself unable to utter it; which was as it should be. The space between them was growing shorter by the day. He had only to keep still, and she'd come to him, all of her own accord. Move too fast or too soon, say the wrong thing, startle her in any way and she'd be off.

This afternoon he had set himself to clear away some of the scrub, brambles and ivy that sat like barbed-wire entanglements beneath the trees. Not all of it. He knew that part of the charm of this area, for both the Mariners, lay in its wildness, its air of not being tampered with. At the same time so much of it was not usable. He had a vision of a sort of glade, with paths, ferns and wild flowers. There was a storm-damaged elm, and on more than one occasion he had noticed one or other of the Mariners using the broken branch as a seat. The branch would become rotten in time, but rather than hack it off he intended to reinforce it, while still keeping its natural, rustic appearance.

It was important that he use his initiative, and his imagination. He had no special artistic talent, but he was intuitive—he had an instinct for what would please people. In the mornings, or for as long as was necessary, he performed his prescribed tasks about the place: attending to the maintenance of the house, shed, garden, garage and motor car, and anything that needed doing over at the church. This last gave him a particular pleasure. There was a slinking satisfaction in being the ungodly attending to the house of God. Once he found a small bat, a common pipistrelle, in the folds of the curtain that screened the organist from the congregation, a scrap of crumpled grey leather on the faded red velvet cloth. He had removed it carefully and carried it up through the chancel to the sanctuary, where he repositioned it carefully on the back of the transverse altar-cloth where Mariner would be bound to see it. Though if he did it was never mentioned.

He worked hard. He was often at the house before its occupants were up and about in the morning, and on fine evenings he didn't leave till dusk. He became a presence about the place, not exactly one they took for granted, but which they became accustomed to.

Hilda was the one he had to make sure of. She was altogether less predictable, being watchful and conscious of her status. She was disposed to like him, but equally determined not to have the wool pulled over her eyes. He had to be careful never to appear ingratiating, or presumptuous. He was still a newcomer, not just here but in the village. He was sure to appear quiet and industrious and to show, if not deference, at least the respect due between equals.

Generally speaking he brought his own lunch and ate sitting on the grass at the back of the shed. If the weather was bad, he went inside the shed. Only if specifically invited did he join Hilda in the kitchen.

Very occasionally she would offer him something, if there was extra from the joint, or a stew, or one of her exceptionally good summer fruit puddings. Ashe was not a big eater, something had happened to his appetite during the war and it had never quite recovered, but he could tell that Hilda was justifiably proud of her cooking, and he always expressed appreciation. Carefully, mind—a little flattery went a long way with a woman of Hilda's naturally suspicious nature.

At four o'clock on this particular afternoon he sensed someone coming across the lawn, the rustle of a woman's skirt, but he didn't look round. It was Hilda, wiping her hands on her apron.

'Cup of tea, Mr Ashe?'

'Well—' He straightened up, wiped his brow with the back of his wrist. 'I tell you what.'

'What's that?'

'You wouldn't by any chance have any of your homemade lemonade about the place?'

'I think I very well might.' Her tone was reproving, but playfully so, as if addressing a wheedling child. 'Come along in when you're ready and I'll pour you a glass.'

He continued to work for another ten minutes,

chopping fiercely with the hoe at hawser-like ivy roots. Best not to appear too keen. When he went in, there was a green glass jug full of lemonade on the table, along with two tumblers and a plate of biscuits.

'Sit yourself down,' said Hilda. 'I think I'll join you.'

He sat, and she poured them both a glass, and proffered the biscuits.

'Have a Garibaldi—squashed flies, Mr Mariner calls them. He likes them, so I've always got plenty.'

'Thank you.' Ashe helped himself to one and laid it on the table in front of him.

Hilda sucked her teeth. 'What am I thinking of?' She got up and took a couple of tea plates off the dresser. 'There you are.'

'Thank you,' said Ashe again, and placed the biscuit on the plate. 'Quite a tea party.'

'Well, why not. It must be warm work for you in this weather.'

'I'm in the shade up there.'

He took drink, and a bite of his biscuit. 'Mm.'

There followed a pause, which he allowed to stretch into a silence. He was perfectly comfortable with silence but Hilda was not, and felt compelled to break it. She engaged in one or two small, rustling preliminary gestures before doing so, and then asked:

'So how are you getting on down in the village, Mr Ashe?'

'Pretty good.'

'Comfortable at the post office?'

'It's fair for the price.'

Hilda sucked in her cheeks. 'If you say so.'

Ashe took another sip. 'Is that not what other people say?'

'She's not known for her housekeeping.'

'Maybe not—but then neither am I.'

Hilda glanced at him to see whether or not this was a joke, and decided that it was.

'I don't believe you, Mr Ashe. A man with army experience can always look after himself.'

He smiled and let another pause elapse, which this time he was careful to end himself: 'I've often wondered why you don't live here, the hours you work.'

'I like my own bed,' she said, and when he nodded as if perfectly satisfied with this answer, added: 'Just as well.'

He waited, sipping tranquilly, and was rewarded.

'They don't want anyone else around the place, do they?'

He assumed, correctly, that this question was rhetorical.

'I'm not one to gossip,' she went on. 'You're the same I believe. That's why they've taken to you the way they have.'

'I don't know about that,' he said. 'But I like the work here, and if they're happy so am I.'

'Oh, they're happy, believe me.'

He had now finished both lemonade and biscuit. He put the glass on top of the plate and got up to take them to the sink. Hilda's next words were spoken with an air of abstraction, as though intended not for him, but for him to overhear.

'No, they like their privacy . . . And I'd rather be under my own roof.' She snapped back into the present. 'Don't worry about those now, Mr Ashe, you go and get on with your work.'

313

'Thank you.' He left the things in the sink. 'Much appreciated. That's wet my whistle a treat.'

Back under the trees Ashe experienced a surge of renewed energy, seeing off the clump of roots that had been giving him so much trouble in no time. This was due only in part to the effort of exercising sustained restraint with Hilda. He was used to holding back and keeping his own counsel. Mostly he was energised by the sense of his plan going forward. And now that he'd seen Jarvis that plan had a focus beyond this small, stifling place with its equally small concerns and affectations. He'd do what had to be done here, get out ahead, and claim his free ride on Jarvis's elegant back.

He yanked out the last of the root and threw it to one side. As he rested for a moment on the shaft of the hoe, a swallow darted over the sunlit grass. Watching it from the shadows, Ashe set himself a target: *When they go, I go.*

*   *   *

A few days later the weather turned. Conveniently for Ashe as it happened, though not for the farmers who were short of labour this year and now had another legitimate reason to grouse. After so much fine weather the crops had been standing tall, ripe and ready for an early harvest, but now the rain hammered down out of a gunmetal sky and flattened them so the fields that had been so golden and promising looked dismally dingy and brown, and partially flattened as though some enormous animal had plodded over them. The harvest that had been a sure thing was postponed for the time being. Gutters overflowed.

The sides of the lanes gushed with rivers of muddy water, and the Eaden itself became a voluble, hurtling torrent on which the flustered moorhens bobbed like corks and domestic ducks were unable to swim at all. At Eaden Place it was just as well that numbers were beginning to fall, because the bath chairs and benches had to be brought in off the terrace and lined up in the already crowded conservatory, where the patients gazed out through the steamy, streaming glass like passengers on a storm-tossed ocean liner.

About a week into the wet spell, Ashe arrived later than usual at the vicarage, and knocked on Mr Mariner's study door just after nine o'clock.

'Come in! Ah, Ashe.'

'Morning, Reverend.'

'Not much of a day for gardening.'

'I was wondering whether there was anything I could do for you indoors,' said Ashe.

Mariner frowned, thinking. 'I'm not sure . . .'

'Any painting need doing? Anything need mending?'

'You're a man of many talents, I know,' said Mariner. 'I think you should ask my wife. She's more *au fait* with these things.'

Ashe hoped he'd say this. He closed the door and sought out Mrs Mariner, who was writing letters in her room at the back. The dog was with her and immediately came over to greet him, weaving and wriggling enthusiastically.

She blushed, removed her glasses, and made to stand up from her desk, before recalling herself and staying put, a little awkwardly Ashe thought. He repeated his query.

'I'm sure there must be, let me see . . . Oh look

at that foolish animal, he does love you so . . . why wouldn't he, you're his saviour!' Ashe knew she was looking at the dog to save looking at him, but he did not return the favour: he kept his gaze firmly on her face.

'Perhaps,' she said, 'you could you take him for a walk?'

'I'll do it now.'

'You don't mind, do you, in this awful rain?'

'It's only weather.'

'When you come back, I'll have collected my thoughts—there's the attic, it's simply frightful, I hardly like to ask you.'

'Anything that needs doing,' he said, and slapped his thigh to the dog: 'Come!'

*   *   *

Saxon gazed down at the beginnings of a poem, his first in quite a while. He was attempting to capture his feelings about certain recent events: the memorial, Jarvis, the Clay girl. There was a common thread to the feelings which he was trying to pin down and he had nearly done so, but not yet. Perhaps a short break, to allow the subconscious to do its work. Superstitiously, he turned the page over before leaving the room and going in search of his wife.

Vivien too was sitting at her desk, with a pen in her hand, staring out of the window, though from this room there was very little in the way of a view—part of the garage wall, a sliver of garden, the corner of the shed, all blurred by the downpour. A lighted cigarette lay across the ashtray at her elbow, its thin spiral of smoke like her daydreams.

She started when he came in. 'Saxon!'

'I hope I'm not disturbing you.'

'No . . .' She picked up the cigarette, drew on it, and stubbed it out. 'I was miles away.'

Now that he was in the room he couldn't think why he was there. Had there been something he was going to ask her? Tell her? He walked to the window and peered out into the rain. He had simply wanted to know where she was.

Almost absent-mindedly, she stretched out her hand, opening and closing it once, inviting his. He placed his hand in hers. They didn't look at one another and in a moment her hand fell away.

She said, brightly: 'I sent poor Ashe out into the rain with Boots.'

'He was looking for something to do indoors in this weather and I'm afraid I referred him to you.'

'When he gets back I'm going to suggest he clears out the attic.'

Saxon frowned. 'We don't want him rummaging in our things.'

'He won't rummage. I shall go up there with him and show him what needs to go, and where to put the other things. All those old suitcases and boxes of papers—'

'I don't want the papers touched.'

'They can be put in a trunk so they don't get any sadder and mouldier than they are already. But the main thing is, when the place is tidy he should be able to do something about the holes in the roof. And put more boards down so it's easier to walk around up there.'

'There are limits to Ashe's capabilities. He's a useful handyman, but I suspect a pitched, tiled

317

roof is a job for an expert.'

'We don't have the services of an expert at the moment, but we do have Ashe and we may as well make use of him. I'm sure he'll tell us if it's beyond him.'

'Very well.' Saxon decided that he sounded grudging and added: 'You're right, he's a sensible fellow.'

He leaned forward, peering, pointlessly, out into the rain, brows drawn together.

'I must let you get on,' he said, making no move to do so.

Vivien removed her glasses and leaned back, her hands linked behind her head. 'Hilda likes him, thank God.'

'Thank God indeed. It struck him that he had sought out his wife for reasons that weren't clear even to him, and they had spent the whole time talking about Ashe.

'She says his digs in the village aren't very nice.'

'He can look for others. There must be plenty of families who'd like to let out a room. Think of all—' He had been about to say, *Think of all the rooms left empty by the war* but changed it to: 'Think of all the households who'd appreciate some extra money coming in.'

'I think she feels sorry for him.'

He said cuttingly: 'Then perhaps Hilda herself could oblige?'

'Saxon—you know what she's like, she's so starchy.'

'They might suit each other.'

'I can't imagine it.' Vivien dropped her glasses back on to her nose, and picked up her pen. He was about to leave, and almost didn't hear her when she said: 'Perhaps he could move in here.'

'I beg your pardon?'

'After all,' she went on, 'most houses of this size have someone living in. It's only because Hilda prefers not to—'

'We prefer her not to.'

'It was a little of both. Anyway, I feel sorry for Ashe. He so obviously likes it here and one couldn't ask for anyone less conspicuous . . .' Her voice tailed away, but her cheeks, often so pale these days, were quite pink. It dawned on Saxon that this was no sudden outburst, his wife had been thinking about it. Now she got up and came over to him; he thought she might embrace him but instead she stood facing him, her arms folded.

'What do you think, Saxon—really? This isn't an idle suggestion, I believe it would work very well.'

He held out his hand and after a second she laid hers in it, but would not be drawn closer. 'Let's think about it.'

Back in his study he turned over the sheet of paper containing the poem, and looked at the lines without reading them. That had been a strange and unexpected little conversation with his wife . . . He picked up another piece of paper and began doodling, a childish drawing of a house, a tree, a car that was more like a steam engine . . . Ashe, live here? His old, familiar instinct for caution warned strongly against it; they did not need or want another person in the house, they valued their privacy. But the new Saxon, the writer of this poem, was of a more generous nature, surely. Vivien had always thought the best of him, but only he knew the worst. Here was an opportunity to do the right thing by a stranger, and also (this was by far the most important influence on Saxon) to bring the warmth and colour back to his wife's cheeks, and the light to her eyes. To bring her back to him.

He threw away his childish drawing and addressed himself once more to the poem, which he saw now was quite simply about love: love, and charity.

*   *   *

Ashe walked with the dog for over an hour, along the river bank. The surface of the water seemed to boil under the onslaught of the rain; the trees overhanging the far bank drooped and streamed beneath its weight. Even the dog's exuberance was dampened as he trotted at Ashe's side through the mud, head down and tail hanging, his feathery coat turning to rat's tails.

When they returned to the vicarage, Ashe went in at the back door to find the kitchen empty; Hilda was in some other part of the house. He tied the dog's lead to the boot scraper while he removed his work boots and put on the almost outworn second pair reserved for indoors. Then he took off his sodden jacket and hung it across the clothes horse in the scullery. Finally he rubbed down first his own head, then the dog with the old towel designated for the purpose, and smoothed his hair with his hands before going upstairs.

Vivien was not now daydreaming. She heard the back door, and the scrabbling of Boots's paws on the stone flags, so when Ashe appeared she was able to appear composed.

'You must be absolutely soaked! Did you have a

good walk?'

'We went by the river.'

'And in it, too, by the look of you.'

Ashe said nothing, but passed a hand slowly over his wet, black hair. The collar and cuffs of his striped shirt, and the bottoms of his trousers, were also damp.

'Where's Boots?'

'In the scullery, drying off. I gave him a rub-down.'

'Right.' Vivien got up from her chair. 'It would be so helpful if you *could* do some sorting out in the attic.'

'You just tell me what needs doing.'

'It's really a question of shoring up the roof in places, and laying some more planks so we can walk about up there . . . Is that something you could do?'

'I don't see why not.'

'But before you start you'll need to make some space.'

'Shouldn't be a problem.'

'I'll show you.'

Passing him in the doorway she was acutely aware of the two sides of his face—one pale and calm as a coin, the other a fiery gargoyle.

She led the way along the hall and up the stairs. There was a profound silence on the far side of the study door; Saxon must be writing. Ashe's footsteps were soft as a cat's behind her. On the landing, their bedroom door was open; Hilda was in there, changing sheets, flapping and tucking energetically. Vivien was embarrassed that Ashe should be a witness to this. Something about the intimacy of the discarded sheets lying in a crumpled pile on the floor, the uncovered pillows piled on a chair, the underblanket slewed to reveal the striped mattress ticking, her book, Saxon's water flask and alarm clock, his slippers beneath the bed—

'Hilda!' she said, a touch too brightly, 'I'm just taking Mr Ashe up into the attic, he's going to be doing some work up there—perhaps fix the roof.' She glanced at Ashe for his endorsement, and he nodded.

'Very well, Mrs Mariner.' Hilda came to the door, shaking a pillow vigorously down into its case. 'Is Mr Mariner in his study?'

'He is, so if you could keep a weather ear open for the door bell, please . . .'

'Of course.' This in a somewhat mettlesome tone, as if to say that Hilda did not need reminding. She gave the pillow a couple of slaps and looked pointedly over Vivien's shoulder.

'Morning, Mr Ashe.'

'Hilda.'

'Hope you've got your umbrella with you, it's like a colander up there in places.'

'Mr Ashe is going to change all that,' said Vivien.

'We'll see,' said Ashe.

His manner conveyed, insofar as it conveyed anything, a quiet confidence. It did not seek an opinion. Hilda on the other hand made a sound that was typical of her, which said unequivocally that she wished them well of the enterprise but took leave to have her doubts.

The attic trapdoor was in the ceiling at the far end of the landing. Mercifully, the doors of the two other bedrooms and those of the bathroom and lavatory were closed. A sturdy wooden chair stood against the wall to enable a person to reach the ceiling latch. Vivien went to pick up the chair, but Ashe beat her to it.

'Allow me.'

He positioned the chair, stepped up on to it, and reached above his head to undo the door. The latch was stiff and he had to wrestle with it. Vivien, standing on a level with his knees, smelled the brackish damp of his trousers, but that was all; no sweat—he was always fresh and neat in appearance, his hands immaculate, more like a businessman than a labourer.

The latch gave with a jerk. Unbalanced, Ashe stepped to one side and the chair rocked. Instinctively, Vivien clapped one hand on the back of the chair to steady it, and the other against his leg to prevent him falling on top of her. The touch lasted less than a second but the shock of it shot through her. His leg felt thin and hard, as if beneath the pale skin his blood coursed more quickly, and closer to the surface than others'.

She was burning herself now, not able to look up, but he seemed not to have noticed. He stretched on tiptoe to drop the door down inside the attic.

'There's a ladder inside—it should be to your left, with a torch next to it,' she said, glad to have found her voice and to be able to give instructions. 'Can you see?'

'Got it. Got both of them.'

Suddenly his legs tensed and flexed and he'd levered himself up on to the edge of the aperture.

'All right if I hand it down to you?'

'Ready and waiting.'

Slowly, he lowered the feet of the stepladder. 'Safe?'

'Quite safe,' she replied, shifting the chair aside with her leg. She opened the ladder and climbed up. As she did so, he turned on the torch and laid it on its side on one of the trunks so that it acted as a lamp.

When she reached the top rung and was about to hoist herself up the remaining eighteen inches or so, he extended a hand to help her. She placed her own hand in his and felt its dry heat and the wiry strength of his arm that made her seem almost weightless, floating up in to the dimly lit space. The rain hissed on the slates, dripping and trickling through the gaps.

'Just as well there are a few holes,' he said. 'Makes it easier to see.'

'Heavens, what a mess!'

'That's attics.' He took a wide, sideways, tentative stride, testing the makeshift wooden floor. 'Stay there a moment.'

'Be careful.'

She had become used to his not answering. He meant nothing by it: he was a man of few words, and not one of them surplus to requirements. Moving as he was, with crablike caution, away from her to her right, she could see only the damaged half of his face in the dusty half-light, and it gave her a thrill of fear. Hilda was only a few yards away, and her husband downstairs, but they might as well have been in another world.

'Plenty of bats,' he said, matter-of-factly.

'I suppose there must be.'

'Don't worry, they won't bother us.'

'I'm not scared of them,' she said. 'Sometimes

324

we find them roosting in church.'

He said nothing, but continued his slow, stooping reconnaissance of the floor. When he'd described a circle, of which he tested the centre, too, he was back at her side.

'If it'll hold me it'll hold you. Where do we start?'

Vivien wished she had come up here earlier to look around and evaluate the task: if she had, she might have been able to answer Ashe's question. As it was, she could only gaze around helplessly. As well as the trunks, suitcases and boxes full of the detritus of the Mariners' past, both separate and shared, there were great bundles of old curtains and loose covers tied with twine, some pieces of broken furniture, a stack of pictures, and a wooden crate containing china, still wrapped in newspaper.

'Oh dear,' she murmured, hands to her cheeks in an attitude of dismay. 'There's even more than I thought . . .'

Ashe had been standing next to her also surveying the scene, with his arms folded. Now he said: 'Mrs Mariner, may I make a suggestion.'

'I wish you would!'

'You have a bit of a look round and if there's anything you know right away needs throwing out, I'll move it so I can get it down later. Then I can shift the rest up the end on the good boards. After that the decks'll be clear and I'll take a look at the roof, and how much wood we need for the rest of the floor. And another light, that'd be no bad thing. Once we've done that you can take your time sorting through the rest of this—we can both get on.'

'Yes—yes, you're absolutely right.'

'Start in the far corner, shall we.'

'Yes.'

The attic was filthy, cobwebs festooned the beams, some of them so thick and old they were gobbed with dust like fluffy necklaces. The same dust covered everything else, and there were also the bats . . . She felt him looking at her, and when he spoke his voice was gently enquiring.

'Mrs Mariner, will you be all right in those clothes?'

It was a perfectly reasonable question, and a sensible one, but its implications turned her stomach to water: that he had noticed what she was wearing at all, let alone that he should mention it, or be in the least concerned whether her things got dirty. It was rare for her to consider her appearance except insofar as it affected her own comfort, but now she was made suddenly conscious of her darned cotton skirt and unfashionable blouse.

'These?' Trembling, she looked down at this homely ensemble to avoid looking at him. 'No, nothing matters at all.'

'Right you are then.'

For the next three-quarters of an hour they worked together in near silence, exchanging as few words as possible. She made her decisions, Ashe hefted stuff either to the door-aperture or to the appointed area beneath the eaves. But though they spoke little the dusty air hummed with an intense mutual awareness that Vivien found almost unbearable. She heard every breath of his, every step and strain. She seemed to hear each muscle move, each swallow and blink, each pore open to emit its tiny pearl of sweat. She longed to escape for a moment, to collect herself, have a glass of water, for in spite of the rain there was no air up here and she felt half stifled by the heat and the turmoil inside her.

But escape was not so easy. She was not sure how readily she would manage the ladder—especially coming back—without his help, which she did not want. Or rather which she wanted too much.

Once they brushed against one another, no more than a touch of fabric on fabric, but her skin leapt with shock. Though he showed no sign of a similar response, her instinct told he was nonetheless complicit in hers, not just aware of it but equally aware of his role in provoking it. And yet he had done nothing—had he?—no, nothing, surely, but behave with his usual taciturn civility and restraint. So how *could* he know about the clattering agitation and turmoil going on in her stupid head? She did not recognise herself.

Eventually, unable to bear it any longer, she said: 'I think that'll do for now, Ashe.'

'Yes . . .' He was testing the tiles surrounding one of the holes, and did not look round. 'Leave it to me.'

She went to the door. 'It's awfully hot. Would you like some water?'

'Don't you trouble. I'll come down and fetch some if I feel like it.' He broke off a piece of rotten tile and turned it in front of his face. 'There's your problem, Mrs Mariner. I can patch it up, but you're going to need a roofer up there before the winter.'

'More expense. I'd better break the news gently to Mr Mariner.'

Ashe didn't disagree with this; he appeared entirely absorbed in his task, testing the edges of the tiles between finger and thumb.

Carefully, Vivien sat down with her legs dangling through the loft aperture. Under normal circumstances she wouldn't have given this exercise a moment's thought, but now she was anxious to manage it quickly, cleanly and without embarrassment. She turned to kneel, extended one leg and felt with her foot for the ladder—got it. Then she took the strain on her arms until she was standing with both feet firmly in place. Her legs trembled slightly as she went down.

Back on the landing she paused for a second, her forehead against one of the rungs. She was sweating, her hair in a heavy, damp knot on the nape of her neck.

'All right, Mrs Mariner?'

She turned, swiping her wrist across her brow. Hilda stood at the top of the stairs, carrying a basket with duster, polish and dustpan and brush.

'I'm fine thank you, Hilda.' Flustered, Vivien beat at the front of her blouse and skirt with both hands. 'I'd forgotten how hot and dusty it was in the attic.'

'Mr Ashe still up there?'

'Yes. He's going to do what he can, but he thinks we'll have to have the whole roof seen to before winter. Heaven knows what that will cost . . .' She frowned anxiously. 'Is there something nice for lunch?'

'Liver and bacon,' said Hilda, adding, to show she understood the question's significance: 'Mr Mariner likes that.'

328

Saxon heard his wife talking to Hilda on the landing, and then her footsteps as she came downstairs. There was a slight hesitation at the bottom so that he half expected her to knock on the door, but the footsteps continued, followed by the gentle click of another door. She had returned to her desk.

She had been with Ashe in the attic, for a long time. Over an hour, in fact—Saxon happened to have glanced at his watch when they'd gone up there—and it seemed longer.

The rain had eased off, but only to settle into the sort of even, steady drizzle that could continue all day. The morning dragged.

It wasn't until midday that Vivien heard Ashe come down. Hilda had long since retreated to the kitchen from where a faint but delicious aroma of rhubarb began to float; rhubarb crumble was another of Saxon's favourites. Vivien did hope Hilda wasn't overdoing things: such an obvious embarrassment of delights could very easily prove counter-productive and make him even less amenable to the bad news about the roof, which coming as it did from—

Ashe tapped on the door.

'Come in.'

When he entered, his hair was quite grey with dust, which made her touch her own: did that, too, look grey? What did it matter.

'How are you getting on up there?'

329

'I've used some old material, and cardboard, to cover the holes for now. If it's all right with you and Mr Mariner I'll do a spot of scavenging. There's a bit of stuff down in the station yard, left over from when they built the new waiting room, I think Mr Trodd would give me a good price, as it's for the vicarage. Glad to get rid of it probably.'

'That sounds ideal.'

'I'll go down there this afternoon, then. But Mrs Mariner.' She looked at him obediently. 'You still need to call in the experts.'

'We will, don't worry.'

Vivien picked up her pen. She both did and didn't want him to go; but he remained in the doorway, looking levelly at her.

'Would you like me to mention this to Mr Mariner?' He placed a small emphasis on the 'me'. In anyone else she would have seen this as a touch familiar—the assumption that this was man's business, or that he might in some way protect her from her husband's irritation. As it was, her heart leapt as though he'd saved her life.

'Would you, Ashe? I know how much he respects your opinion.'

He inclined his head and withdrew, closing the door softly behind him. In the kitchen, Hilda invited Ashe to take his lunch indoors in view of the weather, but he declined.

'Shed'll suit me, thanks. And I could do with some fresh air.'

'If you're sure.'

'Dog can keep me company.'

'Now there's a good idea.'

He took his lunch and his newspaper and carried them to the shed, with Boots trotting

330

beside him. Inside he unfolded one of the garden chairs and sat down, with the door open. The dog sat by his legs, hypnotised and salivating. He fed it a piece of bread.

Outside a mistle thrush hopped about, after the worms brought to the surface by the rain. Ashe could hear the faint sound of saucepans, the Mariners' lunch in preparation. He himself hummed with energy and purpose. He had privacy, and power.

He felt like a king.

MESOPOTAMIA

It takes thirteen days. And I was right, we do get to Basra by Christmas, but not before we've made two stops to offload the corpses. It would be all right if that made more space, but then we have to pick up more of the walking wounded who've fallen by the wayside, so the overcrowding just gets worse.

Once any of us gets the runs, he never gets rid of them. Runs or not, men who can drag their arses to the railing do their business over the side. The sides of the boat are festooned with the stuff, all of it encrusted with flies. One chap who sees the boat coming into Basra tells me afterwards that he thought there were ropes attached to it, some sort of special safety precaution. But no, it was just dried shit.

I recover pretty quickly once we've docked. We skinny working men have less to lose than big soft shiny officers, we're evolved to withstand privation. That said, Jarvis does pretty well, too; he's only in hospital for a few days. I say hospital but it's a requisitioned farm building on the outskirts of town, God knows what you might catch while you're convalescing in that place.

And now we're waiting again. Funny how Basra feels like home, scarcely foreign any more after what we've been through. Oh, those old crooks with their smelly food-stalls . . . those same old toast-rack donkeys falling down dead in the street . . . those Buddhoos fooling around, firing into the air at night . . . Home sweet home!

I get back into the old routine, foraging for a bit of decent food, cleaning up Jarvis's kit, mending, polishing, being a proper treasure. Discretion is my middle name, for the time being.

There's no getting away from it, though, we're back to square one. The fun and fleshpots of Baghdad seem further away than ever.

*   *   *

Word soon starts coming down—old Townshend's holed up in Kut with what was left after Ctesiphon, the Turks are tightening the noose on him, and a relief force has to be got up there as soon as possible. How, seems to be the trouble. When I'm foraging down at the docks I keep my eyes and ears open. It doesn't take a genius to see that we don't exactly have a fleet of gunboats ready for the off. What's out there is a collection of scruffy barges, a fair number of the local *mahelas*—pirate-boats we call them and some tugs. Oh, and a handful of paddle steamers, the sort of thing (scrubbed up a bit) you'd take a nice little tootle up the Thames on, back in England. But this isn't Old Father Thames, it's the stinking whore Euphrates, with more hazards on the water and off it than you can shake a stick at. Those of us who were on the hospital ships know, not that our opinion will be asked. What are we going to do? Try and sail up and be shot like fish in a barrel the moment we stick on a sandbank, or march for sodding miles in and out of all those fucking ditches, getting further and further away from the supply wagons? What use are we going to be to old Townshend once we get there? If it was me in charge I'd let him stew. Make or break.

*   *   *

Jarvis is his old self again. Probably thinks I've forgotten our little incident in the heat of battle. We resume normal relations. He had a couple of letters waiting for him when we got back—his mother and the sweetheart—and that's perked him up no end. He's sorry for me, never getting any.

'Who's waiting for you at home, Ashe?' he asks. 'Who do you look forward to seeing again?'

'No one, sir. Both times.'

'Come on, I bet ten pounds that's not true.'

For two pins I'd take that bet, but what would be the point? 'It is, sir.'

'I'm sorry to hear that.' He looks it, too.

'No need, sir,' I say. I'm buffing his tunic buttons, sliding them on to the board and going at them like the devil; my hand's a blur.

'Stop that for a moment,' he says. I stop. He smiles, shakes his head. 'I never knew anyone so busy.'

I say nothing; I'm waiting.

'Now I come to think of it,' he says, 'I don't believe I've ever heard you mention your family—not once in all the time we've been out here.'

'There you are then, sir.'

He narrows his eyes, trying to work me out, poor sod. 'You don't give much away, do you Ashe?'

'Sir.'

'I suppose you did have a mother? You didn't just spring from the ground like the warriors from the dragon's teeth?'

He likes his little classical reference. He may not

334

mean it, but it's a way of pulling rank. I begin polishing again. I spit on the buttons first.

'Hm?' He tilts his head.

'Yes, sir.'

'Very well, I can take a hint. I beg your pardon Ashe, it's rude of me to interrogate you like this.'

'Sir.'

'I'll leave you to it.' Looking down, he shakes his head again. The man who knows about Cadmus, looking at the man who cleans the buttons. 'You're a man of many talents, Ashe.'

Fuck off.

*   *   *

My greatest talent is one he doesn't even know about: hate.

I'm a genius at hating; a natural. But practice makes perfect. I once heard some pompous prick at the newspaper say about a murder we were reporting: 'Of course love and hate are so close, they're almost the same thing.'

What?

If he thought that, then he's never felt either of them. I can't speak for love, never having tried it, or wanted to; but I've observed other people who claim to be at it and it's a stupid, muddy, muddled condition. People in love are confused, not themselves, and (here's the incredible thing) proud of it!

Hate is *pure*. Crystal clear. Perfect. We haters know exactly who we are and what we're up to. And to hide hate, to keep it close and not let on—that's power.

Oddly enough I don't hate Jarvis. You might

think I would, especially with our little shared secret, but I don't. I'm reserving judgement. I don't bestow my hate on just anyone, they have to earn it. The person I hate most perfectly is my mother. She may have meant to hurt me, but when she did that she didn't realise she was doing a disservice to the whole female sex.

Most people I don't care about either way. There may be blokes out there who think of me as a sort of friend, but they're wrong. I don't care whether they live or die.

So no, I don't hate Jarvis. Not yet.

CHAPTER THIRTEEN

His room at the vicarage was pretty cell-like to begin with, and Ashe kept it that way. It was how he liked things: plain, empty, austere. Apart from the bedclothes (always immaculately neat), and his shaving tackle on the washstand you wouldn't have known there was anyone living in it. It had once been the maid's room, and at first this disgusted him. It hadn't been that long ago, either; the previous incumbent would certainly have had someone living in. Bile had come into Ashe's mouth at the thought of some young woman in here, picking, scratching, washing, brushing her hair, taking off her clothes—particularly her underclothes with that distinctive reek that women's things had. The place must have held traces of her: flakes of skin, hairs, nails, bodily secretions . . . It made Ashe's gorge rise. Unbeknown to anyone, even Hilda, he had scrubbed the room from top to bottom with carbolic. There was nothing he could do about the sheets, but he trusted Hilda to be punctilious about boiling.

He was here, under their roof, but they would scarcely know it. His presence would be if anything even less intrusive than before. They would scarcely notice him. The closer he got, the less visible he would be.

It had all happened so easily and swiftly in the end, confirming Ashe in his belief that most events in life were as inevitable as walking. They had a natural rhythm, a preordained movement from balance, through imbalance, and back to balance. Very little was needed except intention, expectation and belief. If you grew and nourished an idea it would soon enough seed out in other people's heads and left well alone it would grow and come to fruition.

He had succeeded in making Hilda his unwitting ally and accomplice. Hilda, who had never wanted to live in at the vicarage, had nonetheless espoused his cause. Of course she did not know the precise nature of that cause or she might not have done what she did.

She might not have said to Mrs Mariner: 'He might as well be living here, the hours he works.' And might not have then pointed out that the maid's room at the top of the old back stairs was standing empty. Or that Ashe could be a great help to her, too, doing the heavier stuff around the house, the grates, carrying groceries and so on. She might not have confided to Mrs Mariner that there were very few persons of her acquaintance, let alone male persons, of whom she would have said this, but John Ashe was someone you could trust with your last farthing.

Which Mrs Mariner knew, of course. She'd said it herself: 'I trust you.'

The vicar had not proved the stumbling block he had expected; that was interesting. If Ashe had been asked to predict a difficulty it would have been in that quarter. But it appeared that he had acceded to the plan the moment it was put to him by his wife. For Ashe was sure that this was the chain of events, though it might have been significant that Mariner, alone, had put the suggestion formally. He had come out to Ashe in the garden and the two of them had stood beneath the trees, in the area Ashe was landscaping.

'This is a large house, almost too large for the two us,' said Mariner. 'It's built for a family with at least one domestic—um—member of staff.'

Ashe waited.

Mariner went on: 'Hilda has never wanted to leave her house—she's a widow and it's her home, with associations for her of her late husband and so on—but I understand that your digs in the village aren't especially comfortable.'

'They're adequate.'

'Perhaps, perhaps, who can say,' was Mariner's rather odd comment. It was clear he was deeply uncomfortable with the whole exchange, but was heading one way and didn't wish to be deflected. 'At any rate I want to suggest—wonder if you'd consider—living at the vicarage while you're working for us.'

Ashe waited again. Considering, as he'd been asked to do. Allowing Mariner the time to be a little more pressing. Which he duly did.

'There would be advantages to both sides,' he said, as if describing some arcane sporting competition. 'You would have no rent to pay, and we should benefit from having you *in situ*, so to speak. You could keep an eye on things, deal with any little problems in the house and garden as they occur. And the church, too of course, let's not forget that.'

Ashe asked the polite question to which he already knew the answer: 'Are you sure Hilda wouldn't mind?'

'No, no, it was she . . . no, I'm quite sure not. My wife, who knows her best, says that she would be all for the idea.'

'Then yes.'

Mariner's pointed elf-like eyebrows flew up as if the startled by the speed of the agreement. 'Good!'

'That's all in, is it?'

'Naturally. With a few extra hours here and there.'

'I understand that.'

'So it's settled then.' Mariner patted his pockets in a nervous gesture as if checking their contents.

'When would you like me to come?'

'What about the weekend?'

'Saturday.'

'Saturday it is.'

*   *   *

It was now early August and Ashe had been living at the vicarage for just over two weeks. The days were beginning almost imperceptibly to shorten. He'd woken before five as usual this morning and it was barely light, though that might have been due to overcast skies.

He slept with the curtains open in order to wake with the dawn. Very often he rose at once, got dressed and went out to work in the garden or the churchyard. Even if he didn't get up, but simply lay in bed for a while as he did now, watching the sky change, he savoured the sensation of being the only one awake in the house—perhaps in the village. Alert and clear-headed, alone with his thoughts, he stole a march on the others.

August was a bad month, he'd always thought so. Ashe was no countryman, but he instinctively disliked this long, stale plateau of late summer,

340

when there was nothing doing. The spurt of growth and greenness was over; the crops had recovered from the beating they'd taken in July and the first of the harvesters were out in the fields; casual village labour, including women and children, had been mobilised to bind the stocks and stone-pick. Nature was in an exhausted stasis, waiting to die.

He was restless. For now, the swallows, his timekeepers, were still around, flitting in and out of their nest just above his window, accompanying their young on maiden flights. The small sounds of their comings and goings reminded him of his promise to himself. Not much time left. By the end of September he should be on his way, ready or not.

This thought galvanised him into action. He got out of bed—naked, as always—poured water out of the jug on his washstand and sloshed it over his face and neck, then scrubbed the rest of his body with his flannel. Cool, his skin tingling, he stood by the window and stretched. The angle of the gable containing the Mariners' bedroom window was upward and to his left, not visible but close enough that if he wanted to he could have leaned out and touched the brickwork. He wondered what they were doing in there. Sound asleep, or stirring, starting to touch each other . . . Or maybe they'd stopped all that.

Looking down at himself Ashe noticed, with dispassionate interest, that the body had a mind of its own.

*   *   *

Vivien had trouble sleeping. Usually it was Saxon

341

who went through phases of having restless nights, rising after midnight to go to the study, or moving to the camp bed in his dressing room for a change of scene. Her own sleep had always been deep and untroubled.

She didn't as a result feel tired, rather the opposite. Her disturbed nights were due to an excess of energy, that would not allow her to relax. Darkness only made it worse, as if switching off the light turned on a different one in her head. When she did sleep, she dreamed—such dreams! She would wake up with a start, damp with sweat and arousal, shocked and exhilarated. Next to her Saxon would be sleeping peacefully, and she never woke him. He was contented at the moment, writing, engaged in his little charitable project with Susan Clay. If she had woken him, what would she have said that wouldn't have spoiled that contentment? Her dreams were not, after all, about him.

If she'd hoped to see more of Ashe when he moved in, she was disappointed. His arrival was quiet, his presence unobtrusive. He worked all day long, quiet and self-contained. There were doors on both sides of the back stairs, and the room he occupied lay beyond both of them, so there was no need for him and the Mariners to see each other at all as they went to and fro outside his working hours. But Vivien was never less than acutely conscious of his presence, which was like a continuous background note, so high and fine that it could only be felt, not heard. That note told her where he was at any given moment, the movement of the air he displaced.

As often as not these days she woke before

dawn, instantly clear-headed, eyes wide in the semi-darkness, and knew, with her recently acquired sixth sense that Ashe was awake, too. She had taken to leaving the curtains half-drawn so she could watch the slow lightening of the sky.

Tonight she had scarcely slept, and at four o'clock was unable to lie there any longer. She got out of bed, slipped her feet into her walking shoes, shrugged on her dressing gown and went out of the bedroom. She crept across the landing like a guilty child and then ran down the stairs, her hand on the banister taking her weight so that she seemed to fly, her feet scarcely touching the treads. Not wanting to disturb the dog, who would in turn disturb Saxon, she unlocked the front door and went out that way.

Once outside, away from the heavily enclosed spaces of the house, it was much less dark. A soft, still greyness lay over everything; here and there floated pockets of low mist. The house behind her seemed like a tall ship becalmed; she half expected to hear its joists creak in the silence. She walked carefully on the gravel and then down the narrow way between the garage and the house, with one simple objective: to stand on the lawn, unknown to Ashe, and stare boldly up at his window as he slept: to take advantage of him; in effect, to spy.

When she reached the back of the house she did not at first look up. Savouring the anticipation she walked at an angle across the grass until she reached the point from which she calculated she would have a clear view of his room. A heavy dew soaked the hem of her dressing gown. She shivered, from excitement as well as the damp.

When she looked up, he was there. In a reversal

343

of the very first time they'd seen one another he was standing at his uncurtained window, looking back at her: indistinct but unmistakable, a thin, white figure in the half light: his black hair, his face that was always half in shadow.

Slowly, head down, like an animal loath to break cover, she crept away. When she reached the side of the house she almost collapsed against the wall, panting as though she'd been running for her life.

*   *   *

Later that morning Susan was on her way to the vicarage. The village at this time of year had a strange, rather febrile atmosphere, its rhythms disrupted by the harvest. And with fewer men these days, people who would normally have been at home were out in the fields. Noises—of shouting, farm machinery, horses, barking dogs—came from unusual quarters. Women were out and about at midday taking the men's bait up to where they were working.

But if the centre of village gravity had shifted, Susan's had not: it remained the vicarage. The house represented her magnetic north, its pull greater than ever now that not only the dog but Ashe too was there. And she had her little jobs in the church, about which she was meticulous: Mr Mariner had said how pleased he was with the way she did them.

Her mother, always alert to the possibility of her being a nuisance, had been doubtful at first, but had gradually grown accustomed to the idea and now thoroughly approved of it. Unknown to Susan, Ted Clay had even gone so far as to mention what

344

Edith would never have permitted herself to think.

'What's the likelihood of our Susan earning a bit?'

'Ted! She couldn't!'

'I don't see why not if she's up there regular and doing a proper job.'

'She's in the church!'

'That Ashe, he's keeping the churchyard tidy, I bet he's not working for free.'

'That's different.'

'Maybe.' Ted looked sceptical. 'He's got his knees under the table at the vicarage.'

'He found their dog,' said Edith. 'They were grateful. Anyway, that's nothing to do with us, and we're not asking for money for what our Susan does. It's good of them to let her help out.'

'Good be blowed,' muttered Ted. 'Cheap labour if you ask me.' And that was where it had rested.

But Susan knew nothing of this, and was blissfully content with her routine, these days one largely of her own devising. Mr Mariner had asked her if she might be able to dust and polish once a week, and help clear up after the flower-arrangers every two weeks. But she derived so much pleasure from what she did that she went there most mornings. Mr Mariner said the church had never looked so nice. She dusted all the hymn and prayer books and hung the hassocks neatly on their hooks. Any creatures she found she carefully caught and took outside. She filled the watering can at the tap and topped up the vases, never spilling a drop.

When she'd done in the church she'd go and tell Mr Mariner. He was worried that she was working too hard, but he said it in a pleased way. One day when she tapped on his study door—a thing which would have been unthinkable a few weeks ago—he took some treacle toffees from the drawer in his desk and gave her one, which she had put in her pocket for later.

Her next port of call was the kitchen where Hilda would greet her with a severe expression and a mug of sweet milky tea or lemonade—always Hilda's choice, not Susan's, but which she accepted gratefully. Then she would find Mrs Mariner and ask to take Boots for a walk. If the answer was yes, there was a prescribed route: down the road into the village, through to the river bank for a short distance, into the village again and back up the road. A circuit around the churchyard was also permitted, especially if Ashe was there. These days the dog behaved well, and walked to heel, but he was never to be let off the lead.

However, there was no fixed time for her arrival and she often dawdled on the way. Excitable sounds came from the field opposite the vicarage which was being harvested. The gate stood wide open and she went and stood with her hand on the post, watching.

When she saw what they were doing she didn't really want to stay, but something kept her there and she found she couldn't move. Most of the field had been cleared, and the stooks collected into sheaves, some tidier than others—the village missed its quick, strong, dexterous young men. The remaining area of wheat looked like an island in the sea of jagged stubble. The boys with their sticks, and even one or two of the wilder girls, stood in a big circle around the island. They'd been stone-picking: the fruits of their labours were dotted around in neat piles, like ammunition, and some of the bigger boys had armed themselves with these as well.

The four farmhands—three young lads and Hubie Dawes, a big middle-aged man who had something in common with Susan—had put their scythes to one side against the shadiest hedge. Hubie had sat down alongside the scythes, and the lads, also now carrying sticks, were walking back to the centre of the field, to the island. The calling and chi-iking that had drawn Susan to the gateway faded away. It was so quiet she could hear the crickets in the grass at her feet, and the whining buzz of a worker bee hovering over the hedge.

The farmhands fanned out round the island of standing wheat. The boy nearest Susan had realised she was there and sent her a wolfish grin and a wink, tapping his homemade cudgel in the opposite palm.

'Ready?'

She shook her head. Not that he was interested. He made a swiping movement with the cudgel; it swished through the air.

'Better stand aside!'

The farm lads stooped forward and held out their arms like cockerels about to fight. Then they began to move forward, slowly, legs apart, towards the standing wheat, tapping the ground with their sticks as they went. With each step they let out a 'Ha!', which started low and got louder, and was picked up by the others until the air shook with 'HA! HA! HA! HA!' and Susan had to put her hands over her ears. The angry noise made her eyes water, but she was too frightened to turn her back on this dreadful war dance in case something should come after *her.*

The lads were in the edge of the wheat now, but not bothering about trampling it underfoot, or banging it down with the sticks . . . Then, suddenly, a shout went up.

'AWAY-AY-AY-AY!'

And the first rabbit shot out of the wheat, ears up at first, startled, looking for an escape, which way to go. It streaked towards the gate, a big boy thrashed at it with his stick, just catching its back leg, slowing it down, the next boy threw himself on top of it with a bloodcurdling yell, and the first one joined him. Now there were dozens of rabbits, bursting out of the dwindling cover of the wheat, so many that some of them ran straight into the legs of the beaters and were snatched up and their necks wrung before they made the open ground. Some of the boys were good marksmen; Susan saw two of the rabbits leap and twist in the air as stones caught them fair and square. Others weren't so accurate, and the rabbits lay squirming and palpitating on the ground until the smaller boys, or the giggling, flailing girls, shrieking like banshees, finished them off. The frantic death-screams of the rabbits, thin and high, were plainly audible above the clamour. Tears poured down Susan's face; her whole body heaved with sobs she felt but couldn't hear. It was horrible, horrible!

At least it was quick. In a very few minutes the fun was all over and the murderous yelling replaced by a busy, cheerful chatter as the killers collected their haul. The sticks had another use now: the boys took string from their pockets, tied the back legs of the rabbits together and then lashed them to the stick. Some had as many as three corpses flopping around, their little grey-white scuts like pussy willow, their pretty ears pricked by gravity, like the leaves of lords-and-ladies.

The boy who had winked at Susan was an expert. He had two rabbits on his stick already, and was picking up another. He came over, the body swinging by its ears from his hand.

'Hey, Susan Clay, what you crying for?'

She shook her head, just as she had to his first question, but they all knew her and didn't mind her ways. Besides, he was a good-hearted boy.

'Don't cry,' he said. 'Here.' He held out the rabbit. 'You can have this one.'

She looked askance, flinchingly, at the rabbit, which was quite small, a young one, and had been alive so recently that its eyes had not yet clouded over and were still bright with alarm. There was a funny taste in her mouth, and she covered the lower part of her face with both hands, shaking her head dumbly for a third time.

The boy gave the rabbit an enticing flourish. 'Go on, Susan. Your mother'd like him. Nice stew for supper, eh?'

This was too much for Susan, the contents of whose stomach threatened to lurch up into her throat. The fear of being sick in public, in front of this boy and all the others, was almost as great as her revulsion at the sight of the baby rabbit. If she hadn't been struggling so fiercely to hold down her breakfast she might have seen the boy's expression change as he backed away. As it was she spun round, hands still clamped over her mouth, and bumped into Mr Mariner who was standing right behind her.

Then several things happened at once, all of

them unpleasant for both parties.

*   *   *

Saxon had been finding it hard to concentrate on the parish finances. They constituted an area where his imprimatur was required but which he took largely on trust from the estimable parish treasurer. Still, it was important to go through the accounts, and to have understood whatever implications they had for the coming months. Today he was finding this task even heavier going than usual. Vivien had begun having wakeful nights and last night had been particularly unsettled. To avoid discussion, he'd feigned sleep a good deal of the time, not dropping off properly until some time after three. Consequently he'd overslept, and woke to find that Vivien had breakfasted early and gone out, he didn't know where.

As a result of all this Saxon felt distinctly jaded. So at first it was only dully that he noted the goings-on in the wheat field. He knew of course that these things happened; this particular activity was one of the harsh, heartless rural activities that made a nonsense of the lyrical Wordsworthian view of the countryside. This showed nature red in tooth and nail, displaying the human animal (in Saxon's view) at its least prepossessing. But the same small, unedifying drama would be acted out in almost every field in the neighbourhood over the next couple of weeks and it was not his business to stop it even if it had been in his power to do so.

It was Susan's arrival that arrested and

disturbed him. Since she had been helping at the church he had got to know her for the simple, gentle soul she was; as one of nature's Christians. She might be a country girl, born and bred in Eadenford, but she was a friend to all living things. He had seen himself the infinite care with which she carried butterflies, birds, spiders, even bats, out of the church, and the tenderness with which she placed them on the grass outside, or released them into the fresh air. Now he literally shuddered to think of what she was about to witness even if, as in all probability, it wasn't for the first time.

Once the anxiety about her had taken hold, he couldn't shake it off. When the shouting and thumping began—for all the world like some bloodthirsty pagan rite—he tried to turn a deaf ear to it. But as the noise reached a peak, he got up to close the window and caught a glimpse of Susan, her hands to her face, looking wretched. This picture stayed in his mind as the tribal chanting gave way to the shrieks and yells of random slaughter. Saxon could stand it no more. Impatience and bottled-up irritation overcame him and he marched out of the office, and the house, and down the driveway. The mayhem was beginning to die down, but as he crossed the road he could see Susan in an attitude of despair, the boy advancing with his wretched haul, another limp corpse dangling from his outstretched hand . . . Saxon accelerated his pace and as he caught the boy's eye assumed his most withering expression of disapproval.

The boy retreated. Susan Clay turned round blindly and stumbled. To prevent her from falling Saxon had no alternative but to put his arms round her. As he did so, she made a choking sound, which was accompanied by a horribly familiar rank smell and a warm, wet sensation penetrating his waistcoat.

Saxon only kept his own stomach in check by assuring himself that this was a true test of Christian charity. He had come over here to make sure Susan was all right, to rescue her in effect, and this extra travail of hers made the rescue all the more important. Keeping one arm firmly round her for both their sakes, he steered her back over the road and towards the kitchen door.

* * *

Hilda's concern had been all for her employer and the appalling *lèse-majesté* to which he'd been subjected. She had taken charge at once, sitting Susan down with a glass of water, a problem to be dealt with in a moment, when she had helped the reverend remove his waistcoat and given him a damp cloth to remove the worst excesses from the rest of his clothes, and his shoes. She then sent him upstairs with strictures as to where and how to leave his dirty things.

When he'd gone she turned her attention to Susan, surveying her with hands on hips.

'Well, missy, and what are we going to do with you?'

Susan, still green at the gills, looked wanly over her glass. 'I'm sorry.'

'I should think you are!'

'Can I go home?'

'I think you'd better had!' Hilda sounded a good deal more spirited than she felt. She rather balked at the prospect of accompanying Susan down the High Street in her current state, but she could scarcely send her off on her own, for the same reason. Her face crimped with distaste, she rinsed out the cloth and dabbed with sharp pecking movements at Susan's dress. It wasn't as bad as the reverend's waistcoat, anyway . . . Hilda sucked her teeth. Edith Clay was going to be mortified—mortified!

'Anything I can do?'

Ashe had appeared at the back door, come out of nowhere as he was wont to do, and just at the right moment.

'It's Susan here, she's not well.'

'I can see that.' Ashe came in. He addressed Susan: 'Saw you coming over with the vicar. Poor old rabbits, eh?'

Tears oozed down Susan's cheeks.

Hilda tutted again and raised her eyes heavenward for Ashe's benefit.

'I don't know where Mrs Mariner's got to this morning—'

'Taken the dog out,' said Ashe, and then to Susan: 'Why don't I walk you home?'

At once, rather unsteadily, she got up.

'Looks like you've got yourself a job,' said Hilda. 'I'm afraid her mother's not going to be too pleased.'

Ashe winked his good eye at Susan. 'We'll see to her, won't we?'

Susan nodded. Ashe took her elbow—extremely gentlemanlike—and steered her out of the door.

'Back in a bit.'

Baffled, Hilda watched them go. She washed her hands for a full two minutes and returned to her pastry with a sense of relief. That was quite enough surprises for one day.

* * *

It was almost lunchtime when Vivien returned, and the scent of apple pie was wafting through the house. She let the dog off his lead in the hall and he galloped away to the kitchen in anticipation of scraps, his paws skidding waywardly on the polished floor. The study door was ajar but when she looked in she found the room empty; the drawing room also. There was no sound from the floor above. She went to the top of the stairs and called down to the kitchen:

'Hilda! Have you seen the vicar?'

'He's in the garden, ma'am . . .' Hilda came to the foot of the stairs, wiping her hands on her apron. 'There was a bit of an accident with young Susan.'

'Accident?'

'Nothing to worry about.'

'But what sort of accident?'

Hilda lowered her voice, brows drawn together to indicate the extreme delicacy of the subject. 'She was taken very poorly. Poor Mr Mariner—he was in a mess.'

'You don't surely mean that she was sick?'

'Yes, ma'am.'

'But what had that got to do with Mr Mariner?'

'I've no idea.' Unwilling to elaborate, Hilda waved her hands in the air, as if it was all beyond her. 'Anyway, Mr Ashe took her home and the vicar's sitting outdoors.'

Vivien was baffled. 'I'll go and see.'

She did not, as would have been logical, go down the stairs and out into the garden that way, which was the shortest route, but retraced her steps via the front door. This was to allow herself time to prepare a suitably sympathetic manner for Saxon, and to stifle the disappointment into which she'd been plunged on learning that Ashe was not in the house. She could almost taste the sourness in her own mouth. It was terrible to realise, and to acknowledge, that she was jealous of poor, fat, simple—and now sick!—Susan Clay.

*   *   *

Edith Clay's embarrassment made her brusque.

'I see. Well, better go and get out of that dress, girl. Thanks for bringing her back.'

She would have closed the door but Ashe remained standing on the step.

'It wasn't her fault,' he said. 'They were flushing out the rabbits in that field by the vicarage. It turned her stomach.'

'That's nothing new.' Edith's hand was still on the door handle. 'She shouldn't have been hanging about there.'

'It's all right, Mr Mariner was with her.'

Now he had her undivided attention. 'The vicar? What was he doing there?'

Ashe shrugged; his turn now to look as if the conversation was over. 'They're friends.'

'Friends?'

'He likes your Susan.'

'I dare say.' Edith's eyes flicked over Ashe's face, trying to gauge the weight of what was being said. 'She's a willing, well-brought-up girl and she works hard, but that doesn't make them friends.'

'You're right,' agreed Ashe. 'She's willing.'

There followed a short pause.

'Right then.' This time Edith was firm. 'Thanks anyway.'

They parted company. Edith closed the door. Her expression as she did so, and that of Ashe, walking up the High Street, could not have been more different.

There were some things that you did for no other reason than the simple, perfect one: that you could.

*   *   *

'How on earth did it happen?' asked Vivien.

'Does it matter?'

'No, but I'm interested.'

He sighed and rubbed his face wearily. 'They were killing rabbits in the field. I saw she was watching. It didn't seem like a good idea, so I went over to tell her to come away, before she became upset. Unfortunately, I was too late. With the results that you now know about.'

Vivien looked at him doubtfully. 'It was very kind of you, Saxon.'

'Not really. The poor child wouldn't be coming here if it wasn't for me. And the Clays are an extremely nice and respectable family who deserve help.'

'You used to find her rather a nuisance.'

'Did I? She's not a nuisance now, quite the opposite. In fact I'd go so far as to say I've grown genuinely fond of her.' He looked down at himself with a dark little smile. 'What's a waistcoat

356

between friends?'

Vivien could tell that he intended these as the last words on the matter, and it was nearly one o'clock so she let it lie. Besides, her mind was elsewhere.

Where was Ashe?

*   *   *

After lunch, unable to settle to anything, she set off round the village on her bicycle. Her pretext was making calls, but in reality she wanted only to get out of the house. As she pedalled out of the driveway she encountered the parish treasurer coming the other way, his files beneath his arm. She gave him a cheery wave but didn't stop. Poor Saxon, he hated money matters . . . And yet his servitude lent extra savour to her freedom, and sped her wheels down the High Street.

She rode as far as the school, for no other reason than that it was a good distance from home. Once there she got off the bicycle, opened the gate, closed it after her, and strode purposefully across the schoolyard. Anyone noticing her would say they'd seen Mrs Mariner dropping in at the school in her own time, and attribute to her any of a wide range of exemplary motives.

Behind the gabled, grey-brick schoolhouse was a small garden where the children, under direction and supervision, grew simple flowers and vegetables. In theory these were supposed to be watered during the summer holidays, with a rota for the purpose, but in reality only the hardiest plants survived.

Vivien fished cigarettes and matches from her

357

skirt pocket, and lit one.

But it was not the smoking of the cigarette that brought her here this afternoon; however much Saxon disliked the habit he would not have dreamed of forbidding it. She simply wished to be alone with her thoughts, which these days were strange, wild things that it was quite alarming to let loose. A short time ago, no more than a few months, there had been a pattern to her life, a rhythm to the present and a shape to the future. She shared the pattern with her husband. She and Saxon, whatever their differences (the differences that fuelled and fanned their intimate moments), had forged a durable partnership. They'd taken a certain unspoken pride in this, and in each other: they moved forward together. To Vivien, that picture of her marriage had become a strange one—a curiosity, like an old photograph lit by the baleful glare of hindsight. She barely recognised it, or herself. Every minute of every day she was taut with the anticipation of some momentous external change that would mirror the one inside her.

No, thought Vivien, Ashe had done nothing to advance himself. He had simply cast a spell, and they had done it all themselves.

She finished her cigarette, stubbed it out in the soil at the edge of the vegetable border, pinched the end and put it in her pocket. The waistband of her skirt sagged. She was burning up.

*   *   *

On the way home she had to pass the Clays' cottage and it seemed the very least she could do, as   well   as   providing   some   retrospective justification for her outing, to stop and enquire about Susan.

Edith said her daughter was quite recovered, thank you.

'Perhaps we'll see her tomorrow, then?'

'I shouldn't be surprised.'

Vivien detected something prickly in the other woman's manner. 'I do hope so. Mr Mariner would miss her these days.'

'I dare say.'

'He thinks the world of her.'

'Does he.'

This was not a question but Vivien chose to treat it as one. 'Yes—you might not think it but they get on like a house on fire.'

'I'm glad to hear it.' Edith's face gave nothing away.

Seeing that she was obviously not going to be invited in, Vivien said goodbye and left. Even in her present, distracted frame of mind she thought it odd that no mention or apology had been made concerning the morning's 'accident'.

*   *   *

Ashe called in at the Waggoner's two or three times a week. He was a moderate drinker and no great talker; his reasons for being there had less to do with the Hogg's ale than with being seen as a regular, which conferred a certain modest status. He always sat at the left-hand end of the bar so it was the good side of his face that was on show. Matters were discussed, in the cryptic, codified manner of the village, in front of him, even if without his direct involvement. If he wished to contribute anything he could, but this was rarely the case. His habitual silence lent a certain weight to whatever he might choose to say. The other patrons knew John Ashe didn't speak lightly, so they paid attention.

This evening, talk was of the harvest. The weather looked set to hold for another week or so, but with manpower reduced the work was slow. Ted Clay had already said he could spare his lad for a few days if need be.

'But not your Susan, eh?' joshed one of the others.

Clay looked embarrassed. 'She shouldn't've been there.'

'Right opposite the vicarage though, weren't it?' said someone else. 'She couldn't hardly not see.'

'Poor old vicar!' There followed a good deal of unmalicious merriment at Clay's expense, and his face reddened.

'Give over . . . Anyway he owes us, he gets a lot of work out of our girl, and for no pay, neither.'

'He paid good and proper this time!' It was no good, they liked nothing better than a spot of genial bear-baiting and Ted Clay—who along with his missus was apt to be a bit self-righteous—was the perfect subject.

Ashe waited till the laughter had died down, then said:

'He gets a lot else out of her, too.'

He spoke just loud enough to be heard, but not quite loud enough for them to be certain *what* they'd heard. They looked his way, their faces still wearing the tail-end of their laughter. Except for Clay's, which was red and angry-looking.

Someone asked, 'What's that, Ashe?'

360

He sipped his beer slowly, comfortably, as if it had been nothing, the most casual comment.

'What did you say?' This time it was Clay.

He wasn't going to repeat it. 'About the vicar—he likes your Susan.'

'She's a worker, if that's what you mean.'

'She is . . .' Ashe took another sip. 'And she's not a girl any more, either.' At once, before Clay could pick him up on this, he went on: 'You're right, she's a young woman doing a day's work.'

In the past few minutes the atmosphere had shifted from warm jocularity to the chilly beginnings of unease. Now it shifted back slightly towards more comfortable territory. To signal he had nothing else to say, Ashe pushed his glass forward.

'I'll have the other half if I may.'

The conversation became, without him, general once again. Ten minutes later he got up to leave. One or two of the patrons wished him good night. Ted Clay met him by the door.

'John Ashe—can I have a word?'

He stopped. Waited.

'You work up at the vicarage. Live up there these days. You know what goes on.'

'I mind my own business.'

'Our Susan—she's all right up there?'

Ashe shrugged. 'More than welcome, I'd say.'

Clay's eyes narrowed. 'Only—you saying she's a woman. She's not, is she? Not up here.' He tapped his temple. 'She knows nothing.'

'You have to be careful,' allowed Ashe.

'We are, always have been.'

Ashe waited. The other man's mood, a combustible mixture of suspicion, anxiety and

361

battened-down anger, swirled round them.

'As I say,' said Clay. 'You're up there, you'll keep an eye on her.'

It was in his voice, that he wasn't accustomed to ask favours and could scarcely bear to do so now.

'I'll do my best,' said Ashe. 'Good night.'

Calmly, he stepped outside. The days were beginning to draw in; it was very nearly dark.

Not much time to go.

MESOPOTAMIA

Jarvis wasn't in dock for long. The brave (and the not so brave) boys of the Relief Force are on the move. Rumours about Kut have been flying—how they've only got rations for another five days (that was three weeks ago, but never mind), how rats for the pot are changing hands at inflated prices, how they're making tea out of stable straw, and blokes are shooting themselves in the leg at the rate of a dozen a day—though why they should do that when they're stuck there anyway is a bit of a mystery. It's in our interests to keep the stories going; makes us realise that a) there are worse places than Basra and b) we're going to be the heroes of the hour, the saviours of Kut. In fact Kut takes on a sort of mythical significance, almost like Baghdad, except even we can't fool ourselves.

Reinforcements have been arriving thick and fast and completely unprepared, the poor bastards, from India, from Egypt, from France, straight from England, God help us. As per usual it's taken them bloody nearly as long to disembark in Basra as it has to get there in the first place. As soon as they're on dry land they're off, with no idea what they're up against, and I'm not talking about the Turks.

The brass have decreed that all the troops move up overland, so they can use the river boats for supplies and ammunition. As few animals as possible because of lack of forage. Just a few officers' horses and so on. A couple of aeroplanes are buzzing back and forth doing recces and making maps, so we're told. Maps? Of what? If you see anything resembling a natural feature round here it's a topic of conversation all day. We're marching with a company of Norsets—Norfolks and Dorsets, fresh out of basic training on the Wiltshire downs. It's tricky deciding how much to tell them: nothing at all and let them find out the hard way, or the full SP and risk them getting shot for desertion first time out.

*   *   *

Our company arrives when it's all over bar the shouting at Sheikh Sa'ad. It's like Ctesiphon all over again.

The Indians take it particularly hard; they seem to feel betrayed. The very least they expected was decent British organisation and here they are, wounded in the service of the Empire, lying in the mud and their own filth waiting for help to arrive. Hoping it does; wondering if it ever will.

I take myself for a little walk behind the lines, out of curiosity. It's a facer, I don't mind admitting. I'm shaken. There's hundreds of the Sikh troops lying back here and they don't know what hit them. A week or so ago they looked bloody marvellous, so tall and dignified, just their whiskers were enough to scare the living daylights out of you. I was glad they were on our side. Now they're behaving like—no other word for it—like beggars. Surely they can see I'm not worth bothering with, but there's men pawing me and catching at my legs, and wailing and whining, 'Water, Sahib! Sahib, blanket! Help me, Sahib, help me!' For the first time I feel angry. Angry with them for losing

364

their pride and even angrier with the generals who reduced them to this.

One of the Sikhs is just lying there on his side. He's got a nasty shoulder wound, but his eyes are open. His arms are out in front of him, wrists crossed, and his hands are beautiful, with smooth skin, long fingers and filbert nails; the palms are like that old, stained ivory you see on cigarette holders. He's absolutely still, which reminds me of how sick animals just close down and retreat inside themselves, waiting for the end.

Because he's the one not making a fuss I crouch down next to him for a moment. His lips move, I think he's praying.

'You'll be all right, squire,' I say. 'They'll get here soon.'

He rolls his eyes in my direction. They're almost black, with whites the colour of buttermilk.

'Why do we need it?' he whispers. 'This Satan-like land?'

Good question, and I've got no answer for him.

*   *   *

We're ten miles closer to Kut at a cost of four thousand men. And the weather's terrible. If we don't get there in the next few weeks we'll have drowned before they've eaten their last rat, if they haven't done so already. So, naturally, we hang about.

Some bright spark's written something called 'The Cynical Alphabet', that's doing the rounds. Just leafing through . . . Take 'W':

W stands for the wonder and pain

365

With which we regard our infirm and insane
Old aged generals who run this campaign
We are waging in Mesopotamia.

Give that man a medal.

It's a funny thing: that Sikh can ask the real question, and use a poetic turn of phrase while he's about it—'Satan-like' land, I like that. Whereas Tommy, simple soul that he is, trusts his superiors and grouses about the weather and the food. Safer, I suppose. Here it is, under 'R':

R are the rations 'by order' we get,
Though no one I know has sampled them yet -
And I don't think we will, so it's best to forget
That they're somewhere in Mesopotamia.

Jarvis thinks that verse is funny, but not the one about the generals. Not exactly on his high horse, sort of more in sorrow than in anger.

'Would you want their job, Ashe? All those difficult decisions, that terrible responsibility?'

'Probably not, sir.'

'Somebody has to make the decisions and carry the can,' he goes on as if I hadn't spoken, so this time, I don't.

He says: 'Let's not forget it's the politicians who put us here in the first place. The chiefs of staff are answerable to them. We're at the end of the line.'

'That's true, sir.'

Notice how he says 'Let's not'. *Us.* It's incredible how he's managed to put what happened right out of his mind, and talk to me as if we're chums, brothers-in-arms or something. It appears I overestimated Jarvis. I don't mind him being a

366

coward, nobody in their right mind wants to meet a sticky one. What gives me the creeps is him never mentioning it again, hoping if he doesn't that it'll all go away. And I don't mean thanks, fuck thanks! I mean shame. A bit of good old dishonest, slimy crawling and bartering. I couldn't have promised anything but who knows? It might have paid off.

As it is, the more he takes this all-water-under-the-bridge, least-said-soonest-mended attitude, the more carefully I tend my little nugget of unsavoury knowledge.

He's doing pretty well at the moment: keeping the men's spirits up, his speciality. We've had a couple of bashes at Kut, both pretty inconclusive, and the conditions are worsening by the day. It's bally freezing at night, rains like you wouldn't believe. The blokes from France say they feel quite at home, except there's no proper trenches and dugouts here. Just the odd *nullah* and drainage dyke and whatever foxholes we can scratch out in the mud. Though that's like building sandcastles as the tide comes in. One night the hospital tents just filled up with water, a couple of the Indian sepoys and myself had to rally round, baling out, shifting the wounded and collecting any old thing to use as ballast; dead men, even. You couldn't move the tents, there was nowhere to move them to. The Indian troops are a study. Those wounded men lying in the mud waiting for help to come were about as stoical as dishrags. But they're brave as lions going into battle. And the way the sepoys look after their officers is way beyond the call of duty. It makes my humble efforts look quite paltry. One chap was out in no man's land with one of his officers—a subaltern straight out of boarding school—for more than twelve hours, patching him up, protecting him, all this under fire. Eventually he manages to carry him on his own back to the hospital tent. What makes them do it? Not power, not fear . . . It must be devotion. Eerie, in my opinion. Lieutenant Morrish copped it at Sheikh Sa'ad and as far as I'm concerned it's one less to worry about.

We keep banging away at Kut like a ram at a wall, except we're nowhere near the walls yet. Every yard has to be fought for across open, featureless desert—correction, quagmire—giving the Turkish machine gunners plenty of time to get a bead on us, so the casualties are terrible.

Last night the rain was torrential. The river overflowed and the camp's under water. Every single trench and defile is full. When I come out at daybreak to try and make breakfast there's a bloke lying outside without a mark on him, his face in a puddle, stone dead. And he's just one of hundreds. Hardly a shot fired overnight but it hasn't been possible to do the usual tidying-up operation and these chaps have just died of exposure.

The rain slackens off while we have tea and porridge, but it's like eating in a churchyard after the gravediggers have been. I've forgotten what it feels like to be dry, let alone warm. Not long ago we were dying of heat. Now we're dying of cold. 'Satan-like land' is right.

It turns out our side's asked for a truce to collect the wounded and bury the dead. I've developed some respect for the Turks, but you wouldn't expect them to say 'Yes, carry on' just like that, even if there are as many of them as there are of us out there. They're going to think about it, make us

368

sweat for a while.

Our white flag goes up while we wait, and right away the Arabs are out there in no man's land doing what they do best—looting, stealing, finishing off anyone lucky enough to have survived the night. No way of telling if the bastards are enlisted men or just jackals, but it's too much for some of our men, who charge out there to see them off. Weaponless (the white flag's up and you have to play fair), so the inevitable happens—they get attacked and robbed, too. It's threatening to turn into a full-scale incident when a handful of Turkish generals comes out and calls off the Buddhoos.

The rest of the day we spend bringing in the bodies. To protect themselves the Buddhoos have used a different method of keeping their victims quiet: a handful of wet sand stuffed into the mouth, suffocating the poor buggers. It's not even quick, one chap is still gagging and struggling, but even though we get a lot of muck out of his mouth he's already swallowed too much, and he's shy half his stomach, so he's a goner.

On one of our trips back to the hospital area I see Jarvis, wandering up and down the lines, taking names and numbers of the casualties. Not a cheerful task but even allowing for that he's not looking good, white as a sheet and sweating.

'All right sir?'

'Not too jolly,' he tells me. 'Think I've got another dose of the tummy bug.'

'You want sugar for that. Sweet tea.'

He smiles but it's a bit ghostly. 'You sound like my mother.'

It strikes me as quite funny that I, of all people,

369

should sound like anyone's mother.

'I'll see what I can do,' I say, because that's what he likes to hear. I know what ails him and it's no tummy bug. He's in a funk. Absolutely fucking terrified. Today's goings-on between the lines have reminded him of lying there, waiting for the knife. Very unpleasant I know, because I was there too. That's why he's never going to mention it.

I'm worn out. The sun's dropping along with the temperature. There's the snap! snap! of rifle fire from the wadi. Business as usual.

I can still hear his teeth chattering.

CHAPTER FOURTEEN

Felicity Delamayne, casting a gimlet eye over the small crowd assembled in the Bridgford bookshop, felt compelled to ask after Vivien.

'She's not here.' Saxon appeared somewhat tense, which she supposed was only natural in the circumstances, but still . . .

'I must say I'm rather surprised.'

'She had things to do.'

'Well, if it comes to that—' Felicity bridled slightly—'so do we all, but this is an important event.'

'I don't know that I'd go that far.'

'We don't have so many distinguished poets around here that we can afford to neglect the one we do have. I'd have thought Vivien would have put everything else aside to attend!'

Saxon's eyelids snapped irritably. 'She reads all my work, you know. She doesn't need to come and sit in a bookshop to hear me read it out loud.'

'If you say so.'

'Now if you'll excuse me I need to collect my thoughts.'

'Of course, I mustn't keep you.'

There were not many occasions when Felicity regretted being outspoken, but this one of them. The vicar, poor fellow, was facing a nerve-racking public performance. She fervently hoped her ill-chosen remarks hadn't shaken his confidence; especially as they'd arisen not from censure, but anxiety. She had hoped to see Vivien here, perhaps invite her to Eaden Place again for another woman-to-woman chat. If, in her self-confessedly 'restless' state the girl was not here, then it followed that without the car (which Saxon had driven himself—it was parked outside) she was almost certainly at home; along with the man Ashe, who was *living* at the vicarage these days. This was incomprehensible to Felicity, who, though it was true she would have employed him herself like a shot, wouldn't have wanted him sleeping under the same roof. He wasn't exactly sly; slyness required a carefully constructed self-ingratiation. She could detect no such calculation in Ashe; in fact she could detect nothing at all. He was a mystery, and that of course *was* fascinating . . .

She strongly suspected it was no accident that he had become so chummy with the Mariners; he would have his reasons. She was caught between two equal impulses: one straightforwardly altruistic, to warn Saxon that he and his wife were in some kind of real but unspecified danger (a warning he would certainly brush aside, whatever his private feelings); the other more mischievous, to stand well back and watch to see what happened.

Of one thing Felicity had no doubt: something *would* happen. And her testy little outburst a few moments ago, by putting her in Saxon's bad books, would not have helped to prevent it.

The book-shop owner clapped his hands.

'Ladies and gentlemen, please take your seats . . . that's it . . . don't be frightened of the front row . . . Good . . . Now! This afternoon it's my very great privilege to introduce a distinguished writer whom we in Bridgford can claim as our own.'

Felicity raised her eyebrows—what about Eadenford?—as she sat down firmly at the front. One must fly the flag, and if Vivien wasn't going to, then *noblesse oblige* . . . She only hoped she would be able to understand a word of Saxon's poetry, which she and Sidney recognised as 'deep'. Crossing her legs with a swish she fixed her eyes brightly and intently on Saxon as he picked up his book, and let her mind drift back to her private speculations.

* * *

'Thank you for those kind words.'

Saxon opened *Beyond Self* and took out the sheet of paper he'd slipped inside the front cover. Running his forefinger down the handwritten lines, he tried to clear his mind of irritable and distracting thoughts concerning Lady Delamayne, who was sitting only a few feet away wearing an expression of steely fascination.

'I would like to begin,' he said, 'with a poem I wrote only the other day but which may, God willing, appear in my next collection.' There was a polite rustle of laughter, which he allowed to die away.

'It is entitled: "Caritas".'

* * *

Vivien felt guilty only until Saxon left the house. Fortunately he was preoccupied, and accepted her excuses without question. The instant the door closed behind him, she was caught up in an ecstasy of relief. He would be absent for four hours at least. Susan had gone; Hilda had been sent home. She was alone—or almost alone—in the house. The afternoon opened before her like the mouth of a cave.

She stood in the hall, absorbing the silence. She knew exactly where he was—out in the shed, cleaning tools. He was meticulous about such things.

She heard a click of paws, and looked down to find Boots sitting at her feet, his eyes fixed expectantly on her face, his tail swishing back and forth on the floor. Hilda must have closed the back door on her way out, or he would certainly have been in the garden with Ashe.

'Come!'

She set off in the direction of the kitchen and the dog leapt up and quickly overtook her, pattering down the stairs and jumping up excitedly at the handle of the door.

'No,' she said. 'Good dog—basket.'

He sat down with his head cocked one way, then the other, as if unable to believe his ears. Vivien pointed in the direction of the scullery.

'Boots—basket!'

Miserably, he slunk past her. When he reached his bed he paused, looking over his shoulder in one last, silent plea. Vivien closed the door.

The afternoon was warm, the sky cloudy with occasional glimpses of blue, which made for a soft, changeable light. The shed door stood open but not wide enough for her to see inside.

She walked into the centre of the lawn and picked up one of the badminton racquets and the shuttlecock. She hit the shuttlecock into the air high above her head, and when it came down did the same again, keeping it airborne with repeated strong flicks of the wrist. From this angle she could see the shed out of the corner of her eye, and the suggestion of movement inside, but Ashe did not appear. After a minute or so, when the shuttlecock came down she let it fall to the ground, and dropped the racquet beside it. Slowly, arms folded, she walked over to the shed.

She opened the door wide and pushed it back so that it lay flat against the slatted wall. These days the shed was tidy and ordered, the gleaming mower parked just inside, flowerpots and seed trays arranged to size on a wooden shelf, the hose coiled round the watering can, the tools hanging on nails. Ashe was sitting on a stool at the back, cleaning a pair of pruning shears, head down in an attitude of complete concentration. There was no sign that he'd noticed her arrival.

'Hallo,' she said.

Now he glanced up, but only for a second, and if he spoke she didn't hear him. She didn't think this insolent. This was an encounter on equal terms.

Arms still folded she took a step inside and leaned against the door jamb.

'You're busy.'

He made a little movement with his head, signalling agreement.

'It looks so nice in here these days,' she said, her eyes on his hands. 'You've made such a difference.'

'A lot better for working in.'

The sleeves of his blue shirt were rolled back neatly to above the elbow, the folds encircling the ball of muscle on his upper arm which moved as he worked. His skin was so white that the veins on his wrists showed through beneath. In one hand he held the pruning shears, thumb in one loop, fingers in the other as if about to cut; in the other was the polishing cloth, feeling into the cracks and joints at the base of the handles, wiping smoothly along the blades. Unmarked, he would have been a quietly handsome man. The scar was like a scream in the silence.

'Ah!' he swore under his breath, and jumped up from the stool, dropping the shears and cloth. A bright trickle of blood appeared on his right hand, on the flap of skin between forefinger and thumb and oozed, glistening red, over the white skin.

'Oh no!' Vivien took a half-step forward. 'Let me see.'

He held it out, his eyes on her face, his hand spread as if about to clutch her throat. A drop of blood fell to the floor.

'That's a bad cut,' she whispered.

'It doesn't hurt.'

'But it's deep.'

'Clean, too' His voice was very quiet. 'If these things were rusty it'd be a different story.'

He moved his hand forward a little, proffering it for her closer inspection—nearer to her face, her mouth. The effect, unmistakably, was one of invitation.

Vivien took his wrist in her hand, and closed her eyes as she guided the cut to her lips. The taste of it was warm, and salty, the smell of his skin was clean. She felt the light pressure of his finger and thumb on her cheeks on either side, encouraging her to suck, which she did. No other part of them touched, all sensation was concentrated in that conjunction of mouth and hand. She was faint with it. The rest of her seemed light and insubstantial, so much so that if she leaned forward she would be supported, even lifted from the ground . . .

Slowly, he withdrew his hand, and her eyes opened. She staggered, and he held her elbow for a second to steady her.

'There.'

Her hands went instinctively to cover her face. From his pocket he handed her a white handkerchief, crumpled but spotless.

'Now you know how it feels.'

Tears sprang to her eyes, she mopped and scrubbed at her stained mouth while he calmly looked on. Had she misunderstood? Had she been tricked into humiliating herself?

'It's all gone,' he said. 'Can I have that?'

'I'm sorry,' she whispered, handing back the handkerchief.

He shook his head, wrapping the handkerchief round his right hand. 'Why?'

'I don't know—I thought—I don't know what possessed me.'

He gave her a slanting, quizzical look. 'Yes you do.'

'And you?' She stepped back so that she could lean against the side of the shed. 'What were you thinking?'

He turned away and retrieved the shears and cloth from the floor; when he'd hung both on a nail, he said: 'It was going to happen.'

The simple truth of this required no answer.

He stood before her, hands at his sides as if only waiting for her to step aside so he could leave—a prospect that she could hardly bear.

'We shouldn't have,' she whispered.

'What did we do?' he asked, and when she

377

hesitated: 'We haven't done anything. Not yet.'

He stepped forward and she started violently.

'This afternoon,' he said softly. 'You made sure you were alone, and you came to find me.'

She couldn't deny it. Their faces were only inches apart.

'Well then,' he whispered. 'You come and find me again.'

Weak, stunned, she remained where she was for a moment. There was silence as he walked across the grass, then the sound of the back door opening. He said the dog's name, and a second door opened; a flurry, a disturbance as the dog rushed out; the click of the gate, and they were gone.

*   *   *

Once she'd brought herself to concentrate, Felicity enjoyed the reading more than she'd expected, and approached Saxon afterwards to tell him so.

'Quite wonderful!' she said. 'You had us in the palm of your hand.'

'I wonder.' He smiled anxiously, a great deal more relaxed now, she noticed. 'My poems were not written to be read out loud, and I'm by no means convinced how well they come across.'

'Quite brilliantly,' she assured him, then seized the opportunity: 'Saxon, I do apologise if I spoke out of turn earlier, about Vivien. I've been reproaching myself. I meant no criticism of her whatever.'

He appeared relieved. 'As long as you appreciate that her absence does not mean any lack of enthusiasm or support for my work.'

'I'm sure she's your most ardent admirer,'

378

agreed Felicity. 'And a breath of fresh air about the place, we're very fortunate in our vicar's wife—and our vicar!'

'Please, not another word.'

'Very well then, and do give her my regards. She does too much, I thought she looked awfully tired when I last saw her.'

Saxon eyed the door. There was no sign that he shared her concern. What more could she do?

*   *   *

Vivien washed her hair and changed her clothes. When she heard the car arrive, she went to meet Saxon at the front door. She could tell at once that he was in better spirits than before, and so was unlikely to notice anything changed in her manner or appearance.

'How did it go?' she asked.

'Pretty well, I think. They listened attentively at any rate.'

'I should hope so!'

The book of poetry still in his hand, he went into the drawing room, and she followed, relieved on this occasion that he hadn't wanted to sit in the garden. She held out her hand. 'May I?'

'Please do.' He removed a sheet of paper from between the pages, and handed her the book.

They sat down on the sofa, a little distance apart.

'Which ones did you give them?'

'Oh . . . they're marked in pencil.'

She turned the pages slowly, simulating interest. 'All these?'

'They're quite short.'

Still looking at the book, she said: 'I'm sorry I couldn't be there, Saxon.'

'I am too,' he said, but mildly. 'If you had been, you could have protected me from Lady Delamayne.'

She fell on this distraction. 'Don't tell me they came!'

'Not Sir Sidney. Only her. She interrogated me about your absence.'

Vivien maintained her light tone. 'How very embarrassing.'

'It's none of her business. She said she thought you looked tired last time she saw you, and sent her regards. Anyway,' he turned to her, 'how was your afternoon? Was it productive?'

'Reasonably. I did those things which I ought to have done.'

'And the things you ought not?'

'There were none of those.' She felt almost sick, but his expression was benign and he held out his arm to draw her into an embrace.

'Let's see.' She counted the lies off on her fingers. 'I did the mending, and paid the bills, watered the church flowers—'

'Enough, enough! Come here.'

She moved into the circle of his arm and he pulled her close, his other hand in her hair. How she wished, now, for the sounds of someone else in the house. Why had she sent Hilda home? Her husband's warm, excited breathing only emphasised their inescapable privacy.

'Vivien, my darling . . . Your hair's so beautiful . . .'

Unresponsive, motionless, she let Saxon's hands move amorously over her head, her back. To avoid anything more intimate she put her other arm round him and clung tight as a child, her face buried in his chest.

'Vivien?' He placed a hand beneath her chin and forcibly tilted her face to his. She could scarcely believe that her guilt was not written in letters of fire in her eyes, across her mouth, but whatever he read there, it wasn't that. She heard his murmured 'God help me . . .' before his kiss blotted out the light.

*   *   *

Five days went by before she found Ashe again. Days during which time passed with a glacier-like slowness. The air in the house felt thick, resistant, so that the smallest everyday task became a feat of endurance. Ashe did not seek her out, or make himself available in any way, and this put her in an agony of self-doubt. She could remember, in tormenting detail, everything that had happened, but now she wondered if she had misinterpreted her own shameless behaviour. He, after all, had done nothing. It was she who had ensured the house was empty, who had remained at home when she should have been with her husband, who had sought him out, and taken his hand in her mouth . . . He had said as much himself, he was blameless. But then: 'You come and find me again.' That, surely, was unequivocal.

The minutes crawled by, sticking to her skin like leeches, draining her of vitality. Her hearty appetite deserted her: food appeared intolerable, incomprehensible, a challenge to which she was repeatedly unable to rise. She toyed with her meals, and smoked a great deal. Hilda privately deplored the waste, but as to the reasons for loss of appetite in an otherwise healthy young woman, she kept her counsel.

Saxon (remembering Lady Delamayne's observation) asked Vivien if she was ill.

'Not at all. There's nothing the matter with me, I'm simply not hungry.'

'But this isn't like you.'

She shrugged. 'I should lose a little weight.'

'Not for me. You know that, I hope.'

'Of course I do.'

To deflect his curiosity, she did her best to eat, but could manage very little. At least his concern for her health meant that there was no repetition of that other afternoon. She was even glad of Susan, whose visits claimed his attention. Edith Clay had taken to accompanying her daughter as far as the vicarage gate, presumably to guard against further harvest horrors—although there was little fear of that, as the centre of activities had moved to the fields to the west, at the other end of the village.

Vivien's chance came when Saxon was engaged to attend a diocesan meeting, and elected to go by rail so that he could read the relevant papers en route. He would be gone all day. Ashe drove him to the station to catch the ten o'clock train, and would collect him again at four. It was Hilda's half-day. Not long after the car had left the drive Vivien saw Edith, with Susan by the hand, coming in at the other entrance, and went out to forestall them.

'Mrs Clay, Susan—I'm afraid you've had a wasted journey.'

'Why's that then?' asked Edith, whose manner did not soften with time.

'Mr Mariner's got a meeting, he's just left.' She turned to Susan, whose flat, plain face had already fallen. 'So Susan, there's no need for you to be here.'

'I expect there's odd jobs she can do for you, isn't there?'

'I'm not sure that there are.' Vivien tried rapidly to assemble a plausible excuse. 'I thought I might take the opportunity to go out myself.'

Edith asked bluntly: 'What about Hilda?'

'She's here until lunchtime, but I don't know if there'll be anything to do in the kitchen, she always has things so well in hand.'

Susan brightened. 'Can I see Boots?'

'There,' said Edith. 'That dog, I swear she loves it more than she ever did ours.'

Vivien couldn't escape the impression that the woman was in some way hostile. Now she patted her daughter on the shoulder, ushering her away.

'You run along and say hallo to him while I have a word with Mrs Mariner.'

They both watched as Susan hurried off with her awkward, rolling gait. Anxious to get it over with, whatever it was, Vivien turned back first.

'What can I do for you, Mrs Clay?'

'It's about Susan.'

'I assumed that. She seems very happy.'

'Oh, she's happy enough. But she's growing up.'

'She is, all the time. She's so sensible and dependable these days.'

'I didn't mean that.'

Vivien's heart sank. 'Obviously her physical development—well, her mental abilities haven't kept pace, have they, that's part of her condition.'

'Indeed it is. That's what we all have to

remember. She's only a child, no matter what she looks like.'

'Of course. I think everyone understands that.'

'I hope so.'

'You needn't worry, Mrs Clay.' Vivien adopted a warm, woman-to-woman tone as though no more need to be said. 'Everyone in the village knows Susan.'

Edith returned the warmth with a hard stare. 'She's up here more than anywhere, with the vicar.'

There was an insinuation in her voice which Vivien could not ignore.

'I'm sorry . . . What exactly are you saying?'

'Nothing. I'm not saying anything. Just we want her treated how she behaves, not how she looks.'

'It goes without saying. I understand that.'

'Just so long as everyone does.' Edith nodded in the direction of the kitchen. 'At any rate she'll be right as rain with Hilda. I'll come and pick her up in an hour or so.'

'Right you are.'

Vivien watched her march out of the drive. What she had seemed to be saying was unthinkable. Yet it appeared there were those in Eadenford who had been thinking it.

*   *   *

She was sitting by the drawing-room window when Ashe returned in the car fifteen minutes later. He wore a dark jacket for driving and could easily have passed for the car's owner. When he came out of the garage he looked up and gave her a brief nod.

She spent the morning in the drawing room

384

holding a book. From the back of the house she heard Hilda and Susan, and the dog, going in and out, talking desultorily, doing this and that. She never once heard Ashe's voice. At half-past eleven a smart, crunching step on the gravel heralded the arrival of Edith Clay to collect her daughter, and she heard the two of them leave again. Another hour after that there was a tap on the door.

'Mrs Mariner? I'll be off then.'

'That's fine, Hilda. Thank you for looking after Susan.'

'It was no trouble.'

'Good—oh, Hilda, may I ask you something?'

'Yes, Mrs Mariner.'

'What do people in the village think—about Susan spending so much time with us?'

'I couldn't say.'

'You must have some idea. I'm sure they're interested.'

'I don't know,' said Hilda firmly. 'I don't listen to gossip.'

Vivien let her go. Hilda might deny listening to the gossip, but in doing so she had confirmed its existence.

But now all that went out of her head. He was here, somewhere, and she must find him. She ran down to the kitchen, but the dog was in the scullery, cracking on a knuckle-bone, his eyes half-closed in ecstasy. She shut him in, and went into the garden. The shed was padlocked, there was no sign of Ashe. She flew round to the front of the house but the garage door, too, was closed.

Where was he? Had he gone?

Inside the front door she stood for a moment, trying to gain control of her rising panic. Her heart

385

was banging; there were spots before her eyes. To her right was Saxon's study, to her left the drawing room, both of them empty. The dining-room table was visible, with her covered lunch tray on it. She crossed the hall and opened the door of her small sitting room: no one there. Almost sobbing, she returned to the foot of the stairs, gazing upwards. All was mocking tranquillity. In the silence she could just make out the gnawing of the dog's teeth, down in the scullery.

Then she heard it—the creak of a door, followed by a moment's plaintive whining and scratching: she was not the only one who wanted to be with Ashe. Walking as softly as her shaking would allow—though why should it matter if she was heard?—she crossed the hall and went back down into the kitchen. The dog scratched again, more urgently this time. Next to the range with its gleaming armoury of pots and pans the narrow door leading to the back stairs stood open.

She had forgotten how dark the stairwell was, and how cramped, like a chimney. The treads were shallow, the mean proportions designed for a small domestic servant, a village girl. There was a smell of dust and cooking and something else, a taint of rottenness as if a mouse had died behind the panelling. The stairs curved in a spiral, and ended in the blank dead end of the first landing door. To the right was a vertical thread of light: Ashe's room.

She didn't knock. He was lying on his side on the small, plain bed, his hand pillowing his right cheek, the hideousness of his left side exposed, his eyes on the door. And on her, as she entered.

'So,' he said. 'You found me again.'

*　　*　　*

The time was early afternoon. The sun stood high in the sky and only a few clouds drifted between it and the Eaden valley. But something of autumn, of ending, hung in the air. The harvest was underway. Blackberries were appearing in the more sheltered hedges. The swallows and their newly airborne young were feeling the tug of the south as they assembled on the roof-edge and on telegraph wires, wings rustling and tails dipping, ready for the off.

Down in the scullery the dog had abandoned his efforts to attract anyone's attention and was lying half-asleep, the bone by his nose. Cut roses stood in the sink; the air smelled sweet. By the kitchen door a platoon of ants scuttled back and forth looking for crumbs on Hilda's spotless floor. A spider dangled from the top of the window.

The clocks ticked, measuring time in their different rhythms. The one on the kitchen mantelpiece moved forward in small, tremulous clicks, the second hand shaking slightly with each movement. Upstairs in the hall the stentorian 'tock' of the grandfather clock resembled a slow, sombre footfall in the hush. The carriage clock on Saxon's desk was almost silent, perfectly accurate. His book of poems lay closed on the red leather blotter. In the drawing room Vivien's prized chiming enamelled French ormolu clock lagged languidly, five minutes behind the rest; the pipe-playing shepherd boys and bonneted shepherdesses on its dome gazed at one another with pinprick eyes and O-shaped mouths. In here, the flowers in their brown water were dry, waiting to be replaced by the fresh roses from the scullery.

On the dining-room table stood a tray, covered with a daisy-stitched cloth. A wasp hovered and crawled over the uneven shrouded shapes of Vivien's lunch. In the small back sitting room the desk was open, her Parker pen lay next to the inkwell; untidy sheaves of correspondence and bills protruded from the pigeon-holes. A box dropped in the wastepaper basket had proved too heavy and tipped the basket over. A sloping pile of blankets and folded clothes lay in the corner.

Upstairs, the door of the main bedroom was ajar, showing the bed smooth as a table beneath its brocade counterpane; the small, personal possessions which had once appeared so shockingly intimate to Vivien as she stood on the landing looked innocent and dull.

The door to the attic was closed. The small colony of bats hung clustered together like black ivy under the eaves, above the now-tidy trunks and boxes.

At the end of the landing was the plain, brown door, and the next, its twin, that led to the back stairs and the maid's room. Behind these three doors was the only movement in the house.

Though violent, it was wholly silent. Nothing was disturbed.

*   *   *

After Saxon's long day, it was a pleasant evening. He was particularly struck, on returning from the station, by how handsome and prosperous the vicarage looked, and commented accordingly to

Ashe as he got out of the car.

'It's a fine house,' conceded Ashe, closing the car door after him.

'But not always an especially well-maintained one. It owes its smart appearance largely to you.'

Ashe gave his little bow.

It was the same inside. The house seemed light, fresh, sweet-scented: tranquil. 'This is my home,' thought Saxon, with a frisson of pleasure, and looked up to see Vivien coming down the stairs to meet him—and this was his wife, who at this moment had never, to his eyes, looked more beautiful. She was wearing a loose, pale blue blouse that he had always thought becoming, and a dark skirt. Her glorious hair was coiled loosely at the nape of her neck. Her skin—Lady Delamayne was right—looked unusually pale, but luminously so. Seeing him she removed her glasses and slipped them into her pocket.

The small gesture snagged at Saxon's heart. Now, though it was not his habit to greet her extravagantly, he put down his attaché case and held out his arms to receive her.

She entered his embrace almost submissively. She was definitely thinner, her tall frame slight as a willow against him.

'My darling . . .' He pushed her back gently to look at her. 'It's so nice to be home.'

*   *   *

The time between then and their going to bed, which they did quite early, at about nine thirty, was characterised for Saxon by the same mood of contentment and serenity. After supper, feeling

389

rather stuffy following the long hours in the chapter room and on the train, he suggested a game of badminton, but she didn't feel like it. Instead they took the dog for a walk along the river bank. She slipped her arm through his and he had been pleased and proud as a young buck with his sweetheart. He had felt a real fondness for Boots, the animal's still-puppyish exuberance, running round and ahead of them like the extension of his happiness. They saw a kingfisher plummeting, jewel-bright from willow to water on the far bank and stopped to watch it, admiring its fierce tropical colours against the silver-green.

'I'm reminded of that old story,' said Saxon, as they stood together arm in arm. 'I haven't thought about it for years. About where the swallows go in winter.'

'Tell me.'

'Well, they gather together in the autumn, as they're beginning to do now . . . And when they feel the time is right they fly in a flock to the nearest river bank, to wherever the water is deepest.' Enjoying his role of storyteller, he paused for effect.

She didn't look at him, but said: 'Go on. Then what do they do?'

'They form an enormous ball, a great black rustling sphere of living swallows—imagine!—and they disappear beneath the surface of the water! Far beneath, where it's cold and dark. And there they hibernate, secretly, among the trailing weed and the slippery fish.'

A moment passed while she seemed to think about this. 'And in the spring?'

'In the spring, one fine, sunny morning when the

buds are bursting and the blackbirds are singing, someone walking along the bank, just as we are, might see an agitation on the surface of the river, a flurry of circular ripples growing and intensifying until they form a whirlpool, deeper and deeper, until . . .'

'The swallows?'

'The swallows! The great black ball, with water pouring from it, rising out of the river and then exploding, bursting like a seed-head into a hundred individual birds, back from their months of freezing, dark winter death, each one flying away to its remembered nesting place. Imagine,' he said again, awed by the picture he himself had painted. 'Imagine, Vivien.'

'I can,' she said, as, by tacit mutual consent, they turned for home. 'You describe it very well.'

Saxon knew that it was true: he was, after all, a poet.

*   *   *

That night, though they did not make love, they fell asleep with their arms about each other. Saxon felt a rare impulse to protect and cherish his wife. The storytelling on the river bank had awakened something in him, something that had begun with his renewed appreciation of his house, his home. He felt inspired.

It was this that woke him at about two in the morning. The legend of the swallows, it was the start of a poem! A single line ran through his head:

Wings petrified by water as the fish fly by

391

His eyes snapped open. He must write it down at once: he kept a notebook in the drawer next to his bed. As he rolled over to fumble for it he realised that Vivien was not next to him. The house was quiet, the bedroom door closed. Assuming she was in the bathroom, and anyway too excited by his own thoughts to be concerned, he lit the lamp on his bedside table, and took the notebook and pencil out of the drawer. As soon as he began to write the pencil broke.

'Damn!'

He threw down the pencil and swung his legs out of bed. Not bothering to put on his slippers he went out on to the landing. He must go down to the study and scribble, before he forgot.

'Who's there?'

For a moment he thought he'd seen a ghost. She was standing in the deepest shadow near the door to the back stairs, her hand—surely?—still on the handle.

'Vivien?'

Hesitantly, she took two steps towards him. Moonlight from the tall window on the stairs fell on her, but even now, when he could see her clearly he retained the impression of a ghost. There was a key in her hand.

'What are you doing?' he asked.

MESOPOTAMIA

The word is there were getting on for three thousand casualties at the battle of Hanna, so no wonder it took a long time to clear up. As a result we moved our position slightly, to the side. Where we are now there's an old fort off to our left, to the south-west. Like everything around here the ruins probably look bigger than they are, because there's nothing else on the horizon to give a sense of scale. No relief. Distances can be deceptive too. My guess is it's not less than one mile away, not more than two, but if there's a mirage, that can play all kinds of tricks—make things move forwards or backwards, change their size and shape; heavy rain does the same . . . So you can't be sure.

What we can see from our position is a kind of broad, uneven H-shape. The north wall, the one facing the river, looks quite tall; on the south that falls away to a lower rampart, or maybe just a more broken-down wall, hard to say; further to the south it rises up again, but not so high. Outside Qurna there was a fort, still in good nick, that was like a drum, cylindrical with squat castellated towers, so this one probably looked the same once.

At any rate, it's the only cover for miles around, it's a wonder they're not using it as a field hospital or a holding station or something, but they'll have done a recce. One of the little planes will have been over and taken a look—the fort must be further away or a lot smaller than it looks.

Jarvis is still not right. Very pale, says his stomach is playing him up. I'm sure it is, fear plays havoc with the bowels. He's not even up to doing what he does best: putting on a good show for the men. But he's obsessed with the fort. More than once he says to me: 'We should make use of that ruin.'

'You reckon, sir.'

'It would be useful cover—we could position snipers, use it as a field hospital.'

I've thought it myself, but I'm not letting him know that.

'They must have considered it, sir.'

'Don't bet on it Ashe,' he says. 'Just don't bet on it.'

I say nothing. He shouldn't be talking to me like this, and we both know it. Back in Basra to begin with I quite liked him for it, but things were different then. Now I reckon it's a sign that he might remember what happened, that there's something between us we *don't* talk about.

Another thing he says about the fort: it reminds him of home. Home? Where was home, then, a beach hut on Camber Sands? Then I remember 'Kersney Lee, near Sheringham', that's at the seaside, isn't it.

'Sir.'

'You can walk to the sea in your bathing trunks without leaving our land.'

'That so, sir?'

'When I get back, Ashe, I'm going to pull up the drawbridge.'

'Sir.'

He's cracking up. I've got my eye on him.

* * *

394

We stay here for weeks, while the wounded go back, the reinforcements come up, and the brass decide what to do. We're bored, and some of us are scared. HQ in Basra has a brainwave—improve the fly-catching techniques, to relieve the men's discomfort and give us something to do. Some brilliant scientific brain has come up with this gadget, a box with a revolving triangular panel at the base, coated with sticky stuff. The flies fly in, land, get stuck, you turn a handle and the panel moves round and scrapes them off into the box, the next section's ready and waiting. Clever, eh? But it's not a competition this time, it's just to keep us amused. Most of us can't be bothered. Even the officers think it's a bloody insult. It almost makes us feel kindly towards the flies—we're all in it together. The gadgets arrive by the crateload and we use them for kindling.

Eventually we get marching orders. We're advancing to somewhere called Dujaila, but none of us is fooled by that any more. In Mesopotamia there are names, but no places. Dujaila will look exactly the same as Hanna, and Sheikh Sa'ad and Ctesiphon and all the other godforsaken wastes that'll go in the official history. Sand, stones, scrub and our friends the flies. Looking back, no wonder they thought Qurna was the Garden of Eden. It's all relative.

As a matter of fact Dujaila does turn out to be a little different. There's a kind of valley, a dip in the landscape, called the Dujaila Depression, very apt. To the north west we've got the Dujaila Redoubt, a long ridge, not sure if it's natural or the remains of some old fortified wall. We're camped at the head of the depression, a few hundred yards from the redoubt.

About four miles beyond this is Kut. We're that close. We can't see it, but we know it's there, and that puts everyone on their mettle. Maybe we'll do it this time. We'll be in Kut, a proper town, and a real landmark on the way to Baghdad. For myself I'll be glad if we can reach the top of the ridge, just to get out of this bog. Because the weather's worse if anything. We're half-frozen and soaked through, but at least with the reinforcements there's more of us and a few more rations. Who knows? Perhaps the Turks are living in the open with only flies to eat. Although I don't think so. They'll be waiting for us snug as you like over the other side.

And then they bomb the place. Not us—Kut. They've got wind there's another relief attempt in the offing and they're having a last go at flushing out Townshend's poor sods. If we didn't know precisely where Kut was before, we do now. The air raids take place over two or three days; we have to sit there, bogged down, and listen to the whine and crash of the bombs falling, and watch the smoke and rubble fly up in the air above the top of the redoubt. It's like there are two lots of rain— one coming down, the other going up, the clouds getting mixed up with each other, the man-made thunder and lightning. In the second air raid I start counting, and get to ten. In my rough calculation, forty-odd bombs by the time they're through.

It's during the fourth raid I find Jarvis in a really bad way. I take the rum issue into the tent and he's sitting in the corner wrapped up in his cape, shivering like a jelly with his teeth chattering loud enough to hear. Cornish leaves as I come in, he's got that over-to-you air. He's shivering too, but then we all are. The difference is in the eyes. Jarvis looks wretched, hunted: as close to packing it in as any man I've ever seen.

'Rum, sir.'

He doesn't reply, and I pour him a shot in his tin mug and pass it over. Just as he takes it another bomb comes down, and the mug flies out of his hand, rum everywhere, all over his face, his boots . . . Then another and he gives a little yelp and huddles down.

'Come on, sir. Let's try again.'

This time I hold the mug for him and he manages a few swallows. When I hear another aircraft in the distance I take the mug away. I never saw anyone so changed.

'I'm not well,' he whispers.

'Shall I get the MO, sir?' I ask, but I know what he'll say.

'He can't do anything.'

'You're shaking like a leaf, sir. Maybe you've got marsh fever.' That's a phrase we use for just about anything that doesn't involve broken skin. Any illness—it's marsh fever.

He shakes his head, but more in confusion than anything else. Like an animal again, some poor old moth-eaten bear in a zoo or a circus, sitting there shaking its head, not knowing what the hell's going on.

'I'll make one of my stews tonight, sir,' I say. This is a poor sort of joke, what I can do with bully beef, because here in the depression there's nothing else. Nowhere to scavenge.

Anyway, it doesn't raise a smile, and he shakes his head again. Not long now.

That night as it turns out. Nobody expects to sleep here, what with the cold and wet, half-expecting an air raid, and never knowing when the order will come to advance. Officially we're still on stand-down, but it doesn't feel like it. Everyone's living on their nerves. This is another of those times when I could almost thank my mother. Whatever happens can't be as bad as what she put me through. Poor Jarvis the golden boy, he's been heading for a fall ever since he left Sheringham.

Missing sleep isn't so bad, I can go a long time without it. Most people doze off even if they say they haven't had a wink. In the end it's a quiet night and even the rain's eased off. I'm in the tent next door to Jarvis's, so I hear when someone comes out. This man's trying to be quiet, taking those long, cautious strides that people do when they don't want to be heard. Glooping in and out of the mud. I wait till the footsteps are behind our tent, moving to the right as I lie here ... Then I get up. The bloke next to me swears a bit, but he's not fully conscious. Dog-tired men sleep more than they think. Out I go. For the first time in weeks there's a clear sky, stars sprinkled thick as sugar.

It's Jarvis all right. He's got his cape and cap on so he could be on a top-secret lone mission, but I doubt it. I follow at a distance, trying to match my footsteps to his so he won't hear, and ducking in and out of the tents. Once I think he's heard me, or heard something, because he stops dead in his tracks and looks around. I catch a glimpse of his face, and he looks hunted, terrified.

I'm sure he's running away. But first I have to be

398

absolutely certain, and *then* he has to know that I'm in on his little secret. So I follow him, all the way to the camp perimeter. Now he's got a problem. There are sentries posted, and men standing to in the gulleys at the top of the depression. Which way's he going to go? In the middle distance is the redoubt, with Turkish positions along and behind it, but we don't know how many. We're in a stand-off till we get orders . . . But what's he doing?

Jarvis is going on, trudging in the direction of the redoubt. I think to myself: *He really is mad*. One of the sentries says something to him and he replies, just flings a couple of words over his shoulder. I can see the sentry doesn't know what to make of it. That ingrained 'respect' is written all over him; he lets Jarvis continue, this officer bizarrely marching towards the enemy lines in the middle of the night. He's not going to be so lenient with me, so I stop to think.

Jarvis may be mad, but there's a mad logic to what he's doing. How can you be accused of deserting if you run *towards* the enemy? He must be banking on getting far enough away that he can put on a turn of speed under cover of darkness. But where to? There's just more of the same, in all directions; your chances of survival out here are nil.

Suddenly, I know where, and I'm going to get there before him. There's a chance he may not make it at all in his condition, but that's a risk worth taking. I double back, through the corner of the camp. Weaving between the tents—about five hundred yards—I nearly bump into a bloke taking a slash, but he probably thinks I'm on the same errand because he pays no attention. I reach the six or seven feet of thorny bank at the side of the depression and scramble up. Because of the clear sky I can see the outline of the fort from here, like a broken tooth, thick black against the silvered dark of the horizon.

It turns out not to be so far away, it's smaller than it looks. Taking a wide swing at it, running and walking, tripping over quite a lot, it takes me fifteen minutes. All the time I'm thinking, *We could both get shot for this* but it doesn't put me off, just the opposite. I feel a bit mad myself, mad and free. I've got nothing to lose.

When I arrive it's like a set from *The Gold Rush*, or a bad joke: just a false front. On the far side are some random piles of rocks with scrub growing over and between them. There's a scrabble of claws, a tail flicks, an eye gleams and a small animal scuttles away.

Strange as it may sound, there's something peaceful about sitting down with my back against the wall, and looking at a view with no army in it. When people talk about the beauty of the desert this must be what they mean: what most of the time we hate it for, its utter bloody emptiness. It's like sitting on the skin of the planet. Even with the moonlight there are no shadows out there. Except the one by this little broken wall, where I am.

I hear Jarvis coming quite some distance away. Sound carries in the desert. From the moment I first hear him it's a good three minutes before he arrives. He's crashing and stumbling along like I did—the ground may look flat but it's rough. When he's quite close there's the crackle of random small arms fire from the direction of the redoubt, and I hear him sniffling. Even if they are aiming at him, which I doubt, they're not going to persist. One mad Englishman scampering off won't bother them.

He almost runs into the wall on the other side, and leans on it, his breathing harsh and quick. He's only a foot away from me; he thinks he's all alone. Now he's here I bet he's disappointed. Like me he's seeing what a sad little excuse for a building this place is: not the big, romantic sheltering walls he dreamed of but a broken-down heap of stones in the middle of nowhere. Did he imagine he was going to set up house here, dig for fresh water, live on wild locusts and honey like John the Baptist? Go back to England when it was all over? Now, however crazed he is he can see what I can see— hundreds of miles of nothing on two sides, the enemy on another, duty on the fourth. Is he thinking of going back?

There's another snap! snap! of fire, and he scrambles over. He's lost or taken off his cap and cape as he ran, and he lands untidily, crouching like a monkey, one hand on the ground to steady him on the stones. I just sit there and wait. He sits down with his back to me, his hands over his face, his shoulders heaving, making little sounds of despair and confusion in his throat. My, he is in a state.

It's ages—minutes—before he turns round, and when he does it's on all fours like a dog, presumably because he wants to keep low. The moment he sees me, I say:

'Captain Jarvis, what are you doing here?'

That moment definitely qualifies as among the sweetest in my life. The explosion of shock on his

401

face, and I put it there! Forget drink, this is intoxication. Sod the war, this is what victory feels like. I could die happy.

And I damn nearly do, because the next thing that happens isn't in the plan. He leaps on me, *pounces* like a wild thing, and lands full on me. The wind's knocked out of me, I can feel wet drops raining on my face—tears and spittle and sweat— and he's cursing and swearing. This isn't Queensberry rules: he's got my throat with one hand and is trying to bang my head against the wall and he's gouging at my eyes with the other. But although he's bigger and taller than me he's also softer, and I manage to slip sideways and grab him by his Sam Browne, unbalancing him. Then we're rolling around like a couple of fairground wrestlers, grunting and snarling, biting and scratching. We crash down the pile of rocks and he shrieks, he's caught his back, but it means I land on top. I sit tight astride his chest and hold his wrists down; these things come back to you.

Gradually, we both quieten. When he's stopped squirming I let go his wrists. He's crying, eyes and nose running.

'So,' I say, 'what's the answer to the question? Sir.'

He rolls his head from side to side.

'What did you think you were doing?'

'Ashe . . .'

'Sir?'

'I was using my initiative. Doing a recce. You know that.'

'I don't know if I do. This is a funny old place to spy out the enemy.'

'I wanted to see . . .' He's distracted, his hands

are moving about all the time, wiping his face, rubbing his eyes, catching feebly at the front of my tunic like a drunk trying to make a point. 'I thought this might make a vantage point. Ashe . . . you realise that, you must realise that . . . What else would I be doing?'

'You tell me, sir.'

It's funny but I never stop to wonder why he doesn't ask *me* what *I'm* doing there. I'm so full of my own cleverness I let my guard drop. As he starts to speak again I see his eyes change, just like a red light, but it's too late. His hand comes up and he's holding an entrenching tool—nasty little bugger, we've often talked of the damage they could do with that serrated blade—and I feel the tip at the corner of my mouth.

'Get off me you little bastard,' he says.

'Have you decided on your story, then?' I ask.

'When I do,' he says, 'you'll be the last to know.'

I've lost the initiative and I hate that. My mind's racing, roaring. He's pathetic. I caught him red-handed and he knows it. I've got what I wanted, haven't I? I'm going to get up, leave him lying in his own snot, he's pissed himself too, I can smell it, and I'm going to walk away.

'All right,' I say. And—I can't help it—I laugh.

The tip of the blade slips inside my cheek and I feel it rip through the flesh right up to my ear, not like butter, like raw fish or meat, all those separate fibres tearing, blood vessels rupturing. Blood like a waterfall.

No pain, not yet. Just a single thought.
Get out of this one, Captain Jarvis . . .

CHAPTER FIFTEEN

'I was locking this door,' she said.

'A good idea.'

'It's not as if it's used, anyway.'

'No, indeed.'

'I'm sorry if I disturbed you.'

'You didn't. I had a thought, an idea—I'm just going down to the study to make a note.'

She nodded. Somehow, the key seemed to have disappeared into her hand.

'Here,' he said. 'Give it to me. I'll return it for you.'

'Oh, there's no . . .' She seemed for a fraction of a second to demur, then held it out to him at arm's length, like a child. 'Thank you.'

He took the key and walked away.

'Don't you want your dressing gown?' she asked. 'Won't you be cold?'

'No,' he said. 'I shan't be long.'

*   *   *

Down in the hall, Saxon walked first to the row of hooks near the back stairs where the house keys hung, but having done so he did not put the key there. Instead he returned to the study, closed the door behind him, and turned on the lamp. Then he laid the key on his desk, straight, with its teeth pointing towards him, and sat down.

There was something mysterious about it, as there was about any key. A key functioned both as a keeper of secrets and a means of release. Saxon had read Freud, but it did not take much imagination to see the key as a sexual symbol. Nothing looked exceptional about this one: it was a simple black iron key with a loop at one end. He placed his forefinger on the loop, and gave it a tentative push, as if it were a poisonous insect. A second later he picked it up and put it in the bottom right-hand drawer of his desk, a drawer which itself had a key, which he turned, and placed another drawer beneath the blotter.

He sat upright in his chair, his hands on his knees. He felt a little chilly, Vivien had been right to recommend he wear a dressing gown . . . He frowned. There was no reason on earth why his wife should not decide that the door to the back stairs should be locked. Indeed, with a single male employee living in the house, it was a sensible precaution which he rather wished he'd taken himself, and demonstrated on her part commendable concern for security; and, of course, propriety.

By the time the sky outside began to turn grey, he had not written a single word. When he eventually moved he was cold and stiff, but he nonetheless took out his notebook, more from duty than excitement, to jot down the line of poetry. But it wouldn't come. The swallows— something about wings? Water? He cudgelled his brain but it was no good; he couldn't remember the sequence, the nice juxtaposition of ideas. It would come back to him tomorrow when he wasn't trying.

What he could not forget, as he went slowly up the stairs, was that first sight of Vivien, ghostlike in the dark at the end of the landing, the key in her hand. Why had she been there, locking the door, in the middle of the night? Could it not have waited? What thought process had woken her up and prompted her? And—the terrible thought which he had been keeping at bay leapt out at him and made him flinch—from which side of the door had she come?

Entering the bedroom he went to his wife's side of the bed and looked down at her. She seemed deeply and peacefully asleep, but to be sure he leaned down to within inches of her face. Her lashes were motionless, her breathing long and slow. Her lower lip fluttered slightly. Eyes closed he put his own lips to her cheek, which was warm. She made a little sound in her throat and shifted her position, but did not wake.

By his side of the bed he kneeled to pray. His attitude for prayer was usually formal—back straight, hands clasped, head slightly bowed—but now he spread his arms on the bed and pressed his face into the soft surface of the quilt. There were no words, he wanted only to abase himself, to cast himself on the mercy of God. After a couple of minutes he clambered stiffly to his feet and slumped on to the mattress, pulling the bedclothes ineffectually over his shoulder with one hand. He was utterly exhausted—from sitting up too long, from the pain of that moment's suspicion, from self-loathing—but doubted he would be able to sleep. A few seconds later he fell into complete unconsciousness.

*   *   *

Ever afterwards Vivien remembered that night as

the point of no return. For though she had several times lied to Saxon 'in thought, word and deed' (the prayer book haunted her) in recent weeks, on that night she was telling the simple truth. She had locked the door and had hoped by doing so to lock away herself.

Too late. She had been with Ashe. She had found him, and possessed him; taken him into her with a force and strength she never knew she had. But—and this made her shudder—he, Ashe, must have recognised that force in her, and summoned it from a distance. Her lovemaking with Saxon, the precious, complex intimacy that had always been the barometer of their affections, their secret treasure, was by comparison less than nothing. With Saxon, her pleasure as well as his was within her command. Ashe had gloried in her loss of control.

Images of what she had done, and felt, kept flashing across her mind's eye: her legs, stretched to breaking point—her head striking the wall, then grinding into it—her mouth feasting on that grinning scar, feeling its plushy ridges and fine, silken ripples where no hair grew—her hands kneading and clawing at her own breasts, at his . . . And all the time his silent, imperious acceptance.

She had been, and was still, electrified. On that evening walk by the river Saxon had never been more loving nor more deserving of love, yet she had been barely sentient, riding the aftershocks. Her legs trembled, she had been glad to link her arm through his. When they paused to watch the kingfisher it had been a relief to stand still and lean against him as he talked on, telling her some little story that she couldn't remember. Nothing—

not the walk, nor the birds, nor the evening sunshine, meant anything to her; least of all her husband's tender attention.

She had *had* to imprison herself at night; she did not trust herself not to slip through those two narrow doors into his room, and her other self, under cover of darkness. She had intended to throw the key away. But Saxon had taken it from her, and so it remained in the house.

*   *   *

The next morning Saxon overslept, and Vivien found that the key was missing from its hook in the hall. So he had not believed her. But she knew him so well, knew that he could never begin to imagine the extent of her deception or the depths to which she had sunk. He was a martyr to his own impossibly high standards: his fleeting suspicion about the key would be torturing him.

When he eventually came downstairs he was taciturn and preoccupied. Susan Clay arrived, and he went with her to the church.

*   *   *

For two days she avoided Ashe. This wasn't difficult; he was always elusive, going about his work quietly and industriously, troubling no one, in nobody's way. There was no doubt in her mind, now, that she would find him again. It would happen again not because they willed it but because it *must*.

The key did not reappear, and she neither looked for it nor asked after its whereabouts.

Though he said nothing, Saxon's manner continued to be guarded and a little distant, and she was grateful for the freedom this allowed her to be on her own. The mere sight of her husband filled her with desolation. She remembered, out of the blue, what he had been telling her on the river bank, or at least the essence of it; the words that had meant nothing at all at that moment she took out and put together and examined, like a scientist, and recalled that it had been about swallows, diving into the river and hibernating deep in the water . . . This was sad, too, because at the time she had said something, thrown him some small compliment to flatter his eloquence, and he had been pleased and walked taller because of it. Now, through no fault of his, he was diminished in her eyes.

*   *   *

The second time was in their bedroom; in their bed. Vivien told herself that it was as if by removing the key to the adjoining door, Saxon had somehow made it inevitable. On that afternoon he was conducting a funeral; if she stood very still she could hear the singing of 'Abide with Me' from within the church. At least twenty-five minutes would pass before the congregation came out into the churchyard for the burial. Hilda was doing shopping in the village.

Ashe had gone up into the loft to check his temporary repairs. Vivien came up the stairs to find him lowering the trapdoor above his head. She watched as he stepped down off the chair, and put it back in its place by the wall. When he'd done so he said quietly:

'So. You found me again, then.'

'I knew you were up here.'

'Of course you did.'

Without looking at her he pushed open the bedroom door, and went in. The room was calm and tidy, the bedspread smooth, the pillows plumped. The curtains moved gently at the open window.

'In here,' he said. 'This'll do.'

They came together like dogs on the bare mattress. The spotless sheets lay in a heap on the floor. After they fell away from each other, Vivien turned her back on Ashe. She did not watch him as he dressed, and left the room. She was still shaking as her husband's voice carried from the churchyard on the sunlit air, speaking the solemn words of the committal.

*   *   *

Ashe was getting there. Just as he could push his hand into the vicar's wife and make her cry out, so he was, a step at a time, invading their most private places. Only a little way to go, not far, and the desecration would be complete. Then, if he read things right it would only take a word, the merest suggestion from him to the husband, and her guilt would speak up for itself. The two of them were a tinderbox, there'd be one hell of a conflagration.

Mariner would tell him to go, and they'd hear no arguments from him. He'd go like a lamb—taking with him, in lieu of notice, whatever it was worth to keep the fire contained. For the time being, anyway.

410

*   *   *

His next opportunity came a few days later. He was doing some running maintenance on the mower when he saw Edith Clay arrive with the girl at the vicarage. Five minutes later he raised a hand to Mr Mariner and Susan, as they crossed from the garden gate to the church. Mariner didn't respond, had perhaps not even noticed, but Susan waved back vigorously, like a child.

He returned to his work, putting in autumn-flowering plants around the base of the memorial: wallflowers and winter pansies. They weren't flowers he particularly liked himself, and it was a little early to be planting, but some ground cover was going to be needed over the coming months and he himself wouldn't be around much longer. He liked the idea of leaving this small legacy right here on hallowed ground. He had made a few other preparations, too: chopped all the usable wood from the end of the garden and stacked it in the lean-to he'd built at the back of the shed; set crocus and snowdrop bulbs at the edge of the lawn for the following new year and spring; done running repairs on the garden furniture and a full service on the car, and the bicycles. When the moment came for him to go, they'd have the evidence of his work all around them, every day of their lives for weeks, months, to come.

He heeled in the last of the plants, and tidied up, raking up the debris and stacking the flowerpots in the wheelbarrow. The soil was good round here, rich and loamy, but he hated having the stuff all over his hands, the sooner he could get

411

to a tap—he took out his handkerchief and scrubbed them fastidiously, then threw the handkerchief into the wheelbarrow.

'Mr Ashe!'

Lady Delamayne was walking towards him from the direction of the vicarage. The car must be parked there, so she hadn't come to arrange the flowers. What, then? Ashe could have done without her.

'Mr Ashe,' she said again, with greater emphasis. 'Working away as usual, I see.'

'Morning, your ladyship.'

'I'm a bird of passage, today,' she announced. 'Duty calls elsewhere.'

He waited.

'These will make a lovely show of colour,' she said, not looking at the plants, but at him. He nodded briefly.

'Autumn awaits . . .' She sighed gustily. 'I suppose once the shorter days are upon us there won't be so much for you to do about the place.'

'I can always find something.'

'I'm sure you can, I'm *sure* you can . . .' She stepped up on to the grass. The thick, high heels of her shoes cut the surface. He caught a waft of her scent—too strong for someone who called herself a lady to be wearing during the day—and moved slightly away. Suddenly she noticed something, her eyes fixed on his face.

'Now then, what have you been doing to yourself?' She reached out a hand almost as if she was going to touch the place. 'How did you manage that?'

He covered it with his own hand. 'I got a scratch clearing branches.'

412

'Dear me.'

'Nothing by comparison,' he said. 'Hardly counts.'

'You're right!' She laughed, a little too heartily. 'What a very sensible approach you have to things.'

He waited for her to go. He still couldn't work out why she was hanging around here, wasting his time.

'All settled in at the vicarage?' she asked, this time not looking at him but studying the memorial, running her hand up and down the stone as though it was a thing she was contemplating buying for her house.

'Yes.'

Her hand still on the cross, she slid him a playful sideways glance and adopted a stage whisper: 'Is Hilda behaving herself?'

'Hilda?'

'Nose not out of joint?' He shook his head. 'Not even the littlest bit?'

'Not that I know if. We both have our work to do.'

'Oh, I *know*. Naturally you do. It was a sort of joke—she is notoriously proprietary about the Mariners, and the vicarage has been her fiefdom for so long.'

She paused. Ashe thought, *She thinks I don't know the meaning of proprietary and fiefdom.*

'I was aware of that,' he said. 'The vicar made sure she'd be happy with the arrangement.'

'And of course Mrs Mariner's delighted! The house and garden have never looked better. I've just been talking to her.'

Ashe felt her bright, hard stare on his face. She went on:

413

'We all worry about her, rather. She's not been looking well, lately.'

'I can't say I'd noticed.'

'Why should you? Anyway, between us the vicar and I will be keeping an eye on her.' There was that stare again. Then she said in a different tone of voice:

'But it's the vicar I'm after, and I believe he's at his place of work. So—' Lady Delamayne made a gesture as if heading a column of fighting men, in the direction of the church. 'Onwards.'

She strode off, but the discomfort she occasioned stayed with Ashe as he lifted the shafts of the wheelbarrow, lowered it carefully on to the church path, and headed via the lane to the vicarage.

Better get on with it.

*   *   *

Saxon never regretted taking Susan under his wing. Inside the church, she went immediately to the cupboard and took out the soft broom, suitable for collecting up the dry leaves that gathered beneath the flower arrangements. She no longer needed instructions, which this morning was just as well. Her cleaning was exemplary; she would put a cloth over her finger and painstakingly wipe round the complicated holes and crevices in the carving, her tongue protruding slightly as she did so. She kneeled on the chancel step, her head tipped upside down, face red, hair hanging, to polish the *underside* of the altar rail in what was (all too clearly to the other lady volunteers) a labour of love.

On a morning such as this, when Saxon felt so unsure of himself, the girl's simple loyalty, industry and devotion provided a source of comfort. He wished he could say the same of John Ashe. Though days could go by when Saxon scarcely saw or heard him, he felt his presence, and was surrounded by its beneficial effects. The only deleterious one, and consequently the one that preoccupied Saxon, was the taking root of this ridiculous, despicable anxiety about Vivien . . .

He took his seat near the lectern and opened his prayer book to the collect, epistle and gospel for the day. Sometimes when he did this Susan would sit too, with a book, often upside down, in her hands. Sometimes, as now, she would find something to do that was out of sight and so would not disturb him; she had a natural, an almost motherly, thoughtfulness and discretion which continued to touch him deeply.

He could just hear her mouse-like movements in the vestry but they soothed rather than disturbed him. His little acolyte. He prayed.

When he'd finished he saw that she was sitting at the far end of the front pew, her hands clasped in her lap, eyes squeezed shut.

'Susan?'

She opened her eyes. 'Susan, show me what you've been doing.'

She led the way into the vestry. Everything was tidy: music and books in separate piles, collection bags lying on the plate, all swept and dusted. A couple of the choirboys' surplices still hung on their hooks: the boys were supposed to take them home to be washed but there were some who either forgot or whose parents didn't consider it

415

their responsibility. Both surplices looked limp and greyish.

'Those lazy boys,' said Saxon. 'We should take these over to Hilda and get them washed.' He took them off the hooks, bundled them and placed them in Susan's arms. 'Why don't you do that now?'

'I'll do it now,' she agreed.

He placed a fatherly hand on her head—her hair was thin and fine as a child's—and opened the vestry door.

*   *   *

This was the sight that met Felicity Delamayne's eyes as she entered the church. Quite affecting in a way: the fat, simple girl gazing up adoringly, the vicar's hand laid gently on her head, but Felicity had heard murmurings. It wouldn't do.

*   *   *

'Vicar—there you are!'

'Lady Delamayne, I was expecting to see you later. Run along, Susan. What can I do for you?'

'I wanted—' Felicity paused as Susan lumbered past. 'That's it, off you go . . .' She advanced up the side aisle and met Saxon by the lectern. 'I'm sorry to disturb you. Vivien told me you were here. I shan't be at home when you come up this afternoon, and there are a couple of things I wanted to discuss about harvest home, so I thought I'd drop in en route to the Ladies' Guild.'

'Right,' said Saxon. 'I suggest we go back to the vicarage.'

As they walked together towards the garden

416

gate, Felicity said: 'Your man Ashe has made the memorial blossom as the rose.'

'I must take a look.'

'I tried to have a chat with him, but he's a man of few words.'

Saxon had some sympathy with Ashe here, and said pointedly: 'No, he likes to get on.'

'He doesn't give very much away.' What point was she trying to make? 'How do you find it with him living at the house?'

'Very convenient, it suits us very well.'

'Good! I was talking to Vivien, she seems rather less enthusiastic.'

Really, the woman was intolerable. 'She hasn't said anything to me.'

'And Susan Clay, always bustling about. Doing your bidding.' Felicity glanced sharply at the vicar's grim profile. 'Still, I suppose it's the job of a vicarage, isn't it? Taking in waifs and strays.'

Saxon couldn't bring himself to answer.

* * *

Hilda was cleaning the silver cutlery; she had it spread out on newspaper on the kitchen table and was applying her special solution. Ashe poured himself a glass of water at the sink in the scullery. He watched her as he drank, then put the glass down and wiped his mouth.

'Want a hand with that?'

Hilda bridled. 'I'm sure you've got better things to do.'

'I wouldn't have offered.'

'Go on then.' She tossed him the polishing cloth. 'Give them some elbow grease.'

417

He applied himself. After a couple of minutes he asked: 'Not cooking lunch today?'

'The reverend's going up to Eaden Place, visiting.'

'I just saw Lady Delamayne.'

'She was here.' Hilda jerked her head upward. 'Don't ask me. She's a law unto herself. That's where he's going, anyway, and lunching with Sir Sidney.'

Ashe allowed another minute to elapse, during which he brought the soup ladle to a high shine. He looked at his face in it—a bulging gargoyle. 'Mrs Mariner not eating then?'

'She says she'll make herself something . . . Which means nothing.' Hilda sucked her teeth. 'She's off her food.'

'Less work for you,' he volunteered.

'Out with the dog at the moment.'

They polished a bit more. 'Where's Susan?'

'Her mother came for her.' Hilda nodded at the basket by the sink. 'She brought those over from the church. Little tykes are supposed to take them home.'

'Why should you wash them,' agreed Ashe.

'I don't mind.'

When they finished the job it was half past twelve. They heard the vicar go out, and the car starting up in the drive. There was no sign of Mrs Mariner with the dog—she must have gone miles, as Hilda remarked, adding: 'I'm surprised she's got the strength on what she eats.'

'Speaking of which . . .'

He took his usual bread and cheese, with a bit of ham on this occasion in honour of the polishing, and went out into the garden, where he sat on the

418

grass with his back against the shed to eat.

When he'd finished he returned to the kitchen to find Hilda asleep in her chair. She was sagging half over the arm, threatening to dislodge the cup of tea that stood on the edge of the table next to her. He coughed politely and was sure to be busy dusting the knees of his trousers when she started awake.

'Why don't you cut along home,' he suggested, 'have a bit of peace and quiet while they're out.'

'I can't do that,' she said, 'it's not my day.'

'What's there to do?'

'Not much. Silver's done thanks to you, and supper's cold . . .'

'There you are then,' said Ashe. 'I told them I'd do the grates, so I'll get on with that. If they ask, I'll say you were tired and I told you to. Come back teatime.'

'Do you know,' Hilda rose heavily from the chair, 'I think I will. No point in my sitting about here.' She began untying her apron. 'You make sure to tell them, Mr Ashe.'

'Don't worry.'

'Because they'll believe you,' she said, hanging up the apron. 'They trust you.'

*   *   *

When the house was empty, and quiet, Ashe went upstairs, carrying in one hand a bucket and shovel, in the other the wooden basket containing scourers, cloths and brass polish for the grates.

With Mr Mariner out, it seemed only sensible to start with the study. The fireplace in here was quite small, with a black iron hood and red and green leaf-patterned tiles. He kneeled down and began his work, scraping out the remains of last year's clinker and shovelling it into the bucket. The holy-of-holies thing meant nothing to him, though he knew it did to everyone else in this house. He wasn't interested in prying or poking about, he was cleaning the grate. To show there was no secret, he left the door open.

When he heard her footsteps, and those of the dog on the gravel outside, he didn't look up. He was applying blacking to the hood, rubbing it in with steady, circular strokes. She did not, as he expected, go round to the back of the house but crossed in front of it to the garage. There was a brief silence: she was checking whether the car was there. Then she ran up the steps and opened the front door. She came in with the dog still on the lead and stood in the study doorway. He heard the dog panting and straining in the doorway, but could tell, without looking, how still she was standing, like a statue.

'You're in here.' Her voice trembled.

He sat back on his heels. 'Just doing this.'

'No one—' she began, then said: 'I suppose he won't mind.'

He felt a flare of pure rage, but said nothing, and turned back to his blacking. She pulled the reluctant dog away and he heard her go downstairs, shoo it into the scullery and close the door. When she came back, she said: 'Where's Hilda?'

'Gone home for a couple of hours. She was done in. I said you wouldn't mind.'

He put down the blacking cloth and looked up at her. Her cheeks and mouth were flushed, her pupils dilated.

She walked over to him in her muddy shoes. He saw her eyes flick to the window behind them, back to him. Her breathing was shallow. He could feel the heat coming off her.

'I don't—' she began.

He clasped her ankle, tight and hard like a trap. 'No,' he said. 'In here. Now.'

*   *   *

Saxon returned to find a note on the hall table from Vivien: she was feeling a little below par, and was taking a nap. He went quietly upstairs and looked into the bedroom where she was lying on top of the eiderdown in her dressing gown, her hair in a ruffled pool, her feet incongruous in their thick socks. One of the socks had a hole, and her toe poked through. She looked so innocent and childlike—and so very beautiful—that he was tempted to lie down by her side, to make his peace with an embrace. But he decided against disturbing her. She had had a long walk, the rest would do her good.

He wasn't in a mood to work, but when he went into the study to fetch his book he noticed the fireplace had been cleaned. He was pleased to see it looking clean and bright, less pleased that Ashe had forgotten to wipe his shoes. But it was so unlike the man to be anything but fastidious that he decided against mentioning it, this once. Crouching awkwardly, he picked up the small pieces of dried mud between his finger and thumb and dropped them in the coal scuttle.

At supper Vivien asked about Eaden Place, and Sir Sidney, and he was happy to oblige, although she spoke scarcely at all and appeared not much refreshed after her sleep. Afterwards she went to the drawing room, and Saxon went out into the garden to collect up and put away the badminton set. It looked untidy and besides they'd scarcely used it this summer and it was starting to get on his nerves—a reminder of a kind of accidie on his part. Perhaps exercising the dog had consumed more of the spare energy they'd once spent playing this slightly ridiculous game . . . He thrust the net and its attendant bits and pieces into their canvas bag and put it in the shed along with the racquets and shuttlecock. That was better. The lawn looked more peaceful without it.

The evenings were closing in. Eight o'clock and it was already dusk, a sense of dew falling. The end of the year. Swept by a swooning, not unpleasant melancholy, Saxon looked up at his house. The curtains of the small window of Ashe's room were not drawn, and a soft inverted triangle of light fell on the wall opposite. What was he doing? Even as Saxon asked himself this, a dark shadow appeared momentarily and, ashamed of himself, he looked away.

He returned to the house and went into the drawing room. To his surprise there was no light on and he thought at first Vivien wasn't there. Then he saw her; she was sitting on the sofa with her legs curled up beside her, and a book in her hand. But she wasn't reading—how could she with no light?—she was staring at the ground in front of her, in a world of her own.

He turned on one lamp, then the other. 'Vivien?'

She must have heard, because she turned her face towards him, but the expression on it was distant, the eyes open but still unseeing. For a terrible moment it reminded Saxon of the faces he had so often seen gazing up from coffins: that blank, unreachable, inner absence. Hastily, banishing the thought, he went to sit next to her, took the book from her hands and claimed them himself.

'Vivien, my dear—my darling—what are you doing sitting here in the dark?'

At his touch he heard her exhale, as if she had been holding her breath—or scarcely breathing at all. Her eyes focused, she looked almost puzzled to see him there. He raised her hands to his lips and kissed the fingers.

'I hadn't noticed,' she said.

'You were miles away.'

'Yes.'

Saxon placed her hands back in her lap as if returning a toy to a child, and stood up.

'I am going to suggest we have a tot of whisky.'

'No thank you.' She shook her head and leaned it on the back of the sofa, but he was firm.

'I'm overriding you. A purely medicinal mouthful will do us both good, and help us sleep well.'

He went to the dining room and took the decanter and tumblers from the cabinet. As he poured he remembered that Vivien had had something in the order of two hours' sleep already. And yet she looked so thin and wan.

He returned. She was sitting exactly as he had left her, hands in her lap, eyes gazing at the ceiling. Without lifting her head she turned it towards him.

'Do I have to?'

'Just this once.'

Obediently she held out her hand and he wrapped her fingers round the glass. 'I assure you we shan't be making a habit of this.'

He sat down once more and watched as she took a sip.

'Would you mind very much,' she asked, 'if I had a cigarette?'

'Not at all.' This was not the moment for his usual disapproval. 'Allow me.'

He fetched the silver box from the mantelpiece and proffered it. She took one. They did not have a lighter, and he was obliged to take the box of spills from the hearth. This reminded him of something, and as she took her first deep inhalation, he said:

'Ashe has cleaned the fireplace in the study while I was out today.'

'Has he?'

'I should probably have told him not to bother if I'd been here, but as it is he's brought it up like new. A great deal cosier.'

'Good.'

'He brought rather a lot of earth in on his shoes and forgot to clear it up, which is most unlike him, but I shan't mention it.'

She was silent, and took another mouthful of whisky. The cigarette smoke wreathed around her head. He seemed to have lost her again. Time, Saxon thought, to be direct. It was after all a husband's duty to be solicitous, and it would help to exorcise the disgusting and unloving thoughts

424

that had infested his head over recent days.

'Vivien, forgive me but I must ask, are you quite well?'

She seemed to consider this for a moment, and then replied, carefully: '*Quite* well, yes. Not *very* well, though.'

Saxon was flooded with an ecstasy of relief—his wife was ill! It was no more than that, a purely physical complaint, in all probability one of those specifically female ailments which he could scarcely guess at but which he understood were often accompanied by erratic and unpredictable behaviour . . . An indisposition—that was all!

He tried not altogether successfully to keep this delight out of his voice.

'My darling, I'm so sorry. You should have told me.'

'I didn't want to worry you.'

'But I've worried so much more, not knowing what was troubling you, seeing that you weren't yourself, imagining all kinds of terrible things . . . What are the symptoms? We must take you to the doctor, we'll do so tomorrow.'

'Saxon . . .' She passed a hand across her face, pressing her thumb and forefingers into her eyes as she did so. 'I'm perfectly capable of taking myself to the doctor if I need to.'

'But I should like to come with you. I've felt— how can I explain—a separation between us recently.'

'Yes.'

'And it's because you have been keeping this secret, protecting me in some way.'

She drew on the cigarette as if drawing strength from it. 'Yes.'

Saxon would have put his arm round her but she was occupied with the cigarette and the glass, and was sitting with her shoulders hunched in a way that precluded intimacy. He laid his hand on her shoulder. 'Never mind, nothing is your fault. I've been preoccupied, the reading and so on. No wonder you didn't want to come! You have no idea how much I reproach myself with not having broached this earlier.'

'It really doesn't matter.'

'And anyway, what are your symptoms? I know that you're tired, and you have certainly lost weight. Is there anything else? Are you in pain of any kind?'

She thought again. 'Yes.'

The relief drained from him, sucked away by dread. 'What sort of pain? Where?'

Her hand holding the cigarette rose to her forehead, moved hesitantly down and from side to side, as if she were making the sign of the cross. Saxon frowned.

'I don't understand.' His voice was sharp with anxiety. 'Where—your head? Your whole body?'

'I'm not sure.' She shook her head and with an appearance of effort adopted a brisker, brighter tone. 'I expect a lot of it's in my mind, I'm just run down, though heaven knows why I should be. I'll snap out of it soon.'

'But winter's on its way,' he said fretfully. 'The cold, the dark. And you're buried here, don't think I don't realise that, you with all your energy and fire cooped up with me in this great house, in this stuffy little parish—' He stopped, perhaps he had gone too far. Those things he was so keen to denigrate constituted his vocation. 'Never, ever think,' he said earnestly, 'that you are unappreciated.'

For only the second time since he came into the room she looked directly at him, and this time there was such bleak sadness in her look that it brought tears to his own eyes. 'I do know that.'

'I hope so.' He stood up, to cover the emotion that threatened to overcome him. 'We've had no holiday to speak of since we went on honeymoon. Let's have one. Let's plan it together.'

'But as you say it'll be winter soon, and then Christmas when you're so busy . . .'

'What better time to find some sunshine? Perhaps at the end of October. We could take the train to the Italian lakes.'

She smiled anxiously. 'I suppose we could.'

'Tomorrow!' said Saxon, bringing his hands together to finalise the matter. 'Tomorrow, we shall make a plan, and I will put it into action.'

'Let's see.' She stubbed out her cigarette and set down her barely touched glass. Then she rose and came over to him. He opened his arms and she stepped into the circle they made. But instead of putting her own arms round him she kept them tight to her sides, only lifting her palms to lay them against his chest, and bending her head so that her forehead rested on his shoulder. It was an attitude of—he sought the word—of penitence.

'My darling Vivien,' he murmured into her hair. 'Please don't worry. All will be well.'

*   *   *

The next day, his mind at rest on one score, and fired with enthusiasm for the projected holiday,

427

Saxon was a good deal happier. The problem had been diagnosed, the solution could be put in place. Vivien could see that this improvement in his own morale had projected itself on to her. She declined his offer of breakfast in bed and managed to nibble at enough toast to elicit the comment that she seemed slightly better.

'I think I may be,' she said. All she wanted was for his attention to be elsewhere. Let him dream up holidays, make plans, anything so long as she was not watched.

'But that doesn't mean you shouldn't see the doctor. A complete check-up—'

'Please. Saxon, don't fuss. I'll get in touch with him if I need to.'

'In which case you'll let me know?'

'Yes.'

'What will you do this morning?'

She folded and rolled her napkin. 'I don't know.'

'Not that it matters,' he said hastily. 'But be sure not to overreach yourself.'

'I won't.'

'I shan't be going out, I've got work to do in the study, but perhaps later we could take another walk together—by the river. That was particularly enjoyable.'

'I don't mind,' she said, adding with enormous effort: 'Yes, why not, we might see the kingfisher again.'

'Excellent. And for now, *I* shall walk the dog. Unless you'd like to, of course.'

She shook her head dumbly. Saxon beamed. She had to look away, she did not want his smiles, his pleasure—she did not want his love, which felt like a dusty cobweb, tangling her in its stale, clinging

428

strands. Where had all this renewed affection come from, just when she least wanted it? The moment he had decided she was ill, his mood had altered, she hadn't known him so cheerful and outgoing since the days of their courtship. Why not, she thought, let him be happy, let him make plans, anything, so long as he leaves me alone.

It was only when they'd left the table and she was in the sanctuary of her little sitting room that she considered the implications of her husband's mood. For now she had established a pretext for seeking solitude and rest, like some swooning Victorian lady, but as time went by he would expect her to improve, and their physical intimacy to be resumed. Whereas she—she sobbed and clutched her head between her arms, rocking helplessly back and forth.

Ashe! Where are you?

*　　*　　*

The moment she heard Saxon go out she went up to the bedroom, and stood by the window, the same one from which she'd seen Ashe that first time. It commanded a view of the garden gate, the west end of the church, the south porch and part of the path that led to the war memorial and the road. Almost as if her frenzied longing had conjured him up, Ashe was there! A pair of shears lay on the ground next to him, but he was pulling at the couch and elder that clogged the base of the hedge. As she watched, Saxon came into the picture from the direction of the house, with Boots on his lead. The dog almost pulled him over in its eagerness to greet Ashe, but the moment Ashe was

429

on his feet it lay down, asking to be petted. The two men talked, she could hear their voices—Saxon's mainly—but not what was being said. Saxon gestured in the direction of the church, and Ashe nodded. Saxon gave the dog an encouraging tug and they went on their way.

Vivien stayed where she was, watching. Ashe kneeled down and continued pulling weeds for another couple of minutes then stood up. He picked up the shears and walked across the lawn below her to put them in the shed. Instinctively she stepped back. A moment later he returned, heading for the church. And then, as he closed the gate behind him, he looked up. It was a glance intended, unmistakably, for her: sharp, quick and accurate as a dart.

She sprang back from the window; she was panting; the sweat burst from her, she could feel it creeping between her shoulder blades, down the backs of her legs, through her hair . . . Quickly, she ran from the room and flew down the stairs.

Hilda was in the hall, bearing a tray of breakfast things.

'Careful now, Mrs Mariner!'

Vivien registered the other woman's puzzled expression just enough to make her slow her own pace.

'I'm so sorry, Hilda.'

'If it's the reverend you're after, madam, he's popped out with the dog.'

'I know.' She heard her voice, curt and distracted, and modulated it with an effort. 'No, I've just remembered where I may have left something. Here, let me take that for you, while you finish in the dining room.'

Hilda's face showed a respectful demur but Vivien had already taken a firm hold on the tray.

'Well, thank you madam, if you're going that—'

In the kitchen Vivien put the tray on the table, and went out of the back door, closing it quietly behind her. On the ground by the back gate the weeds pulled up by Ashe were already beginning to look grey and dead on the fresh, green grass.

*   *   *

Hilda was folding the tablecloth when a movement caught her eye beyond the half-open window: Mrs Mariner, skirt caught up in her hand, running like a hare towards the church.

*   *   *

Saxon was full of energy. He could have gone for miles, but he and Vivien would be walking again later, and anyway he had a strong sense that this morning he would be able to do good work, both on his sermon and, God willing, his poetry. He had been planning to walk along the river bank, but changed his mind on the grounds that it would be pleasant to defer repetition of that particular delightful experience until this evening. Having spoken to Ashe, he had at first set off in that direction before changing his mind and heading towards Fort Hill to the west. He walked fast and the incline made him pant, but he had set himself a goal—the wood at the top—and was determined to attain it. Once there, he would have plenty of time to catch his breath while he enjoyed the view.

Just below the tree line he slowed, puffing, to a

431

halt, and sat down. The trudge had been worth it: he had forgotten how delightful it was to be high up, above the small, complex web of parish life of which the vicarage was the centre. This morning he took a special pleasure in contemplating the house, and Vivien's presence in it. As an outwardly dry stick, he had always recognised his good fortune in having such a lovely, if unorthodox, wife: amusing, warm, intelligent—a woman who naturally drew people's affections in a way that he never could. Yes, he had always known that, but reproached himself with not having shown it often enough. Except, of course in the bedroom, but that was a very particular kind of exchange, one in parenthesis to the rest of life, and of which they didn't speak. He should and would make an effort to express his love and appreciation, be sure not to take her for granted. He hated to see her thin, sad and debilitated, and resolved that for however long it took he would cherish her until she was completely recovered.

He sat there for about five minutes while the dog went fossicking about, scratching at molehills and half-heartedly following scents within a safe radius. It was not a great hunter, in fact not an adventurous dog at all. The moment Saxon rose (creakily, he was out of practice) to his feet, it set off down the hill in front of him, quite happy to be going home. He sometimes wondered how on earth such a timid and devoted creature had ever got lost . . . There had been something about it getting stuck down a rabbit burrow, but he'd never seen it show anything beyond a passing and perfunctory interest in such holes when it had been out with him. Of course, it had been smaller then, so who knows . . . Anyway, he was glad that it had been found—that Ashe had found it—because its cheerful, youthful energy and affection was particularly good for Vivien.

*   *   *

This is blasphemy she thought. *Blasphemy, and sacrilege. There can be no forgiveness for this.*

When they were finished they fell apart and lay with awkwardly twisted limbs, chests heaving, mouths agape, like wounded on a battlefield. The pale sunlight filtered through the window above them—*Consider the lilies*—and fell across them on to the altar, burnishing the brass crucifix and splashing the altar cloth with green, white and gold. In an agony of guilt, Vivien reached down to pull up her clothes but he caught her hand.

'No.'

'I must—'

'Wait!'

He leaned up on his elbow, and with his other hand folded her skirt back, neatly and carefully. Then he placed his free hand on the inside of her damp thigh and stroked, this time gently, upwards to the place between her legs, where she was still liquid. There he pushed his fingers into her. When he withdrew his hand it glistened with viscous juice.

'See this?'

She nodded.

Slowly and deliberately he wiped it on the altar cloth.

'Our mark,' he said.

'Ashe!' Vivien put her hand on his arm.

433

'What's that?'

'We're not alone,' she whispered.

*   *   *

'Susan! Susan!'

Susan heard Mrs Mariner calling her name, but she kept running as fast as she could, her heart banging in her chest. She tripped and fell, but scrambled back to her feet, sobbing with terror. Her head was almost cracking open with what she had seen—bare legs, flushed faces, parts of people that weren't supposed to be seen at all, red, gleaming wet and angry-looking, Mr Ashe *wiping his hands* on the holy tablecloth, Mrs Mariner's eyes so terribly, terribly scared! She didn't know what the two of them had been doing there, or what it meant, but the effect on her was like that of the horrible dead rabbit, only much, much worse. She was nauseous with shock. When she reached the gate she looked over her shoulder, but no one was coming after her, and once she was inside she stopped and fell to her knees, crying and gagging.

With difficulty she got to her feet and stumbled on, swiping at the snot and tears with clenched fists. She couldn't carry the awfulness inside her head for a moment longer, it was too big and too dreadful, like a painful swelling that might burst. Someone else must go and look, someone who would understand, who would tell her not to worry, who would know what to do.

The back door crashed open as she went in. The dog, lapping water in the scullery, turned his head, but Hilda, who was peeling things at the sink, hardly glanced at her. By the time she reached the top of the stairs there were spots before her eyes and her legs hurt. She had to stop again before stumbling to the study and bursting in.

Mr Mariner was standing in the middle of the room. His cheeks were pink, and his black hat lay on the desk. He was holding one of Mrs Mariner's big wavy hairpins in his hand. He didn't say anything to Susan about her not knocking, but smiled and twiddled the hairpin in his fingers.

'Susan, my goodness you have been running, look what I found on the floor.'

'They're in the church!' She pointed.

'I beg your pardon? Who's in the church?'

'In the very holy place, lying down!' She began to cry. 'They shouldn't be there, should they . . .'

'Who?' Mr Mariner's voice changed. It got very, very quiet, and he came and stood very close to her and took her hands away from her face, and made her look at him. He was still holding the hairpin, and when he did that it grazed her cheek.

'Who?' he said for the third time. His face wasn't pink any more but grey and white. His eyes looked watery. 'You must tell me at once.'

Susan sensed the enormous importance of what she was about to say. For this one moment *she* was important, and that stiffened her resolve and made her speak up clearly.

'Mrs Mariner and John Ashe.'

He made a funny, frightening sound. He must have squeezed the pin and hurt himself because in the moment before he disappeared she saw blood on his hand. He ran out of the front door and she heard his footsteps crunching across the gravel as she crouched down to pick up the pin which had fallen to the ground. Holding it, she felt calmer.

Here was a job she could do: she could return this to Mrs Mariner, later.

*   *   *

Vivien burst through the garden gate into her husband's arms. For a second only—his fingers bit into her shoulders as he pushed her aside. She staggered and fell, feeling her spectacles break beneath her in her pocket.

'I'm sorry,' he said. 'Get up.'

She did so. His face was shrunken, unrecognisable, the face of an ugly dwarf.

'Where is he?'

She couldn't speak.

'In the church?' He saw what the answer was. 'Were you there with him?'

She was shaking violently now.

'What have you done?' he moaned. 'What have you done?'

She ran on into the house. Susan Clay was sitting at the kitchen table, petting the dog; she held something out to Vivien but she beat her hand away.

'Go! Get out!'

The dog barked excitedly.

Closing the narrow door behind her she ran up the narrow stairs and into his room. She closed that door too—a white shirt hung on the back of it. She took it off the hook and lay down on the bed. Then she wrapped the shirt about her head and over her face, so tight that she could not see, and could scarcely breathe.

There was no trace of him on the shirt; only the smell of clean, washed cotton.

436

LONDON

I found out later that Jarvis was wounded for a second time at Dujaila, but not seriously. I've often wondered about that, but there were no rumours. He came to visit me in hospital, in Basra. I couldn't say when, exactly. Pain's like prison, it's another world, you lose track of time. He took me back, sold them his story of what happened: I got attacked by Buddhoos, apparently when following him on his valiant lone recce. Frankly I felt so bad then I didn't give a stuff. I knew he was hoping I'd concentrate and take it all in, for future reference. Doubtless thought he'd been very clever, getting us both off the hook. He didn't need to worry, did he think I was going to split on him, when I could have all that to myself? I'm a miser, I'd never give it away.

Later, of course, I could picture it all: him lugging me back into camp, both of us covered in my blood, him a hero on two counts, me the simple soul misguidedly keeping an eye on him. His brain must have been working overtime on that little trip. Did they really believe him? I doubt it, but he was a popular chap. They knew he'd got the shakes, but he'd come back, and with a halfway plausible story, too, so they were going to let it go through on the nod, especially as I was in no position to contradict . . .

He sat in that stinking ward, eyes never quite meeting mine, never stopped smiling. Thanks to his handiwork, I'll never stop smiling either.

Mine was a Blighty one, in the end. My face got

infected and I nearly died. For the first and last time I damn near wished I had, the pain was so bad. Like I was being eaten alive. Along with my rotting flesh they must have smelled a rat, because I heard he was transferred on to the staff after that. Got sick in the last months of the war, long after I was back in Civvy Street, and was shipped home a shadow of his former self. It took them months to get him right—the twice-wounded brilliant young officer, breaking the nurses' hearts.

I bet he thought we'd never see each other again. Shows how little he knew. From the moment those metal teeth ripped my face apart, he owed me. And I was going to make it my business to collect.

I never broke any nurses' hearts. Nerve, yes; hearts, no. I'd have laughed if I'd been able to. Did they think I couldn't hear them whispering about whose turn it was to change my dressing? I got a certain pleasure out of lying there, waiting, knowing one of those stupid girls was sooner or later going to have to come over and deal with the monster. I've always known if you keep quiet and wait, people will have to come to you, whether they like it or not.

Once, when two nurses were walking away after making my bed, I heard one of them say under her breath: 'Poor fellow . . . What sort of life will he have?' Looks were so important to her, she couldn't imagine going through life with a face that made people cross the road. Stupid, patronising bitch. Didn't she realise I'd be able to turn all this to my advantage? Not everyone was as vain and stupid as her.

I'll allow there was quite a while when things didn't look too rosy. It was a year—Christmas 1917—when the doctors finally threw their hands up and said they couldn't do any more: sick of the sight of me, in every sense. I was healed, but not mended. I'd been spoiled again.

London at that time was pretty grim, full of wrecks and ghosts and crazies back from the war, and no end in sight; full of families who'd lost their precious son or husband. You'd think that would make them more charitable, wouldn't you? Make them want to be good to people like me, but you'd be wrong. They'd had enough of trenches, and thinking how their lads had died; the last thing they wanted to see was a bloke with a trench on his face.

I swept streets, I collected litter, I cleaned toilets—that didn't last long, the customers complained. Seeing me must have put a knot in their willies. I lived in a hostel. Every night it was full to capacity. After a few months I got a cubicle because I was a regular, but it was then I began to get really angry about what the war had done. The dead ones were lucky, in a way. Not their families, but the men who'd died went out as heroes, or martyrs, they'd always be remembered as the brave young ones who went away. A hell of a lot of the ones who came back, came back to this—menial work, or none at all, nights spent in dormitories that smell of urine and dirty clothes and unwashed skin and hair. The people who ran the hostel were OK, God-botherers, but I didn't hold that against them, they were doing their best. We had to be out by nine in the morning. By five o'clock when we were allowed back in the place was clean and tidy, so they must have worked like blacks. They gave us a cooked tea and a hot breakfast. But what they couldn't give us was dignity. I looked at those men, hundreds of them, lots of them younger than me, and they'd turned into animals, not fierce, wild ones but sad, tame, ill-treated domestic animals, cringing and humble, glad of any crumbs that came their way. It made my blood boil.

There was a lad there for a while, Danny, who'd been in Mesopotamia, like me. He'd been at Ctesiphon, but caught one at Hanna, come back and been pretty much on the streets ever since. One night I sat with him on his bed and we talked about it. He remembered Jarvis shooting his horse—strange to think he and I were standing less than a hundred yards apart back then with no idea about each other, and here we are sitting together in this dormitory. He's a pretty pathetic specimen, skinny and pale with a bad skin (though who am I to talk?) and he bites his nails; he washes up in a hotel in Bayswater. Not a very nice hotel if you know what I mean—businessmen away from home. I asked him about his family.

'I couldn't stay there. My widowed sister and her kids live there and it's only two bedrooms, I had to get out.'

'Do they know where you're living?'

He shook his head. 'I've told them I'm well set.'

I don't often feel sorry for people—we all make our own lives—but I felt sorry for that lad. Lived through all that and came home to find there was no room for him. He'd got to be the big grown-up son and make his way, and look where he wound

440

up—clearing up after those dirty bastards in Bayswater, and sleeping in this place with the likes of me. Except, of course, that I'm different. He was a nice enough bloke, he probably felt sorry for *me*, with my ugly phiz that no one wants in their kitchen, or their office, or their factory if they can help it.

Then one day Danny cheered up. Or at least he cheered up gradually, and one day it was noticeable enough for me to pass a comment.

'Things are looking up, John,' he said. 'I'm moving out of here.'

'What happened?' I asked. 'Find a diamond in the dirty dishes?'

'Sort of.' He smirked. 'I found this man's business card, turned out he was a city councillor from Manchester. When I asked if it was his I used his name: Councillor Pryke, I said, is this yours?' Danny's grin nearly split his face. 'He said it was, and gave me a quid.'

'Then you gave it back, eh.'

'Exchange ain't no robbery. And there's been more since. It's a good little earner.'

Danny, the big blackmailer. Still, he did leave the hostel, so there must have been some truth in it. Never found out how he got on after that . . . Probably ended in tears, he was no brainbox.

Still, he'd given me an idea.

*　　　*　　　*

At long last the show was over. On Armistice Night I stayed in my cubicle and read a book. The streets of London were heaving with drunks. Not long now and they'd be crawling with returning heroes

441

looking for work. That's when I had the idea of clearing off for a bit. I was never one to be part of the herd, I'd seek my fortune somewhere else.

Springtime, I thought, when the sap rises— that's the time to see the countryside.

CHAPTER SIXTEEN

The last time I saw anyone so changed it was Jarvis, that night in Dujaila. But what was sweet about this time was that *I'd* made the change happen. Mariner seemed to have got smaller, and to be getting smaller all the time, right in front of my eyes. His face was like waste paper; his hands were clasped behind his back but his shoulders twitched. Those long fingers would be writhing and twisting like snakes.

He wouldn't let me into the house.

'You're never going in there again,' he said, in a wheezy voice like barbed wire. 'I won't have you setting foot in my house.'

That was understandable. He didn't want me in the house, but he didn't want to be in the church—holy ground, that we'd desecrated—or in the street, where we might be heard or seen. So we were standing under the trees at the end of the garden, that part where I'd been working on and off all summer. My suggestion; I'd led the way up here, and he'd followed. The irony of that wasn't lost on me, and I doubt it was on him, though he was in no state to appreciate it. There were flowers here now, and a little path, and the seat I'd built out of the broken branch . . . all the things I'd made. I stood facing the house, he with his back to it, defensively. The house looked good, too, thanks to me. I didn't know where she was—up in their bedroom, probably, watching us from the window. I'd changed her, too. Nothing was going to be the same in this poxy village—and all my doing.

443

'You've ruined us, haven't you?' he said, as if it had just come to him. There was a funny look in his eyes. It would have been going too far to call it admiration, but he was impressed. Now he took a step towards me, and I could see little gobs of spit at the corners of his mouth. He smelt bad, too; I'm sensitive to these things.

'You are loathsome, John Ashe,' he whispered. He was short of breath, but the barbed wire was still there, snagging and scratching. 'You are a viper.'

I stared back at him. He'd have to do a lot better than this. Of the two of us, I knew who felt worse.

Then he said, in that curious, wondering tone again: 'I've never before spoken of the devil. To do that is to give him credence, to dignify him. But now I know that the devil exists, and that I have given him house room—here, in this vicarage. And in the house of God!'

This was better, he was getting into his stride. I gave him a nod, not exactly agreeing, but acknowledging the compliment.

'I have broad shoulders!' he hissed. 'And I can bear what I must! But you have defiled what is holy: the church, the sacrament of marriage, the innocence of children!'

He didn't fool me. It was himself he was worried about. I recognised real terror, the sort that loosens the sphincter, because I'd seen it before. Right now Saxon Mariner would have slit his wife's throat, and the slow girl's, if it could have saved his skin. As for the house of God, the only part that played in the scheme of things was that it made things much, much worse. There was something particularly poetic in Susan Clay being the one to tell him—a nice little bonus, when all I'd been going to do was have his wife in the church—the final taboo—and then let him know myself, while applying a little gentle pressure to the financial udder . . .

'How dare you smile!' He was so close now I could feel his spit on my face. 'You're mad. I despise you. God will have mercy on us, in the end, but not on you, John Ashe. You will never, ever, be forgiven. Never!'

It was time to break the silence.

'I did nothing,' I said. 'You should speak to your wife.'

'Don't dare to give me orders!'

I shrugged.

'My wife has been ill!' He panted. 'She's not herself, I shall be taking her to see a specialist—'

'She came after me.' I cut across him but I kept my voice very, very low, so that he had to pay attention. 'Ask her. She wouldn't leave me alone. She came after me, and she knew what she wanted.'

He slapped my face! It was wonderful—that fussy, weak, womanish slap that played right into my hands. I scarcely even blinked. I put my hand up to my cheek, but not because he'd hurt me. My hand, unlike his, was completely steady. I pointed.

'See this?'

He scarcely knew what to look at, or what he was seeing, I doubt if he was seeing at all, but I was going to tell him anyway.

'Your wife did that.'

Emotion recollected in tranquillity—William Wordsworth. Mariner was a poet himself, he'd know that quotation, and I was giving Mariner plenty to recollect when I'd gone. Every word, every gesture, every last agonising detail, would come back, when he was alone, and he'd die a death of a thousand cuts. Every time.

I was beginning to get tired of this, though, and tired of him. All of a sudden I could see myself walking away up that hill, shaking the dust of Eadenford from my shoes for ever. I knew exactly what it would feel like to look down on this dull, inconsequential little place for the last time, and that moment couldn't come soon enough.

'Your Vivien drew blood because that's what she likes,' I said. 'In your study and your bedroom as well as your church.'

'Don't say her name!' Yes—I knew that would hurt. He was shaking all over now, and there were tears wobbling down his shrunken face with its big blade of nose like a bird's beak. 'You have no right to speak her name!'

'Oh,' I said, 'I have every right. But I don't have to. Not unless people don't believe Susan Clay.'

He wasn't so crazed that he didn't understand me. I'd seen it in the war, that single, dominating impulse: to survive. The impulse that keeps unwanted babies alive on freezing doorsteps and men running with bullets in their chests, and trapped dogs breathing. For Saxon Mariner, step one in the survival process was first of all to get rid of John Ashe.

'How much?' he asked.

I didn't answer. He turned and walked away over the lawn—my beautiful lawn, I was almost sorry to say goodbye to it—and I followed. He was weaving a bit, I thought he might fall, but he kept going, round the side of the house to the front

446

door. He didn't have to tell me—at the bottom of the steps I waited, while he went in.

I saw the study door open, and his bowed head as he stood at the desk. Susan Clay would be at home by now, she'd have told her story. They wouldn't believe it at first, but it wouldn't take long. I was looking at a man whose life was about to come crashing down round his ears. He bent down, then straightened up; I think he was counting. Then he disappeared and the study door closed.

It was a lot of money—I never expected so much in cash. I thought I might have to come back, or make some complicated arrangement. I wouldn't have minded, I'm very patient. I didn't ask, and I didn't bother counting, just stuffed it in my boot. But it did cross my mind that the money might not be his, that it might have something to do with church funds. He was going to cross that bridge when he came to it. I was going to burn mine.

'Go!' he gasped. 'Now. Go, and never come back.'

He didn't understand, but then he was never supposed to. I *wanted* to go, and I didn't care if I never saw Eadenford again. It had served its purpose.

'Goodbye, Reverend,' I said. He was already walking away from me, back into the ruins. 'And good luck. Give my best to Mrs Mariner.'

A shock went through him. It was as if he'd been struck by lightning. He checked for a split second and put his hand on the wall to steady himself.

He didn't turn round, though. And I left.

*　　　*　　　*

447

A flock of swallows flew over my head as I walked up the hill. Like me, off to better things. At the top, I stopped and took that last look I'd promised myself. Eadenford wasn't much of a place, but back in April I'd told myself, *This'll do*, and I'd been right.

I'd left my few things there, in the maid's room. Someone was going to have to clear those out. I hoped they'd be careful when they made the bonfire, in my garden.

I entered the woods whistling a tune. It was the one about Charlie Chaplin that we used to sing while we were marching, back in Mesopotamia.